"A stunning concoction of political intrigue, found family, and nail-biting tension. *Inferno's Heir* is destined to be a book people obsess over."

—Jaysen Headley (@ezeekat), global top 5 BookTok influencer

INFERNO'S HEIR

INFERNO'S HEIR

TIFFANY WANG

HODDER

HODDER CHILDREN'S BOOKS

First published in Great Britain in 2024 by Hodder & Stoughton
First published in the United States by Violetear Books, an imprint of
Bindery Books, Inc., San Francisco

1 3 5 7 9 10 8 6 4 2

A CIP catalogue record for this book
is available from the British Library.

ISBN 978 1 444 98060 8

Printed and bound in Great Britain by
Clays Ltd, Elcograf S.p.A

The paper and board used in this book
are made from wood from responsible sources.

MIX
Paper | Supporting
responsible forestry
FSC® C104740

Hodder Children's Books
An imprint of
Hachette Children's Group
Part of Hodder & Stoughton Limited
Carmelite House, 50 Victoria Embankment
London EC4Y 0DZ

The authorised representative in the EEA is Hachette Ireland, 8 Castlecourt Centre,
Castleknock Road, Castleknock, Dublin 15, D15 YF6A, Ireland

An Hachette UK Company
www.hachette.co.uk

www.hachettechildrens.co.uk

For my parents,
who believed in me first

CHAPTER ONE

A s Teia strode through the cobblestone streets, her hood tucked over her head, her black cloak flapping against the early autumn chill, she had already decided the man was going to die.

There was simply no way around it. The courtiers in the palace might claim she had sprung into this world with malice in her heart and murder on her lips, but business was business. Teia was no merchant, counting her guilds in some gilt-laden office in the Financial District, but there was a reason she'd asked for the best. There was less room for error, for the messy business conducted behind firmly closed doors.

Around her, the Flats swirled with activity. The Flatiron District thrived during this time of night, with tourists and locals alike packed shoulder to shoulder as they stumbled to their next destination. A twinkling strip of brothels cut through the thick gray mist, far brighter than the iron streetlamps that flickered on either side of the well-worn path. Hoots of delight sounded from the open windows. They mingled with arguments that rang out from the propped doors of alehouses, where drunks quibbled with bartenders.

Enna was waiting by one of the bars, off the forked street that ran to the ruined mansions of Fairweather Banks. Her dark skin glinted under the lamplight, her black curls tumbling down her back. She stretched high on her toes, examining a sheet of paper tacked to the alehouse's weathered wall, although she turned away quickly when Teia drew near.

"Evening, Boss," Enna said. Her grin was exaggeratedly wide as she stepped lithely to block the paper from view. "Excellent weather we're having, aren't we?"

Teia, who wasn't interested in greetings and had less to say about the weather, nodded pointedly over Enna's shoulder. "And that is?"

"That?" Enna rotated back. "Darner's Alehouse. Dirt-cheap prices. Best brewery in Bhanot. Come to think of it, I once nicked an entire row of pocketbooks from the drunkards at the bar—"

Teia's patience dwindled. "Enna," she said sharply. "The poster."

The thief winced. "Er," she said. "You don't want to look at that—"

When had that warning ever staved off anyone? Teia remained where she was, motionless, until Enna ducked aside, feigning an injured expression. "Fine," she muttered. "But you're not going to like it."

It took only a cursory scan for Teia to admit Enna had been right. The paper was damp from the recent bouts of fog, ink smearing down the page, but the words at the top remained starkly legible. Even if they weren't, it wouldn't have mattered. Teia had memorized them three months prior, when Jura first made his declaration on the sweeping balcony of the Golden Palace. Her half brother had been smug in his victory, bathed in sunlight, his green eyes shining with a hard, vindictive light.

I, Jura Carthan, am delighted to announce Teia Carthan's

betrothal to Lord Devon Ralis. As future sovereign of Erisia, it is my honor and my right.

Of course Jura had made copies of the wedding announcement, posting them throughout Bhanot. Of course he found a way to haunt her even here, deep in the belly of the city's worst district.

"Well," Enna said weakly, as Teia tore down the page, scrunching it tight in her hand. "At least your dress is going to be lovely?"

Teia credited this with a withering glare. With that, the pair swept away from the lights of the brothels and bars, into the sagging roofs and weathered buildings that made up the outskirts of the Flats. Enna led the way. Her feet scarcely made a sound as she picked down the worn path. It was among the many reasons the thief had catapulted in rank through the Society of Thieves, amassing enough of a reputation that the banks changed their locks every four weeks.

The building they stopped at seemed in danger of collapse. Great pieces of stone crumbled away from the iron foundation. Faded images were scrawled near the moss-covered threshold, some more recent than others. A rising sun, for the new rebel group that had sprung loose across the country. An old plague symbol with two slashes in the center, from when the Reaper's Kiss had barreled through Erisia nearly a decade before.

Teia glanced at Enna. "This is it?" she said.

Enna averted her gaze. The thief wasn't the type to balk at violence, but there were occasional moments when she could go soft. Her expression was reluctant as she shifted gingerly from foot to foot. "Are you sure you want to do this?" she asked.

Teia's reply was to push aside the door, a flame cast above her palm.

The interior was as decrepit as the outside. Whoever once lived here had left in a hurry, and looters had since carried away anything of value. White sheets draped haphazardly across overturned tables and chairs with misshapen legs. They cast ghastly shapes against the wall, monsters that reared their heads.

She urged her flame higher, nudging the threads of heat outward. A halo of fire expanded in midair and crept toward the chipped ceiling. It illuminated a trail of fresh crumbs, pieces wedged against the uneven floorboards. *Sloppy*, Teia thought, as she padded deeper inside the building.

Erickson Greer might have been a fool, but at least he'd kept his wits about him. She'd barely crossed the second threshold when he lunged at her, surprisingly spry for a man built like a tree trunk. Greer's blade flickered in the light, his blue eyes wild and bloodshot. His knife grazed her shoulder, but she spun away from the worst of the damage. When he swung at her again, Teia sent heat blistering up his arm.

The bruiser collapsed to the ground, wailing in pain. She kicked away his knife and dropped her hood, advancing on him from the shadows.

They'd never met before, but he recognized her immediately. "Princess?" he gasped, as he cradled his injured arm.

She looked down at him—the traitor of a man she'd employed through Enna, the bruiser she'd staked her hopes on. "You tried to double-cross me, Greer. Enna gave you instructions, didn't she? You ambush the Minister of Contracts and Coin. You tell him to soften the terms of my wedding contract. You hold him hostage for a few days, take a finger if he refuses."

Greer had scrambled onto his knees. "Please," he mewled, but she cut him off, rage building in her chest. Three months of planning for nothing. Three months of agonizing nights, banking all she had on her freedom, just for things to end like this.

"But what do you do, Greer?" Teia crooned. "You go behind my back. You try to cut a deal with the minister. You tell him someone has him in their sights—you offer him protection to line your own pockets."

Terror flashed across Greer's craggy face. Teia knew what he was thinking: *witch.* How else could she have discovered what had happened? The bruiser had been careful to speak to the minister alone, sending correspondence written in rough bouts of code.

But for all Greer's scheming, it had taken Teia under an hour in the Golden Palace's passageways to uncover his betrayal. The tunnels snaked behind every room in the palace, including the study of the Minister of Contracts and Coin. After she'd learned from the servants that Minister Lurel Abbott was unusually distraught, Teia had spied on the man as he'd hunched at his desk, a letter quivering in his pudgy fist. One glimpse of the handwriting, and she'd realized at once that Greer was a traitor.

"I'm sorry!" the bruiser pleaded. "If I'd known it was you—"

"I'm not the magistrate," she said softly. "You don't have to beg."

She sensed the water that coursed within him, feeding through his tissue and blood. With one movement, Teia pulled the liquid into Greer's chest. The bruiser screamed. He clawed at his throat as she drew water into his lungs. It trickled out of his mouth, streaming from his nose, choking him where he stood.

"Please," the bruiser managed again. "Please. I have a family."

It would have meant something to the girl Teia once was. Someone kinder, more forgiving. If her father were here, he would have advised mercy. *Power shouldn't be abused, Teia.*

Except that was before her parents' deaths. Before Jura's interim rule. Before his declaration on the sun-spotted balcony, his voice carrying above the sea of people.

"Don't we all?" Teia said, as she closed her hand in a fist.

The moment of death was always quiet—a gurgle, a rasp. Yet as Teia stared down at Greer's body, still twitching against the filthy floor, she felt no sympathy. He'd thought himself clever and taken a gamble. This was simply the price for losing.

"Go to one of the alehouses," Teia said. She hadn't heard Enna approach, but she knew the thief was there, lurking silently by the door. "Buy some bottles, empty them out, and scatter them around the room. Nobody should find Greer here, but it'll look like he drank himself to death if anyone wanders through."

"And you?" Enna said. There was the barest edge to her voice, a question that hovered beneath. *Where are you going? How do you feel?*

Are you sorry?

Teia dusted down her cloak. "Back to the palace," she said shortly. "Abbott has a Council meeting in the morning. I need to see if he mentions Greer."

Enna blinked. Abbott was part of Erisia's triumvirate, but the Council rarely allowed visitors. "They invited you?"

"No."

"But you're going anyway?"

"Yes," Teia said, as she extinguished her flame and stepped back into the night.

The air outside was crisp and clean, the sky layered in a blanket of stars. Empty plague houses stretched over the full crest of the hill. They rotted away in various states of decay, windows smashed in, doors teetering off hinges. No wonder Greer had hidden here. The most hardened criminals treaded lightly in this part of the Flats, flush with superstition and wary of ghosts.

But really, the bruiser never stood a chance. As Teia walked by, she made a point to pass the row of buildings, daring any specters to appear. She didn't fear bedtime stories. In fact, she pitied any creature that made an attempt on her soul. She couldn't imagine there was much left to devour, aside from a few feeble sparks.

CHAPTER TWO

❦

The Council meeting was underway when Teia arrived at the War Room. She heard furtive mumbling as she knelt in the soft dirt of the passageways, arranging her legs to make herself comfortable. As she pressed an eye to a crack in the weathered stone wall, she inventoried the room's many furnishings: stained glass windows set in shades of red, mounted weapons in crystal cases, the stretched pelt of a white stag, and near the very back, a great scarlet banner that fluttered from the ceiling, bearing the Erisian crest with the snarling Serkawr.

It was an undeniably beautiful space, designed to distract from the ugliness that went on inside, but Teia wasn't here for the splendors of interior design. She had come for exactly one reason and one reason only.

Abbott, she thought sourly. *Where is he?*

She craned her neck for a better view before recoiling in shock. While three familiar figures conferred around a gleaming soapstone table, a stranger hovered by the doorway. A scout, judging from the ridiculous striped uniform and colorful plumed hat. He looked ready to wet himself as he gnawed on his lower lip, sneaking frightened glances across the length of the room.

It was Jura who spoke first. Teia's half brother sat tall in his velvet seat. A ruby circlet sparkled in his blond hair. It matched the intricate trimmings of his long silver coat, the gems catching the early morning light. He was the very image of Erisian beauty, of a king to be: the Golden Prince, the Blessed Heir. Even the scout cheered slightly under Jura's radiant smile.

"Go on," Jura said kindly. "We were told you have news about the rebels?"

Teia bit back a sigh. The rebels—the Dawnbreakers, as they called themselves. Ridiculous name, but catchy. They'd been running wild through Erisia, espousing the wonders of democracy to anyone who'd listen.

The scout bobbed his head. "Yes, Highness. The Dawnbreakers have staged another assault on our ports."

"Which one?"

"Anwen Harbor."

"How many casualties?"

"Three."

"Guards?"

"Civilians." The scout pushed his spectacles higher onto his nose. "As usual, the rebels left behind their demands."

He slid a report across the table to Jura, who examined it carefully. "'The monarchy must fall,'" Jura read dryly. "And written in blood at that. How original."

"Preposterous!" Abbott snapped. The Minister of Contracts and Coin's belly shivered over the side of the table, his face purpling with indignation. It consistently baffled Teia why, out of the fifteen ministers in Jura's cabinet, the crown prince had elevated Abbott as a member of the Council. She suspected a bribe or two must have switched hands as the minister added, "How long have the Dawnbreakers said the same thing now? Eight months? Nine?"

"A year, Minister," the scout provided timidly.

"A *year*. Yet we've made no progress capturing their leader and putting an end to this nonsense?"

General Miran nodded. He was the final member of the Council, a time-hardened veteran of the Shaylani War. Jagged scars carved down both his cheeks. They stretched along his jaw and roped around his neck, circling like a noose. Most were souvenirs from his time on the front, although the cloth patch covering his left eye was far more recent.

"Lehm," Miran rasped out, reaching up to tug at the square of fabric.

"That's right!" Abbott said vigorously. "We simply need to flush Cornelius Lehm out. Cut the head off the snake."

Teia rolled her eyes. It was quite the statement from the man who'd sobbed ferociously in the corner of his study just one week before, rocking back and forth, Greer's latest correspondence crumpled by his feet.

Jura, too, was unimpressed by Abbott's declaration. "The issue isn't Lehm," he said mildly, setting his chin above laced hands. "It's the rebellion's base."

"Highness?"

"Think about it, Abbott. You don't rid a nest of vipers by killing just one. If we want to root out the Dawnbreakers, we need to uncover their resources, their manpower." He raised a sharklike look toward the minister, who smiled back wanly. "We burn it to the ground, and we stamp out the Dawnbreakers for good."

From his place before the table, the scout cleared his throat.

"If you please," he stammered. "I do have one more update." He'd gone oddly pale as he clutched his sheaf of files close.

Abbott quieted. Miran folded his arms, and Jura gestured at the scout. "By all means."

"The rebels have rallied around someone."

"Who?"

"A girl."

"A girl," Jura repeated, and Abbott released a single, high-pitched giggle.

"Yes, Highness. Her name is Kyra. Kyra Medoh. She was born on the coast but raised in Set. She'd just turned seventeen when the Dawnbreakers recruited her."

A furrow dipped between Jura's brows. "She's their new leader?" he said.

The scout responded with a wobbly bow. "We believe she's a symbol, Highness. A unifying point. The Dawnbreakers say she's proof of a better future."

"How ridiculous!" Abbott snorted. "What is this *champion* supposed to do? Recite speeches to bolster spirits? Sing songs to lift morale?"

It might have been the beginning of an exceedingly long rant, but Jura coughed sharply, his fingers drumming against the table. The rings he always wore glimmered in the sunlight—a massive star sapphire dredged from the Erisian mines, two garnets for his birth month, and an exquisite ruby cradled by minuscule golden carvings. "This girl," he said, his green eyes narrowed to slits. "Why her? Why now?"

The scout had begun to tremble, quaking harder than any autumn leaf. "Highness," he said. "There's something else you should know."

Jura exchanged glances with Miran. "Well?" he said, his tone exasperated. "What is it?"

The scout's voice had dwindled to a whisper. "Kyra Medoh," he choked out. "It's rumored that she can wield a flame."

Silence swelled in the War Room. On the other side of the wall, Teia stifled a swear.

From his spot at the table, Jura had frozen in his seat. His features were hard, sculpted from marble. He studied the scout with a blank expression before lifting his hand slowly. "Get out," he said.

The scout, who must have been very stupid or very brave, didn't move. "Highness—"

He never finished. The room instantly erupted into flames, and a torrent of pure heat bore down on the scout. The man screamed, scuttling back as the fire pressed closer. Teia watched, unblinking, as Jura pushed away from his chair, shadows lancing across his face. He didn't seem so kingly anymore. Instead, he looked exactly like himself: the oldest Carthan child, playacting as monarch, lost in a murderous fit.

"*Get out*," Jura hissed again. One hand opened as the fire bent into a perfect arch. A slender pathway extended through the blaze, slithering toward the door—wide enough for someone to squeeze through, narrow enough that he would certainly be burned.

This time, there was no pleading, no attempts to change Jura's mind. The scout drew a breath. A stain had spread across the front of his trousers. Tears dripped down his chin. He staggered into the flames haphazardly, his sobs ratcheting into shrieks of horror. Blisters burst open on his arms, popping from the heat. His sleeves melted into his skin, and the smell of burnt flesh trailed into the air.

It was an extraordinarily long minute before the War Room door thudded blissfully shut.

Minister Abbott was still shaking when Jura snuffed out the blaze. "Was that necessary?" he panted, dabbing away at his neck.

Jura merely rolled back his shoulders. "Have someone buff out the scorch marks," he instructed, as he walked around the perimeter of the table, his boots trampling alarmingly close to the spot that Teia knelt behind. She wondered if Jura still remembered the existence of the passageways, the tour their father had given them all those years before.

But if the Golden Prince did think of the tunnels, she doubted that he cared. The passageways were for creatures that went bump in the night, for things that thrived in the dark. They might be the Carthan family's best-kept secret, but what did they matter to the boy who had Erisia at his disposal?

By this point, Abbott had regained some modicum of composure. He angled himself ever so slightly away from Jura, a nervous sweat beading his forehead. "Do we think the scout's information is good?" he hedged.

"That the rebels have found a champion?"

"That she can control fire."

Jura's eyes glinted. "Do you understand what you're saying, Minister?"

Teia hoped Abbott would persist. It would be a spate of good luck if the minister burned as well. Aside from becoming a terrific headache, Abbott was known for cornering servants in empty rooms and bragging loudly about the deed afterward. If the stories were true, he'd recently impregnated a serving maid, who had been thrown from the Golden Palace in disgrace.

But it was Miran who got the next word. The general hadn't

moved during Jura's outburst, radiating a familiar stoniness that announced his presence. Miran was infamous for never smiling, unless in the company of his two young daughters.

"Only the royal family can harness fire," Miran creaked.

"Yes," Abbott dithered. "But the scout said—"

"Didn't you hear the general?" Jura directed the full force of his attention toward the minister. Abbott cringed, flattening himself against the back of his seat. "Facts are facts, Abbott. Fire is my family's inheritance. Nobody outside the Carthan line can command it."

Abbott wet his lips. "Highness," he said. "After your mother passed, the late king took the Shaylani Witch as his wife. It's understandable that he may have strayed, with no one but her for comfort."

Teia stiffened. Any idiot could hear what the minister was implying: that after Ren had married Teia's mother, he had engaged in an affair. That the byproduct of his carelessness was the Dawnbreakers' champion, who had taken up her pitchfork to bring down the monarchy.

If the Erisian court was to be believed, Ren and Calla's relationship hadn't meant anything at all.

Teia had listened to every conceivable rumor about her parents' love story. Yet the prickling anger remained, thorny roots staked too deep to extract. The court swore Calla enchanted Ren, using her powers over water to addle his brain. They said that Ren had been distraught after his first wife passed, leaving behind an infant baby Jura. How was it possible that he had traveled to Shaylan, a country Erisia had warred with for the better part of a decade, and returned with a fiancée? And not just any fiancée either, but the next in line to the Shaylani throne?

It was scandal. It was witchcraft.

What other explanation could there be, for two enemies falling in love?

But it didn't matter what Teia thought, hidden away in the passageway tunnels. Jura wasn't at all concerned with preserving Ren and Calla's reputation. He'd rounded on Abbott, his circlet askew, fixated entirely on another issue.

"Say the rebel girl is a Carthan." Jura spat the words as if they pained him. "Does she have claim to the throne?"

"Erisian law is clear," Abbott said hastily. "The eldest son inherits the throne when he comes of age."

"Your coronation is in four weeks, Highness," Miran added. "We'll double palace reinforcements. Make a direct attack all but impossible."

"That's not what I'm worried about," Jura muttered. He was twisting his rings absentmindedly, his thumb running along the surface of the ruby. "If this is true—if the girl really can control fire—people will flock to her."

"Fools," Abbott sputtered. It was clear the minister was trying to stay on Jura's good side. Perhaps he'd suddenly remembered how flammable his coat was.

"Perhaps. But desperate fools make for dangerous enemies." A thoughtful look clouded Jura's face. "Abbott—how do the coffers look?"

"The coffers?" Abbott said, puzzled. "They're sizable. We collected taxes from the northern villages just last month."

"Excellent. Increase all original bounties on the Dawnbreakers, and send a messenger into town to post the news. As for their champion . . ." Jura paused. "One million guilds for her capture, dead or alive."

The minister gasped. He fumbled at his coat weakly, loosening the last few buttons in a rush. "One *million*?" he echoed.

"Is there a problem?"

Abbott gulped visibly, his throat bobbing as he did. "Highness," he said. "Don't you think we're being a bit—*generous*?"

To the minister's right, Miran surveyed Jura calmly. "What of the Dawnbreaker base?" he said in his gravelly tone. "Money has no sway. We've interrogated prisoners, but they refuse to talk. That, or they take the coward's way out."

Coward's way out indeed, Teia thought. Jura had made a habit of visiting Blackgate Prison to assist with rebel questioning, and the bodies he left in his wake—speckled with ashen burns and pus-filled blisters—made even Teia's stomach churn. If the choice was between a suicide tablet and Jura's interrogation methods, she would pick the former in a heartbeat.

"Guilds won't be enough," Jura agreed grudgingly. "No—there needs to be some better incentive. Something to stir the ones who know the location but won't turn for coin."

At this, Abbott's head snapped upward. "How about a favor?" he said. He seemed incredibly eager to make any suggestion that would avoid further damage to the gold-vaulted treasury.

Jura leaned forward. "A favor?"

"I have a contact in K'val—horribly backward country, as you all know. Dreadfully spicy food. Bugs as large as dinner plates—"

"Abbott."

Abbott pulled at his collar imperiously. "My apologies, Highness. My point is that the K'vali trade in favors. Low-level ones, usually, until their ruler hosts an annual celebration. Nothing as grand as what we offer, naturally, but he uses the opportunity to grant a single villager any favor. Apparently it helps tremendously with keeping the commonfolk in line."

"That's your brilliant plan, Abbott?" Miran said scornfully. "You want the crown prince to throw a party?"

The minister scowled, but Jura held up a hand. "A favor," he mused, and General Miran scoffed.

"Highness—"

"It's worth trying, Miran. We could offer any favor from the Crown—a debt cleared, a family fed." Jura's lips ticked in a humorless smile. "A loved one freed from prison."

"Endless possibility," Abbott said, nodding along sagely.

The smile grew wider, although Teia suspected her half brother was no longer listening. His eyes were fixed high above, on the image detailed within a stained glass panel. The Serkawr was set dead center, its maw drawn into a growl, its fangs tipped in poison. The artist had captured every scale in the sea beast's hide, and the light beamed red onto Jura's face.

"We've been too kind to the rebels," he murmured. The words were low, deadly, meant only for himself. "Too reactive, too polite. We capture one, and another takes its place. We kill two, and ten appear the following day. They've become like rats on a ship, gnawing the planks from inside out."

He rotated toward Abbott with a flourish, dusting flakes of ash off his sleeves. "Have a messenger draft up the decree," Jura said briskly. "Whatever it takes, Minister. I don't care if we roll a thousand heads—I want this over before my coronation."

It wasn't the most inspiring speech, but a bubble of hope rose in Teia's chest.

Her plans shifted in on themselves, concaving, restructuring. Forget the debacle with Greer. Forget blackmailing Abbott for better terms in her wedding contract. Teia had never heard of trading in favors before, but she was suddenly immeasurably grateful for the minister's input. Perhaps he wasn't entirely useless after all.

For all their flaws, the Dawnbreakers were notoriously elusive. Their members took their secrets to the grave or else shared too little information to be of any help. But Kyra Medoh?

Kyra was a new opportunity. She was a fresh nuisance for the Council, a shining beacon of change. Most importantly for Teia, she was a solid lead on the rebel group—a wealth of knowledge, a resource still untapped.

Teia would seek her out. She would gain Kyra's trust. Then she would locate the rebels' base, take the information back to Jura, and trade their freedom for her own.

CHAPTER THREE

Teia plunged through the passageways, her mind alight with activity. Around her, rats squeaked from cobwebbed corners. Stray animal bones crunched beneath her feet. The tunnels were dark, untouched by the gas lamps that illuminated most of Erisia, but Teia knew the way. She had been exploring the passageways since she was seven, guided gently by her father. Ten years later, she'd learned them by heart, memorizing every dead end, every quick turn.

She stopped at an unusually narrow strip of rock, which cut a jutting diagonal across the far wall. Teia reached up. She skimmed her fingers along the diagonal's rough edge, feeling for the notch by touch. When she pressed down, the section of stone swung outward. Teia trotted through the new opening, shaking off the dust of the passageways, her shoes sinking into the springy blue rug.

There were over fifty passageway entrances and exits throughout the palace, hidden behind cabinets or stashed beneath beds, but Teia was especially fond of this one. Calla's old sitting room was private. Nobody—including the more petulant ministers, constantly squabbling for roomier offices—had dared claim the space after she died. Most asserted the sitting room was haunted, that misfortune befell anyone who stepped through the ornate threshold.

Teia harbored no such delusions as she shoved the wall panel back into place. If her mother ever rose from the dead, she certainly wouldn't waste her time in Erisia.

The room was bright and airy, packed with relics Calla had brought from Shaylan. Teia squeezed by a towering jade statue and a hanging set of dainty paper cutouts. There was a loveseat, too, upholstered with deep blue fabric and still smelling faintly of roses. Teia remembered scrunching into the center as a child, gobbling down entire platters of tea cakes while Calla read next to her. Her mother would look up on occasion to show Teia a paragraph or pass her another cake, and Teia would lean against Calla's arm, a warm glow filling her belly.

Teia swallowed hard, dispelling the memory. Her mother might live on here, but Jura had ensured she'd been scrubbed from every other room in the Golden Palace. After Ren's funeral, one of the Blessed Heir's first decrees had been to move Calla's royal portrait away from the palace's main entrance, where the paintings of Teia's other ancestors kept watch over the foyer.

More suitable, he'd said, before giving Teia a razored grin, the kind that showed each of his teeth.

The portrait now hung beside the sitting room door, far from Jura's delicate sensibilities. Calla's gray dress matched the elaborate skeins of pearls in her hair, which spilled over her shoulder and down her waist. Her skin was a shade darker than the Erisian standard, her brown eyes curving at the corners. She radiated the same calmness she'd had in life, an unflappable resolve that Teia always envied.

If asked, Teia could have drawn Calla from memory. And should her recollection ever fail, all she needed to do was look in a mirror. Now at seventeen, she was a younger version of her mother. The poster child of Shaylani beauty.

An outsider in her own home.

A sour taste rose in Teia's throat. She veered away from the painting and wrenched the door open, only for a hand to appear on the other side, catching the polished doorframe.

"Princess."

She didn't bother to hide her annoyance. A palace guard stood before her, tall and unsmiling, no doubt sent by Jura to check in on her. The recent carousel of men materializing at her usual haunts in the palace—the sitting room, the wine cellar—made disappearing into the passageways that much harder, but the crown prince cared little about Teia's discomfort. To him, the guards were a contingency, a way to ensure she didn't spoil his glorious plans for her future.

He'd given her one of the younger soldiers today, a clean-shaven boy about her age, snug in a pressed woolen greatcoat. When the guard glanced skeptically into the sitting room, Teia waved an impatient hand. "I'm sentimental," she said. She pivoted around him gracefully, angling toward one of the palace's back gates—and immediately tripped over a bucket of water in her path.

Water went flying. It drenched her shoes and splashed onto the pristine white tile, positively soaking the two servant girls who'd been cleaning the floor. One let out a squeak of fear, toppling into a curtsy, while the second lost her grip on her mop. It clattered onto the wet floor. Droplets spattered everywhere, and the servant gave a visible wince before shuffling away from the expanding puddle.

Teia groaned. She focused on the puddle, and the water laughed out at her. It swirled into a column, reshaping into a miniature pedestal. The mop billowed toward the second servant girl, held up by shimmering whorls of water.

"Here," Teia said.

The servant reached out, her hand trembling. Teia caught a flash of coppery skin and dark hair before the girl sank into a passable curtsy. The servant kept her gaze fixed to the ground, as still as a figurine.

It wasn't until Teia turned that she felt the weight of the girls' stares. Their eyes followed her as she left, taking in every step of the Halfling Princess, the Shaylani Half-Witch.

Teia would never forget when fire first appeared.

It was shortly after her eighth birthday. Teia had been eating her breakfast, picking at pale slices of melon, when heat erupted inside her chest. A knot of brambles compressed into her lungs. Her cells broiled to ash. Teia didn't fully comprehend what was happening at the time—just that she needed to redirect the burning before it ate her alive.

Her father hadn't minded that she set the table on fire. In fact, Ren had been downright giddy at the sight of the charred silverware. "That can be replaced, love," he'd said, and planted a cheerful kiss on Teia's forehead.

In the beginning, he'd refused to spar with her. Ren had taken Teia to the gardens instead, where the two of them spent hours stretched onto the sweet-smelling lawns. He taught her about the wisps of heat that jostled through the air. They radiated in faint tinges of color, a kaleidoscope of red, orange, yellow.

"Do you see those threads?" Ren had asked, and Teia had squinted at the strands that bumbled clumsily around them.

"They're everywhere because heat is everywhere—but it takes a Carthan to command them. Once we bind them together, we're able to create fire."

He flexed his fingers expertly. Wisps of heat drifted toward Ren, spinning themselves into a knitted pattern. Then the threads disappeared in a magnificent blur, and a scarlet flame blazed into existence.

Teia looked at her father in awe. "How did you do that?"

"You need to draw the threads into you. To connect with the warmth and welcome it in."

She shook her head stubbornly. "I don't *want* to welcome it in," Teia declared. She still remembered the heat bubbling against her stomach, the rasp of fire as it chewed away at her.

Ren smiled patiently as he propped himself up on one elbow. "Look again, Teia. Pay attention to the colors, the patterns. What do you see?"

"It's ugly," she said, after a brief moment of contemplation. "It's ugly, and I don't like it."

Her father chuckled. "On occasion," he said thoughtfully. "There are times when fire can be dangerous. Deadly. There are even some people who still fear it."

Her curiosity got the better of her. "What about you?" Teia asked.

He took her hand then, his palms cupped around hers, his gaze firm and steady. "We're Carthans," Teia's father said. "And Carthans have never been afraid of fire."

It was the start of a very long few months. Ren had repurposed one of the banquet halls for Teia's training. The paintings and tables and porcelain vases were all cleared away, so nothing but the crystal chandelier remained. Even that was hurriedly wrapped in a thick layer of black fabric, although Teia doubted its necessity. She couldn't produce a flame larger than a thumbnail, much less one that would leap forty feet high.

"What about the walls?" she'd said dubiously. Since that day at breakfast, she'd had a recurring nightmare about accidentally setting the palace's foundation aflame, before the whole structure crashed down to squash her.

"Flame-resistant soapstone," her father assured her, rapping a panel with his knuckles. "You don't have anything to worry about."

This was, unfortunately, a well-meant lie. Fire hadn't come easy. Teia had grappled with the threads of heat, hands shaking, chest heaving. Five weeks in, when she'd finally managed to conjure a flame, it had singed the tassels off Ren's uniform and filled the room with a heavy cloud of smoke. Teia had promptly fainted from the exertion. When she woke ten minutes later, her head pounding with a tremendous headache, a rusty tang flooded the inside of her mouth. She'd bitten clean through her lip and hadn't realized until afterward.

Ren had been seated beside her. His tunic smelled faintly of smoke, but he whooped in delight when Teia opened her eyes. "You're a natural," he announced as he caught Teia in a hug, and she blushed with pride, lit from within by a delicious brightness.

A year later, she would control water too.

That transition had been as easy as drawing breath. Teia had been playing alone outside when she'd passed by the garden's central fountain. It was a majestic thing, fashioned from a slab of purple marble and decorated with a host of statues. Most of the sculptures were creatures from the old legends—a giant stamping his feet, a pixie poised to take flight—so lifelike that visiting dignitaries often stopped to gawk at the intricate details.

Teia had been by the fountain a hundred times, yet she'd

been inexplicably drawn toward it that morning. Something about the water, the sunlight sparkling off the ripples, made her pause. It was beautiful. It was the most beautiful thing she'd ever seen, and she was overcome with the compulsion to plunge one arm beneath the surface and feel the coolness against her skin.

When Teia's fingertips met the burbling spout, a weightlessness descended over her. Her bones felt hollowed out, as she became aware of each bubble within the fountain. The water was alive. It moved before her. It was as aware of her as she was of it, cut through with a playful undertone.

Teia raised her hand, and a thousand droplets followed her movement. They spun into an upward swirl, hovering in a spectacular drizzle. They snickered alongside her, mischievous to the end, before emptying over a gaggle of unlucky ministers.

She had begun lessons with her mother the next day. Calla was a far different instructor from Ren: there were no springy lawns or gentle encouragements. Her mother had led her straight to the shores of the Dark Sea, where the tide frothed against the shining sand. She instructed Teia to stand knee-deep in the water, the salt spraying against her face, and directed her daughter to hold back the waves.

"The waves?" Teia squeaked. "Can we start with something else? Something easier?"

Her mother lowered her chin. "Hold them back," Calla repeated, her voice even.

Teia tried. She dashed her arms outward with all her strength. She wrestled with the rhythm of the tide, foam splashing against her knees.

By the end of the hour, Teia had come no closer to connecting with the waves. She was thoroughly soaked, trembling in the shallows and feeling exceptionally sorry for herself. She sensed the water's scorn with each step she took, the tide jeering as she stalked toward dry land.

"Mother," Teia said, wringing water from her hair. "This is impossible. It's the *ocean*."

"The ocean is in our blood. You're as much Shaylani as you are Erisian."

"Maybe I don't want to be!" Teia retorted. And in that second, she found that she meant it. She wanted her father's warmth, not her mother's vague directives. She longed to run up the shore to the palace, past the iron gates and oak doors, to leap into Ren's arms.

Calla's face darkened with a brief sadness. She moved forward, her jade bracelets catching the dying light, and gripped Teia's hands firmly in hers. "Darling, it doesn't matter what you want. What matters is what other people see—and to them, you're Shaylani. You'll always be Shaylani, which means you need to be prepared."

"Prepared for what?"

"Anything. You and I? We don't have the luxury of blending in. People will think of you as the enemy. As a target. It's why you need to learn as much as you can, as early as possible. Lessons like this"—Calla gestured at the sea—"are hard. I know they are. But they might keep you alive in the future."

"Holding back waves will keep me alive?"

Calla smiled, and Teia found herself thinking how lovely her mother was. Lovely and brilliant and so very alone, stranded on an island of her own choosing. "Do you know our family motto?"

Teia nodded. It was embedded in cursive within the Carthan crest, scrawled under the outline of the Serkawr twined around two crossed swords. "'Power incarnate,'" she said, before admitting, "I don't really know what it means."

Calla brushed back a wet lock of Teia's hair. At her touch, a strand of droplets separated, melding into a ball of water that hovered beside them. "Power," she said quietly, "is a funny thing. People collect it. They hoard it." She tapped the tip of her daughter's nose with her finger, and Teia giggled in return. "Power is currency here, Teia. You can buy safety—security. And if you have to split the sea itself to earn that in Erisia, then that's what you're going to do."

Teia nodded again. She hadn't quite understood, but she wasn't about to tell her mother that. In this moment, she felt terrifically grown up. She wanted to hold on to this instant, to remember this first step into adulthood.

Calla gave her daughter a long look, one Teia couldn't quite decipher. Then she set her shoulders and flicked her fingers smartly. The water immediately fell away from the shoreline. The waves curled in on themselves, sweeping back to pull into the air. Algae and pebbles were suspended in the current. A school of orange fish swam overhead dazedly.

A wet strip of sand glistened between the arcs of water, speckled with shells, black against the dusk.

"Now," Calla said. "Let's go again."

Teia had never mastered water. She'd only made moderate progress by the time the plague swept through the country and Calla had fallen ill. The Reaper's Kiss made its rounds throughout the Five Kingdoms, piggybacking on merchant ships through Dvořáki and Ismet to worm its way into Erisia. The skies above the capital had darkened for weeks, as people burned bodies in the streets of Bhanot. By then, the plots had long overflowed, so that none but the wealthiest could afford to properly bury their dead, launching into bidding wars to scoop up empty gravesites.

Calla had fought all she could. She had struggled through the aches and chills for a month, mustering the strength to celebrate with Teia when she turned ten, but the fever soon reached her heart. On that sunny winter day, when the palace healer had covered Calla's face with a linen sheet, something within Teia had flickered out, an ember ground to dust.

There was nobody left to teach her the rhythm of the waves or the flow of the ocean. Without her mother, the best Teia could do was control small quantities of water. The liquid within a bucket, for instance, or some droplets in her bath. Any more than that and her control slipped, fading away at the edges— although she did discover an inherent talent for manipulating the water within people. That realization had been its own brand of surprise, when Teia drowned an assassin that Jura had sent on the eve of her thirteenth birthday.

Parlor tricks and death, Teia thought gloomily as she trudged down the grand staircase, the sitting room guard trailing her like a disapproving shadow. The stately columns were wrapped with bright red banners in preparation for Jura's coronation. Servants roamed the halls with teetering piles of glassware and stacks of neatly folded napkins. Snatches of different languages rang all around her—the heavy tones of the Dvořákians, the soothing syllables of Ismet—although conversations died to nothing as Teia walked by.

Power is currency here.

When she was nine, she hadn't fully grasped what Calla meant. Now, Teia was older and wiser, hardened by her time in the Golden Palace. She was her father's little girl, and her mother's daughter. She had mastered the passageways, eavesdropped on ministers, gathered secret after secret to keep herself safe. The court thought her a monster, and so she gave them one to fear.

In the end, the terms were clear. There were only those who held power and those who didn't—and Teia Carthan would be damned if she ended up on the other side.

CHAPTER FOUR

❦

Teia walked out into blinding sunshine.

The palace's back entrance was a simple iron gate, frequented by servants when running errands. There was a lone soldier assigned to this post, a burly fellow with bushy sideburns and mossy teeth who scratched away at his underarms. He didn't bother bowing when Teia approached, but fiddled at the bronze buttons on his coat while refusing to meet her eyes.

"I'm going to Carfaix Market," she told him curtly, trotting out her favorite excuse for leaving the palace. The soldier merely mumbled his assent, hustling to the stout lever to push the gate aside.

The Golden Palace was positioned in the center of Erisia's capital, surrounded on all sides by the cobbled roads of the Royal District. Mansions packed every inch of space, as the city's most prominent citizens scrambled to outdo one another. Sprawling estates towered over grassy lawns, the insignia of each family etched in the mother-of-pearl transoms. Walkways were plumped with lush trees and trimmed hedges, with hired guards near the front to shoo away any beggars.

Teia had been to several of these estates before. Most recently, she'd visited the Erisian ambassador to Ismet, whom she'd persuaded to issue her travel documentation. He'd nearly had a heart attack when she'd arrived at his door and unfurled a list of each hotel he'd tumbled his latest mistress in, which stretched so long it grazed the ground.

Apparently her demands had spooked him. An extra set of guards was now stationed before the gaudy jeweled trappings of the ambassador's ivory mansion, presumably to keep out unwanted visitors. *Charming*, Teia thought, weaving by without a second glance.

As the estates gave way to stoic gray buildings, gone was the blissful peace so heavily coveted in the Royal District. The Financial District was a hub of commerce and trade, a tangle of noise as carriages rattled through the streets and merchants bustled about with thick pages of documents. To the side, away from the chaos, street performers from all kingdoms drew curious crowds. One boy with the violet eyes and dark skin of a K'vali twirled his hands skyward. A column of wind shot into the air, snatching hats off heads, and his audience surged to toss guilds into the empty cup by his feet.

Carfaix Market hugged the southern edge of the Financial District. It sat at the end of the eponymous street, bordering the wharf where sailors unloaded boxes of goods. Rows of booths dotted the trampled grass. Hawkers shouted their wares, swindling tourists and haggling with locals. Most of the peddlers had been selling at Carfaix for years. Many had inherited their spots, but others had to purchase lots when one became available, in auctions so fierce they were often overseen by bailiffs.

The stands were grouped by country, draped with the colors of each vendor's respective kingdom. Yellow for Ismet. Purple for Dvořáki. Barely a handful of booths, tucked away at the far end of Carfaix Market, flew the steely blue flag of Shaylan, but Teia made sure to visit whenever she stopped by. Her favorite stall was a sweets shop, lined with rows of makeshift bamboo shelves, cluttered with jars of sticky sugared dates and sour kumquat chews. Now, she nodded politely at the owner, accepted a sample of ginger candy, and faced the sitting room guard, who was examining a bag of dried plums with great disinterest.

"Well," Teia said, "this is where you leave me."

"Excuse me?"

She passed a stack of guilds his way. "I need you to get me a few things. Books. A wool cloak. Some of those fried saffron pies from Ismet."

"And you?"

"I'll be right here," she said, making a show of checking her pocket watch. "You should go soon, though. The Ismetian stalls are on the other side of the market."

He didn't look convinced, but he was hardly able to argue. Teia watched him vanish into a whirl of black coats and swirling skirts before she started in the opposite direction, keeping her hood pulled over her head. She sliced through the gaps in the Shaylani stalls, darting past potholes, avoiding the throngs of dockworkers who liked to flirt with any pretty vendors.

Pebbles shifted beneath her boots as Teia stepped onto Mourner's Beach. There was no sand here—only the hardness of stone and the puttering of the tide. She checked her watch once more and held back an irritated sigh. Enna was late again. Perhaps the thief reserved punctuality for special occasions, such as killing men in old plague homes.

She bent to scoop up a handful of rocks, weighing its heft as she meandered to the water. This had become a ritual of hers, something Teia did while waiting for the thief. Skip a stone, test her limits. Try to emulate Calla, who could command the strength of the ocean.

The tide chuckled as she approached. It absorbed the pebbles easily, although one managed to stay aloft. A second later, the waves launched the stone astray. It skittered through the current, where it pinged soundly off the bronze statue installed near the shoreline.

Despite the distance, Teia recognized the statue's serene features and flowing dress. It was one of the many works of art dedicated to the Goddess Armina, who had supposedly helped found the Five Kingdoms. Minuscule shapes were inscribed into the statue's base, which depicted the different elements. Fire, water, earth, metal, air. One blessing for each of the Divine Five—the humans who had endured Armina's trials and been rewarded for their troubles. They had been granted power over a single element and cautioned to use their gifts wisely.

The priests loved to laud Armina's foresight, but Teia disagreed. What type of foresight led to civil war, when each of the Divine Five decided they wanted to rule? Things had become so dire that the Goddess had to intervene. She'd conveniently sent the Serkawr to do her dirty work, which relayed an excellent message to the Divine Five: separate countries would be better than none at all.

And so Erisia—along with the other kingdoms—came to be, thanks to one magnanimous deity and her giant pet sea serpent.

"Competitive rock throwing?" a voice said. "I didn't know you'd taken up a new hobby."

Enna van Apt stood behind Teia, her hair loose, her trousers cut fashionably wide. When she noticed the Goddess's statue in the water, Enna stopped. She lowered her head respectfully before touching her forehead in prayer.

"Why do you do that?" Teia asked. It was something that baffled her, considering Enna's occupation.

"Do what?"

"Worship the Goddess. Isn't it counterintuitive for a thief?"

"I'm a thief with a conscience," Enna said brightly, which made Teia snort. "Armina favors the bold, and everyone knows that's my best quality."

"You once stole a relic from the Temple of Mercy."

"I did?"

"It was right after the Winter Holiday. During a *prayer session*."

"The fang of the Serkawr! I made enough guilds to fill up an entire cottage."

"Still think Armina would favor you?"

"Why wouldn't she?" Enna said staunchly. "I might have stolen the fang, but I did it *boldly*."

Teia's lips twitched. "Glad you're feeling so spry," she said. "I have another job for you. Something big."

"And here I was thinking I'd read the paper wrong."

They communicated through coded notices in Bhanot's newspaper, where they buried their messages within the myriad of advertisements. It wasn't the most efficient way of passing notes, but it was by far the most secure. Teia had never been afraid of being found out; if anything, they were more in danger of the paper going out of circulation.

Enna cocked a brow. "Well?" she said. "I'm at your service, for the low price of my current rate."

Teia wouldn't call it *low*. With the fee Enna charged, she could have purchased any one of the carriages racketing around the

Financial District. But there were benefits to having Erisia's best thief on retainer, not to mention her connections to the Flats' criminal underbelly, and so Teia simply raised both wrists high. The silver bracelets she wore glittered, and Enna's eyes widened.

"I used to have one of those," the thief said longingly. Her words were quiet, almost whisked away in the wind, but Teia heard them anyway. In times like these, Enna looked much older than her sixteen years, caught in the throes of some faraway memory.

She'd mentioned scraps of her past before—a wealthy up-bringing in the Royal District, a prominent merchant father who adored his wife and child. Carver van Apt had made his fortune flipping imported K'vali spices for profit, until a series of bad in-vestments did him in. He'd hidden the damage from his family, brushing off clients and collectors alike, up until he'd steered a ship into the Dark Sea and leapt from the highest mast.

Erisian law forgave Carver's debts, but the loan sharks abroad were far less lenient. They came for his belongings before the month was up, piling furniture into wagons and dividing paint-ings on the stoop. They stripped the mansion of any possible value, before possessing the home and turning Enna and her mother onto the streets.

"It's why I became a thief," Enna had told Teia, on a rare oc-casion when she'd spoken of her past. "How else were Ma and I supposed to eat?"

"What about now?" Teia had said.

"What do you mean?"

"You can't eat diamonds, can you?"

Enna's laugh had been sharp. "Don't worry," she'd said. Her expression had shadowed, as if envisioning her former neigh-bors in the Royal District, who'd watched her eviction from the safety of their windows. "Everything I do now is for pleasure."

Next to Teia, the thief was still inspecting the bracelets thoroughly. They must have passed muster, because she hummed in approval, slipping them away into a hidden pocket. "All right then," she said in a matter-of-fact tone. "Who are we blackmailing today? Another minister of whatever?"

"You don't have to sound so eager."

"I never miss a chance to put nobles in their place. How long have we worked together now? Two years? Three?"

"Four."

"Four years," Enna said, with the utmost satisfaction. "Time flies when you're having fun."

"I'm not sure yesterday's work was *fun*."

The thief's smile vanished. She pressed her lips tightly together. "Today's job," she said. "Do you need a bruiser?"

"Does it matter?"

"You killed Greer, Teia. You could have sent him off with a warning—"

"A *warning*?" Teia repeated. "He betrayed me, Enna. And the contract I needed Abbott for—"

She broke off, fury spiking through her. Enna understood what Greer had cost Teia. She had helped gather information on Teia's dearly betrothed, a noble named Devon Ralis who had broken his first wife's neck and thrown the second down the stairs. All this knowledge, and yet she still defended the bruiser?

"Greer needed the money," Enna said softly. "He had debts to pay off, three children to support."

"He was a liability," Teia said. She ignored the hurt that flashed across Enna's face, as she raised her eyes toward the horizon. "Besides, I don't need bruisers this time. I'm looking for information. There's someone from Set I need to find."

The thief scuffed a foot into the ground. "There's nothing in Set," she said. "Only empty fields and carrot farmers."

What Teia wouldn't give to have sourcing carrots as her greatest concern. "Not just that," she corrected, turning back to Enna. "Have you heard of Kyra Medoh?"

Enna paused. "Who hasn't? People talk, you know."

"People always talk. I'm not interested unless there's something worth listening to."

"They say she's the Dawnbreakers' champion. That she's a sign from the Goddess."

"A sign of what?" Teia said scathingly. "Is Armina about to descend from the skies? Is the Serkawr going to spring to life?"

Enna was unfazed. "A beginning of a new era," she said, "where anyone can control fire." Her stare was clear and focused. It pinned Teia beneath an unwanted searchlight, as the thief straightened her cloak. "Since we're swapping questions—what's with the sudden interest in the rebels?"

"Can't I be curious?"

"You don't care for the Dawnbreakers and their ideas. You never have. So what exactly do you want with Kyra Medoh?"

Teia hesitated.

Trust was a slippery thing, unreliable in even the best moments. Over the years, she'd become accustomed to Enna's presence. The thief knew how Teia protected herself in the Golden Palace, formulating plots and schemes, blackmailing ministers into submission.

Yet there were some things Teia kept hidden, stored away for just herself. Enna might be reliable, but Greer was proof she had her missteps. And with what Jura was offering for the Dawnbreaker base, Teia couldn't afford any more mistakes. A favor from the Crown was an impossibility beyond belief, a prize that would be coveted by all of Erisia.

"It's complicated," Teia said. "But I need whatever you can find on Kyra. Family history, weaknesses. I don't even know what she looks like."

Enna grimaced. "Probably has orange hair from farming all those carrots."

"I'm starting to think you've never met anyone from Set." Teia shook her head. "I need you to move fast. Chances are she might already be here."

"You have eyes on her?"

"Call it intuition. The Dawnbreakers have been targeting locations all over Bhanot. If that's the case, I'm guessing they brought her along."

"Lehm's been busy," Enna muttered. "Thanks to him, your head of military has every guard in the city on alert."

"Miran's committed." It was a nice way of saying the rebel leader had gouged out Miran's eye six months before, which the general had taken rather personally.

"I hope he finds a pastime," the thief replied. "All these guards running around are awfully inconvenient." She blew out an aggravated breath. "As for Kyra, she should stay out of the Flats if she's in Bhanot. The rebels aren't popular there."

"What did they do? Stab the wrong back?"

"Of sorts. A few poked around a bit too much. Tried to recruit for their cause."

"And?"

"And nothing. We told them to bite it. They don't just want

Jura off the throne, you know. They're also insistent on other things. Equality for all. The end of crime."

"Most people would consider that paradisial."

"Most people pay their taxes and bow before royalty." Enna shuddered. "My version of paradise is to die under my weight in guilds. How am I supposed to do that if the rebels clean up the Flats?"

"How philosophical of you."

"I once staked out a classroom at Bhanot University for a week. I'm a natural-born scholar." Enna leveled a shrewd gaze at Teia. "Since I have you, Boss. There's something else I want to ask."

Teia couldn't imagine this would be a lighthearted question. "Well?" she said blankly.

"The Council might hate the rebels, but what stake do you have? Why not allow the Dawnbreakers to win? Let Jura have what's coming to him."

It was a deceptively simple solution to Teia's problems— one she'd pondered over many late nights, as news of the Dawnbreakers trickled into the palace. If the War Room reports were true, the Dawnbreakers had amassed a sizable membership in various Erisian cities, growing outposts and recruiting members. With decent leadership and a bit of good fortune, it wasn't improbable that they could seize the palace.

If Teia joined the rebels now, she might even live to see the aftermath.

But what about after, when the swords were laid to rest and the bullets melted down? Would the palace be sacked, gutted open like a fish, its insides ripped apart to make room for the rebels' precious democracy? Would the throne be toppled where it stood and the pieces used for firewood?

Jura had made Teia what she was—a girl of ash, a ghost in her own home. She'd dreamed of his death since she was thirteen, when the assassin he'd sent rammed a knife toward her neck. Sometimes, Teia fantasized about being the one to flay the air from Jura's chest. She'd sit to the side in quiet observation, watching the life leach from his eyes.

Except what would happen to Erisia then? Relying on the Council wasn't an option, with emergency protocols slating the Minister of Contracts and Coin as next in the line of succession. And unless there was a miraculous reversal in public opinion, the equivalent of another blessing from the Goddess, Erisia would never accept Teia as queen. The Shaylani War ended twenty years ago, in a generation before Teia's, but old wounds ran deep. The court reviled her; the public feared her. They would sooner take an axe to the throne than allow her a seat.

Jura's rule would be nightmarish, but he would preserve their family's legacy. He would safeguard the palace. He would keep Erisia from fracturing without a leader.

Ultimately, wasn't that all that truly mattered?

She dropped her shoulders in a shrug, brushing off Enna's question. "If the Dawnbreakers win," Teia said, "they're clearing the Flats of crime. And when that happens, how will you keep running with the Society of Thieves?"

Enna accepted the answer. She was too smart to fall for Teia's deflections, but they'd stepped back onto common ground now. The exchange of guilds was what had started this relationship, and it was what persevered through the aches and creaks of time, smoothing over any disagreements. Enna wasn't about to push her luck.

"All that for me?" The thief put a hand to her heart. "I'm touched. Truly."

"Does that mean you'll take the job?"

"Do you have to ask?"

Teia pulled two bags from under her cloak. The fabric frayed near the bottom, straining from the sheer number of coins. "I'm trying to be polite. Is three days enough time?"

"Don't insult me. I can get you Kyra's entire family tree in two."

"Two works. As long as you're—"

"Subtle. I know, I know." The guilds disappeared, gone before Teia could blink. "Trust me—if anyone found out you were my secret patron, I'd be beating off con men with a stick."

Teia wasn't so convinced. She'd seen the way Enna fought, transforming into a thing of nails and teeth. The thief carried a dagger in her belt and another up her sleeve. She was especially fond of her bone-handled ice pick, small enough to hide in her shoe, which she'd once used to burst someone's eardrum. When Teia asked later what the man had done, Enna responded that he'd tried to nick her bag.

"I don't think you need a stick to handle yourself," Teia said.

The thief smiled modestly. She hiked her cloak up in her fist and began kicking her way through the pebbles. It wasn't until she'd reached the rugged dirt path, framed by the rows of boats behind her, that she wrenched back, sending Teia a grin.

"I don't," Enna agreed. "It would just give the others a fighting chance."

CHAPTER FIVE

❧

Teia ran into Jura back in the splendor of the Golden Palace. He had changed since the meeting in the War Room. Gone were the silver coat and the casual trousers. His current robes were cut from bolts of black silk, so fine they had to be imported from across the sea. His favorite gold circlet sat upon his head, studded with glinting rubies.

She knew this outfit well. Jura favored black when he attended a prisoner interrogation—the dark fabric helped hide any spatters of blood.

He barely spared Teia a glance as he sauntered past. "Hello, Halfling," he said lazily, stripping off his black gloves to reveal his rings.

How original. The court might scorn her heritage, but Teia no longer ached to please them. She had grown into herself over the years—half-Erisian, half-Shaylani, dual sides of one sword, a Carthan in her own right. She couldn't bleach her skin. She couldn't rearrange the shape of her eyes or scrub away her control of water. She wouldn't, even if given the chance.

Jura might think the nickname an insult, but Teia wore it prouder than any crown.

"Hello, Jura," she responded, peering back at him over her shoulder. "Finished branding prisoners for fun yet?"

"It's my duty to discipline them. Hardly something I do for pleasure."

"Right. Just something you do for sport, then."

Jura stopped. He rotated slowly to face her, blood still speckled along the side of his cheek. "Careful, Halfling," he said, each word clipped and deliberate. "It's a crime to speak so crudely to your king."

"It isn't. And you're not king yet."

"I'm sure we're both counting the days." He smiled at her indulgently. "It'll be a celebration for the ages. Performing acrobats. String quartets. Food and drink and dance—and, of course, the Morning Star on display."

That was a new development. Jura's many plans for his coronation spanned to the exact shade of gold for the tablecloths, but the Morning Star was beyond cutlery and linens. The jewel was famed throughout the Five Kingdoms, left behind by the Goddess when she blessed the Divine Five. It had been stolen and retrieved multiple times, before being moved to Blackgate Prison a century prior, where it had been protected by the Carthans ever since.

"You're throwing the court a toy," Teia deadpanned, "and hoping it distracts them from the Dawnbreakers."

"You mean the vagrants, running about Bhanot like children?"

"They've bombed a dozen warehouses and sunk half your naval fleet."

"They caused insignificant damage, which will be dealt with in time." Jura shook his head sadly. "Although I have to say—it's such a shame when they target civilians. One of our scouts showed up in the infirmary earlier after a run-in with those criminals. Healers say he won't last the night—not with the burns he suffered."

It was hard to forget the scout from the Council briefing, with his nervous ways and awful screams. "Right," Teia said. "You seem terribly broken up by it."

"I did all I could for him, but you know what those barbarians are like. Always maiming and killing without purpose."

"Seems like you have a lot in common."

"On the contrary." Jura's eyes gleamed green fire. A smile glimmered on his lips. "I'm the Blessed Heir of Erisia. My very existence provides purpose."

She laughed aloud, and his expression distorted into a sneer. It was a fool's victory, but Teia savored every second as she said, "You're right, Jura. So purposeful that you've managed to incite a rebellion, which has the country in shambles."

"Internal conflict is a natural part of any rule."

"If you're talking about what Father experienced, the Bhanot Uprising was a group of fifty students, not a movement of hundreds."

"What's hundreds in a population of millions?"

"I don't know. Why don't you ask that outrageous reward that the messengers just posted for Kyra Medoh?"

For all his pronouncements in the War Room, she'd landed upon a sore subject. Jura's stare cut through Teia, but she refused to drop her gaze.

"I'd watch that mouth if I were you," he said smoothly. "You better thank the Goddess that I'm so benevolent, or I would ship you off to Lord Ralis tomorrow. I've heard the Highland Mountains are a marvelous destination this time of year."

Teia's temper rose black within her. Suddenly, she was back on the damned balcony, Jura's voice ringing in her ears. The shame she'd felt hearing the details of her wedding contract came rushing back, prickling against her skin. There had been clauses for the clauses, from the guards that would report her actions to her exile from Bhanot. Jura had even included a section on the removal of her future children, down to the specific method of disposal.

Just as quickly, despair surged to meet her. Teia's original plan was for Abbott to loosen the contract's language, allowing her trips through the Highlands and visits back to Bhanot, providing her space to plot her next move. But in moments like these, backed against a corner, Jura beaming out at her, Teia saw just how fruitless all that would have been.

Goddess. I was doomed from the start.

He must have sensed her helplessness. "Don't strain yourself, Halfling," Jura said smugly. "There are far worse men than Ralis—and *so* many seeking a royal bride. Cross me again, and I'll betroth you to a Dvořákian dignitary. The current representative is fond of strangling prostitutes in bed."

"That's awful."

"That's politics."

Teia dug her nails into her palms. She shoved away a slew of images—Ralis belching in uproarious laughter, the Dvořákian dignitary cleaning his filth-rimmed nails—and tipped her chin upward. "Fine then," she said. "Marry me off to some Dvořákian. Let's see what happens when Carthan fire appears there."

Jura's features curdled at the thought of a white-haired Dvořákian child, manipulating threads of heat. Most members of the Divine Five had spread their abilities freely to their descendants, marrying who they wanted, passing their powers through the generations—but not Erisia. Never Erisia. Teia's family prided itself on fire, clinging to the hereditary secret of the flame, only marrying nobles within the country's borders. It was, in part, why Ren's marriage to Calla had been such a nasty shock.

For all his threats, Jura was a purist. He grimaced in disgust, revulsion radiating from him in waves, which Teia took as an encouraging sign. "Not just that," she continued. "I'm not sure the Council would approve a Dvořákian wedding."

Jura drew himself to full height. "I don't need the Council," he snapped.

"Don't tell me you're forgetting how our government works. Ministers suggest laws, and the Council ratifies them. Until you're king, Jura, you're bound to making decrees—and marriage alliances don't quite qualify."

"My coronation—"

"Will be a wonderful event. Yes, I'm well aware." She smiled at him humorlessly. "Tell me—if you ply the ministers with enough alcohol, do you think they'll finally begin to respect you?"

He wanted to hit her. She could tell from the way his fingers twitched against his side, crumpling into his robes, before he withdrew from her abruptly. "How does it feel," Jura said at last, "to have so much bravado but no real power?"

"I get by."

"I suppose so. But after I ascend the throne, we both know that will no longer be enough."

With that, he stormed back down the golden hallway, toward the main corridor that led to his chambers. The train of his robes vanished around the corner, but Teia remained where she was, motionless. Inside her mind, Jura's words buzzed about angrily, circling like a swarm of hornets.

The assassination attempts. The plotted exiles. Through the

knowledge she held and the favors she swapped, Teia had always managed to slip the folds of Jura's net. And yet he was right. It pained her to admit, as difficult as sawing off her own arm, but once he was king, there was no limit on Jura's power. He no longer needed the Council's vote or a consultation with his ministers. Teia would be his to command, to use how he liked—a pawn for wedding alliances, an example of his eternal benevolence. She had a hunch it was why he'd stopped sending mercenaries after her, at least within the past year.

Jura was nothing if not conniving—and Teia was worth more alive than dead.

She squeezed her eyes shut. Even today, when she was piecing together how she'd befriend the Dawnbreakers, a whispering possibility persisted inside her. A packed bag had been stowed under Teia's bed for weeks, stuffed with valuables and a change of clothes. Right on top, beneath a map of the Five Kingdoms, she kept the papers she'd received from the ambassador to Ismet, which confirmed her identity as a Shaylani immigrant, attempting to seek work within the kingdom's borders.

Yet when she thought of fleeing Erisia, white-hot pain jolted through her. The Golden Palace might be a cage, but it was also Teia's home, her history. It was the last remnant of Ren and Calla, of a life she'd loved and lost. What would be left, if Teia abandoned the place that still sang of her parents? What would she become without her name? Her kingdom?

No. She couldn't leave. She wouldn't, not unless her plan fell apart and she was forced out by the guards, hauled through the gates and thrown into a carriage. Instead, when she brought herself before Jura, Dawnbreaker base in hand, Teia would ask to be left alone. She would request to live in the palace without any disruption. She would swear to stay out of his way and keep to her routines—taking meals by herself, remaining in her room, roaming the passageways like a hapless spirit.

It wasn't a good future. It wasn't even a decent one. But if it was between this and being chained to the Highlands, the decision was the easiest she'd ever make.

When Teia looked to what came next, all she saw was gray.

The next two days crept by, filled with endless reminders of Jura's impending coronation. Florists planned their elaborate arrangements. Cooks rushed around the kitchens, testing recipes and experimenting with ingredients. Teia was hounded by an especially persistent event planner, who insisted on selecting her outfit for the coronation, down to the color of her undergarments.

When Teia suggested all white—the traditional color of Erisian funerals—the event planner fell into hysterics. He staggered dramatically to the opposite wall, wringing his hands and lamenting the indignity of things, before requiring a packet of smelling salts to return to his usual self.

After she picked her dress and chose the style and agreed to stay far away from white silks, Teia was able to slip from the event planner's grasp. A guard escorted her back to the market; she sent him to run her list of errands while she hiked the short distance to Mourner's Beach. The sun hung low in the watercolor sky. Pink streaks shot through the clouds, as sailors poured from their schooners, angling for the Flats' alehouses.

As soon as Enna came into view, Teia rose to her feet. "Please tell me I got my money's worth."

"What a lovely greeting," the thief said. "No 'how are you, Enna?' No 'did you sleep well, Enna?'"

Teia rolled her eyes. "Did you sleep well, Enna?"

"Like a baby, thank you very much." She stooped down to knock pebbles from the soles of her boots and relented with, "I heard Kyra's mixed. Ismetian father, Erisian mother. The mother was out of the picture once Kyra was born, so she was raised by her da."

"In Set?"

"In Bhanot. He died from the Reaper's Kiss when she was nine, which is how she ended up in Set."

"Relatives?"

"Some distant uncle took her in, but he passed when she was fourteen. Some kind of plowing accident in the fields."

"That's bad luck."

"Or maybe Kyra's the bad luck," Enna proposed. "Everyone close to this girl seems to shake hands with death."

Teia sincerely hoped that wasn't the case. "What happened after?" she said. "Once the uncle died."

"Kyra stayed in Set. She was one of the village's tailors, right up to when she went missing three months ago."

"The Dawnbreakers recruited her."

"They did a hell of a job. Kyra was there one day and gone the next. Apparently, the rebels burned her house to the ground to cover their tracks." Enna shrugged. "Gives new meaning to leaving no trace behind, doesn't it?"

"It's smart. Erases any identifying documents."

"There are easier ways to do that," Enna said critically. "They didn't have to light the place up."

"Write them a feedback slip," Teia answered. "In the meantime, do we know what Kyra looks like?"

"Dark skin, dark hair. My contact said she was pretty to look at."

Was this all Teia's guilds had bought her? *Dark skin, dark hair.* It was a generic description that could fit any of the thousands of Ismetians who called Bhanot home. Teia could return to the hubbub of Carfaix Market right now and pick out a hundred vendors who met those criteria.

"Enna. There has to be something else. Something useful."

"Come on, Boss. I've given you enough to write a book about this girl."

"A very short book. For very young children."

"I'll try not to be insulted by that." Enna shook back her curls, which shone against the fading sun. "I do have one more lead. Something you're going to like."

"A better description?"

Enna grinned. "A location."

Teia's stomach dropped. "You know where she is?" she said, her voice heavy with disbelief, and Enna nodded.

"Rumor has it she's doing undercover work in Bhanot, disguised as a servant in the Golden Palace."

It took a full minute for the statement to sink in. "Kyra's in the *palace*?" Teia said. The wind blew back her hair in a wild tangle. A horn sounded far in the distance as a straggling merchant ship sailed into port.

"It's just a rumor, mind you. It's hard to verify something like that, without a direct connection inside the Dawnbreakers."

"But if you had to guess?"

Enna mulled the question over. "It's a good move," she conceded, with no small reluctance. "The rebels have no style, but they're passably smart."

That was the last thing Teia wanted to hear.

◆◆◆

If Teia was cautious before, she was downright paranoid now.

A Dawnbreaker in the palace. Masquerading as a *servant*, no less. In many ways, it was the perfect disguise—one Teia used herself, when sneaking out of the palace for midnight excursions. The nobility didn't pay the least bit of attention to people beneath them, ranking servants somewhere between ugly canvases of art and unsightly pieces of furniture.

When Teia returned from Mourner's Beach, she scrutinized every servant who might be the rebel champion. She spent one afternoon tailing multiple suspects, until realizing her efforts were in vain. Unless Teia could magically duplicate herself, she could hardly be in sixty places at once.

She was in a bitter mood as she slid aside the passageway wall. It skidded cleanly to one side, allowing her to climb out into one of the palace's sunlit back hallways. Teia stalked around the corner. She had wasted the morning following yet another Ismetian servant. It was a lead that had gone absolutely nowhere, and Teia was both frustrated and exhausted, fully intent on returning to her chambers and drowning her sorrows in a nap.

A lone servant knelt at the end of the corridor.

The raven-black braid looked vaguely familiar, as did the copper skin. Teia blinked. It was one of the servants who had been swabbing the floor before Calla's sitting room, the girl who had dropped the mop. This time, she was scrubbing at a stain with a horsehair brush, her stance tense and rigid. She seemed to strain away from the bucket placed beside her, moving with an uncertainty that bordered on pain.

It was enough to make Teia hesitate.

Teia had never been afraid of water. It was one of the advantages of having a parent who could move the tide, the ocean in her voice, her eyes, the sea parting with a single thought.

Jura was different. Teia had a faint memory of her half brother first coming into his powers. He'd been skittish and uneasy, going out of his way to avoid fountains and seek shelter in rainstorms. It had taken several months before fire fully melded into his bones, and he shook off any lingering discomfort.

A discomfort that lined the servant girl's face.

Teia's pulse thumped out an erratic beat. She rapped at the wall loudly, and the servant girl gasped. The brush fell through her fingers as she bent her head quickly. "My lady," she stuttered. "I didn't notice you there."

Teia merely gestured toward the bucket. "Can you lift that up?" she said quietly.

The girl frowned in confusion. "My lady?"

When Teia remained silent, the servant inched forward. Her hand had just curled around the cold metal handle when Teia reached for the water inside. She prodded it awake, heeding it to listen, and it acceded cheerfully to her demands. Water jumped from the bucket. It doused the servant in a tremendous splash, and the girl recoiled, twitching backward in a fit.

It was the closest thing to proof that Teia could have asked for. Her limbs seemed to double in weight. She jerked her head at the girl, nodding back around the corner. "Follow me," she said stiffly.

"The bucket—"

"Leave it."

The girl stood slowly. She plodded behind Teia the way a prisoner approached a firing squad, feet dragging, shoulders slumped. "I should be getting back," she mumbled.

"In a moment. There's something I need your help with first."

Teia led the girl through the palace's various wings, not stopping until they'd come to a mahogany door, its perimeter carved in a pattern of flames. She put her palm to the space above the handle, and the golden cylinders clicked in perfect harmony.

The door opened soundlessly. The room before them was spacious, yet deliberately decorated with simple furnishings. Despite the lock she'd had custom-made from a blacksmith in the Flats, Teia had long feared Jura rummaging through her things, collecting information he could use against her. Aside from a landscape painting from her father and a handwoven tapestry that had dazzled her at Carfaix, the rest of the furniture was standard issue—a canopy bed, a loveseat, a desk pushed against one corner.

Despite the decor, the girl's mouth dropped. "This is—"

"My room," Teia finished shortly. She bolted the door behind her, and the girl whirled at the sound. "You can drop the act. I think we're well past that, don't you?"

"Excuse me?"

Teia would have laughed, if her heart wasn't poised to explode. It was her. It had to be. Nobody else would have such a reaction to water, acting as if it burned her.

Did this count as a miracle? Teia thought so—perhaps she should start making pilgrimages with Enna to Bhanot's temples. She brought one arm forward in a sweeping gesture. She gave the servant girl her best smile.

"Kyra Medoh," she said, "it's time I welcome you to the Golden Palace."

Chapter Six

Kyra took a step back.

One hand tightened near her waist, her fingers curving into a fist. Teia watched the reaction with utter fascination. This girl might be the rebellion's champion, but she was about as subtle as a stack of bricks.

Teia held both hands into the air. "It's all right," she said soothingly. She had once heard the gardener use the same tone on a feral cat, right before it wreaked havoc on his prized rosebushes. "I'm not going to hurt you."

No response.

"If anything, I want to help you. You and the rest of the Dawnbreakers."

Teia would have gladly accepted a nod. A frown. Even an insult or two, if it led to a productive conversation. Yet the girl remained painstakingly silent. If not for the slight rise and fall of her chest, she could have been a statue.

Teia attempted another approach. Jura might be a touch mad, but he had a natural charisma about him, a magnetism that drew people in. Teia tried to embody that charm as she glanced around the room, wondering what she could do to put Kyra at ease. Maybe offer up a cup of tea, or trot out one of the many useless facts she'd learned about Set.

"Listen," Teia said. "Do you want to sit down? I'd love to hear more about the Dawnbreakers—"

In hindsight, it was probably the wrong thing to say. Kyra reeled to the side, her arms pushing out in a frantic motion. A wall of fire instantly lit the space between them, bisecting the room. Teia stared in naked fascination as the flames licked against the ceiling. They burned an unnatural shade of red, far darker than anything she could produce.

Then Kyra was charging through the blaze. A dagger jabbed out at Teia, which she sidestepped with ease before sticking out her foot. The rebel girl went sprawling, and Teia spun her hands outward, latching on to the water within the girl.

The whole affair—A fight? An assassination attempt?—lasted all of five seconds. The rebel girl choked. Her fingers went to her throat, scrabbling as water poured from her nose. She writhed helplessly against the floor, her lips strained in a garbled scream.

As Teia extinguished the fire, she stooped to examine Kyra. Her father's training had included basic combat lessons, but she doubted that was needed to bring Kyra down. *This* was the Dawnbreakers' champion? This was the cause for such alarm, the reason for a million-guild reward?

Goddess. If this girl was the rebellion's best hope, the entire movement was doomed.

With a sigh, Teia cleared the water in Kyra's lungs. She kicked the knife away for good measure, then settled into the loveseat. The cushion was badly burned, the wooden armrest charred into a blackened mess. Teia's tapestry had suffered a similar fate, the bottom melted and scorched beyond repair.

Wonderful. At the rate this discussion was going, she would need to redecorate her entire room.

"You're kidding, right?" Teia said scathingly, temporarily forgetting about channeling Jura's charm. "Fire walls? I've been making those since I was ten."

Kyra was still on the ground, spitting up an ocean's worth of water. She glowered up at Teia and hacked out a chafing cough.

Teia's standards had been low, but this was going so much worse than she'd anticipated. She cleared her throat, desperately racking her brains for a way to win over the rebel girl. "You and I?" she said, fully prepared to launch into a long-winded speech. "We're not so different. We aspire to a common goal. A unified dream. A way to make life better for people—"

"Why didn't you kill me?"

Teia started. "You talk?" she said.

Kyra ignored her. "Why didn't you kill me?" she rasped again. "You could have just now. But you didn't."

"I told you—I don't want to hurt you."

Kyra tapped her throat gingerly, and Teia folded her arms. "To be fair, you came after me with a knife. I'd say that was warranted."

The rebel girl hauled herself to a standing position. She kept a sizable distance between her and Teia, leaving wet footprints as she retreated warily. "What you told me in the beginning," she said. "You said you wanted to help."

"I do."

"Why? You're a Carthan."

"Our families don't define us."

"But why now?" Kyra insisted. She seemed wholly untouched by Teia's declarations. If the door wasn't latched, the rebel girl would have bolted from the room. "The Dawnbreakers have been active for a year. You've had plenty of time to contact us."

"Right. Next time, I'll send word by carrier pigeon."

"Nobody uses pigeons for mail anymore," Kyra said, so earnestly that Teia grimaced.

"It's sarcasm. You have that in Set, right?"

"You know where I'm from?"

"Everyone in Erisia knows where you're from. Your wanted poster is on every building in Bhanot."

Kyra took another step back, her heels meeting the wall. "I don't believe you."

"About the wanted posters?"

"About your motivations. Nobody decides to join a rebel movement overnight."

"Didn't you?" Teia challenged. She was pleased to see Kyra waver, as she plowed ahead determinedly. "Before you came along, nobody outside my family controlled fire. You could have crossed the Dark Sea to Shaylan or gone north to Dvořáki. You could have offered your services to any ruler and made enough for ten lifetimes."

"Why would I do that?"

"Royals kissing your feet? A bucketful of guilds?"

"I don't need a bucketful of guilds."

"A trunkful," Teia amended, thinking of her payments to Enna. "A bucket is likely too small."

"I don't need any of those things!" All of a sudden, Kyra looked more offended than angry, as if her very honor was being called into question. "I stayed in Erisia because it was the right thing to do. People are hurting, and the monarchy doesn't care."

"Governments are usually like that."

"Not the one we want to build." Kyra raised her chin defiantly. "The Dawnbreakers can usher in change. No more thrones or councils or kings making decisions without a thought for the people. We let the commonfolk vote for their leaders. We give them a say in their own futures."

It was the prettiest of ideas, wrapped in brave words and lofty dreams. And if Teia had been a fool, she might have believed it. Because hadn't the people of Ismet—the desert-ringed kingdom to Erisia's south—wanted exactly what Kyra spoke of? There had been an uprising there, too, a movement born out of the same fervid passion that now gripped Erisia. In Ismet, women with pistols and swords led men with colorful banners to storm the gates of the palace. They'd broken down the barred stone doors and overrun the royal guard. The Ismetian queen had fled the country, smuggled out by sympathetic citizens, while her family had been shot in the capital square before a euphoric crowd.

The Ismetian people had rejoiced. They celebrated their newfound freedom. They toasted to democracy, up until their government collapsed not six months later, folded beneath the weight of poor leadership. In the end, the Ismetian queen returned to reclaim her throne, rising like a phoenix to crush the remaining rebels.

Ismet was proof that monarchies were not so easily destroyed.

Kyra Medoh might have never taken a history lesson, but she made an excellent rebel mouthpiece. The other girl spoke with the force of a dozen officials, in a tone flush with utter sincerity. As Teia listened, she found herself stuck between admiration and sheer disbelief. She had known Kyra for all of fifteen minutes, but she was rapidly shaping up to be the most morally just person Teia had ever met.

Teia plucked at the ruined threads on the loveseat.

"Everything you spoke of just now—making life better and furthering Erisia. Is it so hard to believe we'd want the same things?"

"You're a Carthan," Kyra repeated stonily.

"Barely. You've been pretending to be a servant. You know how the court feels."

A hint of shame passed across Kyra's face. "I've heard my share," the rebel girl said guardedly.

"I'm sure that's being generous." Teia's voice caught unexpectedly. Something throbbed inside her, cold and jagged and ugly, until she forced it down quickly. She embraced her ties to Shaylan. She cherished them. Why wouldn't she, when they brought her closer to her mother?

But what about the others? a voice hissed within her. It was one Teia had heard before, a persistent shred of conscience that surfaced during increasingly inconvenient moments. *What about the Shaylani in Erisia? What about people who came to make a living here?*

Usually, Teia's response was swift and unforgiving. She needed to safeguard herself. She had to survive the court. Besides, any Shaylani who ventured to Erisia knew what they would face. Ten years was a long time to have been at war, and while two decades had passed since, too many Erisians still remembered the endless military drafts, the crimson furl of sails as ships departed for the Dark Sea.

But in that instant, Teia's dreams expanded. They rose unexpectedly to loom before her, standing taller than any giant. If she brought Jura the Dawnbreakers, it would be a card she'd never held before. Her demands could go beyond ridding herself of a marriage contract, or decaying quietly within the Golden Palace. There was power to be had here, power that she'd never felt before. She might not be accepted as ruler, but perhaps there were other opportunities, different avenues to explore.

She thought about her mother, an outsider in her own palace. She thought about the lonely years of childhood, wandering the passageways on her own. The Council was a trifecta, spanning back to its inception with Erisia's founder, Eris the First. Yet what if there was another position created, one tailored toward diplomacy? Teia could demand a spot on the Council. She could ask to facilitate relations with Shaylan and craft some sense of belonging for her kinsmen in Erisia.

For the first time, Teia didn't dismiss the voice in her head. What she wanted was still a dream, hewn together from uncertain pieces, but here was a cause that woke something within her, igniting a flame she'd thought gone.

Goddess, Teia thought grimly. *I'm beginning to sound like a Dawnbreaker.*

When she refocused on Kyra, it was with a newfound courage, fanned by whatever had sprung to life. Her voice was steady, her purpose clear. She would give the performance of a lifetime, if it meant assuming a seat on the Erisian Council.

"The nobility hasn't done good in years," Teia said. "The Council is defunct. Jura is too cruel. And I've been here for every second of it. Did you really think I wouldn't want something to change?"

"You've had years to help—"

"I've been afraid." Teia bit her lip. Somehow, admitting this sliver of truth felt so much worse than telling lies. "Wouldn't you be? Jura has everything. Guilds. Troops. I have no allies, no influence over the court."

"You could have tried."

"I know—and I'm sorry. But I'm asking you to take a chance

on me, as the Dawnbreakers did with you. I want to show that I'm dedicated to this cause."

Kyra hesitated. For the briefest moment, her features softened. "How?" she said.

"I have access to nearly everyone in the palace. I can gather information for you. Spy on different nobles."

"And why should I trust you?"

Teia debated her response. "You shouldn't," she acknowledged, her hands folded before her. "But I'd like the chance to prove myself."

There it was—a flicker of hope, a flame against the night. Kyra tilted her head slightly, contemplating the weight of Teia's words. A stifling silence overtook the room, as the rebel girl stood by the door, pondering her decision.

"I have to talk to some people," she said. "Lehm will want to hear about this."

Goddess. Relief mingled with shock, sending a current through Teia. She had her suspicions about Kyra's reach, but she hadn't anticipated the rebel leader's name. Lehm might have masterminded sabotages across Bhanot, but nobody had seen him in months. His last appearance was during a raid on the palace's cache of weapons, when he'd maimed General Miran and made off with a shipment of revolvers.

"Right," Teia managed, struggling to calm her expression. "By all means—you know where I'll be."

It was clearly the end of their conversation. Still, there was an air of reluctance about Kyra. Teia sensed she had another question, something more she wanted to say. The rebel champion's dark eyes were curious as she said, "There has to be something else."

"Such as?"

"A catch. A deal. Something you'd like in exchange for helping us."

Teia had suspected she might ask that. She had planned for this exact instant, rehearsing countless times before the washroom mirror. The smile she gave Kyra was offhanded and unassuming. Gentle. It was a smile that belonged to someone else, someone entirely unfamiliar to Teia.

"Don't worry," she said. She spoke with the confidence of a practiced gambler, a girl who had nothing left to lose. "I just want to see the bastards burn."

CHAPTER SEVEN

Teia didn't expect anything from Kyra—at least, not at first. She spent the next few days replacing a good third of her furniture, which had been roundly flambéed by Kyra's wall of fire. *This girl had better be worth the hassle*, she'd thought darkly, as she unhooked the ruined tapestry and dragged it to the hallway.

She could still feel the charred threads against her skin as her carriage wound through the streets of the Royal District. Barriers had been erected on either side of the road, where the royal guard stood ready with hands on their scabbards. Everywhere, there were people cheering, screaming, tossing long-stemmed roses at the adorned golden carriage, fighting for a better view of the crown prince.

Jura hung out the left window, his fingers gripping the frame, his knee resting on the velvet seat opposite Teia's. He grinned ear to ear, waving to the crowds, and a dozen voices rose around him. Someone begged him to marry her. Another flung a bouquet his way, which Jura caught with a laugh, before sliding languidly back inside the carriage.

"Can I help it?" he said, running a hand through his golden curls. "The people love me."

"Because you distract them with guilds and sweets," Teia

said. She nudged the sack by her ankles, which bulged with an assortment of treats.

He plucked a geranium from the bouquet. "A king lives to serve," Jura said carelessly. "The Autumn Ball tonight is for the nobles, and the parade for the commonfolk. What more could they possibly want?"

"The ability to hold protests. An abolishment of torture."

"I've never heard a complaint."

Correct, Teia thought. Because you string up the ones who object. But she simply rested her elbow against the polished wooden armrest and watched the hordes of people drift past. Set against the glittering crowds, their roars of approval drifting into the carriage, the Dawnbreaker movement seemed miniscule in comparison.

"Maybe you're right," Teia said flatly, prodding again at the bag. "But Father never resorted to such tricks."

His grin hardened, crystallizing against the planes of his face. Jura's moods might be feared within the Golden Palace, but he'd never slipped once before the public. He adored their affection. He craved it. There was something immensely satisfying about seeing him struggle against his rage, as he crushed the flower in his fist.

"Father was far too soft for the throne," Jura said coolly. "All his dithering about reforms and progress."

"He was a good king."

"He was decrepit and inefficient." The flower fell to the floor of the carriage, petals shedding from the stem. "Change is coming, Halfling. When I take the throne, everyone in the Five Kingdoms will know my name."

Teia shook her head. "Throw your parades, Jura," she replied. "If you can't govern, you might as well entertain."

◆◆◆

Jura had despised Teia from the moment she was born.

It began with her mother. Calla was *Shaylani*. She was the *enemy*. Her arrival at the Golden Palace, announced by a hundred brass trumpets and a magnificent parade of white horses, had shaken Erisia to no end. The advisers gossiped about the foreign queen. The nursemaids reminisced about the Shaylani War.

Teia could picture Jura absorbing every barb with those emerald-green eyes. Sometimes, she considered if things could have been different. If he hadn't had those nursemaids, perhaps. If Ren had waited longer to wed his second wife and allowed his son time to meet his new stepmother.

She doubted it. Jura might hate her, but it was far more than a product of his surroundings. She knew the darkness that lurked under the smile. She would never forget discovering his make-shift traps when she was younger, which had been rigged against the open window in his room.

Jura, no older than nine, held tight to one of the cages. A spark danced off his fingers, leaping close to the bluebird inside. The creature screamed in fright. It thrashed against the bars, its little body quivering.

"What are you doing?" Teia piped up. She had been five—an age that she was terrifically proud of—and in the habit of questioning everything.

He didn't bother turning around. "It's nothing," Jura answered silkily. "Just a game I like to play."

"A game?"

"Easy. If my flame is orange, I'll let the bird go. If it's blue, it stays." He rolled back his shoulders. "Do you want to play?"

She crept inside and stretched as tall as she could, trying to get a better view of the cage. "Orange?"

When Jura opened his palm, a flame spun to life. The bottom of the cage instantly came alight. The bluebird's wing singed, its delicate feathers scorching to black. All at once, the room went eerily still.

"Red," Jura said mildly, examining the ruined wing with a scientist's eye. "Oh well. I guess we'll have to play again."

Teia hadn't told anyone. Who would have believed her? From a young age, Jura had dazzled everyone around him. He had a quick wit and an astounding memory. He impressed dignitaries with his advanced vocabulary and excelled at making friends.

No. This was a secret to keep close, buried where nobody would find it. Teia held on to what she'd seen. She nursed it like a grudge. And when the dogs and cats started to go missing from the palace grounds, she kept her mouth shut about that, too, avoiding the cook as he spent a full week going from room to room, calling desperately for his striped tabby.

If Teia was quiet, if she made herself invisible, Jura wouldn't notice her. For a while, her strategy had worked—up until that one particular morning when she'd stolen away to the gardens, eager to escape her lessons. Teia couldn't stomach another lecture on the economic appreciation of Erisian guilds. What did it matter, anyway? She was seven, not seventy. She cared about sunshine and running wild and barreling her way through spiny hedges, her dress so stiff with mud that the maids had to soak her clothes in thick vats of bubbling water.

For four glorious hours, Teia had played outside. She wove a flower crown from white roses. She acted out Eris the First receiving his powers. Eventually, thoroughly worn out, she'd fallen asleep at the base of a towering apple tree, curled up in a patch of dirt.

It was the warmth that woke her. A tickling sensation, like a feather rubbed across the length of her body. Teia jolted awake. She pulled herself upright, fighting back a yawn, to find everything caught in a haze. The world tinged a horrible shade of maroon. Her clothes flaked off in blackened patches, fluttering to the charred ground.

Someone had set her aflame.

There was the shrill pitch of a shriek, followed by the pattering of feet. A bucket of water was thrown over her, but Teia's focus was pinned toward the marble archway.

Jura stood just beyond an arrangement of pruned bushes. His arms were folded, his mouth drawn in an empty smile. His expression was one of absolute detachment, a blank calm used to study a vaguely interesting bug.

Fear slammed into Teia. Her legs locked into place as she huddled against the mass of servants, all eager to swathe her in blankets. Jura didn't care that Teia hadn't burned, just like he wouldn't have cared if she had. Instead, he lit the fire for no other reason than an innate curiosity: he wanted to see what would happen, and so he set out to do exactly that.

It wasn't the first time Teia understood who Jura was. A coldness hid beneath the poise and the grace. It rested somewhere behind his eyes, just like it always had.

But something changed that day in the gardens. That evening, when Ren paced before them, demanding an explanation for what happened, Jura bowed his head. "I don't know, Father," he whispered, tears running down his cheeks. "I wouldn't. You *know* I wouldn't. I wasn't even near Teia when that happened."

Teia watched her half brother as he wiped away his tears. She listened as he proposed other possibilities—that maybe she was coming into her powers and her flame had manifested differently. She waited for a long minute, thoughts searing into her mind, before their father sighed. He opened his arms, kneeling to embrace both his children.

From over Ren's shoulder, Jura flashed Teia a hollow grin. She felt that familiar seize of panic, like she was the bluebird caught in his cage.

Teia understood who Jura was, but she wondered if anyone else did.

◆◆◆

The line of carriages was endless.

They extended far beyond the palace's gates in a rainbow of color, down the streets Teia had ridden through mere hours before. Every noble in Erisia had come to kiss Jura's feet during the Autumn Ball. Teia could see them stepping out near the main entrance, bedazzled in shades of red and gold, their hair teased alarmingly high.

She made her obligatory appearance later that night, sitting to Jura's left in her mother's old seat. Calla had commissioned the throne herself, wrought from silver and lined in blue velvet. It had remained covered in white silks after she'd passed, untouched and unmoved. When Ren died several years later, Teia thought Jura would dismantle the chair. Melt it down in the palace hearth, or whatever ghastly thing he could dream up.

Except Jura kept the throne. Teia needed somewhere to sit during larger ceremonies, as living proof of the crown prince's generosity. In any event, she suspected he enjoyed the distinction between their seats, hers in blue and his a deep crimson. It was an easy way to remind the court of the rift between them, without ever speaking a word.

He observed her now as he took a sip from his glass. "Well, Halfling? Spectacular sight, don't you think?"

It was, although she would never admit that aloud. The ballroom had transformed into a haven of autumnal colors, marking the seasonal celebration. Tawny lights cast the room in an ethereal feel. Flourishing maple trees had been cultivated for this specific occasion, grown in gold planters beaded with jewels.

"I'm surprised the coffers haven't bled dry," Teia said. Across the room, Minister Abbott tossed back a vial of clear liquid, before belching raucously.

Jura followed her gaze with a shudder of trepidation. "Between you and me, I'm counting the days until I take the throne. No more questions from weak-minded idiots. No more waiting for votes to do anything worthwhile."

"My heart breaks for you."

"Show some appreciation, Halfling. We both know I'm destined for great things." He gave her a wink. "Stay in line, and I might keep you around as a witness."

His musings were interrupted by a noble, who called out to him from the base of his throne. A chill wormed through Teia. Jura swiveled away from her, his features delighted as he beamed down at Lord Devon Ralis, who knelt below the dais. "My friend! It's wonderful to see you again."

"Likewise, Highness," Ralis said, standing to press his lips to Jura's hand. When his beady eyes roamed to Teia, she gripped the sides of her chair. There were endless stories about his previous wives, callous whispers about their fates. How the first was found dead in the gardens, surrounded by trampled bushes. How the second had lain at the bottom of the staircase for hours, her skull split open like a pomegranate, her limbs twisted and broken.

Ralis had been tried, with each judge promptly bought off. He had continued living his lavish lifestyle, running the Highlands with an iron fist, until the day Jura announced his engagement to Teia. It was then that he'd given a statement about his other wives, which had been printed in Bhanot's paper in minuscule font.

I lost my temper. Doesn't it happen to everyone?

Teia's mouth was dry. "Ralis," she said.

"Princess," he responded. One more grin, brittle at the edges, and he veered his focus back to Jura.

All it'd taken was a handful of words, but Teia's nerves were frayed. She wanted desperately to leave the room but forced herself steady, her fingers clenched around her wine. *Calm down,* she thought sternly, and cast her gaze toward the rest of the hall. A banquet table spanned one of the walls, cluttered with silver trays of pastries and miniature pies, caviar heaped in little crystal dishes. Nobles flocked nearby, gorging themselves on the Crown's generosity. Foreign dignitaries chatted away, the K'vali ambassador in brightly colored fabrics, the Ismetian diplomat with black braided hair.

To the right, Minister Abbott commanded his section of the room out of pure repulsiveness. There was something riveting about seeing the man guffaw, a hand wrapped around a scallop while the other scratched at his groin. He had a dollop of orange sauce smeared over his left sideburn, and Teia had no earthly idea how it had gotten there.

She was already watching Abbott, which was why she saw what happened next.

The servant boy trembled under his tray, loaded with glasses of plum wine. He was young—around the same age as General Miran's twins, who had recently celebrated their eighth birthday. Certainly not old enough to legally seek work, although that was frequently overlooked. It had been one of Abbott's more passionate stances after Jura had selected him as Minister of Contracts and Coin. *It's the way of the market,* he'd argued in a Council meeting. *If the people want to work, who are we to refuse?*

He'd conveniently excluded details about how the poor were starving, all while the Crown threw its lavish parties. The palace might pay a meager amount, but it offered room, board, and a decent reference for the future. People queued for hours for the opportunity to secure a position, and fights often broke out in line.

The boy continued his tour through the crowd, offering drinks to any courtiers who passed. Things were going smoothly until a flock of Erisian noblewomen pranced by. Their golden hair sparkled with jewels, corsets lacing tightly around their waists. One was twirling a patterned parasol, which smacked into the boy's tray.

The glasses shifted. The silver platter overturned in a rush, and a waterfall of purple wine rained down onto Abbott.

The minister's screech would have put any dying animal to shame. He scratched at the front of his lace robes, wine dripping from his curls. Nobles stopped to stare; the string quintet fell silent. It would have been comical, if Teia wasn't painfully aware of what was to come.

Abbott fixed his bulging eyes on the servant. "*You,*" he hissed, his upper lip sweating profusely.

There was a pointed cough. Amid the chaos, Jura had spotted the scene. "Abbott," he said lightly. "I wasn't aware that purple was an autumnal color."

A ripple of laughter spread through the crowd. The minister

straightened under the interest of the crown prince, gesturing wildly to his clothes. "Highness," he growled. "Look at the mess this boy made. Look at the state of my coat!"

"It's very becoming on you."

"I'm soaked through, and I demand reparations!"

Jura clicked his tongue sympathetically. "I would expect nothing less. Why don't we ask the lad to step forward?"

An eager murmur rose from the guests. They sensed blood in the air, a warped sense of justice that they'd come to expect. Heads bobbed left and right, searching for the boy, ready to push him to the throne.

They were met with a second voice, firm and unyielding.

"Highness."

Teia's stomach clenched. She recognized the voice instantly, the calm tenor that ran throughout. It came from a servant that wasn't, a tailor turned champion. The girl who had a million guilds affixed on her head, the most wanted person in the country.

Kyra Medoh stepped through the chattering crowd.

CHAPTER EIGHT

Teia was going to strangle Kyra.

She felt her fingers clench the many layers of her skirt, nails pressing into her knee. Did this girl not have a shred of self-preservation? Was it really so difficult to fly under the radar and not martyr herself up like some hopeless saint?

Apparently so, Teia thought miserably. The partygoers had split into a perfect semicircle, pressing in around Kyra. They buzzed among themselves about the *audacity* of servants nowadays, who spoke like they owned the Golden Palace. The dignitaries, too, seemed intrigued by the situation, although Teia caught the Ismetian representative making a hasty exit. Perhaps she had already seen a similar scene and had no desire to spectate another.

A crevice formed between Jura's brows. "And you are?"

Kyra set down her tray of appetizers. She dropped into an impressive curtsy, keeping the servant boy shielded from view. "Apologies, Highness. I bumped into Dalton, which is why he spilled the wine. If anyone should be at fault, it's me."

Jura inspected Kyra. The court tittered. Abbott preened.

A second later, Jura stood.

His robes spread behind him in a wave of crimson. The

Golden Palace's outline had been hand-stitched onto the back, displaying each tower and turret as he strode over to Kyra. When he motioned for her to rise, his tone was uncannily gentle. "What's your name, girl?"

As Kyra stumbled over an alias, Teia suppressed a groan. Kyra wasn't just an amateur—she also had the acting skills of a withered shrub.

Jura nodded. Teia doubted he'd registered the name at all, as he said, "Excellent. How long have you worked at the palace?"

"Just over a month, Highness."

"Are you happy?"

"Very."

"Well-fed?"

"Yes," Kyra said, clearly perplexed about where this was going.

"Good," Jura said with a smile. "Good. Now tell me—how would you like to play a game?"

The rebel girl drew a quick breath. "What type of game?"

"Oh, it's very simple." He snapped his fingers, and a page scampered out from behind the thrones. He pressed something into the crown prince's hand, which Jura held up for the room to see. "If the card has a black pattern, we forget this entire ordeal ever took place. If it's red, I let Minister Abbott do whatever he wants, first to your friend and then to you."

Kyra's gaze widened, but the explanation was hardly a request. The cards were beautiful, custom-made and leafed in gold. Dramatically, each movement exaggerated, Jura pulled the top card from the deck. He studied it with a theatrical slowness, before flipping it around for the court to see.

"Blank," Jura said, his voice ringing with false disappointment. Then, before she could react, he jerked his hand aside, backhanding Kyra across the face. His rings ripped open her skin. Welts blossomed on the rebel girl's cheek, the cuts weeping blood.

She recoiled, gasping in pain as Jura advanced on her. The card he was holding collapsed into ash as he reached to retrieve another. "That's poor luck, serving girl," he purred. "Should we try again?"

Teia said a silent prayer. She said two, in case the Goddess happened to have a spare minute to strike Jura down. The last servant who had crossed Jura was a cheerful girl with long yellow braids. After she'd knocked over a pedestal during Jura's coronation rehearsal, he'd forced her to draw cards to decide her own punishment. Teia could still hear the maid's screams as he gripped her hair, scorching her from braids to scalp.

Teia hated Jura for this outburst. She hated Kyra for her hero complex. *Curse this girl and all her ancestors,* she thought fiercely, as she tried to imagine what horrors Jura had waiting when he finished the deck. In the span of minutes, he'd burned through another three cards, all heartrendingly blank. Kyra had crumpled to the ground. Open gashes tore down to her chin, extending to her throat. The left side of her face was so bloodied that it shone.

Teia pushed away from her seat, her heart pounding ferociously. "Jura?" she said. Her voice rang throughout the room, louder than she'd anticipated.

He rotated her way. "Halfling," he said casually, as if they were having a nice chat about the weather. "You have something to add?"

"I do," Teia said bracingly. "This servant. I know her."

"You *know* her?"

"She's my maidservant. I brought her on a few weeks ago."

Jura raised an eyebrow. "You certainly chose a clumsy one."

"You know how new hires can be."

"Inept. Incompetent."

"It's hard to find good help nowadays."

"Indeed. Although this one takes after her mistress."

Loose chuckles scattered across the room. One woman batted her lashes at Jura, and Teia gritted her teeth. Let him have this, then—let everyone here have a good laugh at her expense, if it meant they could all move on from what had happened.

"Yes," Teia said. "I'm sorry, Jura. I'll make sure she's properly disciplined."

"That's all I ask for," Jura said agreeably. Just like that, the cards disappeared into his pocket. He frowned at the blood on the tile and waved disdainfully at Kyra. "Clean that up. I'd hate to leave a mess."

As he strutted back to his throne, the musicians sprang to life. A lilting melody flooded the hall, and any unpleasantness washed away. Courtiers resumed their chatter. Servants whirled about with trays of honeyed fruits and candied tarts. Jura was once again beside Teia, polishing his rings against his tunic. The one on his middle finger—a golden Serkawr wound protectively around a large ruby—had been flecked with Kyra's blood.

Nobody spared a glance for the so-called servant girl. Kyra stood off to the side, a hand cupped over her injuries. Teia could sense the fury rippling off her, could tell how badly the rebel champion wanted to burn. It would have been child's play to take in the heat, coaxing the flames to dance against the golden drapes.

It was a feeling that Teia was well accustomed to.

She managed to catch Kyra's eye. There was no way to communicate further, not without the entire court seeing, but Teia gave the barest shake of her head. She held on to the enduring optimism that Kyra's righteousness would win out, her good nature preventing her from broiling a banquet hall full of people.

Teia's reasons were a smidge less selfless. Either way, though, the general message was the same.

Don't.

It was an excruciatingly long minute before Kyra relaxed. She dropped her hand, her fingers smeared with blood, and melted away into an ocean of skirts.

Teia slid back into her seat. She released a sigh of relief and grabbed for her glass of wine. Nobody else had heeded the exchange that had happened—nobody cared to. The courtiers had their sights set on Jura as they flocked thick around his throne. They kissed his knuckles and knelt before him. They murmured about his potential as king.

Teia downed her drink, while merrymaking continued in the Golden Palace.

Teia knew the knock was coming. She waited for it all night, pacing her room until her legs ached from the strain. At one point, she thought about marching down to the kitchens and demanding to see Kyra, which wouldn't be completely unwarranted. After all, the rebel girl was supposedly Teia's maidservant—and a favored one at that, considering the Halfling Princess had spoken for her. To the endless eyes within the palace, the two of them were now inextricably linked, for better or for worse.

For worse, Teia thought. *Definitely for worse.*

It was early morning when she heard the knock. The sky had broken dapple gray against the windows, casting a pale light over the room. It was enough for Teia to count the cuts across Kyra's face, framed by a smattering of bruises. The rebel girl gripped a burnished tea tray, holding it like a shield before her.

Tension lingered when Kyra walked inside. She chewed nervously on the inside of her cheek and peered up at the new tapestry, which shimmered a gossamer blue. "That's nice," she said.

"I've done some redecorating since you were here."

Kyra, at the very least, had the grace to look ashamed. "I'm sorry about that," she said, setting the tray onto the desk. "When you said you could help me before, I didn't really believe you."

Teia shrugged nonchalantly. It was remarkable acting, considering her palms were slick with sweat. "It's all right. I wouldn't have believed me either."

Kyra offered her a small smile. It was unusually genuine, which caught Teia off guard. Smiles like that were rare in the Golden Palace. "Thank you. For what you did during the ball."

"You don't have to thank me—I'm just glad it didn't go further."

"It would have gone further?"

"I'd say you got off easy."

Kyra sat slowly on the edge of the bed. "What your brother did back there—"

"Half brother," Teia said.

"Half brother. Is it . . . common?"

"It can be."

"And nobody stops him?"

"Not unless they're tired of living."

"So is this it?" Kyra's voice had a shaky undertone. "Did he recognize me? Should I leave Bhanot?"

"Not necessarily," Teia said quickly. A bit too quickly, and she had to hurry to rein herself in. "People see what they want to—and all they saw was a servant, not some chosen rebel champion. I doubt Jura even remembers what you look like."

"Are you sure?"

"No. But if I were you, I would stay. Especially if you feel like there's more you could do." She paused, studying Kyra thoroughly. "That servant back there—the one you took the blame for. He's a Dawnbreaker?"

He had seemed a bit young to be a rebel, but who was Teia to judge? If the boy could brave courtroom politics, perhaps he was ready to swing a sword. She herself had started dabbling with blackmail when she was twelve and hadn't looked back since.

To her surprise, Kyra shook her head. "Dalton? No. I work with him in the kitchens. That would have been his third offense." She touched her cheek gingerly. "He has two siblings to feed. If he'd been fired by the palace, he would have never found work anywhere else."

Teia fell quiet. Her thoughts congealed in an untidy bunch as she pondered what Kyra had said.

Someone else—someone better—might have given up on their plans. They would have understood that the rebels were in good hands, with Kyra Medoh as their champion. They would have reflected on the implications of the Dawnbreaker movement.

But Teia had never claimed to be morally sound. Her freedom awaited—her future. If she wanted to rid herself of Ralis, to better Erisia through the Council, she needed to topple the rebellion first.

Teia exhaled. "Kyra," she said simply. "I want to meet the other Dawnbreakers. I want to help."

Kyra didn't answer. And she might have hesitated forever, discovering infinite ways to stave off Teia's requests, if the sun hadn't parted the clouds outside. A ray of light slanted through the window. They were caught in a blazing swath of gold, something materialized from a fairy story. It was like the Goddess herself was descending from the heavens, returning to extend one more blessing.

When Teia reminisced on things later, she wondered if this was what had changed Kyra's mind.

Kyra nodded. She held Teia's gaze.

She said, "Tonight."

◆◆◆

Kyra had given her a set of strict instructions. Meet at midnight. Go to Sunset Tower. Don't be late.

The palace halls were empty as Teia slipped from her room, wincing at each creak of the stairs. Luckily, the guard stationed at the back gate was one Teia knew well. When he saw the black billow of her cloak, he merely ducked his head and thrust the gates open. She pushed by him without a word, although she sensed his trepidation as he flinched away.

He had no reason to be worried, so long as he kept her goings quiet and his post intact. She'd made the terms of their agreement exceedingly clear the day she caught him lifting guilds from the palace treasury. Teia Carthan might be a source of nightmares, the thing that prowled in the dark, but she'd also given him her word. In her world, that meant something.

The cold hit her first. The wind was a monster, slashing straight through as she hurried down the Royal District's streets, turning east toward the golden gates of the foreign embassies, the weathered buildings of the Carmine District, and in the far distance, the glistening spectacle of the Flats. Toppled metal barricades were stacked haphazardly to her left, remnants of the earlier commotion from the parade. Crinkled newspapers and broken stems littered the gutters. Farther down, closer to where the road bent toward Embassy Row, beggars slept by streetlamps for warmth.

Teia was intensely glad when Sunset Tower came into sight. It stood before the arched bridge that marked the end of the district, notched with flames and built from polished sandstone. During the summer months, the tower was often overrun by tourists who munched on candied pecans and waited patiently for sunset. When the sky reddened and the sun fell, the entire structure gleamed scarlet as a symbol of Carthan might.

The tower was empty tonight, a deadened piece of rock devoid of any tourists. Kyra stood at the base, shivering furiously, but she brightened when she saw Teia. "You came!"

A black strip of cloth hung from her pocket. Teia eyed it apprehensively. This could all be an elaborate assassination plot, which ended with the rebel girl strangling her and dumping her in the Dark Sea. "What's that?"

"I have to blindfold you first," Kyra said apologetically. "Lehm wanted to take precautions."

"Not with a knife?" Teia muttered, thinking again of when the rebel leader had popped out Miran's eye.

"What was that?"

"Nothing," Teia said. "I said it's not a problem."

The rebel girl tied the cloth securely around Teia's eyes, and the rest of the world vanished. There was nothing but the wind and the cobblestones and Kyra's hand on her arm, steering her to the right. "This way."

Teia lost track of time. She counted the corners they rounded at first, but soon realized it was a useless task. Kyra might be an insufferable do-gooder, but she excelled at propelling Teia in seemingly random circles, making it impossible to tell how long they'd walked or the path they'd taken. Before long, everything had blurred into an unending stretch of darkness, punctuated by the occasional whine from a stray dog.

They'd reached the outskirts of the Flats by the time they stopped, where the neatly paved streets transitioned into hard-packed stretches of dirt. There was the sound of a key fitted into a lock, before Kyra guided Teia forward. "This way," she whispered, as a smothering dampness cropped up around them. Teia nearly choked on the cloying scent of floral perfume.

"Hello?" Kyra ventured, pitching her voice louder. She tugged at the blindfold, and the cloth fluttered to the ground. As Teia glanced around, she blinked hard, trying to discern any movement. The room was shrouded in shadows. Bleary shapes moved against them, too vague to make out.

Then an arm hooked around her shoulders. Teia's feet left the ground as someone knocked her off balance, dragging her backward forcefully. Alarm ripped through her, a delayed warning to react. To fight, to burn.

To do anything at all, if it meant escaping the blade pushed against her throat.

CHAPTER NINE

It took everything in Teia not to move. *Everything.* The familiar itch to reach for fire, for water, tickled at her fingers. All it would take was a focused pull, and Teia could sculpt a blistering flame. She might not know where she was, but she smelled the hint of fresh wood, logs piled atop one another. She was in the middle of a tinderbox, a building that begged to become a bonfire.

But Teia pursed her lips. She forced herself to stay still, her arms dropping limp to her sides. She pressed back against the person holding her, hoping to ease some pressure on her neck.

She was rewarded with a boy's voice, low and furious against her ears. "Are you out of your mind, Kyra? You brought a Carthan *here*? Do you know what you've done?"

"The Halfling Princess?" someone else said. A girl this time, with a voice like melted honey. "Goddess, Kyra. I'm not that eager to meet my maker."

There was the scratch of matches, before a lantern blazed above them. Teia's vision stuttered as color faded back in. She was in a cramped space—a warehouse—where slick mold crept along the wooden walls. Crates filled the far side of the room, some rotting with age, others in pristine condition. Several had their lids pried off, swords and revolvers alike sparkling inside.

A cluster of strangers surrounded Teia, none of whom seemed thrilled to be there. The girl in the front, the one who had spoken last, was about Teia's age, although she was a good head shorter and far more developed. She had the type of radiant, full face that men went stupid for, paired with plump lips and piercing gray eyes. A leather belt was cinched around her generous hips, and a string of vials clinked against each other when she moved, sloshing with mysterious liquids.

"We could kill her," the girl proposed at last, in what Teia thought was an insultingly offhanded way.

"I second that," someone thundered from the back. A man with a grizzled beard and patchy skin, twin axes strapped to either side of his waist.

"Great plan," the boy holding Teia retorted. "Except what do we do with her body afterward? Leave it at the palace gates?"

"Is that an option?" the man said.

The boy made a frustrated sound, a cross between exasperation and annoyance. "Don't be daft. We'll be dead before the sun comes up. For all we know, she's led the military right to our doorstep."

"All the more reason to kill her," a second man added through a mouthful of broken teeth. He cracked his knuckles together, just as Kyra pushed through the group, throwing her arms out indignantly.

"Stop it!" she snapped, with a startling amount of vigor. "Nobody's killing anyone. If Teia wanted to turn us in, I'd already be dead. Twice."

The boy snorted. "You're on a first-name basis?" he said, just as the girl laughed.

"Twice already?" she teased. "You've barely been in the palace for three weeks, Champion."

Kyra flushed. "I'm doing my best, Alara."

"And nobody faults you," Alara said promptly, sweeping her mane of blond hair down her back. "Besides, a student is only as good as her instructor."

Teia could hear the full length of the boy's scowl. "Is that supposed to be an insult?"

"I don't know. Are you capable of teaching hand-to-hand combat without absolutely eviscerating someone's self-esteem?"

Kyra's blush deepened. "He didn't *eviscerate* my self-esteem," she protested.

"He sent you crying into your plate at dinner."

"I was homesick."

"You requested another combat instructor the next day."

"Did I?" Kyra said, before hastily adding, "What were you saying about Teia?"

Alara's attention flitted back to Teia. She adjusted her belt, and the bottles chimed in harmony. "So, Princess," she said, "if you aren't about to raid our safe house, why *are* you here?"

"It might be easier for her to speak," Kyra supplied, "if Tobias wasn't holding a knife to her neck."

Alara's eyes flicked down, as if just noticing the blade. Then she glanced over to where Tobias maintained his death grip. "Let her go. I want to hear what she has to say."

"You're kidding, right?" Tobias said.

"Please. It's not like she can control water *and* fire. It's not like she can light this place up with a single thought."

"Thanks for reminding me. That makes me feel so much better."

But the pressure on Teia's throat eased slightly, before falling away altogether. Teia was left standing alone, suddenly feeling more isolated than ever. Kyra gave her an encouraging look from where she sat, balanced on a stack of crates, probably waiting for some brilliant speech. A condensed version of what she'd presented when they first met in the palace.

Instead, Teia went for broke. "I'm here to join the Dawnbreakers," she said, back straight, chin lowered.

She was met with an astonished silence. The others waited for the punch line, their expressions ranging from amusement to outrage to shock, until Alara sucked in a breath. "You're serious?" she said.

"She can't be," the grizzled man jeered. "A Carthan who wants to join the cause? She's either a liar or she's slow. And from what I've heard, my money's on the former."

"Shut up, Swile," Alara said good-naturedly. "I was talking to our guest."

Teia nodded at Alara. "I'm serious," she said. "Kyra said I could help—and I want to. I'm here to speak to Lehm, to make my case."

"He wants to meet her," Kyra chimed in. "Teia has access throughout the palace. She could help us carry messages, run information."

The second man coughed a laugh. "Wasn't aware our champion would be a Carthan lapdog."

Kyra faltered, her shoulders stiffening, and Alara snapped her head toward the man. For the first time, anger sank into her tone. "Fader," she said briskly. "I think it's best if you and Swile leave."

Fader's smile immediately dimmed. "But—"

"But nothing," Alara said. One gloved hand curled close to her belt, fingering the glass vials. The reaction was instantaneous. Swile and Fader all but dashed out, hustling through the wooden door, and Teia watched them go with budding interest.

Just who was this girl, with the authority to throw two grown men from the room?

"Are you allowed to do that?" Kyra asked.

"They're idiots. Bruisers who don't know how to keep their opinions to themselves."

"Still." The rebel champion's voice was tinged with worry. "They can smash skulls with their bare hands."

"That's a rumor."

"It's not. Perry said he's seen it happen."

"Perry is a compulsive liar. I'm more than capable of handling myself."

"Nobody is saying you can't. But that still doesn't explain what we're going to do with *her*." This was from the boy again—Tobias—who rounded behind Teia to sit on the crates. She made the mistake of glancing at him as he did. When he walked into the light, the lantern flickering behind him, her breath caught in her throat.

He wasn't much older than she was, with a combination of sharp, severe features: thin lips, strong nose. A single scar ran white along his jaw, puckering against skin and disappearing into his shirt. His clothes were simple, cut from dark cloth, tailored expertly to fit. He was tall and lean, a creature made of broken edges, a statue carved by an artist's hand.

He was breathtakingly, undeniably beautiful—and that wasn't even the worst part.

"I know you," Teia said, as recognition crashed into her.

"I have one of those faces," Tobias replied blandly.

"Like a waterlogged painting," Alara suggested, "or a bust you'd like to forget."

"I take care of all my paintings."

"You're missing the point, Tobias."

"You work as a guard," Teia interrupted. Normally she would have stayed silent, parsing the Dawnbreakers' dynamic to glean something worthwhile. Yet she remembered Tobias standing outside Calla's sitting room, escorting her to the stalls of Carfaix Market. He hadn't followed her to Mourner's Beach—of that she was certain—but how long had he been skulking around the Golden Palace? How close had she been to meeting the wrong end of his knife?

"I'm undercover," he said tersely. His eyes were a torrential blue, a shade lighter than the sky during dusk.

"For how long?"

"Long enough."

"Spying on me?"

"Doing my job." He pivoted away, his next words addressed to Kyra. "What were you thinking?"

"Tobias," Alara said tartly.

"I stand by my statement. This is a terrible idea, and everyone here knows it."

"Lehm agreed to see her," Kyra said defensively.

"Why?"

"A Carthan ally is valuable."

"It is," he agreed. "And since she's seen our faces, our heads will be on sticks by the morning."

Teia should have allowed it to pass. But some part of her leapt to hit back, if only to settle some unseen score. He might have held a blade to her throat, but she wasn't about to let him speak like he knew her.

"If you're so worried about your death," Teia said flatly, "I'd recommend a priest. They take open confessionals at the Temple of Past."

Tobias's brow lowered. "I'm fine as I am," he growled.

"Oh, yes. You seem tremendously happy. Fulfilled too."

"Do you want to guess my dreams next? Read my fortune?"

"I'd rather not," Teia said. "I can't imagine there's much to predict."

He started toward her, his knife gleaming ominously, but Alara held up her hand. *"Tobias."*

"Alara," he said, outraged. "She's a—"

"Carthan. Yes, I know. But you've already mentioned your points, and Lehm still needs to see her. All in all"—Alara swept a critical gaze over Teia—"she doesn't seem half bad. Nice job, Champion."

The last bit was directed at Kyra. When Alara leaned over, poking the rebel champion playfully, Kyra's cheeks tinted a rosy pink. Ever so slightly, her left hand grazed over her opposite arm, close to where Alara had touched her shoulder.

Tobias remained unmoved. "Fine," he grunted, his fingers wrapped tightly around the hilt of his weapon. "But I want you to remember this moment, when we looked our downfall in the eyes and welcomed her in. Should be a great memory we can all share, when we're waiting our turn for the executioner's block."

Teia met his words with a smile. She couldn't pinpoint what exactly made Tobias so remarkably irritating—but she'd count the days until the Dawnbreakers revealed their base, crossing off the minutes in an invisible ledger. And when she fed names to Jura one by one, each dangling from her lips, his would be the first.

"For you, Tobias?" she cooed. "I'll ask them to go slow."

Cornelius Lehm had been a source of great ire for the Council, far before he cut out Miran's eye. Teia had seen the man's image leering from countless wanted posters in Bhanot. The sketches tended to show the rebel leader as some crazed maniac, with a tangled beard and deranged sneer. The obscene reward for his capture—printed in black block numbers—barely fit across the page.

Yet the man before Teia seemed more courtier than rebel. His upkeep alone must have cost a small fortune, his sweeping greatcoat immaculately pressed, his graying hair trimmed to match the neat beard. Around his neck hung two chains, one silver and one gold. A semicircle charm swung from the silver chain over his simple linen tunic; the second charm was hidden under his shirt, creasing the fabric.

"The Halfling Princess," he said, rising from his seat.

"Cornelius Lehm," Teia answered, as she cast a look around. This was no dingy room with half-opened crates and sputtering lanterns. On the opposite side of one of the warehouse's hidden doors, the oval room was adorned with every luxury, and she wondered what type of sponsors the Dawnbreakers had amassed to afford such finery. There were shelves stuffed with books, and oil paintings of horses hung from the papered walls. Fluffed pillows rested against each seat. A full set of knives lay open on the desk, the brown leather sheath monogrammed with Lehm's initials.

"No need for such formalities—Lehm is fine." He pointed out the velvet chair opposite him. "Please. Sit."

Teia did what he asked, perching on the edge of the green cushion. "Your reputation precedes you," she said.

He peered at her with pale blue eyes, the color of ice before shattering. "Does it, now?"

"You have vision."

"That's not what the Council calls it."

"They might have been a bit more forthcoming if you hadn't maimed Miran."

"About my desire for a republic?" His smile was razor thin. "I sincerely doubt it."

Something about this man unsettled Teia. She couldn't place the feeling, which was similar to plunging her hand into a pit full of vipers. "The Council might not be impressed," she told him, "but I am."

"You?" Lehm set his hands before him. Each nail had been filed to precision. "So tell me—is that why you're here? To make a name for yourself?"

"To join your cause."

"And can you give me a single reason why I should believe you?"

Teia shrugged. "I made your champion a few days ago. I could have handed her in, but I didn't."

"Because you wanted leverage."

"Because I wanted an audience." Teia nodded at him from across the desk. "You could say I received one."

His lip curled. "You do understand what the Dawnbreakers work toward? No more kings, no more princesses."

"Erisia needs a change."

"And what if it ends a six-hundred-year dynasty?"

"So be it. Legacy doesn't matter if Jura ruins this country." How far could she push the rebel leader for information? How much would Lehm be willing to offer? "I assume that's why you started the Dawnbreakers?" she said delicately.

He didn't take the bait. "I have my reasons," was all Lehm said as he inspected Teia closely. "I'm curious. Do you consider yourself a patriot?"

"I do."

"The Halfling Princess. Who would have thought?"

The feeling of unease grew. His pale eyes ran over hers, digging straight into her soul. "I want to help you resolve this as soon as possible," she said. "Assist however I can."

"Out of the goodness of your heart?"

He could tell she was bluffing. She knew it in the way his tone shifted, dismissal clear behind the sentence. She would be thrown out any second now, turned away from the rebels, her future melting like snow against sunlight. For everything Teia had sold to Kyra, Lehm was unwilling to buy.

Except maybe that was it. This was *Cornelius Lehm*. They had just met, but Teia's mind sorted through her knowledge on the rebel leader. The Dawnbreakers might have gained traction, but Lehm wasn't exactly popular with the commonfolk. His bombs had toppled civilian buildings and made a mess of the Financial District. He'd laid traps spiked with nails for the Golden Palace's soldiers and sent back any spies bleeding from their sockets, poison coating the insides of their throats.

He was ambitious, but ruthless. A man who fought without honor. He wouldn't care for Teia's fanciful statements of idealism. She was impressed that Kyra had retained her spirit, sitting beneath Lehm's thumb.

Teia sighed. "No," she said, after a pause. "Not from the goodness of my heart."

Lehm's gaze narrowed. "Finally," he said. "Some honesty."

"I despise Jura."

"I assumed you would."

"He's turned Erisia into a laughingstock. He's destroyed what my parents built." Teia set her jaw. "Most of all, I hate what he's planning to do with me."

"Ah yes," Lehm mused. "The wedding."

"Yes."

"Congratulations."

"Thank you."

"I've heard of Devon Ralis. He killed both his wives, didn't he?"

"And the second's unborn child."

"I see." Lehm stood to pace the length of the room, clasping his hands behind his back. "The wedding is soon?"

"Six weeks to the day."

"So the Dawnbreakers are your way out."

"Yes."

"You would depose your own brother."

"Half brother."

"And what about after?" he said swiftly. "I won't give you the throne. I didn't start the Dawnbreakers to prop up another monarch."

"I don't want to rule." The words landed crisp between them. Teia scarcely had time to contemplate what they meant, to parse fact from fiction. It didn't matter. Nothing did, really, aside from her, the rebel leader, and her need to earn his trust. "I'm not interested in the crown. I never have been."

"I'd hope not," Lehm said. He'd reached her side of the room once again, coming up from behind, and she suddenly felt the scrape of metal at the back of her neck. The point rested at the top of her spine, cold against flesh.

She'd been expecting something along those lines, and so she didn't react. Calmly, Teia turned her head. She saw Lehm's arm in his coat sleeve, the outline of his torso. One wave of her hand, one snap of her fingers, and Teia could send heat soaring through the room. The rebel leader would burn along with his threats—and yet all Teia did was sit a little taller. She reached up to brush her hair from the nape of her neck, exposing bare skin. "If you're going to kill me," she said, "let's get on with it."

She felt him studying her, considering. After a moment, the bite of steel faded away. Lehm returned to his desk. He set the offending knife between them, like some bizarre peace offering, an unspoken test she'd managed to pass. The smile he provided was polite, although his eyes stayed flat and hard.

"Very well, Princess," he said. "If you want to join the Dawnbreakers, you can start by getting me the Morning Star."

Teia took a minute. She took two. She thought she deserved more, actually, for walking into this office and brokering a deal with a madman.

The Morning Star. The jewel the Goddess had left behind when she blessed the Divine Five. The one that sat within Blackgate Prison, encased in several tons of iron and stone.

The same gem Jura wanted for his coronation.

She must have been silent for a little too long. Lehm didn't look amused. His voice was terse as he said, "I have it on good faith that your family has been guarding the Serkawr's Blessing."

The Star carried an abundance of nicknames—the Jewel of Erisia, the Star of the Kingdom. Teia had never heard the Serkawr's Blessing before, but she wasn't about to debate onomastics with the rebel leader. His source might have been correct, but they'd left out one critical detail.

"I don't have access to the Star," Teia said truthfully. The Vault was Erisia's most secure safe, a barrage of locks and codes that even Enna would find difficult to maneuver. "Nobody but Jura has clearance."

"You're the Halfling Princess, aren't you? I have every confidence in your abilities."

Confidence wouldn't help her if she ended up in an early

grave, skewered by a prison guard's spear. "Jura wants the gem displayed during his coronation," Teia said. "Why not steal it there?"

"With guards posted at each corner and sharpshooters poised to strike?"

"On the way to the Golden Palace, then. Any thief worth her salt could break into the transportation wagon."

"And run for the nearest port once they discover what they've taken?" Lehm's laugh was mirthless. "I've thought this through, Princess. This isn't on a whim."

"But—"

His expression grew hollow, sending disquiet rustling through her. "I don't like to repeat myself," Lehm said evenly, "so I'd advise you to listen carefully. When you're with the Dawnbreakers, you step into my house. Here, I tell you what I need, and you go out and do it. This isn't a conversation. This isn't a negotiation. So let me tell you one more time, in a way that any drunkard in the Flats would be able to understand: if you want to join the rebels, you bring me the Morning Star."

She almost left right then and there, her body angled toward the door. Lehm reminded her too much of Jura. He sized her up the way a snake did its prey. If she were a bluebird within a cage, he held the matches, forcing her to a flame.

Yet she couldn't leave now with the stakes that loomed over her. Teia had a goal, and now she had a task. The Morning Star. The Dawnbreaker base. Freedom.

Power.

No matter how impossible it sounded, the rest of her life awaited her.

"I'll do it," Teia said. The words tasted metallic in her mouth.

"I thought so." The anger receded, as if it had never been

there at all. Lehm stitched himself back together with ease, every bit the gentleman he'd been when he first welcomed her inside. "Rennert will be your handler. He'll be in touch, to make sure everything is moving along."

"Rennert?"

"Tobias Rennert."

Teia blanched. She had thought she would work with Kyra, or maybe report to Lehm himself if she was lucky. What she hadn't expected was to be grouped with Tobias. Trigger-happy, knife-wielding Tobias, who'd pressed a blade to her throat.

It was a problem for a later time. Teia offered Lehm a curt smile. "I look forward to working with you," she said.

They shook on it. His grip was solid but cold, and that same sense of dread roiled in Teia's stomach. "As do I, Princess," Lehm said. "As do I."

CHAPTER TEN

Dawn had crept onto the horizon by the time Kyra escorted Teia back to the Golden Palace. As they ducked through the servants' entrance, the dull clunk of pots and pans from the kitchens signaled the start of another day. Morning noises rang through the halls: cooks blustering about, maidservants gossiping as they prepared for their shifts.

Teia stifled a yawn. She was exhausted, the kind of tired that fused into her bones. She fully expected Kyra to part ways with her at the back entrance, but the rebel girl loped down the long corridor, exuding energy as she bounced on the balls of her feet. "Your room?" she said, before Teia could formulate a proper excuse.

Kyra took her hesitation as an answer. She ascended the stairs in twos, pausing expectantly as Teia pressed a reluctant palm to the lock. When they were both inside with the door fastened shut, Kyra offered her a shy smile. "What did you think?" she said.

Your boss is delusional, Teia thought, *and I'm being sent on a suicide mission.*

"If you have ideas on how to bring Lehm the Morning Star, I'd appreciate any suggestions."

Kyra's mouth fell into a perfect O. "*The* Morning Star?"

"Is there any other?"

"Why does he want it?"

"You don't know?"

"The Dawnbreakers operate on a need-to-know basis."

"You're their champion, aren't you?"

"That sounds more impressive than it is. Lehm might use my name to build the movement, but I'm not leading the charge or planning attacks." Kyra plopped down onto the loveseat. "And the others? What do you think about them?"

Teia racked her brains for something positive to say about the remaining Dawnbreakers. At last, she settled on a lukewarm "Your friends seem nice." Even that was a stretch—they *had* debated killing her, and they hadn't been the least bit subtle about it—but Teia thought she should try to be diplomatic.

"They're great," Kyra said, bobbing her head intently. "Tobias can be difficult at first, but he grows on you."

"Didn't he make you cry?"

"Only once," Kyra complained. "I wasn't used to the base yet."

At that, Teia's ears pricked up, any fatigue falling away. Lehm had been impenetrable, unwilling to relinquish even a speck of information, but Kyra Medoh might be a different story.

"It must have been hard," Teia said casually, "adjusting to a new routine."

"Definitely a transition," Kyra said. "Some things have made it easier, though. Hot meals. Daily schedules."

Teia couldn't resist. "Alara?"

Kyra's cheeks glowed pink. She glanced down with renewed interest at the edges of her braid. "We're friends."

"Just that? You seem to get along well."

"She's nice. Easy to talk to."

Teia didn't think *nice* and *easy to talk to* could raise the blush seeping across Kyra's face. "She's very pretty," she remarked. It was true. Alara was the type of girl who knew exactly how striking she was.

"She is," Kyra mumbled. "But she's more than that."

"Oh?"

"She's smart—the smartest person I know, who remembers everything she sees. She cheats when she plays dice but pretends she doesn't. She collects cosmetics, although she doesn't like to use them. She has an entire trunk full of old clothes, because she sews her own outfits. And . . . and—" Kyra stopped abruptly, her fists clenched. She looked ready to sink into the ground.

It was all wildly entertaining. Teia didn't consider herself a romantic, aside from a rather unfortunate incident when she was eleven. She'd taken a liking to the Minister of Defense's son, a stocky, curly-haired boy who ran in Jura's group. She had bottled up her emotions for months. She had savored the fizzy excitement when she glimpsed him in the halls and hoarded each glance he sent her way.

Naturally, things had ended in complete disaster. When Teia approached him, the boy had called her a Halfling. He'd ripped her handwritten letter in two, before scampering back to his friends. Teia had spent the next few days in various states of anguish, before swearing off love for good.

Five years later, she'd blackmail the boy's squadron leader into demoting his rank. He was promptly transferred to hard labor at the Erisian salt mines, until his father relented to her demands. When Teia thought of the son—loud, boisterous, and constantly in the company of others—hacking away at salt crystals in the desolate outpost, she was quite proud of herself. Really, it was some of her best work.

Teia didn't think that story would sit well with Kyra. There was no chance to pry further into the base either, as the rebel girl shook her head. "Anyway—it's not important if things have been hard. I couldn't stay in Set after what happened."

"Your powers?"

Kyra's response was a weary sigh. "Everything was a mess. I accidentally set my house on fire before things came under control."

What had Enna said to Teia? Kyra's home in Set had been torched to the ground, with no trace of the rebel champion left inside. They'd both assumed the fire had been the Dawnbreakers covering their tracks, but apparently the truth was far less complex.

"Just one house?" Teia said. Not bad, considering Kyra had used trial and error.

"A bakery," Kyra admitted. "A farm, the tailor's shop, and my neighbor's apple orchard."

Goddess—no wonder Kyra had to leave. At that rate, she would have incinerated every building in Set. "That's when the Dawnbreakers arrived?" Teia asked.

"I'm still not sure how Lehm found me."

"The row of charred buildings was probably an outstanding clue." Teia frowned. There had been something bothering her, a timeline that didn't match up. "If Lehm recruited you three months ago, what took you so long to make an appearance?"

"I was training."

"For what?"

"Tasks. Errands."

"You're telling me the rebellion's champion was sent on produce runs?"

Kyra reddened further. "No."

"Then for what? Picking up Lehm's shoes? Hemming his coat?"

She fiddled nervously with her braid. Her voice pitched a fraction lower, barely audible above the crackling hearth. "I was sent as an assassin."

Teia burst into laughter. "You?" she said.

Kyra seemed vaguely insulted. "What about me?"

"Do you even kill spiders when they crawl into your house?"

"Sometimes," Kyra said. "But usually I take a broom and shoo them outside—"

"You're making my point for me. Why would Lehm send you as an assassin?" An image sharpened in her head, formed from what she knew about Kyra's abilities. She stopped laughing at once and said, "You were supposed to kill me, weren't you?"

"No."

"That doesn't sound the least bit convincing."

"Not you." Kyra paused, before muttering, "Jura."

If the rebel girl had been a fraction more violent, it would have been a decent plan. Kyra could burn, which meant she could survive Jura's flame. One dagger through the heart, and Kyra could flee the palace in secret, with all the anonymity her servant's disguise afforded her.

Privately, Teia thought the whole thing was hopeless. The Dawnbreakers would have a better chance of Jura drowning in his bath than Kyra carrying out an assassination. But all she said was, "And what happens after?"

"After?"

"Let's say the Dawnbreakers win. I get the Star, Lehm frames it on his wall, and you lop off Jura's head. What happens once all that's done? Do you become the new queen? Do you sit on the throne?"

"Republics don't have thrones."

"Sorry. The palace curriculum neglected to cover rival forms of government."

"It's been mentioned," Kyra said, "but I don't want to govern. When this is over, I'd like to be a scholar. Follow in my da's footsteps."

Professors often cut through the Royal District on their way to the university, books spilling loose from their satchels, half-eaten pastries dangling from the pockets of their austere gray robes. "He taught at Bhanot University?"

"In the geology department," Kyra said fondly. "Sometimes in the morning, we'd walk Mariner's Cove together, just before the tide pulled in. He'd collect huge buckets of rocks and wade into the shallows to retrieve all types of stones. We'd line our windowsills with them, and he'd tell me stories about the lands they came from."

Her expression was distant. Unwittingly, Teia remembered the rebel girl's background, her father who had died of the Reaper's Kiss. At the time, Teia had accepted the information with a weathered indifference. Thousands had died from the plague, their bodies wrapped in sheets and set ablaze in the streets. In the end, what was another tragedy? People suffered and erred and felt horrific pain, just to soldier through life like always. Like usual.

But something split open inside Teia, a memory that forced itself to the surface. She was buffeted with a vision of mourning silks and silent rooms, fireworks lit by people who celebrated the Shaylani Witch's death. When Teia had crept away from the window, her bare feet puttering against tile, she'd found Ren collapsed in the chair behind her. His breath stank of spirits, his hand fixed around the neck of a bottle. She'd tugged at his sleeve to wake him, and he'd barely stirred before turning away.

No. She was no longer that terrified girl, watching her father slip into an ocean of grief. "The rocks on your windowsill," Teia said gruffly to Kyra. "What did you do with them?"

"I'm not sure. I think they were left behind." An undercurrent of admiration swelled in Kyra's voice. "Lehm brought me replacements. He said they were from his hometown."

"He's from Set?"

"Ystrad."

Teia was familiar with Ystrad. It was a tiny village near the eastern coast, where the waves lapped black from the Dark Sea. According to Erisian lore, the Serkawr had first risen from the waters there, which had cemented Ystrad as a fervent tourist destination. There was an entire museum built around the Serkawr's footprint, where visitors could learn more about the sea beast. Vendors sold piping-hot cakes shaped like the Serkawr, and guides regaled visitors with old Erisian folk stories.

Good on Ystrad's population for making a living, but that hardly provided Teia with any reassurance on Lehm. "You trust him," she said. She didn't think that was a strong frame of reference—the rebel girl seemed the type to trust a robber in an alley—but Kyra was unwavering.

"He took me in after Set. He's been good to me." She reached out uncertainly to touch Teia's arm. "The rebellion is Lehm's life, Teia. I don't know why he wants the Star, but he must have his reasons."

I'm sure he does, Teia thought darkly, and the fire in the hearth scorched a dangerous shade of orange. But for all her questions, her unease in the oval room, the tip of his knife against her neck,

Lehm's motivations could wait. Blackgate Prison hovered in the distance, with the Morning Star trapped inside.

The day was young and her purpose clear. The Halfling Princess had work to do.

CHAPTER ELEVEN

Teia learned what it meant to have a handler later that night.

She was plucked from a marvelous dream about a three-tiered cake when an incessant knocking drummed its way into her sleep. The sound continued, thundering on with a steadfast persistence despite the pillow she yanked over her head. Eventually, realizing this was a losing strategy, Teia sat up groggily. She rubbed at her eyes and grabbed for her robe. Goddess. What kind of assassin knocked before they entered?

Teia opened the door to Tobias Rennert, who peered down at her stoically.

"What are you doing here?" Teia hissed. She grabbed at his sleeve, dragging him into the room without any further fanfare.

"The guard barracks are two floors down. It's easy enough to slip away."

"And then you wander around the palace? Keep people from a good night's sleep?"

"I'm your handler," he replied crisply. "It's my job to relay updates back to Lehm."

"It's been sixteen hours," Teia snapped, pointing to her drawn curtains. "I haven't exactly figured out how to steal the Morning Star yet."

"You might want to work faster."

"So tell him to hire a magician. I'm doing the best I can."

"The bar is low."

"Then invest in some spectacles. From where I'm standing, Lehm's asking for the impossible. If you're so brilliant, go steal the Star yourself."

He shook off her reply with a noise of disgust. "Maybe nobody's mentioned this, Princess, but this is a war. Not a game, not a pastime. If you need a hobby, there are easier activities to pick up."

Teia blinked innocently. "Is there a point to be made here?"

"Kyra might believe your act, but I don't. A Carthan joining the Dawnbreakers?"

"If you're about to tell me how much you hate my family, you'll have to wait in line. Take a ticket while you're at it."

He scoffed. "You really are just like him."

"Him?"

"Your brother."

"Half brother."

"Does it matter?"

Anger lit through Teia, as she lost whatever peace of mind she'd managed to hold on to. She resented Tobias's statement, the message he so clearly meant to convey. "I'm nothing like Jura," she snarled.

"Aren't you? You throw around your big words and grand gestures. You hide behind your powers as if that gives you the right to rule."

Her laugh was scornful. "You're awfully confident for someone who seems unusually afraid of those powers."

"Who said I'm afraid?"

Teia flicked her fingers. A flame unfolded in midair, weaving into existence.

That was all it took. Tobias moved faster than lightning, leveling his blade directly at her chest. She glanced down with a practiced disinterest. It was a gorgeous weapon—too short to be a broadsword, but longer than any regular knife. The metal reflected an ethereal shade of blue. The hilt was wrapped in soft leather cords.

Yet it was the silver markings along the blade's surface that caught Teia's notice. The image was faint, cut near the bottom, a hound howling against a crescent moon. Her retort died in her throat. She waved away her flame and reached out cautiously, flipping the knife to the side to better see the etchings.

"St. Clair."

Tobias went an alarming shade of gray. "How did you—"

"The hound on your knife. It's the symbol on the St. Clair crest."

Memorizing the sigils of Erisia's many noble families had been a mandatory part of Teia's schooling. When she'd lamented about it to her father, Ren merely patted her on the head before sneaking her a piece of ginger candy as consolation. *Keep at it, love. There'll be some use yet.*

Years later, Teia had to concede that Ren had been right—the lessons *had* been useful. It was much easier to extort nobles when she could instantly identify whom she was eavesdropping on.

Except Teia was unsure what to make of the blade. Part of her wished she'd never seen it at all, given what she knew about the St. Clairs. She hoped that Tobias Rennert moonlighted as a grave robber, or he had obtained the knife through some morbid pawnshop in the Flats. The other alternative—the one written across his face—made her somewhat ill to think about.

"You're a St. Clair," she asserted. "A noble."

He gave her a bitter smile. "I *was*."

"The fire. You were—"

"Thirteen." Tobias exhaled softly, his eyes glittering. "I was thirteen."

There was nothing else to say. The St. Clairs had become a cautionary tale throughout the palace—a warning, for anyone who might defy Jura. When the Golden Prince had begun his interim rule at seventeen, he had promptly rolled back Ren's reforms. And after Isaac and Liana St. Clair made their case against the Crown's new allowance on torture, the entire family died in an estate fire just weeks later.

The papers claimed that the incident was due to a toppled oil lamp, but even a fool could connect the dots. After that, there were no more objections, no more requests. Jura had proven what kind of ruler he was going to be, and the court fell neatly in line behind him.

"How are you alive?" Teia said in disbelief. It wasn't the most sensitive thing to say, but she chalked it up to reactionary shock.

"At the will of the Crown, of course." Tobias's voice was flat, stripped bare of any emotion. "He forced me outside, away from my parents. He made me watch as the house burned to nothing, and when that was done, he said he wanted to play a game."

"A game?" Teia said, as her heart sank. She might as well have been five again, hovering in Jura's room as he prodded at the bluebird's cage.

It's nothing. Just a game I like to play.

"He had cards with him. An entire stack, but he drew the one on top. Red to live, black to die." Tobias cupped the side of his neck, where the pearly scar shone under the lamplight. "The card was red, but he slit me open to my ribs anyway. A true test of chance, he said. A reminder of Carthan might."

She hadn't realized she was shaking. Tobias glanced at Teia, his dark eyes meeting hers, and she saw the anger that ran black beneath the surface. It swirled like a current, a well that refused to bleed dry. For a second, Tobias was her mirror.

"What happened afterward?" Teia said, her voice tearing against her throat.

"A family nearby found me. They took me in. I adopted my mother's maiden name and recovered in secret. As soon as I heard about Lehm and the Dawnbreakers, I was on the first train to Bhanot."

"You want Jura's head."

Tobias's smile was empty. "Not just that," he said, "but it'll be a start."

He said it simply, as if it was the most obvious thing in the world. The sky was blue, the grass was green, and the singular thing keeping Tobias afloat was the possibility of Jura's undoing.

And Teia understood. Ever since the wedding announcement, when the lull of her life had been blown to pieces, she knew what it meant to cling to a goal. It was the way of people who had been broken but tried desperately to pretend they weren't. The trouble was that the cracks always showed sooner or later, fissures that ran beneath the surface, tremors undercutting solid ground.

"Whatever you do," Teia said, "it will be a long time coming."

His look was one she couldn't decipher. Skepticism? Doubt? Any malice had drained from his voice as Tobias said, "I suppose that's why you and I are here."

"It is."

"You really don't care about all this?" He beckoned around the room with his knife.

"Not as much as everyone assumes."

"That's hardly a straight answer."

"This is all I know. But I'd like something different. Something more."

"You think the Dawnbreakers can give that to you?"

It was all a fabrication—a fantastic story she was still in the midst of writing. Yet deep inside, light as a feather, fluttered a strange new pulse, an ache that perched gently within Teia. In some other world, she might have joined the rebels under sincere circumstances. She might have walked a separate path.

Teia nodded. "I hope so," she said, with so much conviction she nearly fooled herself. The lie settled inside her, the pulse beating onward.

She wondered what would happen if it ever took root.

CHAPTER TWELVE

Teia breezed through the back gate into the growing dusk. Around her, long shadows lanced through the streets. Nobles hurried home in packs, giggling into their fans and dragging frilly sleeves behind them. Some tugged along tiny dogs, which yapped shrilly in protest, on diamond-encrusted leashes.

Teia wasn't expecting any trouble. She'd worn a servant's uniform today, which she kept stashed beneath the false bottom of her wardrobe. It was risky to use the disguise at all—her features were too recognizable in Bhanot, despite her hood—but the evenings provided some semblance of cover.

So when a hand fastened around her arm, Teia practically leapt from her skin. She whirled to face her attacker, almost summoning a flame, before a great peal of laughter rang out.

There, caught under the light of a streetlamp, stood Alara. She was stylishly dressed—ribbons trimming the front of her white linen shirt—with her golden hair curling to the small of her back. The leather belt was still clasped securely around her waist, but the bottles had been filled with an assortment of colorful powders today, purples and yellows that settled near the glass bottoms.

"I almost missed you," Alara said happily. "Great disguise,

by the way. Nobles don't pay attention to anyone but themselves, do they?"

Teia scowled. "You're my babysitter now?" she said, without an ounce of grace. "What happened to Tobias?"

"I take it working with him is going well?"

"Well enough," Teia said. It wasn't a complete lie, considering the revelation about his family history not two days before. She didn't inquire further, and he hadn't attempted to stab her. It was the closest they would get to a truce.

"You sound amazingly excited." Alara adjusted her belt. "He has that effect on people. All work, no play. Incredibly dull, if you ask me."

"And you?"

"I'm working now, aren't I?" Alara said begrudgingly. "And to answer your question—Tobias is at the front gates today. A bit of an annoyance, but we have eyes on the palace constantly. Everything's about teamwork."

"In other words—you drew the short straw?"

"I don't think about it like that. Anyway, we should probably get to know each other, since you've decided to join the Dawnbreakers." As she spoke, she flung a smile at one of the passing bankers. The poor man stumbled over his own feet, his mouth agape, before dropping his top hat in a puddle of sludge.

Teia watched him retrieve the hat, shaking it mournfully before stuffing it inside his satchel. "Are you usually this easygoing around your mortal enemies?" she said to Alara.

"You aren't my mortal enemy. I have very few of those. Bad hair days. Corsets. Uneven lipstick."

"I don't think eradicating bumpy lipstick is part of the Dawnbreakers' agenda."

"Stick around. I'll make sure Lehm gets to that next."

The mansions had dwindled in size. Few carriages remained on the increasingly empty streets, the windows covered in heavy black curtains. Ministers sought refuge inside, as a quiet place to escape their spouses and tumble their mistresses. Unfortunately, the curtains weren't soundproof, which was exhibited by the periodic moan that would drift into the streets.

Alara straightened her bronze cloak pin. The point was unnecessarily sharp, studded with gemstones. "So, Teia. Can I call you Teia?"

"Um," Teia said.

"Are you really just taking a walk? Or is there some other reason you're sneaking out of the palace?"

"Would you believe that I needed some air?"

"With seven hundred sixty-three windows in the palace?" Alara shook her head. "Try again."

Teia chose her next words carefully. "I'm checking on a lead," she said with a noncommittal shrug. She didn't know how much she wanted to tell Alara, especially without confirmation. It was the entire purpose of her current detour—to verify a tentative hunch.

"Ah." Alara bobbed her head wisely. "For stealing the Morning Star?"

"It's not technically stealing if it belongs to my family."

"Funny you should say that. And yet all this"—she waved at the servant uniform—"implies that you plan on stealing something." Alara winced. "Although your palace seamstress needs a new pair of eyes. That dress is cut like a potato sack."

Teia lifted the hem of her skirt with a self-conscious frown. "Not all of us can wear matching colors," she said, nodding at Alara. The other girl's gloves and belt were cut from the same dark material, both trimmed in bright red.

"You noticed!" Alara framed her hands against the sky, catching a patch of orange between them. "I love these gloves. I'm trying to keep myself in check, since I wore out my last pair in a week."

"A week? Did you put them through a shredder?"

"That might actually be more sustainable," Alara said thoughtfully. "I handle poisons. Toxins. Deadly stuff, and I never know when I have to get my hands dirty. It's why I usually keep these"—she wiggled her gloved fingers at Teia—"on at all times."

Teia missed a step. "*You're* the Poisons Master?" she said.

Alara bent into an exaggerated bow. "You've heard of me?"

Goddess, who hadn't? The Council had sent countless spies to infiltrate the rebellion, all of whom had been returned to the palace's gates, their bodies coated in boils and their jackets laced in nightshade. Most had died horrible deaths, raving mad and in unspeakable pain. The ones who managed to survive had blank spaces in their memories. They couldn't remember their own names, much less the Dawnbreakers' location.

After a while, the Council learned its lesson. They stopped sending spies to slaughter, and the Poisons Master became the stuff of legend.

"Messy work," Teia said finally, which caused Alara to glow with pride. "Where did you learn about these things? Is there some secretive rebel handbook for new recruits?"

The Poisons Master's smile waned. For an instant, sadness seeped into her face, turning down the corners of her mouth. It was the look of someone who had been twisted apart and clumsily reassembled, the pieces incorrectly welded together.

Then the nonchalance locked back into place. "We had a garden when I was younger," Alara said casually. "It was something I grew up around."

Teia didn't think the leap from gardening to poisons was particularly intuitive, but she wasn't about to argue with Alara— not when the leather belt hung tight around her waist. "That's why those Dawnbreaker bruisers were afraid of you?"

Alara cocked her head. "Which bruisers?"

"Swile and Fader."

"Oh. Them." She dismissed the men with a flutter of her hand. "Those two would run from their own shadows."

"Is this before or after they crush skulls?"

"Talk is cheap. I'll believe it when I see it."

The palace's spires faded behind them. They passed the short row of embassies—Shaylan's stood at the very end, one of its walls smeared with red paint—and crossed the Magnus Bridge, where any opulence evaporated on the other side. The Carmine District was named for Carmine Carthan, one of Teia's ancestors who had advocated for corralling the poor into their own patch of land, out of sight of the palace. Here, the buildings were jumbles of residential blocks, constructed from stoic gray rock and strung through with wired clotheslines. Flea-bitten cats roamed the streets, spitting at each other territorially.

One turn later, and everything else had fallen away.

The slick walls of Blackgate Prison cut high into the sky. They stretched endlessly down the streets, crowned with whorls of barbed wire. Guards stood fast at their individual posts, weapons out and at the ready. Prison wagons rumbled through the narrow arched entrances.

There had been a tremendous fuss about Blackgate when it was first announced. The architect insisted on this specific spot in the Carmine District. *For the vision*, he had written in his memoir, as if anyone would be commentating on the artistic placement of a prison.

The residents had been scandalized. They'd rallied together in protest and organized makeshift roadblocks. They had spent an entire season petitioning the Crown for a stay of construction, citing an inevitable decrease in quality of life, but their efforts were in vain. After a while, things were solved the old-fashioned way: a few threats here, a few beatings there, and Erisia's most infamous prison was up and running.

"Teia?"

Alara's voice pulled Teia from her thoughts. The Poisons Master had gone unnaturally pale, the blood drained from her cheeks. "What are we doing here?"

"Gathering information."

"On the prison?"

"On a target."

They dodged into a nearby alley, heaped with overflowing waste bins. Teia leaned against the chipped gray wall, as far from the litter as she could manage. If she blocked out the stink of garbage, the alley was a fairly decent lookout spot. She had an outstanding view of Blackgate's tallest side gate, where guards clocked in for their shift. There were no lines—not yet—but the queues would begin soon enough.

Beside her, Alara swatted at a fruit fly. "I hate this place," the Poisons Master grunted.

Teia didn't take her eyes from the gate. "The alley?" she said.

"Blackgate."

"Everyone hates Blackgate. That's the deterrent of going to prison."

"Maybe," Alara said venomously. "But I'd burn it down if I could."

The bells from the prison's watchtower had started clanging

loudly, marking the top of the hour. A group of guards arriving for their next shift had lined single file against the wall. Each was dressed in full uniform, armbands denoting their rank, grated iron masks secured over their faces.

The masks were a relatively new addition. They had become standard practice about five years back, after a rogue inmate bit off a guard's nose during an escape attempt. While the masks were meant for physical protection, they also did a respectable job of concealing each man's identity, at least from a distance. Blackgate was extraordinarily secretive about the people they hired, and there was a taboo to seeking employment here, even among the commonfolk desperate for work.

The line dragged onward. When the last man had stepped up to the gate, night was filtering fast over Bhanot. The streets had mellowed into darkness.

The light was low, but Teia glimpsed what she'd been waiting for.

At first glance, the final guard seemed identical to the others. He was of normal height, normal build. A grated mask hung over his face, obscuring his features, and his uniform was predictably spotless. He was painfully average, in almost every way.

Every way but one.

A blotchy birthmark spread over the man's neck. It snuck down to his collarbone, inching into the folds of his coat. It was tinged with red and mottled at the edges—and just about the most wonderful thing Teia had ever seen.

"Beautiful," she whispered. Alara looked over at her, likely worried she'd gone mad, but Teia didn't care. She examined the guard as he held out his papers and laid his weapons out for inspection. A second later, he was allowed inside, where he vanished into the depths of Blackgate.

His name was Johns Pembrant. He was one of the officers at the prison.

And he was about to become Teia's ticket to the Morning Star.

CHAPTER THIRTEEN

Teia had noticed Pembrant's absences gradually.

He was a veteran of the Shaylani War, which had left him with an abundance of night terrors and an iron medal for his troubles. After the war ended, Pembrant had married his childhood sweetheart. Teia presumed it was a lovely ceremony, with doves released at the end and a guild buried in their cake for good luck. Yet the wedding bed was still warm when Pembrant kissed his wife goodbye, marched straight back to the palace, and reenlisted with his old squadron.

These days, there was no front to defend. The military tended to funnel soldiers back to the Golden Palace as guards, which was where Pembrant worked now, rotating between different posts. The back gates. The throne room.

The halls of Blackgate Prison.

Few guards were ever stationed in the throne room, and Teia made it her business to know about each of them. After she realized Johns Pembrant was disappearing from the palace every other day, she began to harbor her suspicions. Pembrant excelled at swordplay. He believed in the Crown, knew how to fight, held the respect of his superiors.

He was, in many ways, the ideal candidate for a Blackgate guard.

It was why, several days after her excursion to the prison, Teia was currently in the palace library. She'd staked out one of the side rooms with Kyra and Alara, the one flanked by overflowing oak shelves. Historical records packed the bookcases. Cheerful bronze lanterns dangled from alcoves. A statue of Ren towered in the corner, its head scraping the ceiling.

Teia had taken one look and picked the seat farthest from the sculpture. She had a feeling her father would roll in his grave if he could see what she was up to.

Kyra cast a nervous look at the door. "You're sure nobody will suspect anything?" she asked for the fifth time, her leg jostling the table.

"Positive," Teia answered, as she skimmed through another tome. "If anyone asks, the two of you are shelving books. The kitchen loans out to the library staff often enough."

Alara groaned. Teia had enlisted her help as well, and the Poisons Master had snuck into the palace earlier with a set of forged work documents. Now she, like Kyra, was dressed as a servant. She was spectacular under the dim light, her blond hair wound back, the neckline of her dress cutting dangerously low.

"Teia," she said emphatically, grabbing at a book, "I'd rather face a firing squad than put all these back."

"Not so loud," Kyra muttered.

Alara grinned. "Don't worry, Champion," she said, and thumped herself on the chest. "If anyone wants you, they'll have to go through me first."

"All five feet of you?"

"What can I say? I'm small but mighty." Alara pushed away the ledger she was holding and directed her gaze at Teia. "There are some palace guards listed in here, but they're all from fifty years back. You want the more recent ones?"

"Twenty years at most."

The good news—each worker in the palace had their information inked into the royal ledgers. If Teia searched hard enough, she would find everything she needed on Johns Pembrant. His birthday. His family history.

His address.

The bad news—the ledger organization system left something to be desired. The royal recordkeepers were unreliable at best, with blots and doodles dotting the margins. A single page might contain records spanning multiple decades, before jumping back to a different year. Names were scattered about haphazardly, and alphabetization was nothing more than a friendly suggestion.

Alara cracked her neck expertly. She shivered as her joints loosened, stretching her arms up high. "Goddess, Teia," she grumbled. "I have paper cuts on every finger."

"You're wearing gloves," Teia said.

"Emotional paper cuts."

"Which means?"

"That poisons are so much *easier* than this. You mix a few things, chop up some roots, and that's it. You're done."

"That sounds like an oversimplification," Kyra said.

"How would you know? You never come into the lab with me."

Kyra shook her head. "I've heard about the things that happen in your lab."

"Groundbreaking discoveries? Incredible work?"

"Someone fell into a coma, didn't they?"

"Once," Alara said indignantly. "And I *said* I was sorry."

"That doesn't fill me with confidence."

Alara laughed. She leaned over carelessly to tuck a stray lock of hair behind Kyra's ear. "Would it help if I promised to keep you safe?"

Kyra let out a squeak. Her hand brushed her ear, touching the strand of hair that had fallen out of place. She looked like she might burst into flames, or else collapse into a heap.

Teia decided to take pity on her. "Any luck?" she asked.

"Luck?" Kyra repeated dazedly.

"Pembrant's address?"

"Right!" the rebel girl said, all but diving back into the stack of ledgers.

They hunted in silence for a while longer, until Alara shifted aside a fat stack of books. "I can't do this anymore," she declared, dropping her head onto a tome. A puff of dust clouded upward, and Alara recoiled, pawing at her face miserably. "We're three hours in, Teia. Are you going to tell us why getting this man's address is so important?"

"I will once we find it."

"You're stalling."

"I'm not."

"You *are*." Alara stacked another book onto the pile. "Does this have anything to do with our trip to Blackgate?"

Kyra flinched. "You visited Blackgate?"

This wasn't how Teia hoped things would go. Any plan she had was still shaky at best, and she wanted to fit as many pieces into place first before the grand reveal. Come to think of it, maybe the Carthans *did* have a flair for dramatics.

But with Kyra staring intently and Alara on the verge of a boycott, it was useless to drag things out. Teia set aside the tome she was holding and nodded reluctantly. "The Morning Star is kept inside the Vault. It's supposed to be the most secure safe ever built, guarded by ten men around the clock."

"Vault, with a capitalized *V*?" Alara said.

"I have a feeling this is about to get worse," Kyra ventured.

"The Vault," Teia continued, "is housed within Blackgate Prison."

"And there it is," Kyra said, sounding none too happy. She gestured to the piles of ledgers. "Except what does Pembrant's address have to do with all this?"

"It's hard to explain," Teia said. "I'm working on the details, but the sooner we get the address, the better."

She expected them to argue. Alara, at the very least, would have some fresh remark already prepared. Yet when Teia glanced over, the Poisons Master's expression was distorted in pain. Quietly, her voice nearly inaudible, Alara said, "You want to break into Blackgate?"

"Um," Teia said. "Theoretically."

"It's a mistake. People don't come back from that place."

"I'm hoping to break that streak."

"Then I'll start picking the spot for your grave. Any words you'd like me to say at your funeral?"

Kyra hesitated. She stretched out a hand—To comfort Alara? To calm her down?—but the Poisons Master pulled away. "Don't. You think I don't know what I'm talking about? They took my brother to Blackgate. Six weeks later, they sent him back in a body bag."

A shocked, dull tension filled the air. "You had a brother?" Kyra said.

"He attended a protest against the Golden Prince." Alara studied her gloves closely. "Sai never stood a chance. They clapped him in irons and threw him in Blackgate. I was the last one to see him alive." Her laugh was drained of good humor, a coarse sound that caught in the middle. "He asked me to take care of his garden."

Teia thought of the girl Alara had once been, living in a nondescript house with a carefully weeded garden. She could imagine plots of thriving herbs and flowers in varying shades of the rainbow. How long had Alara tended to the garden after her brother's death? How many times had she raked her hand through the soil, praying for his safe return?

Teia might have sat in silence forever. Kyra, however, stood immediately, moving closer to Alara. Before the Poisons Master could bat her away, Kyra leaned forward to envelop her in a hug. "I'm sorry," she said.

"It doesn't matter," Alara said, swiping at her nose. "It was a long time ago."

"That doesn't change anything."

Alara sighed. "Are you always like this?"

"Like what?"

"Positive. Supportive."

"Are those bad things?"

"No," Alara said. Gently, she unfastened the rebel champion's arms from around her neck. When the Poisons Master turned back, her gray eyes searched Kyra's, like she was trying to memorize every detail. "Definitely not bad."

Watching them made Teia feel oddly invasive, as if she'd stumbled upon an intensely private moment. There was a radiance between Kyra and Alara, a brilliance that burned with new hope. They moved with a natural ease, echoing the familiarity of two people who had known each other for years, not months.

Kyra might be dazzled by Alara, but it seemed the Poisons Master had met her match.

Teia's heart lurched unexpectedly, twisting with longing. She gestured awkwardly at the ledgers strewn across the wooden table. "I'll be back," she said to no one in particular, rising from her seat to lunge for the door.

The library was a maze of books and artwork, with cracked busts and framed portraits arranged along the walls. Teia found it unnerving—too many eyes, not enough souls—but Calla had loved it here. When her mother hadn't been in court, she had been down in the stacks, rummaging through the aisles. Ultimately, her persistence managed to win over the scholars working within the library, a trio of crotchety women who could name each title in the Golden Palace.

After Calla's funeral, Teia had wandered down here, still wrapped in white mourning silks. She had run into one of the scholars somewhere past the classics section. On impulse, she had asked what her mother liked to read. Fiction? Folktales?

"No," the woman had answered, pushing her half-moon spectacles high on her nose. She, too, wore white, which had surprised Teia—few Erisians bothered to pay their respects to Calla. "The queen wanted every book we had about Shaylan. Would sit here for hours, right there in that chair, and reread the same pages over and over."

"Halfling?"

A voice deposited Teia back into the present. She looked up to find Jura not six feet away, as he snapped the book he was holding shut. "I didn't expect to see you here."

"I could say the same," Teia said. She motioned to the bronze placard drilled to the shelf. "Since when have you developed an interest in Erisian history?"

His response was a punctuated laugh. "You know, Halfling," Jura said, ignoring her question to lean against the bookcase, "there's something that's been weighing on my mind."

"Your inability to catch the Dawnbreakers?"

"Your engagement to Ralis. I heard you're dissatisfied with the match."

"He murdered both his wives."

"Accidents," Jura said. "And I wasn't aware you'd grown a set of morals, what with the members of my court you've been terrorizing."

The blackmail. She had suspected he'd known for a while. He must have, between all the demands she'd made—strategic moves to counter exile, increased protection after the assassination attempts. Yet he had never taken her seriously, even when officials bent to her will. To him, Teia was nothing more than a petulant child, an irritating thorn in his side.

"Anyway," Jura went on, casting aside any mention of blackmail with one shake of his head. "Since you're so slighted about Ralis, I've decided to do you a favor."

"Which is?"

"I've called off your wedding and canceled any plans to send you to the Highlands. After all, you're my baby sister. My last remnant of family. How could I ever bear to part with you?"

He sounded far too smug for the statement to be innocuous. Panic rumbled through Teia. All her dreams flashed before her, fragile as panes of glass. A seat on the Council would necessitate her staying in the palace—yet there was an ominous tint to how Jura emphasized the last sentence, each syllable speckled with victory.

"What do you mean?" she managed, afraid of not knowing, terrified of learning the answer.

"It's simple, really. There's a far more suitable match here. A man who meets all your needs and keeps you right at home in the Golden Palace." He paused for effect, before finishing with a gleeful, "I believe you're acquainted with Lurel Abbott?"

A great rush of noise rang out in Teia's ears. "Abbott?" she said, and the minister's face spun before her. She remembered the serving boy he'd berated. The maid he'd impregnated. Rumor had it he'd once beaten a servant girl half to death with a break-fast tray because she'd brought him the wrong order of scones.

"The one and only," Jura confirmed, as he shifted the book away from the crook of his elbow. As he flipped smartly through the chapters, he must have found what he was searching for. Jura stopped, placing three fingers on the page before tilting his head at Teia. "He's absolutely *thrilled*. Has all these excellent plans for the wedding."

"When?"

"The day after my coronation."

"That soon?"

"I like to be efficient." Jura tapped at his temple. "That re-minds me. There will be changes once your wedding takes place. More guards, more time by Abbott's side. Although he men-tioned he's prepared to share you with other members of the court, as a gesture of good faith."

Of everything she'd heard, this was by far the worst. "*Share* me?" Teia said, repulsed.

"He's open-minded," Jura said. "A man with vision."

With that, he ripped two pages from the book, slipping both into his pocket. He started to say something more to Teia, no doubt another gloat, when a voice interrupted him midway.

"Highness!"

A woman came stamping up the aisles. Her silver hair was coiled into a strict bun, and she walked with the help of an oiled wooden cane. She was older, more wizened, but Teia recognized those half-moon glasses perched on the edge of a rounded nose.

It was the scholar she had spoken to after her mother's funeral, the one who wore white and knew of Calla's reading habits. She exuded the same no-nonsense attitude she'd had seven years before, resting heavily against her walking stick.

"Highness," the woman said again. "What are you *doing*?"

Jura held up the book. "Reading," he said. "It's what one does here, if I'm not mistaken."

The scholar's nostrils flared. "The book you're holding is priceless," she said. "It's been in our library for generations, since your father's father—"

Jura's smile was angelic. He reached down deliberately and tore another page from the binding. His expression was childlike as he dangled the paper before him, its edges beginning to char.

"I think there's something you don't understand," he said. The entire book had begun to smoke in his palms. The cover caught alight, blue flames eating away at the leather. "This book might be valuable, but it's also mine. This library is mine. Your purpose—your sole reason for living—is to serve at the command of your king."

He tossed the book's withered remains to the ground. A cruel light had appeared in his eyes as bits of ash scattered against the carpet. The scholar inhaled sharply. She opened her mouth to respond, but Jura spoke first.

"Give me your hand."

Teia's spine prickled. "Jura," she said, but his attention was entirely fixed on the old woman, who met his unwavering stare. After a long minute, the scholar set her cane aside. When she hobbled over to Jura, her knotted veins shone against her skin.

"Jura!"

He huffed impatiently before spinning around, seizing Teia by the side of the neck. His thumb dug into the hollow of her throat, his other fingers bracing against her shoulder. Jura's breath smelled like honeycomb, like cinnamon and melted sugar. Spots erupted behind Teia's eyes. She had the dreadful thought that he would kill her right there and leave her body in a grave-yard of books.

One minute she was fighting for air; the next, she was being thrown backward into a shelf. As Teia's skull collided with wood, the blow knocking breath from her lungs, she saw Jura's hand envelop the scholar's. The old woman was trembling, her shoulders hunched, but there was a steely acceptance etched into her face. Slowly, the smell of charred flesh leaked into the air, followed by a wailing scream.

"You move," Jura said, "and I'll take your other hand too."

Maybe it was her time with the Dawnbreakers—the stories from Alara and Kyra, the emptiness in Tobias's eyes when he spoke of his parents. Teia had watched Jura's moods before, but something shifted for the first time, breaking through the numbness that encased her. When Teia heaved herself upright, she reached on instinct for the water within his blood. She was ready to threaten him by force, to act in a way she never had before, when he stepped away from the scholar.

"There," Jura chirped. "Was that so bad?"

The woman crumpled. Jura surveyed her with distinct dis-interest before patting the pocket that held the torn pages. He dusted off his robes absentmindedly, humming a disjointed tune as he moved toward the exit. At the door, though, he looked back at Teia, who stood frozen by the bookshelf.

"Congratulations on the engagement, Halfling," he said. "And don't forget to wear orange when you can—it's Abbott's favorite color."

The threads of heat loosened as Jura walked away, collapsing without a proper master. As Teia rushed to the scholar, she balked at the sight of the wound. The flame had scorched through the woman's wrist. It had destroyed muscle and sinew, leaving nothing but a withered stump behind. It was a wonder she was still conscious, gesturing at Teia with a clawing movement, tears streaking her cheeks.

When Teia bent down, the scholar's eyelids fluttered. *Legends of the Serkawr,*" the old woman whispered, her voice a dry husk.

"What?"

"The book he burned." A sob. "That's the title."

Legends of the Serkawr? Teia thought wildly, as the scholar went still. In all her seventeen years, she had never known Jura to take an interest in Erisia's lore. True, the crown prince hauled himself to the palace temple on occasion, breaking bread with priests and reciting devotional hymns. But Jura's ego was a deadly thing, and she doubted he'd truly found faith—certainly not enough that he'd be reading about the Serkawr for pleasure.

It was a question for another day.

Teia sprinted away, desperate to return to Alara, to see if the Poisons Master had something—anything—that might save the old woman. Yet as she tore through the stacks, past the leering busts and endless aisles of books, Jura's words replayed in her mind, a chain around her neck, a cycle that refused to break.

You're my baby sister. My last remnant of family. How could I ever bear to part with you?

Bastard, she thought as she gritted her teeth. Her throat smarted in pain, chafing with each breath.

She would call Jura a monster. A nightmare. One day soon, she would even call him king.

But until the end of her days, Teia would never call him family.

CHAPTER FOURTEEN

The first snow of the season fell the next day.

Wind swept through Bhanot like a banshee, screeching at the top of its lungs, rattling against the windowpanes. It was so cold that the palace fountain had frozen overnight, with icicles clinging to each statue. Teia was shivering within minutes of venturing outside. Frost clung to her hair, her lashes, as she trekked out to the gardens, teeth chattering uncontrollably.

The dead were never buried on palace grounds. The superstitious said it was bad luck; the skeptics claimed it was to avoid the stink of decaying corpses. Either way, all bodies were hauled a respectable distance away. The nobility went to the Splendid Graveyard, accompanied by a hand-selected honor guard. The poor were rolled into whatever grave was available—behind abandoned shops or into unmarked plots.

Yet the palace staff held to their traditions whenever one of their own passed away: a single candle would be propped against the garden's gate, kept in place by a small cairn of stones. It was a poor replica of the rows of candles that stood within the temples, but the gesture still remained. In Erisia, a candle for the dead meant respect. It was a final goodbye, a promise to meet again in the next life.

It was why Teia was here today, paying her respects to the old scholar.

She sent a burst of heat toward the candle, but the wind whipped it away effortlessly. Around her, the storm raged on, the lights of the palace barely visible. Teia clenched her jaw. She spurred another lick of heat forward, watching as it faded away in midair. Again. *Again.*

It was hopeless. *This* was hopeless. Beneath the wool of her scarf and a fine layer of powder, the bruises Jura left had yet to fade. Teia could still feel his hand clamped around her throat, cutting off her windpipe, and she thought once more about the packed bag stowed under her bed. Would it be easier to leave? To disappear without a trace, to wander stateless, to renounce her parents in exchange for freedom?

As quickly as the thought appeared, something inside her pushed back. She wouldn't go. She couldn't. Council members might be constrained to their spheres of influence, but some power was better than none at all. In the palace, Teia could keep track of the ministers, of Jura. She could operate as she had for years, moving the pieces behind the curtain.

The marriage to Abbott was a separate problem, one she'd deal with in time. Although she doubted he'd want a wife who was his political equal, the thought of being linked to the Minister of Contracts and Coin made Teia want to scream. If she spent too long pondering the situation, she'd fall into utter despair.

It was far better to focus on her plan. She needed it to work more than ever, before she was swallowed alive into the belly of the beast. She would steal the Star. She would win the Dawnbreakers' trust.

She had no other choice but to succeed.

Teia drew her scarf tighter. She directed another thread of heat toward the candle. It caught for the briefest instant, before snuffing out. Teia swore, and someone behind her cleared his throat.

"Is that the type of language they teach in the palace?"

Tobias. She didn't know when he'd appeared, but she recognized the scratch of his voice. Over the past week, they had settled into a terse routine. He asked for updates. She gave him none. And he would bestow her with a look of complete disappointment, as if she was dooming the Dawnbreakers with her lack of action.

"Aren't you supposed to be on patrol?" Teia asked.

"I'm making my rounds," he answered flatly, "and you have a meeting with Lehm tomorrow."

"I know."

"You sound thrilled."

"I'm busy."

"You're trying to light a candle in a snowstorm."

"Smaller miracles have happened."

"Yes," he agreed, "but never at the Golden Palace."

After the catastrophe of the last day, Teia hardly needed Tobias Rennert's input. "If that's all you came to tell me," she said, burrowing into the fur lining of her cloak, "I'll take your advice under consideration."

Teia started stomping her way down the mosaic path, setting course for the warmth of the palace. She was almost to the door when she made the mistake of turning back. Tobias had knelt to the stone cairn, snow crowning his dark hair. He wore no gloves but cupped his bare hands around the candle. From between his fingers, there came the spark of flame as he touched match to wick.

What did she care if the rebel boy succumbed to frostbite? Better for her if the Dawnbreakers had to peel his body off the street tomorrow. But some traitorous part of Teia revolted. She watched him bow his head, still guarding the candle from the roaring wind. And she heard her voice speak on its own accord, issuing a challenge, weaving a lie. "Well?" she said, as she yanked open the door. "You want an update for Lehm, don't you?"

It was enough to rouse him from the snow. He followed her through the hallway and up the staircase, their footprints wet against the steps. When Teia unlocked her door, she hustled Tobias inside and pointed at the hearth. Immediately, a hearty flame crackled against the blackened logs. They crowded by the fire wordlessly, her on the loveseat, him standing.

It took a while before Tobias spoke again. "Thank you," he said stiffly.

"That sounded like it hurt."

"It did."

A fresh gale howled outside. Tobias clasped his hands together, holding them in front of the fire. "Thank you," he said again, his tone a touch less pained. "The storm wasn't this bad when I was out earlier."

Teia had the absurd image of Tobias winding through Bhanot, heaving around a sack of groceries. "You were running errands?"

"What do you think I do all day?"

"Clean your knives. Glower at people."

"I don't glower," he said imperiously.

"You've never looked in a mirror before, have you?"

His cough sounded suspiciously close to a laugh. "No errands today. I was off duty in the morning and had some things to take care of."

"Like?"

"Are all nobles this intrusive?"

"Curious," Teia corrected. "This is how a discussion works."

"I never asked for a discussion."

"I never asked for a rebel handler who threatened to slit my throat."

The smallest smile tugged at the corners of his mouth. "If you must know," Tobias said, "I was at the cartographer's shop."

Teia had expected something a tad more mysterious. Training rebels in an underground cavern, for instance, or conducting drills by some rocky shoreline. "You like maps?" she said.

"I study them."

"Bhanot's streets are grids. That's easy enough to memorize."

"Not just Bhanot. I wanted to be an explorer when I was younger. See new lands."

"You still could," she pointed out. The Dark Sea remained largely undiscovered. Kingdoms frequently commissioned sailors, offering them ships and gold in exchange for their labor.

He shook his head. "Not when I'm with the Dawnbreakers," he said. "When I promised to fight with Lehm, I meant it."

There was no reverence when he spoke of the rebel leader. In fact, Tobias seemed hardened. Resigned.

"What do you think of him?" Teia hedged.

"He's dedicated to the cause."

She blew on her fingers to warm them. "For personal benefit?"

"His sister," Tobias said. "She was killed in the Bhanot Uprising."

A warning bell chimed in Teia's head. She had studied the Bhanot Uprising briefly, the fifty university students who had camped before the palace gates, throwing smoke pellets and brandishing weapons. The uprising had taken place just one month after Ren ascended the throne, although her father had never spoken of the incident.

Teia swallowed. "They wanted to overthrow the monarchy."

"It wouldn't have worked then," Tobias said. "Ren was popular—all the Carthans were. But his guards were quick to act, slow to forgive."

"They shot into the crowd."

"They killed twenty people and injured almost as many." Tobias sighed. "Some of the older Dawnbreakers—the ones who've followed Lehm for years—say he was there too. He was just a kid who'd gone with his sister to have company. In the end, he escaped, but she didn't. He's been chasing vengeance ever since."

"He wants to finish what she started."

"I'd say he's doing a decent job."

"Is that the general Dawnbreaker consensus?"

He shrugged. "Some disagree with his tactics. They think he's too bloody, too cruel."

"But Kyra likes him."

"Kyra likes everyone," Tobias said dryly. "She would like an assassin if they greeted her before firing."

Teia bit her lip. "And you?" she said. "Do you like Lehm?"

He contemplated that as he shook frozen droplets from his sleeves. "I need him," Tobias answered at last. "I suppose that's close enough."

As he'd been talking, she'd removed her gloves and unwrapped the scarf from around her neck. Tobias's gaze darkened. His eyes trailed her throat, and Teia gripped at her scarf. *Dammit.* The powder she'd applied must have rubbed off with the melting snow, the bruises Jura left purple against her skin.

She didn't want his pity, nor his remorse. "I saw you outside,"

Teia said instead. "I thought a lit candle in the storm would be a miracle."

"Sometimes a miracle is what we deserve." He dropped his eyes to the hearth. "I light a candle every morning at the Temple of Past, right before sunrise. I'll make sure to burn an extra one tomorrow."

Teia stared into the flames. "You heard what happened?"

"Alara told me. Safa was a good woman."

The scholar who had died. *She cared for my mother,* Teia thought, *and I didn't even know her name.*

They were silent for a while. Teia inspected the lines on her palm, crisscrossing over one another. "Things won't be like this forever," she said.

Tobias dipped his chin. "I know," he said. "But sometimes it's hard to imagine."

"Not being part of the rebellion?"

"Not having something to work toward."

She knew what he meant. "You could travel the Five Kingdoms," Teia offered. "Draw maps to your heart's content."

"Maybe not the second part. I'm not talented enough to draw anything."

"You didn't have an instructor?"

"Oh, I did. He quit after the second lesson."

"That bad?"

"Beyond your wildest imagination. He said he'd met salamanders who were more artistically inclined."

"Gifted salamanders."

"Dream crushers," Tobias said, so sourly that Teia hid a laugh. She draped her damp cloak against the back of the loveseat and smoothed out the folds in the fabric.

"What were the Highlands like?" she asked.

For a second, she was afraid she'd overstepped. Then a true smile lit Tobias's face, brightening his eyes, loosening his frame. She knew he was picturing the blue mountains, rising past the horizon. The great eastern cliffs, craggy and imposing, soaring over the frothing shores of the Dark Sea. It was his old home— the land that the St. Clairs had overseen for centuries, until Jura gifted it away to Devon Ralis.

"Busy," Tobias said. "Loud. There were always couples in town, honeymooning during the warmer months. They would sightsee near the manor and sail out in the evenings."

"The Highlands has a port." She'd never been but had studied enough maps with her father.

"The second largest in Erisia, outside the one in Bhanot. It was the most wonderful place in the world to me. My friends and I would sit near the dock entrances during the high season, offering to carry bags for a few guilds. For me, it was an excuse to trail the sailors who worked there. I'd run behind them, begging for a story." He shook his head ruefully. "Most of them ignored me. But some would tell me about their lives back in K'val or Shaylan. One Ismetian even moved the earth, just for a second, so I could feel what it was like."

Gone was the rebel soldier, the boy weathered by time. Teia could envision Tobias as he used to be, young and carefree, hounding sailors for a few minutes of their time. For some reason, this struck an odd chord with her, and the revelation that followed was quick and unforgiving, tumbling like a waterfall through rocks. She suddenly yearned to hear more, to retain descriptions about the bustling harbor and the salt-streaked ships, the foghorns that blasted over the teeming docks.

I could listen to him speak forever.

"Maybe you have some merchant blood in you," she said. "Carrying bags for a story is a decent trade."

"Not quite," Tobias admitted. "They ended up barring me from the docks, after I dropped a visiting noble's bags into the water."

"That doesn't sound too bad."

"No," he agreed, "until the clasp came undone, and all his undergarments floated to the surface."

This time, Teia couldn't hold back her laughter. "In front of everyone?"

"*Everyone.* Vacationers, shopkeepers. I thought I was going to faint from embarrassment. The patrolmen were pulling silk shirts from the bay for weeks, embroidered with these enormous pink flowers. My father—" Tobias's voice caught, before he continued roughly, "He came to the docks to see what the commotion was. I'd never seen him laugh so hard. He shook the noble's hand and said he had a wonderful sense of style."

Teia's chest tightened. Before she could stop herself, she said, "My father was the same way."

He tipped his brow. "Ren?"

"He was always laughing, always joking. There was one story he loved to tell, about how I'd snuck under the banquet table before he was set to dine with his officials. I was little—three, maybe four. I must have gotten bored and fallen asleep. When I woke up, I grabbed someone's calf to stand, and the minister almost flipped the table. Kept screaming about rats the size of people."

Tobias's jaw dropped in astonishment. "You're lying."

"I'm not! It was a disaster. There was food everywhere."

"Wine on the floor?"

"On the walls too. One of the ministers lost his wig."

He was laughing now, the sound filling the room, drifting like music. "You," he said, "are a terror."

"Criminal."

"Menace." He gave her a sideways glance, a smile pulling at his lips. "You don't actually have an update for Lehm, do you?"

"About that," Teia said, after a brief pause. "I don't suppose he'd like to hear about rats of unusual size?"

And it was around then, between the warmth of the room and the fire popping in a merry cadence, that a dreadful understanding came over Teia. This was different from how she and Tobias had been before, beyond disgust or apathy or even a tentative truce.

This was something strange and new, the fragile weight of a friendship. Built from the barest of bones, spanning the thinnest tightrope—and yet unequivocally there nonetheless.

Chapter Fifteen

When Teia returned to the Dawnbreakers' warehouse the following day, she was ready for what was to come.

After yanking off the blindfold and reorienting herself to her surroundings, Teia allowed Kyra to direct her into Lehm's hidden office. Alara sat in one of the squishy velvet chairs, framed by a massive painting of stampeding mustangs. She was inspecting a powdery substance with great concentration, although she grinned when Teia and Kyra entered. "About time you two showed up."

Teia eyed the powder. "And that is?"

"A work in progress."

"That sounds reassuring."

"Not really," Alara said blithely. "It's been four days, and my test subject hasn't woken up yet." She patted the chair beside her. "Sit. Lehm and Tobias will be here soon."

She was right. Teia had barely sunk into the seat when Lehm marched into the room. Tobias was a few paces behind him, his expression disinterested. There was no sign of the boy by the hearth, the one who'd told stories by the fire. Instead, this was the rebel through and through, the soldier with an unshakable mission.

Alara wriggled one of her eyebrows at him. "You seem happy."

"I am," Tobias deadpanned. "Can't you tell?"

Lehm clapped his hands impatiently. "Well, Halfling?" he said, skipping straight over Alara to speak to Teia. "I was promised a brilliant plan."

It *was* brilliant, especially considering the timeline she'd been given. Teia stood, pulling at the roll of butcher's paper on the rebel leader's desk. She selected an expensive-looking pen, still snug within a satin-lined case, and began sketching out a rough overview of Blackgate Prison, connecting the lines into the shape of a pentagon.

"Blackgate is built in a hub-and-spokes design," Teia said, channeling her overnight expertise in the prison's architecture. "The main command tower is here in the center, overlooking the five cell blocks. It gives guards a vantage point on each of the buildings—and all the exits and entrances to the prison."

If Lehm was impressed, he didn't show it. "And this is relevant how?" he said.

"You want the Morning Star, don't you?" Teia set the pen's nib on the northern tip of the pentagon. "It's here, inside the Vault."

Tobias leaned over the drawing. "It's a smart setup," he conceded. "Think about the security in Blackgate. Scheduled patrols. State-of-the-art weapons. Nobody in or out without being accompanied by a guard."

"Oh," Alara said. "Is that all?"

"What more do you want? A fire-breathing dragon?"

"Those," Alara said haughtily, "are extinct."

Lehm studied Teia for a long moment. The vacancy behind his gaze unsettled her, but she tipped her head to return his stare. "Which building is the Star in?" Lehm said.

"Block C," Teia said. Her voice was quiet, no louder than a rustle of silk, but it seemed to carry throughout the room.

Kyra took a ragged breath. "Block C?"

Blackgate might be notorious, but Block C had gained its own type of infamy. It was the prison's resident torture building, designed to break the most stubborn of prisoners. It was said an entire section of the block had been specifically repurposed for interrogating Dawnbreakers. Teia had heard rumors about the acts carried out there, led by specially designated guards: needles pricked through eye sockets, teeth plied raw from gums, knives jammed into different limbs.

It had been enough to keep her far away from Block C, until this current lapse in judgment.

"All of Blackgate's entrances are guarded," Teia said. "There are fifteen gates in total, and two guards stationed at each one. Anyone who wants access to the prison needs to get past them first."

"Do you happen to have any good news?" Alara interjected. "Aside from potentially dying a long, painful death."

"Weren't you the one who asked for more?" Kyra said.

"I've changed my mind, now that I've had time to think things over."

"Nobody's dying," Teia said, with far more confidence than she felt. She took a crinkled sheet of paper from her pocket, smoothing it flat on the table to show Pembrant's address. Teia had managed to find it after another trip to the library. When she'd discovered it hidden away near the end of an overflowing ledger, squeezed in minuscule script near a margin, she'd almost wept tears of joy.

Kyra's features clouded. "'Johns Pembrant,'" she murmured,

reading the name scrawled at the top of the page. "Weren't we searching for his address?"

Teia tapped the paper smartly. "Correct. He's a guard at the palace, but he also works at Blackgate."

"Right. So why would he help us get the Star?"

"Because he'll be properly incentivized."

"Meaning?"

"Meaning I'll apply the necessary amount of pressure. The details aren't important."

Kyra didn't waver. "They *are* important," she said staunchly. "What do you plan on doing to him?"

"I'm going to ask nicely."

"Teia."

"You don't think I can behave myself?"

Kyra's knuckles were white. "You aren't going to hurt him, are you?"

It depended on what her definition of *hurt* entailed. "Not exactly," Teia said delicately.

"Then what?"

"It's really not important—"

"*Teia.*" Kyra was upright by this point, her palms flat on the table. "What are you going to do?"

Tobias had been watching Teia closely from his chair. As he rested his cheek against the curl of his fist, his dark blue eyes settled onto hers. "Blackmail," he said.

Kyra wrenched around. "What?"

"That's the plan, isn't it?" Tobias's thumb brushed over the scar on his neck. "If you aren't going to torture Pembrant, you need him to comply in some other way. Blackmail would be the easiest option."

Kyra hesitated. She gazed desperately at Teia, waiting for her to rebuke the statement. When it was evident that there was nothing to refute, the rebel champion's brow lowered. "This is a joke, right?"

"Kyra—"

"I can't believe you!" she raged. "You're going to ruin someone's life over a *gem*?"

"I think," Teia said, feeling unusually defensive, "that there's a bit more nuance than that."

"Is there?" Kyra's entire frame stiffened. She appeared to come to some ghastly realization, as she said, "You've done this before, haven't you?"

Teia could infer what the rebel girl meant. After all, shouldn't this be expected from a Carthan? Wasn't this what royals did best? They schemed and they manipulated. They cut down rivals to come out ahead, pistols roaring, swords swinging. It was why they needed to be cast from power, replaced with a gentler sort of future.

But Teia's plots were also why she was alive. She would make the same choices, walk the same path, if it brought her where she needed to be. Under Kyra's piercing judgment, Teia held her ground.

She lifted her chin. She said, "Yes."

Teia was twelve when she first blackmailed someone.

She still maintained it was an accident. Teia had been exploring the passageways when she overheard the Minister of Agriculture drunkenly lamenting the pitfalls of marriage. Teia had recognized his voice instantly—there was a whiny texture about it, reminiscent of an exceedingly unpleasant baby.

"I'm a whole new man, gentlemen," the minister had slurred. "You wouldn't believe the fun Pearl and I have together. I can hardly stand straight when she's finished with me."

He went on to describe each excruciating detail, down to the placements of their legs on the bed. His friends hooted with laughter, the Minister of Agriculture grew increasingly animated, and Teia listened to every word from the other side of the wall, kept in place by a disgusted fascination. It wasn't until the man began heartily throwing up in a vase that Teia melted back into the shadows, brimming with her newfound knowledge. She hadn't understood everything the minister had said, nor did she want to.

What she *did* know were three things: the Minister of Agriculture was married. His wife was pregnant.

And her name was Lissa, not Pearl.

Teia cornered the minister's maidservant the following afternoon. When she made her request, the girl was understandably reluctant. "I'll be thrown onto the streets, my lady," she kept saying, right until Teia offered up her sapphire necklace.

Things spiraled from there. The maidservant stole away scraps of proof for Teia: a handkerchief here, a garter there. Teia collected the trinkets under her bed, squirreled beneath a loose slat. The minister's wife had swelled to an impressive size by the time Teia assembled her things, stuffing the items into a sack to confront the minister.

She had sidestepped his page and pounded on the rosewood door to his office. When the minister cracked open the door, Teia pushed past him, ignoring his protests to dump her mountain of evidence onto his desk.

The minister reeled back. "This isn't mine."

"I wouldn't dare to presume," Teia said. She picked up the garter between two of her fingers. The name was clearly embroidered in white lace, decorated with tiny sparkles. "It's Pearl's."

"I don't know a Pearl."

"Don't you? You said it yourself—you like it when she pulls your hair."

The Minister of Agriculture exploded into a string of curses. He proceeded to call Teia an entire host of names, most of which would make a sailor's ears blister. After a bit, she grew tired of standing, so she sat down instead, picking a comfortable seat as he rattled off his threats. It took a good while before he stammered to a halt, his thin face ruddy with exertion.

"Are you finished?" Teia asked. She took his vehement stare as confirmation and added, "Because if you are, I'm here to make you a deal."

Teia had learned of the flowers a few days prior. They had recently been discovered along a muddy riverbank near Set, the snowy petals tipped in oceanic blue. The flowers were said to be exquisitely lovely, so beautiful that the country's best painters couldn't fully capture their likeness. Naturally, there had been a tremendous fuss about what they should be called, with every scholar, official, and noble in the kingdom sending in their suggestions.

It was what Teia had decided on, as she beamed up at the minister. "I'd like them to be named after me," she explained.

He gaped down at her. "You want—a flower?"

"Is there an issue?"

"Not at all, Princess," the minister said. He reached out hurriedly and swept her pile of evidence beneath the desk. "*Flora teian* will be christened within the week."

The Minister of Agriculture might have been a lecher and a cheat, but he stayed true to his word. The announcement was made just hours later, scandalizing horticulturalists across the country and leading to a spate of protests. There were demands for the minister to resign for this apparent gaff, all of which the man promptly disregarded.

Of course, *Flora teian* was later found to be poisonous, after two horses and a goat dropped dead along the riverbank. But nobody had known that at the time, and Teia had been immensely proud of her hard-hitting bargain.

So that was how things started: with an overheard conversation and a crop of plants. It was Teia's first taste of power, and she instantly lusted for more. She explored the passageways with a revitalized interest, finding different entrances, uncovering where the walls were thinnest. She kept a steady group of servants at her disposal, who received bonuses for each piece of information they brought her.

Then came Ren's death. Her father had been self-medicating for years, staving off Calla's passing with the help of a bottle. When the alcohol eventually caught up to him, it had poisoned his liver, his blood, tingeing his skin a sickly blue. He died convulsing in his bed, with Jura and Teia standing beside him.

The wake had been its own type of awful. Teia had dressed in white silks for the second time in three years. She sat next to Jura, who wore a pristine set of ivory robes and carried a dozen red roses. Dignitaries approached the crown prince throughout the ceremony. They whispered their condolences, while ruminating about how Ren would be missed.

"Thank you," Jura would say each time, shaking hand after hand. "I appreciate the sentiments. I hope to do him justice."

After the priest concluded his droning speech, filled with

generic descriptions of a monarch that sounded nothing like Ren, Teia and Jura were nudged toward the casket. She was standing behind Jura as he set the roses over the crystal lid. She saw him raise his hand in farewell. She saw him bow his head.

And she saw the grin that stretched ear to ear, his lips pulled back, his teeth glittering in the candlelight.

Teia was only thirteen, but she knew what that smile meant.

Ren had favored compassion. He'd been changed by Calla's death, thrown off balance and knocked astray, and yet this particular characteristic never faltered. Even on his worst days, stinking of alcohol and weaving on his feet, he met with commonfolk to discuss their needs. He reduced taxes. He expanded infrastructure. Once, he'd stopped his royal procession to help a street vendor save his cart, kneeling three inches into muck to haul out a wagon wheel.

But kindness was a quality neither of his children had inherited. Jura Carthan preferred to rip things out by the root, to remake them in his likeness. Within a month of his interim rule, he'd broken tradition by sacking the old Council. The ministers were replaced next, as members of Ren's government were weeded out one after another, forced into early retirement or met with untimely accidents. The court contracted in on itself, devouring the weak, sculpting around this new dynamic. Nobody dared question the crown prince, especially after news spread of the St. Clair family's fate.

What started as flower names snowballed into something far larger. Teia's secrets became more than a hobby, offering her protection against the world outside. It was how she learned in advance of the other assassins Jura would send—one when she was fifteen, another a year later. It was how she dismantled his plot to exile her to the Southern Fortress, after speaking to the

Minister of Defense and using his son as leverage to claim the fort for military drills.

One thing led to another, didn't it? Each event was a tidal wave, rearranging what was truth, molding Teia into who she was today. She learned that every person had a breaking point, no matter how well hidden it might be. And if Teia needed to hit that spot with a mallet, if she had to shatter someone completely to get what she needed, then so be it. She had made peace with her actions. There was an irredeemable fracture in her soul, a blackness that brought her a bit closer to Jura.

Except she was still alive. She might be the Halfling Princess, scorned by the court, hated by her country, but she had built her tower of thorns high. She would keep herself safe, staying in its fold for as long as she could—and when Jura finally pried her out, he would not be prepared for what he found inside.

Kyra strode the length of the room. She had been at this for ten minutes, moving jerkily from wall to wall with both hands clasped firmly behind her. Teia thought she resembled a rather agitated house cat, although she was wise enough to keep her observation to herself.

"There has to be another way," Kyra said, as she came to an abrupt stop.

"To get into Blackgate?" Teia shook her head. "Not unless you want us strung up on the spot."

"How can you be so calm about this?"

"Hangings are considered entertainment at Blackgate."

"Not about that," Kyra snapped. "I meant the people you extort."

"The Dawnbreakers are hardly saints, Kyra."

"That doesn't make this right."

"If you wanted to argue morals, you should have studied philosophy, not joined a rebel movement."

"Or I can act as a conscience for people who seem to be lacking."

"Enough." Lehm's voice was sharper than any whip. As Kyra fell silent, he rose to his feet, pondering the sketch of the prison. "This Johns Pembrant—how will he get you into Blackgate?"

Teia pointed at the drawing. "He's posted at one of the gates. All he needs to do is unlock it and let us inside."

"There are two guards at each entrance."

"I'll leave the second one to Pembrant. If it comes down to a fight, I've heard he's an excellent swordsman."

Kyra winced, but Teia didn't care. After so much unfamiliarity, here was a language she understood. This meeting had become all business now, transactional in a way she excelled at. There was something Teia wanted and a price she had to pay.

If Lehm needed the Star to prove her loyalty, she would move the damn moon to bring it to him.

"An interesting proposition," Lehm mused. "Which gate does Pembrant guard?"

"I'm not sure. But I plan on paying him a visit tomorrow."

Lehm nodded. "The East Gate."

"Excuse me?"

"Use the East Gate when you enter." Lehm tapped at the right corner of the Blackgate sketch, somewhere near Block E. "It's the safest route into the prison."

"Why?"

"We have scouts posted nearby. They can extract you if you run into any trouble."

Teia felt a twinge of surprise. She hadn't anticipated Lehm making such an offer, but she wasn't about to refuse the help. "The East Gate," she agreed, as she returned to the sketch. "When we're inside, Pembrant can guide us through the prison. Blackgate is intentionally designed to be confusing, and it's best to have someone familiar with the layout. After we finish with the Vault, we can exit from its emergency door and leave through the same gate."

She reached into the folds of her cloak for another roll of paper. Teia had discovered the map of the Vault while rifling through Miran's office. The poor general had no idea that a passageway entrance was fitted behind one of his bookshelves, allowing easy access into his locked study. Teia had simply waited for Miran to retire for the night before stepping out of the tunnels and searching each of his cabinets.

A hiss whistled out between Alara's teeth as she scanned the Vault's blueprint. "Your family doesn't skimp on security, does it?"

"Is that a positive or a negative?"

"Most definitely a negative."

Teia traced one finger along the rows of notes crammed at the top. "The Vault is protected by ten guards, who rotate out on the hour. They're trained in hand-to-hand combat. Sharpshooting. There are traps, too, which can be activated as a fail-safe."

"Goddess," Kyra swore.

"Such as?" Alara said.

"Poisonous gas. Spikes from the ceiling and the floor. Don't take my word for it, though. This"—Teia indicated at the cramped writing—"says that the traps are cycled through each month. Keeps any potential thieves on their toes."

"Makes sense," Tobias reasoned. "There's probably nothing else left to bury."

Teia plowed on. "After that, there's the safe. State of the art, built with a two-ton iron door. It can be unlocked with a combination, which nobody knows in full. Sections of the code are distributed to different officials around Erisia."

"I don't suppose you know how to pick locks," Tobias said.

There'd never been a need to learn, when she employed Enna van Apt's services. Yet this time, Teia wouldn't be relying on Enna. Lehm might be one smug bastard, but he'd made fair points when he'd first demanded the Star. There was too much risk involving a thief. If Enna decided to bolt with the Star in hand, Teia wasn't confident she'd be able to catch her.

"I have something better than a lockpick," she said, as she lit a single flame above her open palm. "My father built a fail-safe for the Vault. A white flame can override the lock without the combination."

"What about the guards? The traps?"

"I can extinguish the lamps before we get inside. We take out the guards, grab the Star, and go on our merry way."

Alara frowned. "But if the lanterns go out and the Star goes missing, won't everyone know it was you?"

"Not necessarily. Kyra can manipulate fire, so she could theoretically open the safe." Teia dragged her finger back to the Vault's entrance. "When the Morning Star disappears, people will suspect the Dawnbreakers. We just need to let them draw their own conclusions."

Tobias's lips quirked. "There's a lot of *we* being thrown into this plan."

"I've been saying that the entire time. Have you not been listening to me?"

"I have. I just don't recall agreeing to this death trap."

"You didn't," she acknowledged. She rotated toward Alara,

and then Kyra. "But I'm asking the three of you to come with me."

Alara's look was disbelieving. "You want us in Blackgate with you?"

"Yes."

"Why?"

"I can't fight ten guards alone. I need your help, if you're up for the task."

Asking Alara had always been a risk. There was too much history for the rebel girl in Blackgate, too much bad blood. But a sudden determination ignited behind the Poisons Master's eyes. Her hands loosened from her knees, settling into her lap. "All right," she said. "I'm in."

"You are?" Kyra said.

"On one condition."

This didn't seem promising. Teia braced herself. "What?"

"If we see any Dawnbreakers, we try to help them."

"Help them?" Teia parroted in astonishment. They would barely be able to help themselves in Blackgate, much less any inmates they came across.

"We have people in there, ones we haven't heard from in months."

"They knew the risks." This was from Lehm, who watched Alara with undisguised displeasure.

"They did," Alara said. "But they don't deserve torture."

Teia was going to throttle the Poisons Master. "We can plan something else for them. A second trip once we have the Star."

"Don't play me for a fool. This isn't the kind of job someone pulls off twice."

"The Star is our priority."

"There are human beings in there." Alara's lower lip trembled. "People with families."

Fine. Teia didn't need four people for Blackgate. Alara would have been nice to have, with her knowledge of toxins and poisons, but she would be too unfocused inside the prison. Distracted, unmoored. *Yes*, Teia thought. Perhaps this was for the best.

But then Kyra dropped back into her seat, a familiar steadiness reflected in her face. One look, and Teia knew the ultimatum was coming. "We help them," the rebel champion said. "We help them, and we don't hurt the guards—Pembrant included."

"The guards are murderers, Kyra," Tobias said. "Torturers."

"Not all of them," Kyra said. "Blackgate pays well. Some people join because they need work. If it's that or sleeping on the street, what do you think they're going to choose?"

Tobias shook his head. Teia could sympathize; at this point, she was tempted to wave off the rebels and try her luck on her own. Stage a prison break? Coddle the guards? She could feel their chances of survival plummeting with each additional request.

But she couldn't fight the Vault's ten guards by herself, especially if she sustained any injuries along the way. Even if Tobias did agree to help, higher numbers would assist with their odds. As much as she resented the notion, Teia needed Alara and Kyra for her plan to work—which meant listening to their fanciful, reckless ideas.

"Fine," Teia growled. "We help any Dawnbreakers that we see, and we do our best to minimize casualties. No more, no less."

"That's all I ask," Alara said.

Kyra nodded.

That left Tobias. Unthinkably beautiful, dependably irritating Tobias, who took her in with his torrential eyes. "I still think this is a death trap."

"Does that mean you're not coming?"

"That's not what I'm saying."

"You'll have to forgive me. I've never been the best at deciphering riddles."

This earned her a ghost of a smile. "I'm your handler," he said. "I go where you go."

Alara coughed. "I don't *quite* think it works like that," she offered.

While they were negotiating terms, Lehm had moved to the other side of the table. He was surveying the map of the Vault again, tugging absentmindedly on his pendants. A grimace played around his lips. He seemed a thousand miles away, caught in another world, but his next words were clear and focused, directed to Teia alone. "I want the Star before the week is over."

"I wouldn't have it any other way," Teia said.

She held out her hand, which the rebel leader took after a beat.

Teia couldn't shake the feeling of his eyes boring into hers, long after she had left the room.

CHAPTER SIXTEEN

Johns Pembrant had no vice. He didn't gamble or drink. He worked hard, believed in the law, made an honest living. He actually loved his wife, which was a rarity in itself. She had a fondness for apple blossoms, and so during the spring, Pembrant would occasionally travel outside of Bhanot in the early mornings. He would wander the orchards, gathering armfuls of pink flowers to adorn their windowsills.

Aside from his wife, Pembrant harbored only one other weakness.

"Her name is Wynter," Enna had said to Teia, as she slid a bulging pouch of guilds into the depths of her cloak. "She turned three last month."

"What's she like?"

"Talkative. Blond." Enna flipped a guild into the air before testing it between her teeth. "The spitting image of her da."

"Do you think she'll go quietly?"

"Do I seem like someone well-versed in the mannerisms of children?"

"Don't you have a cat?"

Enna had rolled her eyes. "I'm going to pretend you didn't just try to equate the two."

When Teia arrived at Pembrant's house, dusk was bleeding into night. The Southern District was mostly for the working class. While the houses varied, this part of the district pushed up against the Flats, which meant the homes here were built for practicality, rather than aesthetics. There were endless rows of thatched roofs and brick walls, each identical to the one beside it. Every house had its curtains drawn, with sturdy metal bars affixed to the windows.

"I had no idea blackmail was done out in the open like this."

Teia's pulse jumped. She turned back to see Tobias, who dipped his chin in greeting. "Hi," he said cheekily.

She seized him by the arm, dragging him to a nearby alleyway. "What are you doing here?" she hissed.

"Following you."

"I told you I could handle this."

"What if I'm interested in the art of extortion?"

"You?"

"I have many interests."

She didn't have time for this. This wasn't the place for being lighthearted, nor for tunneling into whatever fragile friendship they had somehow achieved. She didn't want him here. She didn't want him to glimpse this side of her.

Before Teia could concoct a proper excuse, a sparkler whirred in the distance. A moment later, a circlet of light imploded high above. To any of the district's inhabitants, it was nothing out of the ordinary—one of the many fireworks that children around here set off for fun. Erisia might have regulations about who could purchase sparklers, but any street merchant worth his salt would overlook them for a quick guild.

Teia knew better. The sparkler had been bright blue, a color that wasn't typically sold by peddlers. Unless an exceptionally lucky child had gotten hold of a rare firework, the clock had started ticking.

"Stay here," Teia ordered. She swept from the alley with a prevailing sense of dread, all too aware that Tobias wouldn't listen. She should have let him freeze to death in the snowstorm, rather than setting off this unfortunate chain reaction.

Teia reached Pembrant's stoop in record time. She rapped on the door before treading back into the shadows. From the other side of solid oak, she felt a pocket of flames spring alive as someone lit a lamp. It was easy enough to tug lightly at the threads, grinding the fire to cinders as a figure walked outside.

"Johns Pembrant?" she called out.

"Yes?"

She could make out some vague features: hooded eyes, a trimmed beard. It was too dark to see anything more, for which Teia was grateful. It was far more productive to think of Pembrant as an empty husk, instead of grappling with what made him human. No personality, no character traits. No favorite season or greatest ambitions or interesting quirks.

"In a few minutes," Teia said smoothly, "your wife is going to come home. She'll be frantic, likely in tears. She'll tell you that Wynter is missing."

"Excuse me?"

"That's your daughter's name, isn't it? I know she and your wife like to go on walks together. They take the path to the canals so they can watch the sunset."

Anger crept into Pembrant's voice. "I think you should leave," he growled.

Teia didn't bother to argue as she kept the brim of her hood tucked low, ensuring her face stayed hidden. "I will. But if you want to find Wynter, I suggest visiting Fairweather Banks before dawn."

Pembrant's hand strayed closer to his waist, hovering near where he kept his sword. "Leave," he said again. "Now."

"Remember what I said. Fairweather Banks. Come alone."

Pembrant shut the door without another word. As the bolt clicked soundly in place, Teia's feet were already moving beneath her. "Let's go," she whispered to Tobias. "We don't have much time until he comes searching."

Tobias kept her pace as they sped along the shuttered streets. There was a heaviness that hadn't been there before, a fresh uncertainty that hung thick between them. They had reached the Flats, the lights from the bars and brothels blazing brighter than the sun, when Tobias caught her by the wrist.

"Teia."

It was the first time he'd said her name. Something tensed inside her. She forced her gaze to his, pulling at her hand halfheartedly. "We shouldn't stop here."

Tobias didn't move. "This is important."

"You want to know what I did, don't you?"

"Yes."

"I thought you were curious about blackmail."

"I'm serious."

"So am I." Teia planted her feet, refusing to feel any shame. "I know a thief. The best thief in Erisia, who will steal anything for the right price."

"Including a little girl?"

Teia nodded.

Tobias's face was a mask. "And what happens after?"

"To the thief? Or to the girl?"

"Both."

"The thief makes a fortune in guilds, and the little girl spends a few nights in the penthouse of the Imperial Hotel."

There was a hint of recognition. "You sent Kyra and Alara there earlier."

"We'll meet them when we're done."

Teia waited for a reaction. A response. When she received neither, she simply snatched her wrist from Tobias's grasp and resumed her trudge forward, steeling herself against the wind.

No more distractions, no more interruptions. It was time for the Halfling Princess to live up to her reputation.

Fairweather Banks had once been beautiful.

In a time well before Teia's, Fairweather had been a place of incredible splendor, favored by select wealthy families for its stunning ocean view. Despite its location at the edge of the Flats, the residents found this all very adventurous. They'd swept the crooks and con men right off their front porches, hired whatever guards they needed, and erected glistening manors behind soaring silver gates, each more extravagant than the last.

Of course, this had all been prior to a series of floods sent by the Shaylani during the height of the war. Fairweather Banks had been drowned under the crushing weight of water, its statues beheaded, its buildings ripped apart. After that, the wealthy inhabitants learned their lesson. They moved inland toward the Royal District, and Fairweather was left to rot along with the rest of the Flats.

Now, anything salvageable was long gone. Fairweather was nothing more than a dumping ground, filled with the carcasses of old homes. The only people who still frequented the area were criminals seeking solace from prying eyes.

Teia didn't know what that made her. She came to Fairweather Banks more often than she cared to admit, particularly during the warmer months. Mourner's Bay became too crowded in the summer, overrun with stray tourists and laughing children, and so Teia would meet Enna here, among the decaying estates and crooked iron skeletons.

"Watch your step," Teia said. She summoned a flame, more for Tobias's benefit than her own, as they picked their way to the center of the ruins. A mansion rose from the gloom, dashing into the gray clouds. Fractured statues protected either side of the gaping threshold, although the door had long been torn off its hinges.

Teia lowered herself onto the crumbling stoop. Tobias sat beside her, scanning the rubble that surrounded them. "You've been here before?"

"You missed your calling as a detective."

They didn't wait long. It had scarcely been an hour when someone came sprinting their way, using the hovering flame as a guide.

Teia stubbed out the fire just in time. Johns Pembrant was in front of them not a minute later, a blade in his hand, a pistol clasped to his belt. She didn't need a light to feel his glare of pure hatred.

"You took her," he spat.

"I told you that, didn't I?"

"Where is she?"

"You don't actually expect an answer, do you?"

He took a shaky step in her direction. "*Where is she?*" he bellowed.

Words or threats or swords. In the end, they were all just as useless.

"Safe," Teia said back, the reply dancing off her tongue.

Pembrant released a wordless scream and drove his broadsword toward her. She didn't flinch, and he didn't waver. At the very last second, he shifted position, just as she'd known he would. The blade plunged into the dirt, less than an inch from where Teia stood.

"You're a monster," he snarled. "A coward."

"Maybe a monster," she conceded, "but certainly not a coward."

She dropped her hood back, and an arc of moonlight shone onto her face. Pembrant's eyes widened. His features jumbled in a kaleidoscope of confusion, fear, bewilderment. He immediately abandoned the sword. As his knees sank into the soft-packed earth, he dropped his head to the ground. "Princess," he whispered.

"Soldier." If they were trading titles, she could do this all night.

"You took her?" he said, sounding as if he didn't quite believe she was there. "You took my Wynter?"

"Yes."

"But—why?"

"I needed to get your attention." She nudged the sword delicately. "I'd say it worked."

Pembrant jerked his head upward, a burst of rage breaking through his expression. "Return her to me," he said. He sounded passably confident, and Teia pitied him for it. "If I don't get her back, I'll go to the crown prince."

"Go ahead," she challenged. "You want to speak to Jura? Tell the court? Set your guard friends on me, like I'm some deer in the woods?" She ground her heel into his blade. "Trust me, soldier. By the time you gain an audience, I'll send you your girl's ashes to bury."

Pembrant sagged. A noble might have thundered through her speech. They would have sunk into a horrid tantrum, blustering that she would regret this slight.

Except Pembrant wasn't a noble. He was a soldier, trained to respect the Crown, inundated with the importance of loyalty. He had been told to trust his leaders and serve the royals.

He was a good man, entirely unprepared for what Teia had brought onto his shoulders.

"Please," Pembrant said hoarsely, as tears slid down his cheeks. "Please tell me where she is. Anything you want, anything I have. It's yours."

"Anything?"

"Yes. Anything at all."

"I expect utter discretion."

"I swear on my life. Nobody will know about any of this."

She drew out the moment for as long as she could. "You're a guard at Blackgate?"

He hesitated, clearly confused by the question. "I am," he said haltingly.

"I understand you're posted at one of the gates?"

"One of the side entrances."

"Not the East Gate?"

"No. Gate Thirteen. It's near Block C, by the stables."

So much for Lehm's insistence on the East Gate. Teia brushed away the thought—the rebel leader's ire was the least of her current concerns—and smiled down at Pembrant. "Good," she said. She spoke airily, as if his daughter's life didn't hang in the balance. "This is going to be a very enlightening conversation."

Pembrant listened to Teia outline her needs, one after another. He seemed stunned at first, then perplexed, then dazed. When she'd finished describing all that he had to do, the soldier kept shaking his head in a half-swiveling motion, like one of the broken windup dolls in the Flats' many pawnshops.

Not that Teia blamed him. Her plan did sound somewhat more intimidating against the backdrop of the drowned mansions.

"Princess," Pembrant spluttered. "Please. Your idea—it simply can't be done."

"And why is that?"

"This is *Blackgate*. The prison is designed to be impenetrable."

"Maybe for someone who isn't correctly motivated. But for you?" She brought forth a filmy headband, stitched with a pattern of smiling snowflakes, and tossed it unceremoniously into the dirt. Enna had plucked it from Wynter's nightstand the day before, slipping past the locks on Pembrant's door with ease. "I suspect you won't have that problem."

Pembrant trembled. His lips moved soundlessly as he scooped up the headband, cradling it to his heart. Was he praying? Apologizing? Was he trying to seek solace in what he needed to do?

The tears had dried on his cheeks when he looked up once more. "I do what you ask," he said, "and you promise you'll return her to me?"

"You have my word."

"Then you have mine." Pembrant lifted his right fist and placed it over his chest. Out of the many parts of a guard's oath to the Crown, this was the last step. It was a motion that signified sacrifice—to protect the royal family above all else, to put kingdom over self.

"Two days," Teia said. Her tone was made of iron. "We'll come to you."

He nodded brokenly and turned on his heel. As he vanished into the ruins of Fairweather Banks, Teia felt the barest pang of regret. Was this who she'd become? There was a time when she'd thought she could be fair and just. Now here she was, terrorizing people in the dead of night, transforming into the very creature they expected her to be.

Her mood grew darker as she swung back to face Tobias. He'd been observing her silently throughout the conversation with Pembrant. He hadn't said a word—not yet—but annoyance surged through Teia's blood. She hadn't asked him to come. In fact, the opposite. Who was he to judge her, when she'd warned him to stay away?

"If you have something to say," Teia said, "I'd advise you to hurry up."

"I don't."

"Really? No words of wisdom? Nothing about how cruel this is?"

"No."

"All the staring would imply otherwise."

He merely glanced beyond her, to where Fairweather's cliffs gave way to an empty stretch of ocean. "There's nothing for me to say," Tobias said, "because I would have done the same thing."

The assertion should have comforted her. Instead, she understood then just how damaged they both were. There was no hiding the terrible things they had done, their hands so bloody it would take an eternity to scrub clean. They had plunged head-first into a battlefield, a war zone, for survival or for vengeance—and she doubted they could ever come to terms with what they had become.

◆◆◆

Teia was welcomed at the door of the Imperial Hotel's penthouse by Kyra. The rebel girl was positively livid, her braid whipping behind her as she advanced on Teia. "You kidnapped a *baby*?" she fumed, her voice pitching higher with each syllable. Any more words, and Kyra would have become completely inaudible.

Tobias threw Teia a meaningful glance. He had backed halfway out the door, almost overturning a vase of flowers in the process. "I'll let you handle this one," he said.

"Thanks for the help," Teia muttered, as she revolved toward Kyra and said, "A toddler."

"What?"

"You said I kidnapped a baby. I'm letting you know that that's technically incorrect."

"You're arguing semantics when we have someone's child in the next room?"

Teia stabbed a finger at the wall. Wynter's cheerful gurgles could be heard from here, followed by a spate of affectionate crooning. "Wynter is doing fine—much better than the rest of us, if I'm being honest. She has three gourmet meals a day, all the toys she could play with—not to mention the temporary care of a dedicated Dawnbreaker nanny."

"Lise is great with babies," Alara added from her spot on the couch. When Kyra sent her a glare, the Poisons Master fell silent, scrutinizing her gloves with a renewed enthusiasm.

"This is your master plan?" Kyra said to Teia. "We hold Pembrant's baby hostage until he guides us through Blackgate?"

"Toddler," Teia corrected again. "And yes—that's a decent summary. It's not a bad idea, is it?"

"It's highly unethical."

"The best things in life are."

"This isn't a joke."

"Then maybe you should change your perspective. I thought you wanted to make it out of Blackgate alive."

"I do."

"Well, this is how we do it." Teia fell into the seat beside Alara, swiping for one of the champagne flutes on the table. "Wynter will spend a few nights here, and when we return from Blackgate, I'll take her back to Pembrant's house myself. You're welcome to come along, since you seem convinced I'll drop her off the closest bridge."

"And if we die?"

"Glad to see you've been channeling positive thoughts."

"I am. That doesn't mean I'm not practical."

"If we die—which I'm sincerely hoping we don't—my contact returns Wynter to her parents, and nobody is the wiser."

"Your contact is the thief that brought her here?"

"You don't have to be so skeptical. Thieves can be incredibly honorable."

"Sure," Alara grumbled. "Right before they pinch the clothes off your back."

Teia paid no mind to the Poisons Master. "Any more questions?" she asked Kyra.

"I don't like this."

"Noted," Teia said. "Although that's not a question, and you've already mentioned that."

Kyra made a noise of immense disapproval, one that came from the base of her throat. Teia took a sip of her champagne as the rebel champion stomped into the adjoining suite. The door slammed shut behind her, rattling the remaining glasses.

Alara whistled. "Well done, Teia. I've never seen her this angry before."

"Maybe it's a hidden talent."

"I hope not. I thought she was going to set you on fire."

"I don't think she has it in her."

"She doesn't," Alara said affectionately. She picked up a glass as well, clinking hers to Teia's. "I saw her try to put down a mouse once."

"I assume it went poorly?"

"You assume correctly. You'd think she was being asked to cut off her own leg."

Teia laughed. "Goddess," she marveled. "And the Dawnbreakers sent her to the Golden Palace as an *assassin*?"

The good humor evaporated from Alara's expression. "It wasn't a collective decision," she said. "I advised against it."

"Lehm."

"Yes."

There was enough strain in her voice to pique Teia's interest. She wanted desperately to pry but settled for a more subtle approach. "Have you worked with him for a while now?"

Alara smiled wryly. "Are you testing my moral compass?"

"I'm gauging how well the needle spins."

The Poisons Master's response was to down her drink. When she set the flute aside roughly, she reached for a nearby tray—piled with what looked like every pastry in the Imperial Hotel's kitchen—and yanked apart a cherry tart. "Did you know both my parents died from the Reaper's Kiss?"

Teia bit her lip. "No," she said softly. "I'm sorry."

"They passed overseas, in one of the first waves. They were

traveling merchants to Ismet, and I didn't see them much growing up. Sai was the one who raised me. We had this old book on edible plants, and he'd take me to the forest to gather roots for our meals. In the summer, we'd boil these skinny blue tubers to make dye, and buy canvases from the market to paint on. I always made a mess, but he was an amazing artist."

Alara's sigh was pained. She grabbed for a chocolate pastry, pulling it open before setting it next to the discarded cherry tart. "When they sent back Sai's body, it was the middle of winter. It was freezing—the shovel didn't make a dent. The best I could do was tuck him into bed and light a candle by the door. The next morning, I was on a train to Bhanot."

"You sought Lehm out."

"I begged him for a chance to prove myself. He decided I could earn my stripes in interrogations."

"You accepted."

"I was angry, but I didn't think I could do it. Not at first. Not until I walked into the room and saw one of the Council's spies tied to the table."

Teia set down her glass. She'd been holding on to it for support, gripping it so hard she was afraid it might break. "Alara," she said. "You don't have to come with us to Blackgate. Your brother—"

"Would have been proud. He would have loved being in the action—and he would have thought you were a genius." She lifted her shoulders. "Lehm is a package deal. He tolerates me; I endure him. I don't think he's the best choice for Erisia, but he's better than what we have now."

Somewhere in the distance, the bells of Sunset Tower were ringing. Dawn would come soon enough, with the sky dissolving into the lightest gold. It was Teia's cue to clamber to her feet. Her limbs were stiff from disuse as she retightened her cloak. She had one final place to visit before darkness fell away.

"Keep Wynter out of trouble," she instructed. "I'll try to stop by later."

Alara shifted aside a heap of pillows. "Busy day?"

"Unfortunately."

"Let me guess," Alara said. She touched her forehead with the utmost concentration, similar to the fortune tellers who harassed unsuspecting tourists from booths at Carfaix Market. Just like that, the Poisons Master was as blasé as ever, cheerful and carefree, without a hint of the grief that lay within. "Coronation rehearsal? Dress fittings?"

"Not quite," Teia said, pushing at the door. Then she was out of the room, winding through the patterned halls of the Imperial Hotel, slipping into the shadowed streets quieter than any specter.

CHAPTER SEVENTEEN

The Temple of Past was silent when Teia walked inside.

She hadn't been religious since she was nine. When Calla had fallen ill, coughs racking her body, blood spattering her handkerchief, Teia had gone straight for the palace's temple. She'd collapsed before the pulpit, begging the priest for an audience. The man had listened unenthusiastically to her requests, before providing a tepid recommendation. *Pray to the Goddess. If she deems it, this shall pass.*

Teia had listened. She'd made endless bargains with Armina—promises that she would heed her parents and attend her lectures. She even slipped in a few sentences about being a better sister to Jura, if it meant keeping Calla among the living.

When her mother had died anyway, Teia had stopped praying altogether.

But here she was, voluntarily treading through the stone entryway, drawn toward the temple's center by an invisible string. She passed the vestibule to enter the main chamber, which was decorated with stained glass murals. A statue of the Goddess overlooked Teia, her arms outstretched to the empty pews. Rows of candleholders huddled at the base of the statue, some caked with melted remnants of wax.

Teia knelt beside the boy at the front. Her legs pressed into the red cushion, feeling the coldness of marble beneath.

"I've never done this before," she confessed. Her hands moved deliberately, rolling two candles from the sandalwood box, setting them into holders. Everything felt uncomfortably natural, like she'd waited years to make this precise motion.

Tobias looked over at her. "You're telling me nobody lit a candle for Erisia's monarchs?"

Teia glanced away. "They did. Everyone did. Just not me."

She tugged at the heat dancing around her, illuminating both candles at once before gesturing at Tobias. "May I?"

When he nodded, the two candles before him flamed awake. They danced blue in the darkness, puckering against a draft. She watched the fire lick at the air, the smoke winnowing upward in thin gray wisps.

"I wasn't following you," Teia said at last.

"That's good. I'd like to think I'm a bit more perceptive."

"Don't flatter yourself."

"I'm not. I'm only stating facts."

"I'm not sure you know what that word means."

A smile darted across Tobias's face. "So aside from following me—which you would clearly never do—what exactly are you doing here?"

Acting a fool, Teia thought, as she sat back on her heels. Once Pembrant delivered on what she asked and they retrieved the Star from Blackgate, all pretenses would vanish. The smoke screen would disappear; the veil would lift. She couldn't afford more stolen midnight conversations or casual jokes by the fire. She didn't deserve them, if things went according to plan.

It was stupid to be here. Reckless. And yet Teia remained anyway, keeping her eyes on the flames.

What exactly are you doing here?

"You mentioned you came here before," Teia said. "I thought I would do the same."

"To keep tabs on me?"

"To pay my respects."

She waited for something surly, but nothing came. Tobias's next words were gentle. "Your parents?"

Sadness welled in Teia's chest. "At least they're together now."

She could hear his reluctance when he spoke again, the discomfort that threaded throughout. "There are rumors, Teia—"

She finished the thought for him. "About my father having an affair, which is how Kyra can control fire."

"You don't believe them?"

"Not for a second."

She tried to think of how to describe Calla and Ren together— the looks they'd exchanged. The differences in their smiles when they were reunited. Her father used to stride through the Golden Palace's halls, stories flying, his presence beaming larger than life. He would catch his wife's hand, kissing each of her knuckles until Calla swatted him away. *You're distracting me,* she would say with a laugh, and Ren would grin back.

Isn't that why we fell in love?

There was no fathomable way to summarize their relationship. All Teia could do was cobble together a few sentences and hope it was enough. "He wasn't the same after my mother passed. Her death broke his heart."

The flames stuttered. Teia's memories clung like phantoms, refusing to scatter. Some days Ren would be fine, marching around the palace with his former energy, commissioning projects and meeting with diplomats. Then he would come across some reminder of Calla—an old note, her favorite sweet—and his entire body would grind to a halt. Sorrow would split across his features, any control sliding from his grasp.

The downside of true love was it really could last forever—and the ones left behind always suffered.

She forced her gaze away from the candles. There had to be something else to talk about, some way to ward off the knot in her throat. She said the first thing that came to mind, as she scrutinized the statue of Armina.

"This is my first time here," Teia said.

His brow quirked. "Really? The Minister of Tourism would be scandalized."

"Not a lot of time to sightsee when you're stuck in the palace."

"You seem to do a fair job of sneaking away."

"If I didn't know better, I'd say you sound impressed."

"Must be the echo in here," Tobias said. He, too, had rested on his heels and was now examining her carefully. Something about this made Teia feel strangely vulnerable, peeled apart layer by layer. "You're not what I expected."

"From a Carthan?"

"Yes." His voice wasn't spiteful as much as it was puzzled. He seemed taken aback at his own reflection.

An unwelcome warmth cascaded into Teia. "What *did* you expect?" she said. "Someone who eats babies? Breathes flames?"

"I'm still not entirely convinced otherwise."

"We'll take it day by day. I'll send you my breakfast order as proof."

His laughter was a cadenza, spooled straight from a symphony. Teia drank in the sound. For a ridiculous, reckless moment, she might have told him whatever he wanted, just to hear that laugh once more.

"Let me guess," Tobias said. "Tea cakes?"

He remembered, she thought in astonishment. The miniature cakes were served at every banquet, topped in honey and smothered in sugar. She had mentioned her obsession with the dessert that day by the hearth, although it was a comment meant in passing, a detail to be listened to and then forgotten.

"Not just regular tea cakes," Teia said eagerly. "My mother used to have the kitchen fill them with different ingredients. Red beans, lotus paste. They have something called mooncakes in Shaylan. I think it was the closest she could come to eating one again."

Tobias tipped his head to the side. "What's it like there?"

"The palace kitchens? Hot. Lots of broken dishes."

"Not the kitchens. Shaylan."

She couldn't identify the sensation that washed over her. "I haven't been," she said finally. The sentence felt strange in her mouth, as if signaling a defeat. She hated to think about how an entire country lay out there with a family she'd never known, rife with culture and history.

"Really?"

"It's shocking. I know."

"Sorry. It's just—surprising. I thought you would have visited."

"My mother wanted to. We would talk about it when I was younger, before I went to sleep. She would describe the way the mountains reached straight into the sky. She said there were dragons that lurked in the clouds."

"You could still go," he said, after a pause. "Shaylan isn't that far. All you need to do is cross the Dark Sea."

"You make it seem like a nice stroll through the park."

"But people do it, don't they? Merchants travel when needed. Officials make the occasional trip." His eyes were bright, eager. "It isn't impossible."

It is right now, but not once I'm on the Council.

The thought was so fierce it almost hurt. Hope buoyed inside Teia, painted the deepest shade of red. It took all her might to swallow the words down, as she turned her head to focus back on Tobias. "We'll see," she informed him. "I'm not overly fond of boats."

"I'm the opposite," he said. "Can you imagine what you might see on the water?"

"Schools of fish?"

"The old myths come alive. There are people that think the Serkawr is still beneath the waves."

Teia had no desire to ever test that theory. "Is that supposed to be a selling point?"

"Didn't the Carthans take the Serkawr as their symbol?"

"Just because it's on our crest doesn't mean I want to meet it." She pointed toward Tobias's knife. "Would you want a run-in with the Dormarch?"

"Absolutely not," he answered immediately. When Teia stifled a grin, he frowned. "What?"

"Nothing. It's just hard to picture the Dawnbreakers' star rebel being frightened by a dog."

"The Dormarch is a *hound*. And I wouldn't say I'm afraid— just that I was chased by one when I was eight, and I've never fully recovered."

"A true catastrophe!"

"I'll have you know that it ate my entire birthday cake, before licking away half my face. I've been permanently scarred ever since."

He spoke with a mock seriousness, and Teia found herself speculating about that unfortunate birthday, trying to fill in the rest of the tale. It scared her that she wanted to keep listening, to learn about his childhood and the hound that had bullied him and each story that might come after that.

Yet before she could ply him with questions, a fresh gust of wind whistled through the chamber. The candles fizzled out, one after another. Tobias reached for a match, but Teia stopped him.

"Don't," she said. "Let me."

Heat whirled all around her, nudging against her fingertips. The strands wished to come alive. They pleaded to become something more, and so she obliged. She warped the threads with a single push, and sent them careening though the space.

The entire temple blazed awake, brightened by the shine of a hundred candles. Some were little more than stubs. Others were partially ground away, the wicks weeping into the holder. Even so, each flame pulsed steadily, eager to prove its worth. The walls were bathed in gold, the statue of Armina doused in light.

Tobias rose beside her. She saw him take in the sight, saw the wonder written on his face. "It's lovely," he said, in a way that made her think he was saying something else.

"It is," she said back.

Teia wasn't sure when they left the Temple of Past—only that they stood there for the longest time, the Halfling Princess and the rebel boy, until the very last candle had burned down to nothing.

CHAPTER EIGHTEEN

Jura Carthan never missed a chance to throw a good party.

The public courts hadn't started as a joyous affair. Rather, they had originally been dreamed up by Eris the First as a way to connect Erisia's most prominent families. Eris would gather the nobility together once a month for routine status updates. Nobles would report on the condition of their lands, the auspiciousness of their crops. Generals would proclaim their most recent military conquests.

It was as dry as it sounded, but the nobility clung to the public courts. *Tradition*, they said haughtily, like that one word could explain away any detractors.

The upside was that the public courts had evolved throughout the years—or devolved, depending on who was surveyed. There was still the ritualistic pomp and endless hours of updates, but the free flow of alcohol made things marginally tolerable. Courtesans tipped back imported spirits. Lecherous husbands hovered close by, ogling any serving girls that walked past. The throne room's center aisle had been cleared for presenters, with nobles mingling on either side.

Teia stood near the back, waiting impatiently for Jura to

arrive. She wasn't required to be here, but she made a point to attend every public court. There was a surprising amount to learn from the updates given—which noble was being praised, which courtier had fallen out of favor. That, and the plum wine was always delicious.

As she took a practiced sip, swirling the liquid within her glass, her eyes drifted toward the ceiling. A magnificent chandelier hung overhead, constructed from a thousand crystals and surrounded by elaborate frescoes. Each panel detailed a chapter of Erisia's history. To the left, the Serkawr awoke from its slumber. On the farthest end of the room, above the throne, Ren laid his signature on the Shaylani Peace Treaty.

It was only a matter of time before Jura was up there too. He would be forever memorialized in paint, made unforgettable by some gifted artist. The thought made Teia somewhat ill, and she tore her gaze away, refusing to dwell on the notion.

She'd finished her second drink when a commotion came from her right. Someone shoved through the crowds, brusque and impatient. A minute later, Minister Abbott had materialized by her side. He stank of foul-smelling spirits, flushed and starry-eyed from his previous glasses of whiskey.

"Abbott?" Teia said, taking a step back.

"My future wife," he crooned. He lunged at her, angling for her neckline. She felt his hand clamp on her breast before she managed to react, her arm slicing forward.

The minister howled in pain. He jerked back, clutching at his wrist. His fingers had begun swelling from the burns, patches of skin peeling back at the ends.

"Touch me again," Teia snarled, "and you won't have any fingers left."

He ran his tongue over his lips. "I'm about to be your husband, Halfling," he panted. "I wouldn't get so feisty—in less than two weeks, I'll own you."

She snapped heat into his hand again, just to hear his shriek. Heads turned and courtiers whispered, but nobody came to her aid. They all knew of Jura's amended wedding announcement, which had been printed on flyers and pasted throughout Bhanot. Abbott might be a sorry excuse for a man, but he was telling the truth: she was his future wife, and he, by unspoken law, could lay his claim to her.

It was a blessing when the trumpets blared out, marking Jura's entrance. The court broke into applause, and guests parted to let the crown prince pass. As Jura strutted down the aisle, Teia pressed a hand to her chest. She was composed on the outside—all frozen smiles and blank looks—but her heart still raced from what Abbott had done. He had fled from the room to lick his wounds, but that helplessness he'd brought on, that piercing sense of shame, would not soon be forgotten.

I'll handle him later, Teia vowed, as the trumpets blasted again. For now, she needed to hone her rage. There was no room for error, what with their trip to Blackgate planned for the following night.

If she took the Star—if she earned the Dawnbreakers' trust and entered their base—Teia would be free of Abbott for good.

At the front of the throne room, Jura cleared his throat. He looked out at the crowd, his golden curls slicked down. "The Crown," he pronounced, "invites General Samos Miran forward."

The more boisterous courtiers fell quiet, setting aside their glasses. There wasn't a single person in attendance who wasn't familiar with Miran's heroics, from his innovative strategies during the Shaylani War to his ongoing fight against the rebels.

The general had come to the public courts with his twin daughters tonight, tucked protectively on either side of him. The one on the left hugged a stuffed bear, while her sister clutched a book. Miran patted them both tenderly on the shoulders as he moved them aside to sink before Jura.

"Highness."

"Rise, General. I look forward to hearing your updates."

The medals on Miran's jacket gleamed with a dull luster. He was in full uniform today, a scarlet sash across his chest, his remaining eye glittering with satisfaction. "I have news on the rebels."

The crowd broke into excited hisses. Jura tilted forward in his chair. "Oh?"

"My men received word on a recruitment camp in Elden. We raided the site and arrested a handful of Dawnbreakers. They await processing at Blackgate."

"How many?"

"Six."

"So few?"

"The pills, Highness."

Miran didn't have to say more. The suicide tablets the rebels carried were a persistent, frustrating blow for the Council. Teia had listened to Jura vent about the tablets time and time again, complaining ferociously about a waste of perfectly good information.

The Golden Prince's rings twinkled under the chandelier. "And what of the rebel base?" he said softly.

"Nothing yet. My men will pursue any leads once the interrogations are complete."

Teia exhaled in relief. Jura, however, was still contemplating Miran. "One last question, General."

Miran nodded.

"Why did the rebels set up in Elden?"

"We believe one of the Dawnbreakers was a blacksmith there."

"A civilian?"

"Yes, Highness. Other than that, there is no immediate connection."

"Interesting," Jura said. The barest smile pulled at his lips as he dipped his hand into his pocket, lifting a single playing card into the air. The spiral design glinted red beneath the chandelier's light, before Jura closed his fist. When he reopened his palm, only a handful of ash remained, which scattered black to the base of the throne.

"Miran," the crown prince said. "I'd like you to make an example out of Elden."

The silence that followed wasn't just deafening. It shrieked across the entire length of the throne room, blistering through Teia's body. She could imagine the full extent of the massacre—bodies strewn like dolls, houses looted and mangled. It would be destruction for the sake of sending a message, violence sanctioned by the Crown and carried out by the military.

But maybe public opinion didn't matter anymore. Maybe Jura didn't care about the cost, as long as the prize was worth the carnage. In the end, the crown would fit regardless.

"General?" Jura said.

No response.

"Miran. I gave you a direct command, didn't I?"

Miran had gone the color of chalk. This was a man who had dedicated his life to the Crown, who had built his entire identity around it. He had served under Ren; he had served under Ren's father. Teia hadn't ever seen him disregard an order, despite the many questionable acts that Jura had asked for.

Except never anything against innocent civilians. Never against children.

Even men like General Miran had their breaking point.

Miran bent his head. "Highness," he said.

It wasn't defiance, but it was close enough. Teia could read every trace of coldness across Jura's features. He rose to his feet swiftly, his robes pooling around him. As he descended the steps, coming to a stop before Miran, he radiated nothing short of absolute power.

Deliberately, his movements unhurried, the Golden Prince flicked a long look to the corner of the throne room. Miran's twins watched from their seats, their hands laced together. As Miran followed Jura's gaze, the muscle in his jaw tightened.

"Miran," Jura said. "I won't ask a third time."

A bead of sweat wormed down the general's temple. Perhaps he thought this was merely a brief bout of insanity. The crown prince would move past this whim, and all would be forgotten.

But this wasn't insanity. Not exactly. This was Jura being the truest version of himself—the boy who'd dissected cats for fun and set birds on fire to hear them scream. He had been no different then than he was now; the only change was that Jura no longer needed to hide his impulses.

He was, after all, about to be king.

Miran lifted his hand. He placed his right fist to his heart as he nodded slowly. What else could he do? Jura had laid his intentions bare—the safety of Miran's twins had been called into question, caught in the web of courtroom politics. The general might have his morals, but he was a father first. There was no other choice.

Jura flashed a broad grin. "I'm glad we came to this agreement."

And that was that. Jura pivoted away, dismissing Miran with one movement. The other nobles fell into scattered murmurs as the general returned to his chair. He settled firmly between his daughters, an arm stretched over each of their shoulders.

Teia remained behind the crowds. Her vision spun before her. Her lungs heaved with a terrible emptiness, like someone had taken an axe to her chest.

She wasn't sure why—shouldn't she, of all people, have anticipated Jura's decision to raze Elden? Wasn't this the next logical step? Jura had already declared war on the Dawnbreakers with the bounties, the imprisonments. What was a decimated town and a few hundred casualties, should it send the intended message?

Yet the despair Teia felt almost took her off her feet. Was this all Erisia had to look forward to? Jura would burn down the kingdom to get what he wanted. He would slaughter his own people— their people—and the court would nod along the entire way.

That was when a whispering voice slunk into Teia's mind.

It was the same voice that had been steering an uncanny number of decisions as of late. Infiltrating the Dawnbreakers. The position on the Council. If Teia listened closely, she wondered who the voice sounded like. Her mother? Herself?

For the first time since eavesdropping on the War Room conversation, Teia didn't think about her own freedom. She didn't think about her marriage contract or betraying the rebels or even her life beyond that, championing a cause Calla would have been proud of.

A dryness filled her mouth. The room compressed into a great twist of color, as the circlet on Jura's head gleamed invitingly. It was embellished with rubies, hypnotically beautiful beneath the lights. It called her name, teased her forward, presented a challenge for her to accept.

Teia thought, *Why Jura?*

She thought, *Why should he rule?*

And she thought, *Why not me instead?*

CHAPTER NINETEEN

*T*here *are easier ways to lose my head.*

For the next day, this was the mantra that looped through Teia's mind. It played in an infernal cadence. It ricocheted through the crevices of her skull as an image of the crown hovered behind her eyes, sparkling innocently under an unseen light.

There are easier ways to lose my head. There are easier ways to lose my head . . .

It was an especially distressing consideration, since Teia was rather fond of having her head attached to the rest of her.

Of course, this new, intrusive thought was accompanied by all the usual worries. Yes, she'd daydreamed about the throne. Yes, she'd fantasized about her own coronation, imagining the weight of the crown and the rustle of the crimson mantle. Who in the Carthan family hadn't? But Teia's problems were beyond any normal royal's. Unless Armina was prepared to offer her a direct blessing, neither the commonfolk nor the court would be willing to accept her. She'd no sooner lay her claim than be dragged off by the military, thrown into the catacombs beneath the palace.

Still, the possibility of the throne haunted her. She thought about it incessantly, when she ate her meals and sat through

coronation rehearsals and listened to the daily Council briefing from the passageways. Miran had embarked on the military
campaign to Elden, and so his second-in-command—a beefy,
balding fellow named Kashan—took the general's seat, bobbing
his head to the rhythm of Jura's speeches.

When Teia finally left for Fairweather Banks, it was almost a
relief to escape the palace. None of her musings would matter if
she was killed within the next several hours, which remained a
distinct possibility.

Teia wasn't keen on dying, but she was able to spot a silver
lining. At the very least, it would offer her some peace and quiet.

The sight of Tobias, standing in the doorway of one of
Fairweather's dilapidated mansions, sent a shiver up Teia's
spine. He was already dressed in one of the guard uniforms
that Pembrant had procured. Kyra had outdone herself with the
tailoring—the uniform clung to Tobias as if made for him. With
the iron mask over his face and the Carthan crest on his chest, he
was the spitting image of a Blackgate guard.

"Kyra and Alara?" Teia asked. She accepted the parcel that
he passed to her and took another uniform out of the wrapping.

"They'll meet us there."

"They're not having second thoughts, are they?"

"I'd be worried if they weren't. This plan is still a death trap."

"Glad you're as upbeat as ever." She frowned when she saw
him pause. "What?"

"Lehm isn't pleased," he said reluctantly.

"This is about the East Gate?" Teia said, before adding, "I
can't manifest a guard's post into existence."

"I know that. I'm just saying he isn't pleased."

"We don't need scouts or safeguards. We'll be fine."

"Can I get that in writing?"

"Spoken like a true cynic."

Teia undid her cloak and let it flutter gently to her feet. As she started slipping off her tunic, she was rewarded by a strangled sound from Tobias. "You're changing here?" he said.

"Do you see a dressing room anywhere?"

Tobias rotated away, his cheeks burning pink. Teia felt a thrum of satisfaction as she stepped into the scratchy fabric, yanking it past her waist and fastening the buttons securely.

"How do I look?" she asked.

Tobias considered her seriously. "Short," he said, and she flipped him a quick, efficient gesture.

When Teia pulled on the iron mask, the world dispersed into pieces, gridded by the metal that crisscrossed her face. She adjusted it carefully, attempting to orient herself. The mask wasn't foolproof—anyone who was close enough could make out her features—but it was better than nothing.

They stashed her discarded clothes under a pile of rubble before beginning the trek to Blackgate Prison. The air was tantalizingly cold, and a thousand stars dotted the sky. Everything seemed brighter, more vivid. Even Fairweather's rotting estates had regained some of their old charm, standing straighter beneath the starlight.

"Are you afraid?" Tobias asked suddenly. His gaze was fixed on some distant point, to where Blackgate's towers would soon creep into sight.

"Yes," Teia said truthfully, the word reverberating into the night. Then a beat later, "Aren't you?"

"It's hard to tell. I haven't felt much of anything in a long time."

Her brow creased. "So what happens if someone hits you?"

"What kind of question is that?"

"One you haven't answered yet."

He kicked at a stray clump of dirt. "I'd hit them back," he said, after a moment's deliberation.

"Naturally," she agreed. "But wouldn't you be angry? Upset?"

"I'd be thinking of ways to do the most damage possible." He motioned to his knife, which was strapped to his leg. "Uppercut to the chin. Feint under the arm. One slash to the stomach, one to the side. Final blow delivered against the neck."

It was far too detailed to have been thought of on a whim. "You must be excellent at parties," Teia said.

Tobias cracked a smile. "Not many chances for that, when you're alone in the Flats."

That got her attention. "The Flats?"

"I lived there after I first got to Bhanot."

"Once you joined the Dawnbreakers?"

He shook his head. "I was in the city for a year before I tracked Lehm down. I convinced some of the sellswords to give me lessons while I searched for him."

"You ran with the sellswords?" Teia said, trying and failing to hide her admiration. The mercenaries were infamous for their ridiculous rates, which none but the absurdly rich or the unthinkably stupid would pay. They were said to be skilled enough to cut apart a butterfly in midair, although Enna swore that was an exaggeration.

Tobias shrugged noncommittally. "They taught me how to fight, and I worked for a roof over my head. I hadn't had any luck finding Lehm, so I figured I would let him come to me."

"It worked," Teia said. "You became the Dawnbreakers' star recruit."

"Yes."

She glanced over at him. "You don't seem too happy about it."

"There's nothing to be unhappy about."

"Other than being devoid of any normal human emotion?"

"I'm not."

"If I placed a basket of kittens in your path, what would you do?"

"Walk around it."

"Goddess," Teia said. "Maybe you *are* beyond help."

He nudged at her arm, and she clutched at it dramatically. "What about you?" Tobias said slyly.

"What *about* me?"

"You'd help a basket of kittens?"

Teia thought that one over. "It depends on my mood," she disclosed. "I've never liked cats."

A laugh shook his shoulders. "Teia," he said, before hesitating, her name resting between them. He stopped walking, and she did too. They turned to face each other, their breaths drifting before them in translucent puffs. Above, the moon hung high in an arc of silver.

It shouldn't have mattered what he'd say next, with death hovering over them and Blackgate in view. But for some unknown reason, Teia wanted nothing more than for Tobias to finish his sentence. They were so close that she could see through the grids of his mask, the dark blue of his eyes shining out at her.

What, Tobias? she wanted to ask. *What is it?*

They were questions that belonged to another girl, one with the luxury of time and the proper courage to use it. Teia had neither as she forced her legs forward, swinging herself away from Tobias. "We should go," she said, staving off the puzzling feeling of disappointment. "We don't want to keep the others waiting."

◆◆◆

The Carmine District might be quiet this time of night, but Blackgate was a hub of activity. Wagons carted in new prisoners. Lanterns flared from the weathered black walls. Guards stood firm at their assigned posts, although some broke their stances to frighten away the rats that twitched in the shadows.

Their chosen meeting point was in one of the narrow alleys by Block C, marked by a set of broken clotheslines that fluttered in the breeze. Kyra and Alara were already there. The Poisons Master raised her hand at Tobias and Teia, but Kyra kept her eyes on a stray piece of litter drifting limply by the gutter.

"How's Wynter?" Teia said bracingly.

Kyra didn't meet her gaze. "She ate an entire bowl of caviar for dinner."

"*And* a pheasant leg," Alara provided. "*And* a box of K'vali chocolates."

"Expensive tastes," Teia muttered. "The four-course meal that the Imperial provides wasn't enough for her?"

She was rewarded with a faint smile from Kyra. It was hardly anything, but Teia's heart lifted all the same. Maybe the rebel girl was wary of carrying grudges into the next life. "It's on the Crown's tab, isn't it?"

"That it is," Teia affirmed. "I hope you ordered one for yourself too."

"Two of everything," Kyra said. "Alara insisted."

The Poisons Master, in the meantime, was tugging murderously at the collar of her shirt. "This uniform is awful," she griped. "You'd think Blackgate could spring for more breathable fabric."

"I'm sure that's a top priority," Tobias said.

"It should be," Alara shot back, pulling a face as she curved around to examine the back of her uniform. "I'd start a revolution over these elbow patches. They're burlap, Tobias. *Burlap*. Do you know how impractical that is?"

Teia shushed them both and peeked out at the gate opposite the alleyway. Gate Thirteen was identical to all the other entrances, shaped from heavy black iron to seal off one of the alcoves. Two guards stood before the gate, their weapons at the ready, their masks glinting under the lantern light.

"This is the right one?" Kyra asked.

"This is it," Teia confirmed.

"Let's hope we live to see it again," Tobias said.

"We're the craziest bastards to ever grace Erisia," Alara mumbled.

They glanced again at the guards, who hadn't moved a muscle. Teia sucked in a breath, each bone in her body protesting what she had to do next. "Ready?" she said.

"If I said no," Kyra said nervously, "would that change anything?"

It wouldn't, although Teia understood the sentiment. She inhaled once more, savoring the night air, and walked out toward the gate. When she strolled from the alley onto the street, the guard on the left tensed. His hand went to his rifle, ready to strike at a moment's notice. "Identity checks are at the North Gate," he barked.

It was the last thing he said before his features crumpled into a look of shock. One palm went to his neck, cupping the blue-feathered dart that had pricked into his vein.

The man toppled to the side, and the second guard sprang forward. Pembrant stowed the pouch of darts into his pocket. He caught the sleeping man carefully around the waist, while Teia took his legs. Together, they dragged him into the alleyway, dumping him out of direct view of the street.

"He's going to wake up, right?" Kyra whispered.

"Give it four days," Alara assured her. "He should come around by then."

This statement did nothing for Pembrant's nerves. The guard's eyes were panicked. His breaths came out in shuddering fits as they stole their way back to Gate Thirteen. "We have to be quick," he said, fishing a key from his breast pocket and fitting it into the padlock. "We have forty minutes before the next shift starts."

The gate creaked open ominously. Blackgate's courtyard stretched before them, with the top of the central command tower poking above the massive prison walls. There were no guards outside at this hour, but the grass was worn along well-traveled paths. Weapon racks lined the perimeter, stacked with polished bayonets and fresh rifles.

Pembrant led them to a simple iron door, inlaid against the gray cinder-block building. He pushed it open hastily and stepped into the darkness.

Teia's feet propelled her over the threshold, plunging her through the entrance to Blackgate Prison.

CHAPTER TWENTY

The smell hit her first.

It was the musk of a thousand unwashed bodies, crammed into far too little space. A hint of sewage lingered beneath, mixed with the stench of something that had long rotted away. Teia stumbled, her pace faltering, bile rising in her throat.

Then came the sounds. Voices were everywhere, flooding out from the cells. Prisoners begged for water, for sunlight, for grace. They pleaded for their mothers, their fathers, their wives, the moans condensing into a cacophony of noise as arms clawed out from the metal bars.

"Goddess," Kyra croaked, and Pembrant shook his head wearily. "The pay is good. I'll say that much."

The gray walkway was wide enough for all five of them. A few guards milled about on patrol, but nobody spared a second glance for the impostors. Teia's group was halfway down the corridor when a set of spindly guards teetered by. They wore three green stripes on their left sleeves and carried a man's body between them. The one on the right strained under its weight, flinching as the corpse's arm flopped about listlessly.

"Greenies," Pembrant explained, when Teia cast a look his way. "They're responsible for cleanup."

"And the key?" she asked, eyeing the bronze key that hung at one of the greenie's belts.

"A master key. The head greenies each have one. It unlocks every cell in the block."

A pity that it couldn't magic them all to safety, with the Star in hand and their memories wiped. Around her, the prisoners' cries seemed to magnify. They spiraled toward the ceiling in a wordless wail. The stench intensified, thick enough to taste, so strong that Teia's eyes watered.

When the walkway had emptied out and the greenies receded from sight, Alara quickened her stride to match Pembrant's. She was pale but determined, as if seeing the body had spurred her into action. "These prisoners," she said. "What are their crimes?"

"In this block? Murderers. Rapists."

"No Dawnbreakers?"

Pembrant barked a laugh. "That's what you are, then? Dawnbreakers?" He rounded on Teia. "Do you sleep well at night?"

"Like a baby."

"You're betraying your own country."

"And you're awfully conversational for someone who should be guiding, not talking."

A second door lay at the end of the hall, with a half circle seared into the wood. A staircase extended beyond it. The steps were hewn from craggy rock, each reaching up to Teia's calves.

Pembrant held tight to the burnished handrail. He started to climb, bracing himself against the railing, and the others fell in sync after him. Bit by bit, the sounds of the first corridor dwindled behind them. Teia exhaled a sigh, savoring the silence that washed over her.

It was a feeling that was extraordinarily short-lived.

"You wanted Dawnbreakers?" Pembrant said roughly. "This is where they're kept."

On the second floor, the walls were no longer gray but a piercing white. The ceilings had been replaced with marble, as unblemished as fresh snow. There wasn't a trace of dirt or grime to be found, and the floors glistened with a recent coat of polish.

Up ahead, a row of doors hung open. *Cell doors*, Teia realized as they moved down the hall. Alara stiffened beside her, angling away from the doors, but Teia drew closer. She was driven by some macabre urge, a desire to peer into one of the empty rooms.

She was met with a tidy space, similar to the inside of a healer's office. A metal cart rested in the corner. A drain had been fitted to the white tiled floor.

But it was impossible to overlook the iron slab that was bolted in the center of the room. It rose on sturdy legs, fitted with metal cuffs at all four corners. Thin scratches lashed across the slab's surface. They were interspersed with gouges, some carving several inches deep.

Every horror story Teia had ever heard thundered to life. There were the Dawnbreakers who had been set alight, their blackened corpses displayed from the towers of Blackgate as a gruesome warning. There were the dissections and the whippings, the vivisections that Jura came to personally oversee.

And, of course, there were the interrogations, which caused indescribable pain before the relief of death. As Teia stared at the slab, she knew immediately that this was what took place here. People had died on this slab. People had been strapped to the sheet of metal, not five feet away, and tortured for secrets, their blood running onto the floor and down the drain.

Someone touched her shoulder. Tobias stood behind her, his eyes on the slab. "This entire prison's a tragedy," he said tonelessly.

Teia didn't reply. Instead, she told herself that this was fine. They were right on schedule, and things were going astoundingly well. The white rooms, all of which were uncannily pristine, were rock bottom. She could keep going. She could survive this.

Then they reached the end of the open doors, and Kyra released a scream.

By some stroke of luck, nobody came to check on the noise. The final white room was closed, the door firmly sealed. A rectangular window had been cut from tempered glass, and a guard was visible inside.

He must have noticed he had company. The guard clomped to the door, pulling it open with obvious annoyance. He hefted a bloodied pair of shears, swiping greasy tufts of hair back from his mask. "Yes?" he said, with the impatience of someone eager to return to work.

Any excuse Teia had prepared stuck in her throat. There, beyond the guard, were two more figures, almost hidden from view. A man was fastened to the table, whimpering faintly through bloodied stumps of teeth. In the corner, a woman had collapsed in a heap. She wasn't tied down, as she clutched at her knees to rock back and forth senselessly. A tangled mess of curls hung before her eyes. The same garbled word was being repeated over and over, meshing into a river of noise.

"Mercy. Mercy mercy mercy mercy mercy."

Alara reeled back. She pressed against the opposite wall, as far from the prisoners as she could manage. Kyra went to steady her, and the guard inside the room edged back, his voice tightening in suspicion. "Who's your squadron leader?"

Anything else he might have said was cut short. Tobias's blade sliced forward, embedding into the side of his chest. The guard gasped. He looked down at the wound, the blood spilling from his uniform, before losing his balance, pitching unceremoniously onto the floor of the white room.

They could have left him to bleed out. The guard was wheezing for breath. He tried to drag himself away from them, clawing for handholds in the floor, but Teia stepped inside the room, cutting off his path.

He looked up at her, blood trickling down the bottom of his mask. "Please," he rasped. "Help me."

She closed the door behind her gently. She felt the threads of heat sing out around her.

"Burn," Teia said.

The man came ablaze in a tongue of flames. His shrieks were like an animal's as he tore at the iron mask and twisted on the ground. His uniform melted into his back. Blisters popped against his blackened skin.

It took less than a minute before Teia opened the door again, leaving the smoking corpse of the guard behind. Pembrant fell aside, all but shrinking away in fear. "Princess," he quavered, his mouth flapping open. "You . . . he . . ."

She shoved by him, shouldering past the soldier without a second thought. Alara was still hunched by the wall. Tobias stood over her, but it was Kyra that Teia looked toward. She knew at once that the rebel girl had seen everything, witnessing the scene behind a sparkling piece of glass.

She hadn't promised to spare the guards—not exactly. But she was aware of what the rebel girl would say about that. *Semantics.*

"Kyra—" Teia said, but the rebel champion shook her head.

"It's all right," she choked out. It might have been a lie, but it was one Teia would accept. Besides, none of them were truly all right as long as they were in Blackgate. "Alara—"

"I'm fine," the Poisons Master gasped. She was massaging

furiously at her chest, but she managed to straighten, clasping the pouches sewn into her belt. "Teia, the prisoners. We have to help them. We have to get them out."

Teia desperately wanted to avoid this conversation. The white room was seared into her memory now. The man on the slab, the woman in the corner—both had watched the guard burn without a sound. Whatever they'd endured had broken not just their bodies but their minds, and in another life, Teia hoped she would have abandoned her mission. She hoped she would have helped.

But there was no possibility for that here, with time slipping away like grains of sand. Killing the guard was one thing, but detouring to assist two prisoners would bankrupt their schedule. Teia felt each minute tick down. The seconds melted by, one after another, and she clenched her teeth hard, biting down on the inside of her cheek.

The Star, she thought. *The Star.*

"Alara—" she began.

That was as far as she got before the bells started to chime.

Chapter Twenty-One

Bells thundered all around them, breaking into blasts of four. The sound was excruciating, loud enough to deafen Teia. She resisted the urge to clap her hands over her ears as she pushed off the wall, veering away from the Dawnbreakers.

"Pembrant?" she shouted.

His eyes spun in their sockets. "It wasn't me! I swear. It might be a drill. Or . . ."

The soldier's voice died. Teia lurched forward. She seized him by the front of his uniform and forced his gaze back to hers. "Or what?" she demanded.

"There might be something in the white room. A hidden alarm that was tripped."

She hadn't seen the dead guard call for reinforcements, but anything was possible in this wasteland of a prison. Teia swore, releasing her hold on Pembrant. The noise had grown more furious, ricocheting into an uproar. "What do the bells mean?"

"Four bells," he garbled. "This is a Red Alert—a potential intruder alarm. Every cell will be checked. Central command will distribute teams of guards to each floor."

"And the gates?"

"The locks have all been triggered, but they can be manually opened with the key."

"Your key will work on any of them?"

"Yes."

It was the smallest of mercies. "How long do we have?" Teia said.

"Five minutes?" he said feebly. "Maybe less."

Five minutes was nothing. It was a slow walk down a long hallway, the line to pay for a merchant's wares at the market. But she hadn't come this far for nothing, and she would be damned if she scampered back to the palace empty-handed.

"The Vault," Teia said. "How far away is it?"

"Close."

"Good. Let's go—we're against the clock now."

A hand closed around her wrist. Teia spun to see Alara, her feet rooted to the floor. "I'm not leaving," she said, her voice thick with conviction.

"We need to get to the Vault."

"What about them?" Alara gestured to the open room.

"Alara," Teia said witheringly. "Did you happen to miss the alarm? The one that's going to send every guard in Blackgate our way?"

"We can be fast."

"You can't help them if you're dead."

Alara didn't move. "You go, then. I'll get them out myself."

Teia was ready to scream. "What about after? Do you have a poison that will magically teleport everyone to safety?"

"How would we have gotten out before?"

"Through the stables. The door is by the staircase, marked with a horseshoe."

"Then that's what I'll do."

"You're going to drag two people by yourself?"

"She won't be by herself." Kyra had appeared beside them. "I'll stay with her."

Where did the line between heroics and insanity blur? This was the worst potential outcome, a decision that would doom them all. Teia would lose manpower to fight the guards in the Vault, and Alara and Kyra were going to get themselves killed, all for a pair of unknown rebels. Teia was at a loss. She was prepared to bind them both in chains and haul them with her, when Pembrant spoke up.

"We need to go," he said, casting a petrified look at the door. "Reinforcements will be here soon."

Their five minutes were grinding down to nothing. Teia threw up her hands in exasperation. "Tobias?"

He didn't hesitate. "I'm with you."

Gratitude flooded through her, but she didn't have time to dwell on the feeling. *Fine, then,* Teia thought as she turned to Pembrant. "The key."

He removed the silver key from his pocket, and she palmed it to Kyra. "There are two gates by the stables. The one on the right is a checkpoint; the one on the left, a regular entrance. Use the one on the left—you'll cause less of a scene. Take out the guards, get through the gate, and wait for us there. We'll need you to let us out."

Kyra tucked the key into her fist. "We're doing the right thing," she said.

"I know," Teia replied, although it didn't make her feel any better.

There was no time for goodbyes. Teia allowed Pembrant to guide her and Tobias forward. They took a sharp right into another corridor, and Kyra and Alara disappeared, lost within the prison.

"They'll be fine."

Teia glanced over at Tobias. "Will they?" she said.

"Alara knows what she's doing, and Kyra is decent in a fight."

"Let's hope it doesn't come to that."

They both knew it very well might.

Another turn later, the walls had started sloping inward, white fading to gray. They were nearing the upper point of the pentagon, and a flood of worries erupted inside Teia's head. What if the white flame failed to open the safe? What if there were additional guards? Tobias had lost so much because of the Carthans. Was he about to forfeit his life too?

The door that emerged to their right was plain and unassuming. Pembrant reached out. He twisted the handle expertly to reveal a slender hallway, so narrow that the three of them would barely fit side by side.

"Through here," the soldier said.

Tobias went first, with Pembrant close behind. Teia was at the rear, her mind still on the Vault. She had just approached the threshold when the door banged shut in her face, closing with a sudden force.

Panic exploded inside Teia. She lunged for the handle, her fingers wrapping around brass. The metal was cold and smooth, and she yanked on it with all her might.

The door gave way, groaning as it did.

Lanterns dangled from iron hooks. The hallway was dim, but Teia could see all she needed to. There was Pembrant standing behind Tobias, one arm caught around his chest.

And there was the barrel of his gun, pressed snugly beneath Tobias's chin.

CHAPTER TWENTY-TWO

"Pembrant!" Teia snarled. "What are you *doing*?"

"Step inside," he said flatly, "and shut the door behind you."

He had a hollow, deadened expression that sent a chill down her spine. Quickly, in rapid succession, Teia's brain fired off her choices, none of which were particularly good. She could send a wave of flames toward Pembrant, but burn Tobias in the process. She could drown Pembrant where he stood, but he might pull the trigger as a reflex.

Gingerly, she raised her hands in the air. She moved into the corridor carefully, evaluating the scene, trying to find some advantage. Tobias's mask had been torn off. A bruise was forming near his temple. His knife was still strapped to his leg, but it was out of his immediate reach. By the time he grasped the hilt, a bullet would be in his skull.

"Pembrant," Teia said. She wasn't gifted in small talk, but she was more than willing to stall for time. "You're making a mistake. Remember your daughter—remember Wynter."

Pembrant's voice quivered. "How dare you," he said venomously. "After everything you've done?"

Had he gone mad? Teia thought she must have misunderstood the soldier—perhaps this was simply a hallucination, brought on by the terrors of Blackgate. Yet when she blinked hard, her vision swimming, her eyes watering, he was still there, the revolver jammed to Tobias's chin.

"Pembrant," she tried again. "What are you—"

Tears leaked down his face. His hand quaked so hard she was afraid he'd accidentally fire the gun. "I thought I could trust you. You gave me your word."

Around them, the bells chimed on. There were no guards pounding at the door, but it had to be only a matter of time if they were doing a sweep. How long did Teia have to talk the soldier off this cliff? A minute? Less?

"Pembrant," she said firmly. "Tell me what's wrong."

"Lies," he mumbled. "All you do is lie."

"What do you mean?"

"I trusted you!" he roared. His eyes glistened behind the mask, and Teia saw then that Pembrant couldn't be reasoned with. He'd gone insane, trapped in whatever delusion had overtaken him. He would shoot Tobias out of sheer spite and turn the gun on her next.

Teia called to the heat around her. She snapped it into the handle of the revolver, and the metal flared a dazzling red. Pembrant bellowed in agony. He dropped the gun to clutch at his ruined hand. His fingers were covered in blisters the size of grapes.

Tobias dove to the side. He kicked the gun out of reach as Pembrant lashed out with his sword. The blow went wide, nearly embedding itself into the opposite wall, and Pembrant coiled back, readying himself for a second swing. He'd just loosened his arm when Tobias ducked beneath the blow, slipping his knife upward.

The first cut ripped through Pembrant's sternum, the second

his stomach. The soldier dropped to his knees. He grabbed frantically at the shredded mess of his torso. Blood pooled over his uniform as he wheezed for breath, his insides leaking onto the floor.

As the soldier became still, everything else fell away. Teia should have been indifferent. Happy, even. This was the way of traitors. A knife in the gut was too good for Pembrant, especially after what he'd done.

Yet the mantra did nothing to ward off the regret, which came to rest within Teia's chest. Wynter. The little girl was safe and warm in the Imperial Hotel, happily scooping caviar out of a crystal bowl. She had no idea how her life had changed, that her father was now a corpse in the halls of Blackgate Prison.

Tobias stood motionless over Pembrant's body. When Teia came closer, he sent her a bewildered look. "What *happened*?"

She wrung her hands helplessly. "Maybe he snapped?"

"From what?"

There were any number of possibilities. But as Teia recalled Pembrant's expression when she'd exited the white room, ash flaking off her skin, smoke wafting from her clothes, she thought she had an answer. "He saw me kill the guard in the white room."

"You think that was it?" Tobias said dubiously. "Pembrant was a soldier. He spent time on the front."

"They might have been acquaintances. Friends."

"Hell of a place to make friends," Tobias grunted. He seemed prepared to say more, when a rattling echoed from behind the door. Teia paused. She was hoping it was an overzealous rat, but the commotion came again, louder than before. Unless the prison's rodents had evolved to turn handles, the sound was a warning of what was to come.

Tobias put a finger to his lips. The clattering intensified while they retreated deeper into the corridor, taking care to keep their footsteps silent. As Teia and Tobias rounded the corner, she made a fervent wish that there would be another door. An exit.

The hallway was a dead end.

There was murder written across Tobias's face. "Please tell me this is part of your plan," he hissed.

"About that," Teia said back.

Then came the crack of a door thrust against a wall. Two dozen boot steps thundered over stone, advancing on Teia and Tobias in perfect unison. In a matter of seconds, they were surrounded by a horde of Blackgate guards. The soldiers came in rows of three, squeezing beside each other in the tight space. Teia and Tobias were corralled toward the far wall, positioned within a misshapen semicircle.

"As expected," the man in front gloated. "The intruders." He wore the black uniform of a commander, with the winding figure of the Serkawr stitched up his left sleeve. Teia prayed it was too dark for him to make out her features, that a combination of distance and bloodlust would dull the man's immediate senses.

Tobias lifted his hands. "This is a mistake," he said. "We're—"

"The reason a Red Alert has been implemented around Blackgate," the commander interrupted. "Impostors, who decided to impersonate prison guards but didn't bother with the regulation weapons." He motioned his revolver toward Tobias's waist. "No broadsword, no gun. Any other excuses you want to feed me?"

The knife dangled loosely from Tobias's fingers. "Well," he said, "I don't suppose you want to talk this out?"

The commander lowered his head. He cocked his gun

leisurely, aimed it at Teia's thigh, and gestured to his men. "Nonlethal force," he barked. "The crown prince will want them questioned."

How generous of Jura, Teia thought, just as the commander squeezed the trigger.

The bullet missed, but only because of Tobias. He thrust her back in a single movement, his blade extended to deflect the bullet. She listened to its *ping!* as it clanged to the floor, and she stared at him in open astonishment.

"You can do that?" Teia said, as chaos erupted around them.

Most of the guards fell on Tobias in a frenzy. They were easily twice his size, built with bulging muscles and towering forms. It was too crowded to risk more gunfire with the crush of bodies, so they swung a variety of weapons instead: massive swords with wicked blades, spiked metal balls on iron chains.

He swept them aside effortlessly, blade flashing against the light. Teia had never seen someone fight the way Tobias did, parrying blows with a fluid precision. There was no warning of his next move—just the scream of a guard or a short wail of pain. A body would thud to the ground and Tobias would dart away, his knife cresting in another arc.

She couldn't afford to watch any longer. It was wonderful that Tobias was making progress, but Teia had no such talent in swordplay. She was quite literally backed against a wall, debating what to do as three guards sneered down at her.

The one to the left grinned through chapped lips. "I'll be damned," he said. "Looks like the Dawnbreakers recruited a girl."

"Not just any girl," another put in. "A Shaylani."

"I didn't know the Dawnbreakers were recruiting across the sea now."

"I didn't either. But I've always wanted to tumble one of them water witches."

The third chuckled. "Maybe we should have some fun first."

"With a rebel?"

"I'm sure the crown prince won't mind."

The words had hardly left his mouth when Teia struck. She was determined to forgo water—there was no other option if she wanted to impersonate Kyra—so she swiped one hand downward, sending a spurt of heat into each of their uniforms. Knees, shoulders, shoes. Fabric gave way to fire; the flames blossomed a deep orange. The three men howled, their voices cracking in anguish. They ripped at their burning clothes and dropped to the ground, screeching as they did.

She realized her mistake when every head turned toward her. As smoke seeped into the corridor, the commander devolved into a tirade of curses.

"That one," he said. "I don't care what it takes."

Tobias was beside her in a heartbeat, countering a blow that would have hacked off Teia's arm. They fought together now, him with metal, her with fire, tearing through the guards that approached. Everything was blood and noise and death; Teia could feel sweat streaming down her back, soiling her clothes. Her arms ached; her legs wavered. The smoke was so thick she could barely breathe, and she knew Tobias was tiring, too, his movements slower than before.

They were boxed in from all sides, their backs together as guards pressed toward them. These soldiers were more skilled than their predecessors—or had learned more quickly from their mistakes. They fought nimbly, jabbing with their blades before retreating hastily. This was a game of cat and mouse, a wager of numbers. The soldiers were biding their time, taking the gamble that one of them would make contact.

And, eventually, someone did. The guard to the far right had been wilier than the rest. As Tobias blocked a strike to his chest, the guard maneuvered down to ram his second blade forward. The metal slashed into Tobias's calf. He swore, his leg buckling beneath him, and Teia spun around. She saw the guard raise his sword again, flush with triumph as he prepared to claim victory—

Teia didn't stop to think. She acted on impulse, on instinct, her shoulder knocking against Tobias, pushing him away to block the sword with her body.

When the metal speared into Teia's ribs, nothing felt particularly real—not the red on her shirt nor the sounds of the fight. She floated, borne by a spurt of adrenaline that put her heart in her throat.

Then the pain hit.

A circle of fire ripped outward from Teia, searing blue and white as it blasted through the room. The remaining guards screamed against the heat. Their skin sagged like taffy, bodies convulsing wildly. Some of the men at the fringes sprinted for the door but were trapped in the inferno as it roared in glee.

It was over in an instant. As the shrieks gave way to a crackling quiet, Teia stretched for the strands of heat. She could feel the world slipping away as she pulled, unraveling the flames clumsily. When she turned to look at Tobias, she had the sudden, stupid thought that she could create entire oceans from the blue of his eyes.

"You need to go," she gasped, as her vision dimmed to nothing. When she hit the ground, her body colliding against stone, Teia was overcome with a muted sense of acceptance. In some strange way, this was how things were supposed to be.

Violent beginnings, violent ends—yet another legacy of the Carthan family.

But in the next moment, a hand closed around her wrist. Tobias's voice was clearer than it should have been, underlaid by a furious determination. "Get up, Teia," he growled as he hauled her to her feet. Through a blurred haze, she saw his blade still extended before him, dripping scarlet with blood.

They hobbled past the sea of bodies, maneuvering by blackened limbs twisted in agony. As Tobias steadied her with one arm, thrusting open the door with the other, she had the dreadful sense that they might both die in here.

"You should leave," she whispered. "I'll slow us down."

He responded by sheathing his knife. He threw a single glance down the hallway, devoid of any guards, before he stooped to pick her up gently, folding her to his chest. She felt the beat of his heart through his uniform. For a second, she swore it was all that was keeping her sane.

"I'm not going anywhere," Tobias said, "so we'll just have to suffer together."

Past the gray tunnels, the doors slicing into shadows, the halls blurring into one. She didn't know where they were or how far they had gone. The bells screamed louder than before, accompanied by the patter of boots. Guards yelled orders; prisoners pleaded in their cells. Tobias cursed under his breath, each word ground out between his teeth, and a burst of light illuminated around them.

"Tobias?"

"A flash bomb. Everything's fine, Teia. We're almost there."

"How far?"

"Close. Trust me."

She shouldn't, but she did anyway. All of a sudden, she was

breathing in clean air, so different from the stink of Blackgate. He was running now, cradling her tight, insisting she stay awake, demanding she talk to him.

"About what?" she managed.

"Anything. Tell me about how you terrorize the palace ministers. Tell me what you'll do when we win."

"Penance."

"For what?"

There were too many grievances, a list of sins that would take a lifetime to review. Teia closed her eyes, her thoughts drifting on a cloud—and the last thing she heard was a female voice, bordering on the edge of hysteria, screaming that someone was still inside.

CHAPTER TWENTY-THREE

Teia waded through a fog of faces. Fragments of her parents lingered, each memory cropping up around her. Ren spinning a flame. Calla kissing her good night. Those were the ghosts of better days—the phantoms of what could have been, the ones she wanted so desperately to follow.

"Teia?"

The voice seized her around the waist. It lugged her back toward the pain, as an ache pierced through her ribs. The images that rushed in were faster, unrelenting. A healer pulled a cloth over Calla's face. Ren slumped sideways on his throne. Jura bestowed her with a pearly grin, cradled protectively into their father's shoulder.

It's nothing. Just a game I like to play.

There was a white, blinding pulse. She was no longer in the Golden Palace, but on the shores of the Dark Sea. The water here was far from kind—it hungered to sink ships; it longed to submerge her beneath the waves. She could glimpse a creature in the distance, its red scales shining against the water, beautiful and majestic. The Serkawr had frightened Teia all her life, ever since she'd first seen it on the Carthan crest. But as she stood in the shallows, rain pattering onto her face, cold seeping into her skin, she felt an inexplicable connection to the sea beast. A keening stirred in her blood, a call to some otherworldly force, a yearning for control, for power.

A tremor started in her side, splitting her apart at the seams. Everyone wanted a piece of her, wanted her gone or dead or exiled, wanted her secrets, wanted the Morning Star. The pain expanded, cutting a trail through her chest, battering her skull.

"Teia," the voice said, more insistent this time. "Goddess, Teia. *Wake up.*"

When she opened her eyes, all she saw was gray.

She thought she was dead at first, but reconsidered almost immediately. Death shouldn't be this uncomfortable. Every inch of her ached, as if wrung out by a giant washerwoman.

"I'm alive?" Teia grated.

"Not too loud—I'm afraid you might jinx it."

Kyra sat beside the bed, wedged uncomfortably into a rickety wooden chair. A chipped mug was clasped in her palms, and a furrow seemed permanently entrenched between her brows. In the next instant, though, she had flung the cup aside, shooting to her feet to throw both arms around Teia. And Teia had enough time to register an enormous sense of relief, the weight of the world lifting away, before she was hugging Kyra back, a sob catching in her throat.

They were all right. They had made it.

"Where are we?" Teia creaked, when Kyra finally released her. The room was small, with furniture in various states of abandonment. Boards had been nailed over the windows, which were framed by threadbare curtains. Water damage dotted the ceiling, and paint peeled in chunks from the walls.

"One of our safe houses," Kyra answered. She walked to a sagging dresser to take out a flagon, busying herself with pouring a lavender liquid into a tin cup. "You were lucky. When Tobias carried you out of Blackgate, I thought you were dead."

"Tobias," Teia said quietly. Her last moments in the prison were wreathed in uncertainty—and yet she remembered the beat of Tobias's heart, the sharp burn of his voice. Despite the throbbing in her side and the tightness in her chest, something about the memory stirred a warmth inside her, like the glow of an ember against a hearth's blackened ashes. "How is he?"

"He's . . ." Kyra trailed off before setting the flagon down. "He's coping."

"Which means?"

"Tobias was—er—a bit *distraught* when he brought you here. After the healers told him to leave, he put his fist through the wall."

"He punched a *wall*?"

"He punched two," Kyra informed her, placing the cup in Teia's hands before she could ask any more questions. "Here. Drink. Our healers said nothing vital was hit, but you've only been out a few hours. If we want to leave for the palace by daybreak, you need to rest."

Teia thought about setting the cup aside, but Kyra had a steely look in her eye, identical to the kind her nursemaids used to get before they unleashed one of their lectures. She accepted the cup and took an obedient sip. The mixture tasted sickly sweet going down, similar to candy that had melted away in the afternoon heat.

"Kyra," she said heavily. There was something more she needed to ask, something she was dreading. "We didn't get the Star, did we?"

To her credit, Kyra didn't try to spare her feelings. "No."

"What did Lehm say?"

Kyra's lips thinned. "He wasn't happy," she answered, dropping into her seat. The rebel girl also held a cup, although hers was filled with a tawny, golden liquid. "Not with everything that happened."

"Things could have gone better," Teia acknowledged. "But we can try again, find a different way to reach the Star. Lehm knows that Jura wants the Star at his coronation. We ambush the escort unit, hire someone from the Flats—"

"Teia." Kyra paused. She closed her eyes and took a shuddering breath. Tears clung to her lashes, glistening like jewels. "Teia," she said again, her voice splintering. "Alara's gone."

"Gone?"

"Yes."

Disbelief split through Teia. This was some kind of catastrophic misunderstanding. The Poisons Master would barge in at any moment now, with her silver tongue and relentless teasing. She'd prop her feet on the rickety table and opine about her newest tincture or powder. She'd bring along a bottle for celebration, before flirting so ruthlessly with Kyra that the rebel champion would flush the same color as the wine.

There was no possible way that Alara—brilliant, radiant Alara—was *gone*.

Teia could see why Kyra had been nursing a drink. She wanted one, too, as she sank back into her pillows. "What *happened*?"

The rebel girl wiped at her eyes. "We were trying to free the two Dawnbreakers. We'd almost gotten to the end of the hall when the first patrol arrived."

"And then?" Teia said.

Kyra looked away. "And then nothing. We gave the prisoners our suicide tablets—and when the patrols turned the corner, Alara said she'd be right behind me. She told me she'd hold them off because she was the better fighter. I tried to argue, but she told me to trust her. That, after I requested to switch instructors, she was the one who trained me."

The glass had begun smoldering against her palms. Kyra set it down with a loud thud. "They'll torture her, Teia. You saw what happened back there, how they treated the other Dawnbreakers. What do you think they'll do to the rebellion's Poisons Master?"

Nothing good, Teia thought, envisioning the sterile white rooms of Block C. Grief expanded inside her, as cold and dark as the halls of Blackgate. She had done this. Her plan had brought them no closer to the Star. Any shot at a better future was blown to hell, with this string of events now set in motion. Alara was gone, locked away in a cell, chained to an iron slab.

But as Teia stared at the cracks on the ceiling, wishing the sleeping draught would take effect, wishing the floor would open beneath her, the barest shred of hope sprang to life. Alara had smuggled in her poisons; she'd have fought with them, using the pouches hidden within the borrowed uniform, color coded by substance. Kyra was right—the guards would know her identity and notify Jura about her capture.

The Golden Prince might be a murderer, but he was cunning. Smart. The Poisons Master was worth something. She was a bargaining chip, a hard-earned victory against the Dawnbreakers. There was no payoff in her immediate execution when Jura could flaunt his new trophy.

He would keep her alive, at least for now. He would strategize what to do next, and then he would make his announcement to all of Erisia.

As long as Alara lived, so too did hope.

◆◆◆

When Teia and Kyra exited the Dawnbreaker safe house, they were deposited onto the lawn of one of the Royal District's manors. From the outside, the safe house was nothing more than a gardening shed, with an inscription of a rising sun carved against wood. As dawn broke over Bhanot, swathing the grounds in gold, the carving became all but invisible, washed out against the dark slats.

The walk to the palace wasn't far, but Teia was hobbling by the time she and Kyra reached the back entrance. They hid in a crop of trees in sight of the palace, waiting until the guard on duty wandered off to relieve himself in a flower patch. *Useless,* Teia thought, as she and Kyra slipped through the open gate. The rebels could sneak an entire battering ram inside, and she doubted the guard would notice.

They took a shortcut through the neatly trimmed hedges, snaking past the stables toward the kitchens. They'd stepped onto the dirt path when voices floated their way, accompanied by the thump of equipment thrown roughly in a pile. A horse nickered indignantly, stamping its hooves against the floor.

"Soldiers?" Kyra breathed, and Teia shrugged. Miran was known for his infamous sunrise drills, which started before dawn and continued well into the afternoon. On occasion, Teia would hear the soldiers during early trips through the palace tunnels. They would grumble bitterly about the host of exercises, with some bemoaning how they couldn't lift their arms the following day.

Today, there were no quibbling complaints. A grim mood lingered by the stables, penetrating through the hedges. There was the scratch of a leather scabbard being undone, before a reedy voice ventured, "What a night, eh?"

"I'll say," another soldier said. "My da owns a pig farm, and

I've never seen slaughter like that. You couldn't tell it used to be a village."

"We'd vacation there in the warm months," someone else murmured. "My ma would take us to the lakes. It's what Elden is known for, you know."

"Was."

"What?"

An embittered laugh. "Well, it's not anything anymore, is it?"

Elden? Kyra mouthed, but Teia just shook her head wordlessly. Any exhaustion had seeped from her body. She was more awake than ever, the pain in her side dwindling to a whisper. In the pandemonium that had taken place at Blackgate, she had somehow forgotten about Jura's decree on Elden.

If there was anything more to relay, the soldiers weren't forthcoming. They seemed to have depleted any further avenues of conversation, as they set to work sweeping the floors and replacing the tack. After a while, the stable door squeaked. The soldiers trekked out, one after another, some yawning into their shirts as they filed back to the barracks.

Teia parted ways with Kyra inside the palace. She staved off the rebel girl's many questions, pleading ignorance as best she could until another servant recognized Kyra and dragged her back toward the kitchens. It was only after the rebel girl vanished that Teia started for her mother's old sitting room. When she ducked through the door and stepped into the passageways, Calla's portrait seemed to follow her every move.

Teia took this as a positive sign. Out of anyone, her mother would have understood what she was about to do.

Most officials kept their individual offices on the southern side of the palace. It was far enough from the residential wing to avoid a disturbance, but close enough to the sprawling wine cellar for a quick libation. A minister once described it as *the best of both worlds*, before he'd promptly thrown up over the contract he was signing.

After Teia passed the space behind the War Room, she took the central fork, veering into a mustier section of the tunnels. Everything was damper here, water dripping from the ceiling, mildew thickening the air.

By the time Teia arrived at her intended spot, she was panting from exertion. Whatever numbing poultice the healer had given her had worn off. Her side throbbed horribly, sweat trickling down her back. She held down a wince as she knelt into the dirt, her palms fumbling against an inch of gray dust.

On the other side of the passageway wall, General Miran paced in his study, fresh off his military campaign to Elden.

Teia was here on a hunch, on nothing more than a gamble about Miran's inner dilemma. His hesitation during the public courts, his sheer uncertainty. Had it not been for his girls, would Miran's ethics have won out? Would he have refused the order to march on Elden?

His defiance before Jura had meant something—Teia just wasn't sure what yet.

Whatever the case, Miran was in no hurry. The pacing continued, steady and persistent, his boot steps rounding out the stiff edges of the room. Teia's calves had cramped by the end of the first hour. She sat by the second. She was in the midst of regretting her decision, wondering if her intuition had been wrong, when a gruff noise ricocheted into the passageways.

Teia didn't trust her own ears. She scanned the wall, hunting feverishly for a fissure. When she discovered one with a respectable view into the study, she jammed her right eye against the crack, flattening herself against stone.

Miran had fallen into his seat. He'd swept his files to the ground, where the papers covered the rug like fallen flakes of snow.

He cradled his head in his hands—and he sobbed like his heart would break.

CHAPTER TWENTY-FOUR

Time had come to a standstill.

It had been two days since Alara's capture—two days where Teia learned how the minutes could limp onward, dragging second by second. She spent a disproportionate amount of time bribing nobles from the court, trading jewels from her personal clutch for information. There had to be something she'd overlooked, a secret to uncover that might save the Poisons Master.

To make matters worse, the voice in Teia's head had returned, this thread of her subconscious that refused to die. *This is just the beginning*, it insisted. *What do you think Jura will do to the others once you give him the base? What happens to Kyra? To Tobias?*

Shut up, Teia thought back. She had enough problems at the moment without adding another to the fray. And just when Teia suspected she might implode, her feelings in disarray, her nerves shot through, the knock came on the cusp of the third day, as dawn filtered over the horizon.

She was still half awake, dazed from lack of sleep, her feet freezing against the slick tile. She'd barely opened the door when Kyra came rushing in, clutching a cluttered breakfast tray. "We have to go," she said. "Lehm has news."

Normally, this would have been a net negative. Today, though, Teia was willing to set aside her qualms about the rebel leader. They left under the guise of an early morning trip to Carfaix Market, bringing along an empty woven basket for good measure. As they ventured into the Flats, revelers were making their way home. Several had passed out on the side of the street, their skin blue from cold. One Dvořákian had his hand wrapped protectively around the thin neck of a bottle, his pale hair spread around him as he shivered in his sleep.

The safe house—the one where Teia had first met the Dawnbreakers—was as sparsely furnished as she remembered. She'd never cared before, but now she wished there was more to see, a distraction while they waited for Lehm. Anything had to be better than the silence that lingered here, a reminder of the Poisons Master's absence.

Kyra must have been thinking the same thing. As the rebel girl surveyed the empty room, her chin trembled. A packing crate caught fire, the hay stuffed inside igniting with a *pop!*

"Goddess," Kyra swore. She swatted at the flames. When they refused to extinguish, she hissed in frustration, balling her fists as she stalked toward the crate. "Jura has her," she said fiercely, and the words seemed to burst from somewhere deep inside, guided forth by an invisible hand. "He has her and he knows it and he wants us to hurt."

"It's what Jura does," Teia deadpanned. "He invented sadism."

"If this is what he's like now . . ." Kyra trailed off in a frustrated growl. "I would take anyone else on the throne, Teia. A general. A minister. The tailor next to Carfaix Market who upcharges for his shoddy services."

It might have been an overstatement, but Teia's muscles tensed. A familiar vision cracked open in her head, as it had every hour since spying on Samos Miran. Taking the crown. Ruling Erisia. Leading her country into something new, something better.

What was a seat on the Council, when Teia could become something more? She could leave behind the shroud of Jura's shadow. She could work alongside the Dawnbreakers, not betray them.

I can shield them, Teia thought. *Pardon them.*

Because there was opportunity now—a path to the throne that hadn't existed before, which glinted in the far distance. Unbelievably, inconceivably, the rules of the game had changed. The court and the military had always supported Jura. It was their unspoken gift to him, a symbol of trust in Ren's son. Yet ever since the strike on Elden, the many rooms of the palace were alive with whispers. People hissed that the Blessed Heir had taken things too far. Soldiers mumbled of mutiny, and Miran wandered the halls like a ghost.

For a split second, Teia almost spoke her dream aloud. The image of the crown was so vivid that a ferocious longing sliced through her chest. She felt the sentences hovering on the tip of her tongue. They were lovely, dangerous things that she longed to share with someone else—a forbidden language she yearned to speak.

In the end, she didn't. How could she? Kyra Medoh was many things, but she was a Dawnbreaker through and through. She was the hero from a fairy story, a champion plucked from obscurity to spark inspiration in the rebels. She had her own dreams of a republic, a government where leaders weren't born but chosen. She would never support a Carthan on the throne, not with all the damage Jura had caused.

Not even if that Carthan was Teia.

The door creaked behind them. Cornelius Lehm entered the room, with Tobias at his heels. Kyra jolted forward, her face haggard, but Teia stayed where she was, watching Tobias watch her. It was the first time she'd seen him since Blackgate, and she found herself searching him for injuries, taking inventory of the scrape on his cheek, the bandage around his arm.

I'm not going anywhere—so we'll just have to suffer together.

Lehm clapped his hands sharply, shattering Teia's thoughts. "Briefing room," he said. "Now."

This door was farther down the winnowing hallway, away from the spaciousness of the main chamber. Teia followed Kyra and Tobias as they funneled into the cramped room. A simple wooden table stood in the center, flanked by a half dozen chairs. Several atlases sat on a wobbly shelf.

Lehm cast a disdainful look at Teia. "You want the Halfling here?" he asked Kyra.

The rebel girl was resolute. "If this is about Alara, Teia might be able to help."

"I sincerely doubt that," Lehm said crisply. He withdrew a single sheet of paper from the folds of his coat and laid it down on the table. The ink was blurred from a rushed print job, but it did nothing to blunt the page's message.

"Jura Carthan," Lehm said, "has offered us a deal."

Tobias picked up the sheet. Disgust lined his face as he said, "He wants to trade Alara for Kyra?"

"So it seems."

"This can't be real."

"There are copies posted throughout Bhanot. Messengers are taking them out of the city as we speak."

"Has he lost his mind?" Tobias seethed. "What makes him think we would ever agree to a deal?"

"He's confident," Lehm said.

"He's insane."

"If you ask me," Kyra interjected softly, her eyes on the table, "I think we should consider making the exchange."

Tobias dropped the paper. "Please tell me you're kidding," he said.

"If we get Alara in return—"

"But this is *Jura*," Teia said. She wanted to grab Kyra by the shoulders and shake some sense into the rebel girl. Hadn't she learned anything from the Autumn Ball? "If you make the exchange, he's going to double-cross you. He'll shoot Alara in the back and ship you off to Blackgate."

"Do you happen to have any better ideas?"

"He doesn't have a clear picture of what you look like. We send in a decoy—a fake."

"And risk someone else's life?" Kyra said. "Not a chance."

Teia sighed. She should have known better than to offer the suggestion. "Something else then. We can find another way—one that doesn't involve making you a martyr."

The rebel girl pointed to the deadline on the poster. "In one week?"

"Anything is possible."

"Unless you can stage a divine intervention, I'd say we're out of good options."

Lehm rapped his knuckles against the table, cutting their argument short. An uneasy quiet fell over the room as he craned his neck toward Kyra. "Child," he said, in a voice slick as oil. "This isn't something to take lightly. You've become a symbol of the Dawnbreakers. When people hear your name, they're reminded that a Carthan doesn't need to lead this country."

Teia, who was very much a Carthan, folded her arms tightly.

"And what about the people we care for?" Kyra said. "What if they become collateral damage?"

"You aren't the only one who cares about Alara," Tobias said stonily. "But taking this deal is absurd."

She glared at him. "Funny you'd say that now."

"What's that supposed to mean?"

"You weren't this calm when you were carrying Teia out of Blackgate, were you?"

Tobias stood, his eyes blazing, but Lehm made a harsh sound. "Enough!" he thundered, before resting his head above clasped hands. When he spoke again, his tone was at an absolute neutral. "Kyra. You're certain you want to make the exchange?"

"Lehm!" Tobias exploded, but Lehm ignored him.

"Well?" the rebel leader prompted.

"If it means bringing Alara back," Kyra said stubbornly, "I'll do whatever it takes."

Teia hated how Lehm inspected Kyra, with a material disinterest that a banker used for his coins. And similar to a merchant finishing a deal, Lehm nodded curtly before sliding the page back in his pocket. "I'll send word. One week from now at Fairweather Banks, as the crown prince requested."

Teia gritted her teeth. "This is a mistake," she said.

He rounded on her with a tight-lipped smile, one that pushed the very limits of condescension. "Tell me, Halfling," he said. "How many men should we anticipate at the exchange?"

If Lehm's intention was to throw her off guard, he'd gotten his wish. "What?"

"You heard me. You, out of any of us, would know the crown prince best." He adjusted his pendants. "Family ties, and all that."

Anger hummed inside Teia, daring her to hit back, but she refused to allow Lehm the satisfaction. In a way, the rebel leader was right. She *did* know Jura best, which was how she was certain this would be an utter catastrophe. "He'll bring an army."

"How many?"

"Fifty, sixty men. You should expect high-ranking military officials, trained to react if anything goes wrong."

"Good. Then that's what we'll do as well."

Tobias's expression was bleak. "We can hardly match the Crown in resources."

"We have enough to put on a show of force," Lehm said. He selected an atlas from the shelf, laying it on the surface of the table. A map of Fairweather Banks spread across the wrinkled pages, with the dilapidated ruins displayed in all their former glory.

Lehm pointed to the gated entrance, which had long been reduced to scrap metal. "Jura Carthan has no option but to enter from here. His party will stop short of coming inside—too many places for snipers to take cover—which means the swap will occur along the central path. We position sharpshooters here, hidden in the trees"—he made an X to the right of Fairweather—"and here, where the road leads back into town."

"And?" Tobias said.

Lehm offered the same biting smile. "And when the exchange is complete," he said, "we open fire."

"With Kyra on the other side?"

"She'll be perfectly fine. Our very own Halfling Princess will be there to keep her safe."

"Me?" Teia said incredulously. "I won't have a sanctioned reason to be at the exchange."

"I trust you can find one. I'm sure your brother will understand."

Half brother, Teia thought, although the distinction would be lost on Lehm. Instead, she spread her hands in a halfhearted attempt at reconciliation. "Lehm—I can't control the path of a speeding bullet."

"I have every confidence you'll think of something." Lehm's gaze was unfaltering. "You want to be a Dawnbreaker, don't you?"

"Lehm," Kyra said. Worry had crept into her tone, as what the rebel leader was saying settled into the room. "If Teia defends me, she'll reveal her cover. People will know she's working with us."

"I suppose subtlety will be key."

"And what about the other Dawnbreakers?"

"What about them?"

Kyra hesitated. "If you open fire on the military, they'll shoot back. Anyone that accompanies us will be caught in the crossfire."

Lehm's shrug was almost imperceptible. "An acceptable loss, if we accomplish what we set out to do."

"Which is what, exactly?" Teia said. She was unconvinced that she hadn't hallucinated this entire conversation. Maybe she would wake up snug in bed, to find all this had just been a faraway nightmare. "Jura will be planning something similar— Alara is too important for him to let go."

"And too important to allow him to keep."

"He'll expect a trap."

"We'll move fast."

"He'll scout the area."

"Our sharpshooters will be well hidden."

"You won't have a clean shot on him."

"We receive Alara, you protect Kyra. If we take out enough military in the process, we might be able to reach him."

This couldn't be a plan. And if it was, it had more flaws than the average Erisian courtier. What Lehm had proposed was a mishmash of irrationality. Where was the exceptional strategist who had outfoxed the Crown for the better part of a year? Had all those coordinated attacks been the work of someone else? Had Lehm simply gotten lucky?

Yet the rebel leader seemed thoroughly unconcerned with unsolicited feedback. As he showed where his forces would be stationed, depicting them with makeshift wooden tokens, the pendants around his throat shifted. The golden chain lifted slightly, and the charm hidden beneath Lehm's tunic swung free from his collar, dangling into open air.

It wasn't a traditional charm. A ring had been threaded on the glinting chain. The Serkawr rested atop a diamond band, sculpted from soft gold, its fangs bared in a growl. Its claws were curved protectively around a glimmering ruby, which was the size of a fingernail.

The sight sent panic stampeding through Teia.

In the background, Lehm droned on, harping on the details of his glorious plan. While he did, he roped the pendant between his fingers, replacing it under his shirt. It was a casual movement, a discreet one, easily irrelevant for anyone who might have been looking.

Except Teia recognized the ring. There wasn't another piece like it in all the Five Kingdoms. There never would be again, after the jeweler had been shot to death in a mysterious mugging. Before he'd died, however, the man had visited the Golden Palace countless times. He had taken meticulous measurements and expressed his utmost excitement, buzzing enthusiastically about what an incredible honor this was.

Few jewelers were ever commissioned by the crown prince.

How is this possible? Teia thought. She combed through her memories, trying to recall when she'd last seen Jura with the Serkawr ring. He hadn't worn it in the library, nor at the public courts. The most recent time she could remember was the night of the Autumn Ball, when a servant boy had spilled wine on Minister Abbott. After Jura had struck Kyra, he'd walked back to his throne while wiping the ruby clean, the jewel almost black under the chandelier.

Had Lehm blackmailed Jura for the ring? Had he wanted it stolen as a trophy, just like the Morning Star? *Yes,* Teia thought numbly, as she forced her eyes back to the map of Fairweather. *Of course. That must be it.*

While she'd been lost in thought, Tobias had been listening to Lehm's plan with a deepening frown. "This will be a bloodbath," he said, tracking the movements of the wooden tokens. "We aren't prepared for a direct confrontation."

"A victory," Lehm asserted, "if carried out properly."

"Tobias is right." Kyra sounded beseeching, like she could somehow dampen Lehm's enthusiasm. "I can carry out the exchange, Lehm. I don't need anyone's protection. The sacrifice that we'll make here—"

"Will be worth it," Lehm finished. "Child. Don't you trust me?"

Kyra flung a frantic glance at Teia, as if pleading with her to provide some kind of input. Teia said nothing. She didn't need to. Even if she had, it wouldn't have made a lick of difference. Lehm had the look of someone who'd stared into the void and come away empty, drained of anything that once made him human. What remained was a gaping hollowness, intertwined with an uncanny sense of conviction, the steadfastness of a man wholly set in his ways.

The assurance scared her more than she cared to admit.

There was something fundamentally off-kilter about Cornelius Lehm—secrets that lay beneath the surface, lurking just beyond reach. What he was proposing was a massacre of his own followers, a disaster that would decimate his forces. And as Teia sat stiffly in her chair, trapped beneath the rebel leader's deadened glare, the same question she'd had earlier rose from the depths.

How had Lehm gotten Jura's ring?

"It's a terrible plan," Kyra said.

"I know."

"Terrible may not be a strong enough word."

"I know."

"It's going to get us all killed."

"I *know*," Tobias snapped for the third time. "And I'd prefer not to use the limited time I have left to dwell on my impending death."

He, Teia, and Kyra had chosen one of Fairweather's gutted mansions to debrief in. It was a decent spot—isolated, private— although a smidge too close to where Teia had blackmailed Pembrant. She didn't bring it up, and neither did Tobias. The soldier might be dead and gone, his daughter safely returned to his widow, but it was a subject they'd both avoided. Neither cared to reminisce about traitors.

From her spot on the floor, huddled against the collapsed frame of a marble column, Kyra groaned. "Why is Lehm so set on this?" she said. "Firing on the military makes no sense. *None* of this makes any sense."

"Maybe he has some greater strategy?" Tobias said.

"You don't actually believe that."

"I thought you supported an exchange."

"Because I want to get Alara back," Kyra said. "Except what good is the swap if she's shot in the crossfire?"

"What do you want me to do?" he countered angrily. "Bash Lehm over the head and hope he changes his mind?"

"Is that an option? Because I'm failing to see a better solution."

A better solution.

Kyra's words jostled something within Teia. As her fingers brushed against the stone walls, dislodging a puff of dust, the first inklings of an idea took shape inside her head. She tried to shoo it away, eager to latch on to something more logical, but the idea stirred again, louder than before.

It was a risky plan. Delusional, in fact, to anyone who harbored the slightest drop of sanity.

I don't have to, she thought furiously. For all her sentiments earlier about thrones and pardons, Teia didn't owe the rebels anything. At the end of the day, there was still Lehm's gaff of an exchange—she could gamble her nonexistent luck there. Throw caution to the wind and pray everything worked itself out. Or she could bet on herself, just as she always had. The kingdom. The crown. What did one girl matter, when an entire future awaited her?

But deep inside, Teia knew the truth. Saving Alara was more than Kyra's poor influence or a guilty conscience. It was more than repaying a debt, from when Tobias rescued her in Blackgate.

That damned voice in her head had been right. Teia hadn't been the same since she met the Dawnbreakers, and now something had changed. *She* had changed. She saw it in the way she shared stories with Kyra, when she swapped barbs with Alara and sat quietly beside Tobias. Somehow, against all odds, she'd grown to like the Dawnbreakers. Perhaps she even cared about them, in a way that terrified her.

In her seventeen years of life, Teia had experienced many things. Yet not once had she known the weight of friendship, the sharp joy of belonging.

At the very least, she owed them this much.

"We're going to get our girl," Teia said, interrupting Kyra and Tobias. When they glanced toward her simultaneously, she hoped she looked more authoritative than she felt. "Not on Jura's terms—on ours."

Kyra started. "You have a plan?" she said, and there was such optimism in her voice that Teia winced. She wondered if the rebel champion would feel the same way in a few minutes.

"Yes," Teia answered, with as much confidence as she could muster. "We're going to break Alara out of Blackgate."

CHAPTER TWENTY-FIVE

It was a somber walk back to the Golden Palace.

Teia was grateful for the silence—but when she reached her room and peeled off her cloak, the world had begun contorting at an alarming rate. Her pulse rattled out in unsteady fits. Each revelation was like a riptide, jerking her into unfamiliar waters, yanking her under the murky surface.

The Dawnbreakers. The throne. Jura's ring. And now this impossible promise Teia had made to Kyra and Tobias about attempting another trip to Blackgate. When she closed her eyes, images of the prison beamed through the darkness. She could smell the dampness of Block C, the white walls rising to box her in.

If she stood still any longer, she was going to go mad. Teia strode across the length of the room, her body thrumming with energy. She wedged herself against the windowsill and threw back the latch. Night air streamed in, cold and crisp. It wrapped around her, soothing her nerves. She'd just convinced herself that everything was fine, when a knock came at the door.

Any sense of peace dissipated. Teia's heart leapt, almost prying free from her chest. "Come in," she managed.

A second later, Tobias let himself inside. His shirt was

rumpled, his hair untidy. As he shrugged off his jacket and draped it against the loveseat, he shot her a crooked smile. "You really should lock your door."

What could she possibly say in return? That she was relieved he was alive. That she needed to thank him for not leaving her behind. That, in truth, she'd left her door unlocked every night since Blackgate, caught in some stupid hope that he might visit. It was a foolish practice. A dangerous one. She hadn't kept her door unbarred since she was thirteen, too green to know any better. So what was she doing now?

Teia lifted her chin. "I knew it was you," she said blithely. "Who else would stop by this late?"

"Thieves. Assassins."

"Friends of yours?"

"Naturally."

A pause. Teia adjusted her position, moving to the center of the windowsill. She dangled her legs into open air and motioned to the space beside her. "Do you want to sit down?"

"Is that a trick question?"

"How so?"

"Like I accept the invitation, and you push me to my death."

"Oh, please. If I wanted you dead, you'd know."

"Fair," Tobias conceded, and then he was loping onto the windowsill with a dancer's grace. All at once, she found that he was close—too close, his body radiating an uncanny warmth. He reminded her of summer, of a glimmer of sunshine on an overcast day.

He gazed out at the distance, somewhere past the estates of the Royal District. Blackgate was just a speck, practically invisible against the night. "We're really going back there," Tobias murmured.

"We have to," Teia said. "Alara needs us."

A sigh escaped his lips. "Did you know she was the first person I met after joining the Dawnbreakers? Showed up at my room with a pair of dice and a bottle of whiskey, demanding to be let in."

Teia could imagine Alara, dice flashing in her palm, one hand placed on her generous hips. "You listened to her. I'd say that was your first mistake."

"I had to. She said she'd poison my dinner unless I played a round."

"Did you?"

"We played six," he said promptly, "and she cheated her way through each one."

"She admitted that?"

"Of course not. She told me I had rotten luck and that she'd teach me to place a proper bet the next day." Tobias exhaled, his breath steaming against the bitter chill. "If anyone can survive Blackgate, it's her."

"She'll have updated all the uniforms by the time we return. We'll find her rallying the prisoners and charming the guards."

"Spewing bits of wisdom at anyone who asks."

"And to those who don't."

"It's one of her greatest talents." Tobias sighed again before glancing over at Teia. His eyes were the color of a hurricane, a maelstrom as it tore a harbor apart. "How do you feel?" he said, nodding down at her side.

The wound still throbbed beneath Teia's bandages. "Better," she lied. "You?"

"Fine," he said. His fingers brushed the cut on his cheek absentmindedly, like he'd just realized it was there. "I got lucky."

"We both did."

His gaze hardened. Something glinted behind his eyes, flickering black against the lantern light. "You beat me to it," Tobias said.

"What?"

"The guard from the hallway. The one who hurt you."

She could no longer recall the man's face—just the bite of the sword, the pain that followed. "I killed him," Teia said slowly. Of that she was certain.

But Tobias shook his head. "I wish you hadn't," he told her. And when Teia frowned at him, confused, he set his jaw, looking up at the midnight sky. "I only needed five minutes," Tobias said, "to teach him what suffering truly means."

She smiled faintly. "Five?" Teia said. "I showed him in one."

"And you took a sword for me in the process." Tobias turned then, his expression furious. The wind ruffled at his hair, sending it in every direction. He was close enough that he might have kissed her. "Why?"

Pieces of the prison flashed through Teia's mind, cascading one into another. The guards, the hallway. The drip of her own blood. And always, always, the sound of his voice, demanding she stay with him, telling her to hold on.

She didn't know why. That was the truth, as best as she could tell it. Sometimes, she thought, there was no explanation for the things people did. They hurt one another; they acted on impulse. They fell in love, one foot from the grave, hearts open, eyes clear.

Even now, pain seeping through the bandages, adrenaline racing through her veins, Teia would have saved him again.

She coughed. "Temporary insanity," Teia said. Was it her imagination, or did disappointment dart across Tobias's features?

In the next moment, it was gone. "It came at a good time," he said coolly. "I happen to like my insides where they are."

"You're welcome. I accept gratitude in guilds."

"You're speaking to a rebel, not a merchant."

"Tea cakes, then," Teia amended, and Tobias put a hand to his chest, as if pledging an oath.

"I'll make sure they're stocked in all our safe houses," he promised, "including the one you first barged into."

Teia sniffed. "I was invited," she reminded him, "and you tried to cut my throat."

"But I didn't."

"What unparalleled self-restraint."

"I appreciate the recognition."

She grinned, stretching her arms high above. "And to think you used to hate me," Teia said. She took in the lights of Bhanot, the thin slice of the moon.

He shook his head in response. "I didn't hate you." His voice was low, so quiet she strained to hear. He sounded as if he were confessing to a sin. "I've never hated you."

"Not even at first?"

He pondered the statement. "Well," he said, "maybe a little at first."

She nudged him indignantly and he returned the gesture, his shoulder grazing hers. It was a tiny movement—barely anything at all, to someone bolder. But for an instant, all of Teia's inhibitions faded away. If she had the courage to take Tobias's hand, to thread her fingers through his, what would he do in return?

"Teia," Tobias said suddenly, and she glanced over at him, startled. "When all this is over, what will you do?"

"I'll move to the countryside. Revel in the peace and quiet."

"Peace and quiet?" he repeated lightly. "That's really what you want?"

Teia faltered. She scarcely held back the words as they welled inside her, begging to break loose. *I want you,* she thought about saying. *I want this.*

She shoved the thoughts aside. "It would be a nice change of pace. I'm tired of being stabbed at."

He grinned slyly. "There are some vicious birds out in the wild."

"So?"

"Pointy beaks. Lots of casualties."

She scowled. "I'll go north. The snow will keep them away."

"Do you know a single thing about surviving in the tundra?"

"Start a fire. Seek shelter."

"You're doomed," Tobias declared. "I think you're better off with the birds."

She rolled her eyes at him. "We'll all go," she replied. "We'll need a vacation after we break Alara out of Blackgate."

"If we go to the tundra, she'll complain about the parkas."

"She'll think they're hideous," Teia confirmed, "but we'll have one custom-made for her."

"And what will we do once we get there?"

"Learn to ice fish. Drink our weight in liquor." She arched an eyebrow. "Hunt stray birds with pointy beaks."

"Menace."

"Criminal."

Tobias's laugh rang throughout the room. And when he cast a mischievous glance her way, his face aglow beneath a pattern of constellations, Teia told herself to hold steady. To steel herself against him.

She would not let this drown her.

CHAPTER TWENTY-SIX

"Let me get this straight," Enna said. The thief was perched on a misshapen boulder with undeniable elegance, fluffing out her windswept curls. "You want to stage a rescue mission."

"An extraction."

"A rescue mission," Enna persisted, "from Blackgate Prison."

"An undertaking," Teia suggested. "A detour."

"A suicide pact."

"Come on, Enna. Where's your sense of adventure?"

"Safe in bed," the thief retorted, "along with my will to live."

They had been at this for twenty minutes, and Teia had made no progress. She had met Enna at Mourner's Bay under the watchful eye of the Goddess statue. It was late in the day, the sunset painted in pink and gold, a breeze snapping over the docks. Vendors at Carfaix Market were taking down their wares, while the midday crowds had long since scattered. Gulls soared overhead, diving for a snack as the waves crashed against the shore.

Teia had rehearsed her request. She'd assembled a fortune in guilds. She had brought along a set of massive ruby earrings, which she knew Enna was especially fond of.

Nothing. The thief was a lot of things, but she was certainly no fool.

"*That* Blackgate," Enna stated again. She thrust a finger in the prison's general direction, somewhere beyond Carfaix Market.

"Yes."

"The place that people don't come back from."

"That seems like a stretch."

"Don't play dumb with me. Even the sellswords wouldn't touch this job. I'd be lucky to find a single person to sign on to this, much less a typical crew."

It was the break in conversation that Teia had been waiting for. She made an ambiguous sound, something close to an innocent hum, and Enna immediately sharpened her gaze.

"That's what's interesting," Teia wheedled. "I'm not looking for a bruiser."

Enna went from skeptical to downright incredulous. "If you're asking what I think you are, the answer is no."

"But—"

"Actually, the answer is *hell no*—nothing in Erisia will make me step foot in there."

"You can pick any lock, breeze past any guard. I need you there for this to work." Teia reached into the velvet drawstring to scoop out a handful of guilds. The coins shimmered as they caught the last rays of the sun, the Carthan crest stamped on both sides. "I'll double your usual rate. By the end of the week, you'll have enough guilds to bathe in."

"Contrary to popular belief," Enna said, "that sounds incredibly filthy."

"I thought it was every thief's dream."

"I'm not a common thief."

"Enna—"

"Forget it," Enna said resolutely. She eyed Teia mulishly, crossing her arms to keep any additional negotiations at bay.

"Like I said—strong will to live. All the guilds in the world won't help me if I'm dead."

Luckily for Teia, she had anticipated a similar response. It was why she'd brought something else to bargain with, an offer no proper thief could refuse.

"What if I told you," Teia said cagily, "that this isn't just an extraction?"

"I'd say you're full of shit."

"Am I?" Teia slid a creased page from her bag. She passed it to Enna, who scrutinized it dubiously before unfolding it against her knee.

The thief's eyes widened as she read through the sheet. She sucked in a breath, gripping the corners so hard that the paper began to tear. "Teia," she said weakly. "I must be having a stroke. If I didn't know better, I'd say I'm holding a blueprint of the Vault."

"Which also happens to be inside Blackgate."

"The Vault is *inside* Blackgate?"

"At the northern point of the pentagon."

"Block C."

"That's the one." Teia blinked innocuously. "Still think I'm full of shit?"

"Less and less now," Enna mumbled. There was an unmistakable hunger as she absorbed the writing scrawled into the margins. No doubt she was memorizing everything she could before she needed to relinquish the blueprint. "You do realize what's in the Vault, right?"

Here was the clincher, the point of no return. "Enna van Apt," Teia said grandly. "How would you like the chance to steal the Morning Star?"

It all came down to this—an opportunity of a lifetime, worth more than gold to someone like Enna. This was no nobleman's watch or stray temple relic, no ordinary heist that would be forgotten within the week. If Enna van Apt stole the Morning Star, she would cement her place among the greats. She would become a legend, not only in the Flats, but throughout Erisia. The girl who had achieved the impossible. The greatest thief of this generation.

Enna's groan was full of anguish. She pinched at the bridge of her nose, waging a losing battle against a splitting headache. "In a purely theoretical scenario," she said, "let's assume that I'm interested."

"That's promising."

"What happens to the Star after I steal it?"

"Keep it, sell it. Sew it into your coat and carry it around as a good luck charm. What matters to me is getting into Blackgate. Once we're inside and have Alara out of her cell, you can head to the Vault."

"How much time would I have?"

"My guess? Ten minutes."

"That's a tight timeframe."

"I thought you were the best."

"I *am*. But this is madness. Absolute madness."

"Think of it as a calculated risk."

"Sure," Enna said. "We get caught and I lose my head."

"Or you pocket the Star and there's not a criminal in Erisia who won't know your name."

An excruciating minute crept by before Enna heaved a sigh. It was a theatrical sound, something dredged from the bottom of her soul, but Teia's pulse skyrocketed. She knew what that sigh meant.

Enna stood. She gave her legs a firm stretch, as if already feeling the walls of Blackgate. "I'll probably leave in a body bag," she groused. "But this"—Enna gave the blueprint a good shake—"might just make things worth it."

"Is that a yes?"

"Only because you brought me the greatest prize in the Five Kingdoms."

"I do what I can."

"You've really outdone yourself. A shot at stealing the Serkawr's Blessing?" Enna whistled. "They'll hear about me as far as Shaylan."

The nickname struck an odd chord with Teia. Her brow knit together, remembering her first conversation with Lehm. He'd called the Star the same thing—and while she'd thought it an interesting quirk at the time, it had hardly been relevant to the conversation at hand.

"That's an unusual name for the Star," Teia observed.

Enna laughed. "Blame my da," she said, her tone affectionate. "He grew up in Ystrad. It's one of those seaside villages to the east. Small, superstitious place. Horrible screeching goats that keep you up at night. I visited once when I was young and heard enough about the Star to last a lifetime."

"Ystrad," Teia echoed. The town, too, sounded vaguely familiar, like something transplanted from a dream. Hadn't Kyra told her that was where Lehm hailed from?

Enna bobbed her head. "It's where the Serkawr first appeared, after the Divine Five began their civil war."

"Right," Teia said. "They tore up the land, until the Goddess sent the Serkawr as a warning. The Star was given to the Divine Five after they stopped fighting."

"Depends on interpretation. People usually think Armina was the one who left the Star behind, but Ystrad locals swear it was a gift from the Serkawr. A blessing, if you will."

"It's a point of pride."

"More than that. Locals claim it could raise the sea beast itself."

Teia's laugh was cynical. "And what happens then?" she said. "The Serkawr scrounges up treasures from the deep? It offers free rides across the Dark Sea?"

Enna scrunched one eye closed as she contemplated the question. "I suppose it depends," she said seriously. "Legend says the sea beast is at the will of whoever summons it."

Uncertainty clawed its way up Teia's spine. She was struck by the sudden memory of Calla, dressed in her trademark blue, the wind sweeping at her embroidered hem. Her mother had instructed Teia to hold back the tide, her expression unreadable as she gazed out at the sea.

What had her mother said, long ago on that glittering beach? *The ocean is in our blood.*

"The Serkawr is a myth," Teia said, more breathless than she would have liked. "And even if it wasn't, how is a gem supposed to bring it to life?"

"I'm not sure. I was ten, remember? I was more concerned with dodging those damn goats than listening to old stories."

"Hell of a story."

"You're telling me."

Teia shook her head. "Do you think it's real?" she said. "About how the Morning Star can summon the Serkawr?"

She'd been hoping for a lighthearted answer, a response to shatter her growing unease. Instead, Enna inclined her chin toward the statue of Armina, who kept a peaceful watch from the shallows. "Why tempt fate if you don't have to?"

Teia had no intention of doing so. There wasn't a single shred of her being that wanted to see the Serkawr, and the thought of raising the sea beast from its grave—a hundred feet long, maw dripping with poison—was utterly unappealing.

But there might be someone else who felt differently.

Teia's thoughts jumped to Lehm. The rebel leader had asked for the Star, hadn't he? It had been his singular demand of Teia, her audition to join the Dawnbreakers. He hadn't cared about the risks. He hadn't cared if obtaining the gem meant breaking into Blackgate or sending along his champion. The Morning Star had been a fixation. An obsession.

He hadn't shared his reasons, but Teia had made her assumptions. Clout. Satisfaction. Greed.

Except this was something new, a possibility she hadn't considered. If Lehm had grown up in Ystrad, did he know about the legend? Did he, like his kinsmen, believe the Star might actually summon the Serkawr?

Ridiculous, Teia thought. Lehm might be prone to questionable tactics, but he didn't seem the type to run around the countryside, attempting to raise an ancient sea beast. Not to mention that the Serkawr wasn't *real.* It was a creature of a different era, a piece of the past best left undisturbed.

She faced Enna with renewed conviction. "Maybe the Serkawr used to exist," Teia said, "but it couldn't today."

"And why is that?"

"Because it's impossible," Teia spluttered. It wasn't a remotely good defense, but she needed to say the words aloud, to solidify the statement as fact. She tried not to think about how her voice frayed, worn apart at the edges, a sentence away from unraveling.

Enna smirked. "Spare me, Boss," she said. "You can spin flames from thin air and drown men where they stand—I'd say you're hardly in the position to pass judgment on the impossible."

◆◆◆

When Teia returned to the palace, she made a beeline for the library. She dug out every tome on the legend of Armina and the blessing of the Divine Five. She spread them before her in a semi-circle, a makeshift wall of knowledge, and then she began to read.

They all told the same tale. Armina, descending from the heavens. The Divine Five, receiving their abilities. Fierce in-fighting, which ended when the Serkawr scared the Five into an uncomfortable peace. There was little mention of the Morning Star, aside from what was commonly known. It had been left be-hind by the Goddess. It was the most valuable jewel in the Five Kingdoms, irrevocably tied to each of the founders.

Teia read until her eyes were dry and the words started roil-ing into an indecipherable mess. She had found nothing out of the ordinary, which was the best flavor of reassurance. It was as she'd expected. The Ystrad locals were nothing more than a wildly superstitious bunch, who treasured their heritage and doted on their goats more than their own children.

She exited the library to venture into the main hall. The pal-ace was quiet at this hour, aside from the occasional guard left on patrol. Unwittingly, Teia wondered where Tobias was tonight—if he was stationed in another wing, or had already been dismissed to the barracks. Their conversation on the windowsill had been just one night before, but it felt like an eternity had gone by since.

She swerved to her right, yawning into her sleeve as she pushed open the doors to the throne room. They gave way with a pained rumble, and she stepped soundlessly inside. This nor-mally wasn't a shortcut she would take, but Teia was exhausted and Jura long asleep. There was nobody here but her, and some-thing about the silence gave her pause.

The room was beautiful under moonlight, stripped of any noisy partygoers and demanding officials. The ceiling frescoes glowed with a breathtaking vivacity. The floor tiles were newly waxed, and someone had secured the heavy red curtains with a tasseled cord, so that Bhanot was visible through the arched windows.

And there, in the center of the adorned wooden dais, was the throne. It was exquisite—a piece of Erisian history passed through the generations, upholstered in velvet, trimmed in gold. A chair fit for a monarch, a ruler. How would it feel to climb those engraved steps, to look out the windows at Erisia and be able to call it hers?

Impulse overtook her. Teia's feet moved her to the center of the room. She glimpsed the wooden flames etched along the throne's base, stretching toward the cushioned seat. For some reason, this exhilarated her. She wanted to remember this moment, this illusion of peace in the eye of the storm. She took a deep breath, running a hand through her hair, tilting her head to the ceiling.

She froze.

Teia had seen the fresco above her a thousand times. It was supposedly commissioned by Eris the First himself, although a painter was brought in for restorations every other decade. The image showed the Goddess standing alongside the Serkawr. Armina had a hand resting on the sea beast, which bared its fangs down at Teia. Spikes rippled outward from its body, creating a hide of scarlet armor. Its claws sank into the springy earth.

And there, in the very center of its forehead, gleamed a jewel. Red as blood, cut with four points. Minuscule in comparison to the rest of the creature, but there nonetheless.

The Morning Star.

Teia swore. She had seen plenty of depictions of the Serkawr, but never with the Star. Yet there it was, cleverly camouflaged among the crimson scales, unmistakable once she knew to look for it.

There was something else, too, Teia realized as she focused on the painting. She conjured a wreath of flames, which climbed diligently toward the ceiling, illuminating the fresco. The fire highlighted a thin string of words inscribed along the Serkawr's back. The sentence had been printed in a spidery script, worn away with the flow of time, barely legible beneath the light.

The sea beast, raised by commoner's flame and noble's water, brought together under the Morning Star.

That was it. No smoking gun or irrefutable evidence. *Hardly proof of anything,* Teia thought, with a giddy jolt of relief. She hadn't heard of commoner's flame or noble's water before—they sounded like gibberish to her, written for the sake of being ambiguous and artistic. Not to mention that none of the Divine Five had been noble. Armina had chosen her champions from a lot of commonfolk, yanking them from pastoral villages to bless them with incredible power.

No. No, that wasn't quite right. *Most* of the Divine Five had been peasants, but not all. The singular exception was Mei, the woman who had received control over water. She had been the daughter of a high priestess, who'd served as the town's unofficial leader. Teia admitted that, with a bit of flexibility, Mei could pass as noble.

But that meant commoner's flame had to be from one man.

Teia swiveled around slowly. A portrait of Eris hung on the far wall. A golden circlet rested over his curls, his fist clamped around a hulking broadsword. He surveyed her impassively, a half smile plastered against his lips.

Disbelief whistled through Teia, strong and sharp as ever, but it did nothing for the numbness that had blossomed in her chest. All her life, she'd been told Eris was a man of unbreakable will. He was cunning and brave. He was power incarnate. It showed in his kingdom, his ambitions—but just how far did that extend? What if the Serkawr hadn't been sent by Armina, as the old legends claimed?

What if Mei and Eris had raised the sea beast with the Morning Star?

It was a scandalous theory, if not completely blasphemous. Teia could think of several high priests who would drop dead from the shock alone. The ones that survived would likely chase her from the temple, livid that she would dare make such a suggestion.

Except why else would Teia's family guard the gem with such dedication? Was this a secret that she hadn't managed to uncover, one that had been safeguarded throughout the years, told directly to the Carthan heir?

The Carthan heir.

The air evaporated from Teia's lungs. Lehm might be aware of the Star's power, but was Jura? He had never said a word, never mentioned raising the Serkawr. But she had run into him in the palace library, standing in the history section, researching Erisian lore. He had torn those pages from the book he'd held—Teia even knew the title, gifted to her by the scholar the crown prince had mutilated.

Legends of the Serkawr.

Goddess, Teia thought. Suddenly, she was picturing the exchange request, the many posters pasted throughout Bhanot. A life for a life—Kyra's for Alara's.

What if there was a secondary reason for the exchange,

extending beyond striking a blow to the rebels? Kyra might be able to control fire, but she had been born to a tailor and a refugee. She didn't have a drop of royal blood within her. She was, by all accounts, as much of a commoner as Eris had been.

Teia's eyes shifted down. She examined her palms hesitantly, taking in the lines grooved into her skin. Despite the bruises and scrapes earned in Blackgate, the old scars collected from falling in the passageways, Teia's were still the hands of a noble. She could bend water to her will. She could stir the tide.

And if the fresco was to be believed, she could summon the Serkawr with Kyra.

Teia's legs nearly buckled beneath her. Her mind rebelled against the statement, scrambling for some alternative explanation. The Serkawr didn't exist. It was a story invented to scare children. It was a myth that the naive fell victim to.

But what if it's not? something whispered inside her. *What if it's real? What happens then?*

Teia already had the answer, which reverberated loud and clear. It would be a disaster beyond imagination. A calamity that would destroy her kingdom.

Because if both Jura and Lehm thought they could summon the Serkawr, they would rip Erisia apart to get to it first. *Maybe they already are,* Teia thought, as she recalled the recent string of reckless decisions, each more erratic than the last. There had been the slaughter in Elden from Jura, the dubious exchange plans from Lehm. And the ring—the damned ring. If Lehm had it stolen from Jura's nightstand, it was a slight the Golden Prince wouldn't take lightly. A direct message, a knife in the side.

Had each choice been made with the other in mind? Were they intended to be warnings, shows of bluster and might, an indication that the other was willing to sacrifice everything to win?

Teia stepped away from the throne. She had been running from a monster all her life, but she no longer knew which way to turn. The walls felt very close, the frescoes blinding her with their splendor. Something lay ahead, stretching to engulf Erisia, threatening to catch Teia in its midst.

Her nightmares were full of the red of flames, of the coolness of water and the silence that followed.

CHAPTER TWENTY-SEVEN

It was an exceedingly poor time to be breaking into General Miran's office.

Teia was a mere twelve hours away from her return to Blackgate. Her bandages needed changing. Her side throbbed. She hadn't enjoyed a last meal or visited the wine cellar or swiped a final platter of tea cakes from the kitchens.

Yet for all her flaws, Teia considered herself an opportunist. And as she rotated the wall behind the bookshelf, stepping out from the passageways, she had one more loose end to resolve—a task to take care of, in the slimmest chance she lived through Blackgate.

In the days following the Elden military campaign, Samos Miran had experienced a religious reawakening. The servants under Teia's retention reported they'd seen Miran in the palace temple for hours at a time, his head bent low before the statue of Armina. One altar boy claimed he'd caught Miran weeping uncontrollably, although he later confessed that may have been a trick of the light.

Teia didn't think so. She suspected Miran needed his time after Elden. Perhaps communing with the Goddess made him feel better about all those people he'd cut down for Jura.

Either way, where others viewed a broken man, Teia saw a gift. Miran was someone who had glimpsed the Crown's writhing underbelly. The events of Elden had transformed him into a man without purpose, floundering in the dark, at war with himself. His faith in the monarchy had been fractured, splintered beyond repair.

He might just listen to what Teia had to say.

When Miran returned from the palace's temple, she had already made herself comfortable in his office, sitting in his wooden chair like it'd been built for her. He didn't seem shocked to find her there, as he bowed by the door. "Princess," he said.

"General."

"You seem well."

"I've never felt better."

It was a lie if she'd ever told one, and it took all Teia's concentration to keep her voice steady. She had blackmailed and bargained and negotiated—she had rubbed elbows with the best the Flats had to offer and threatened more ministers than she could count.

But that would be child's play compared to this.

"Do you want to sit down?" Teia asked graciously. She beckoned to the second seat, positioned across from Miran's desk.

Miran didn't move. "Is there something I can help you with?"

"There is, actually. It's been a while since we've spoken, and I wanted to check in on you."

"How generous."

"I try my best." Teia offered a dazzling smile. "How have you been? I know you're busy nowadays, running around as Jura's errand boy."

Miran ignored the jab. "I've been well," he rumbled.

Teia rested her cheek against the curve of her palm. "Really?" she said.

"Yes."

"And your girls?"

"They're fine."

"Just fine?" Teia asked. "You can be more candid than that. I see them running around the palace, stealing sweets, reading books. How old are they now? I heard they recently celebrated a birthday."

"They turned eight last month."

Teia snapped her fingers. "What a wonderful age to be. So adorable—so *inquisitive*."

"They're very bright."

"Almost *too* bright." Teia tsked sympathetically. "What did they think of what happened in the public courts?"

Miran's good eye burned in its socket. "They were frightened," he said at last. The words seemed to physically pain him.

"I can imagine. Their father—the man they admire most— cowed before Jura like a dog. I'm sure it would terrify anyone." She looked up at the general unwaveringly. "Is that why they left the palace the next day?"

"They were due for a holiday."

"A *holiday*," Teia marveled. "And in the most remote part of Erisia, no less." She spread her palms over the surface of the desk, where a map of the kingdom lay under a protective layer of glass. It had been drawn in remarkable detail, down to the ridges of the Highland Mountains and the quarries by the coast. "I wouldn't have taken the Northern Pass to reach the Summer Isles," Teia continued. She traced the route that the twins' carriage had taken, snaking along the narrow gorge. "Too isolated, too dull. It can be a hard trip to make for children that young."

"They found ways to amuse themselves."

"I suppose they had to. They might have been bored, but at least now they're safe."

Miran's fingers twitched against his scabbard, and Teia leaned back in her seat. "You don't have to look so nervous, General. I know they're all you have since your wife passed. I wouldn't hurt them. I would never."

"Is that so?"

"It is. I'm not my half brother."

She let that stew for a while, as they both pondered the implications of what she'd said. The general wasn't one for wearing his emotions freely, but doubt had worked its way into his features. His shoulders were rigid, his eye skittering to the spot above Teia's head, where a miniature of Armina hung on the wall. He was as rattled as she had ever seen him, rapidly approaching the tipping point, the moment he might shatter.

She just needed to push him a bit further.

"Miran," Teia said thoughtfully, dipping her head at the map. "When was this printed?"

"Two, three years ago."

"Ah," she said. "That's too bad—it's due for some updates."

She tapped one finger down, rolling a spark of heat forward to leave a smoky stain on the glass. When she'd finished, Teia admired her work. She withdrew her hand with a dramatic flourish, shifting aside so Miran could see what she'd done.

The blemish was right where Elden used to be.

"No need to thank me," she said magnanimously. "Although, tell me—is this similar to what you did in Elden? Because I've heard stories, you know. The way your men rode in on horseback, with you at the helm. The way you set fire to fields and homes, barring doors so nobody could leave, running through anyone who tried to escape."

Miran was whiter than a ghost. "We didn't—"

"You did. What's the point in denying it? The entire palace has heard by now." She lit a flame above her palm, letting the heat squirm playfully before extinguishing it in her fist. "There are rumors that even the children weren't safe. That your soldiers hunted down each one—babies in their cradles, toddlers who hid under their beds. You dragged their corpses out into Elden's courtyard, and then you set the entire town ablaze."

The general swayed on his feet. His breaths were shallow, his chin trembling, and Teia understood that this was it—there was nothing more she could possibly say. It was up to Miran's conscience now, or whatever pieces were still intact. The general would either give an inch, or not at all.

He pulled out the second chair and dropped like a stone, his hands clasped over his face. She glimpsed his lips moving as his shoulders shook violently. He was praying, she realized. Trying to do penance, it seemed, for the actions he'd carried out in Jura's name.

When Miran glanced up at Teia, his eye was bloodshot. "Goddess forgive me," he whispered, "for the things that I've done."

"It's not the Goddess you should be pleading forgiveness from."

"I had no choice. His Highness made a demand. A *public* demand."

"I understand, Miran," Teia said soothingly. "You don't have to rationalize your choices to me. You made a decision that you were backed into. You traded the lives of other children for your own. And it might have worked this time, but what about the next? And the next?" She scuffed the soot across the glass, smudging the stain as wide as it could go. "You know the truth as well as I do. This is a taste of what happens when Jura doesn't get his way, the first of many tantrums. He'll burn the entire country down to get what he wants, and he'll sleep more soundly than you or I ever will."

"The Dawnbreakers," Miran rasped. "They've weighed on the crown prince—"

"Yes, I'm well aware. But what about the threat after that? What about protests from villages or petitions to the Crown? What happens when the Council is no longer there to check Jura's power?"

Miran's hands were clenched so tightly they must have lost all circulation. Still, he gave a firm shake of his head. "I serve at the will of the Crown," he ground out.

"And when you're asked to massacre children?"

"There's nothing to be done."

"There is, if you'd be willing to listen."

The barest hope flitted across Miran's face, as a blotchy red bled into his cheeks. He sat a little straighter in his chair, following each of her movements, waiting for the idea that would somehow reduce Jura's disposition for murder.

Teia took a deep breath. She ignored the hammering of her pulse.

She said, "Put me on the throne instead."

Miran went stiff. His eye darted around the room, inspecting each corner, ensuring this wasn't a trap. When he was satisfied no spies skulked behind the furniture, he focused back on Teia. "Princess," he said, his voice almost imperceptible. "What you're suggesting is treason."

"Maybe," Teia said. "But it's also a solution. I'm a Carthan. The throne is my birthright."

"The laws are clear. No woman—"

"Is eligible to rule Erisia." Teia clicked her tongue impatiently. "Those same laws also say that brothels are illegal, and rulers must protect their subjects. There's evidently some flexibility within the system."

A vein throbbed against Miran's forehead. "Is this about Abbott?" he said. "Your new arrangement with him—"

Arrangement. How easy it was to reduce the engagement to a single word. How simple. Despite having two daughters, Miran would never understand the fear Teia had felt when Abbott cornered her at the public courts.

"No," she bit out. "It's because I can be a better ruler. I'll reopen relations with the Shaylani. Reshape our foreign policies and strengthen our alliances."

"It can't be done."

"Better relations?"

"You assuming the throne."

"It can. It just hasn't yet."

Teia could feel Miran's indecision as he stared her down; his reluctance was enough to suffocate her. Even so, she refused to give in. There was too much to gain here—an agreement that could tip the scales. If she had the military's support, she would have no real fear of mutiny from either the court or the commonfolk. Teia didn't want to be the kind of monarch that wielded sword in fist, always ready to strike, but she would if she needed to.

"Think about it, Miran," Teia said. "There's no love lost between Jura and the military—any fool can see that. And your soldiers will follow you. If I have your backing, I have theirs."

"You aren't asking for a handshake. You're asking for a *coup*."

"You would rather have Jura on the throne?"

"He's young. He'll learn."

"He ordered the slaughter of an entire village. That's not something a person grows out of."

"The Council will advise him."

"Once Jura becomes king, the Council becomes nothing more than a friendly suggestion and a circle of old men."

Miran rose to his feet abruptly. His mouth was set in a firm line, his body tilted away from her. "Respectfully, Princess," he said curtly, "what you're asking for is impossible."

She stood, too, drawing herself up to full height. She barely met Miran's chest, but she would do her damnedest to tower over him. "Is that your final answer?"

"I serve at the will of the Crown. I took an oath."

"Where was your oath in Elden?"

"I carried it with me."

"Through the madness?"

"Through whatever challenges I may endure. It's what sustains me." He bowed once more, placing a fist to his heart. "I trust you can find your own way out."

Teia wanted to laugh at Miran's dismissiveness. He was convinced that she'd bargained with all she had, each card laid bare on the table. The general was ready to put this discussion behind him. He would pack it away with his other ghosts, stowed securely in the past. Maybe he would even reflect on what she'd said from time to time, as he made his morning pilgrimage to the palace temple.

Except Miran was only human. He might be a decorated veteran and a respected hero and a member of the glorified Erisian Council, but he, too, had his limits. In many ways, he wasn't much different from the other nobles that Teia had blackmailed.

Every last one of them had underestimated her.

Two paces from the door, Teia pivoted around smoothly. "Miran," she said. "What if I could offer you something else?"

"There's nothing that I want."

"Nothing?"

"I'm more than content as I am."

But he wasn't, not really. She could sense his anger whenever he reached to adjust his eyepatch, could glimpse the pain that remained after all these months. The rounded piece of cloth did little to hide the scars that had been left behind, from where a knife had been taken to Miran's face. Scars lanced down his cheek. They hacked horizontally across his chin and clumped in white tissue along his neck, like someone had tried to carve a message with a blade.

People could always be swayed by something. By love. By greed.

By vengeance.

Teia watched her future shift once more, solidifying into something new. And in the end, all it took were six words, sweeter than honey, colder than ice.

"I can give you Cornelius Lehm."

Chapter Twenty-Eight

That same night after her talk with Miran, Teia found herself walking toward Sunset Tower, toward Blackgate and Alara and near-certain death. Clouds hung low in the sky, and the air was strangely muggy. As Teia reveled in her last minutes of freedom, she had the good sense to wonder what the hell she was doing.

She had survived one tour of the prison, and that was by the skin of her teeth. Now, she was injured, shaken, ready to plunge back into Blackgate with every guard on high alert.

How had Enna described this job?

Right, Teia thought. *Madness*.

Enna was already waiting by Sunset Tower. She was shuffling from leg to leg, rotating out the joints in her wrists as Teia approached. "I was getting worried you'd stand me up."

"You're never early for anything," Teia replied. "You once staged your death and were late to your own funeral."

"What can I say?" Enna said, shrugging off the retort easily. "It's a beautiful night to become a household name."

It was far preferable to the alternative. As Teia drew her cloak tighter, the streets were eerily empty. The merchants that usually scampered home at this hour, weary from concluding their business, were nowhere to be found. Rows of iron lamps creaked from the corner of each building, and Teia could make out the distant outlines of two figures, growing closer by the minute.

"Enna," Teia warned. "Play nice."

Enna responded with a sharklike smile. "Who?" she said. "Me?"

Kyra and Tobias broke through a gray swirl of mist. Both were dressed in dark clothing: black tunics, comfortable trousers. Tobias had no reaction to Enna—she might as well have been another streetlamp—but Kyra did a visible double take. "You're from the hotel," she said cautiously. "The one who brought us Wynter."

"Enna van Apt," the thief said, sticking out her hand.

"Kyra Medoh."

"I know." Enna's grin flickered as it landed on Tobias. "And you are?" she said.

"Nobody important."

"Oh, I doubt that."

"And why is that?"

"Because anyone acquainted with Teia is either terrifically important or utterly stupid—and you don't strike me as dense."

Tobias's mouth twitched. "So which one are you?"

Enna huffed a sigh. "At the moment? Probably the latter."

"Quiet," Teia said tersely. The bells atop Sunset Tower had begun to ring. They didn't have much time, and she tipped her head toward the cobbled path. "If we live through this, I'll buy everyone a pint. You can swap stories until you can't stand straight."

"A *pint*," Enna said, aghast. "You better buy me the damn bar with what we're about to go through."

The wind nipped at their backs as they started toward

Blackgate. Soon, the slick walls had risen up before them, although Teia took care to shepherd her group clear of the gates. They stuck close to the rickety alleys and mottled buildings of Carmine, away from the open streets. The prison's entrances were each manned with four guards now, who kept their hands fixed to their weapons. It seemed the wardens weren't taking any chances with intruders after the debacle of Teia's first visit.

And that was just fine with her. She made a generous loop around the prison before veering to the left, staying solidly within the shadows. Before long, Blackgate's walls fell behind them. Empty land stretched ahead, the soil hard and clumped, puckered with deep grooves from where prison wagons had rumbled over dirt.

Someone tugged at her sleeve. Kyra pointed back toward the prison in bewilderment. "Er—Teia?"

"What?"

"Are we lost?"

"No."

"But isn't Blackgate over there?"

"Yes," Teia answered, and continued on her way.

They saw the metal fence first. It was an ugly thing, built from prison labor, the different sections clumsily assembled. The chain links spread across several acres of land, roping off countless rows of unmarked graves. A mausoleum had been constructed at the end of a simple dirt path, barely visible behind the fence.

"A cemetery?" Kyra asked in a hushed voice.

Enna released a mock gasp. "Is everyone from Set this observant?"

Teia elbowed her in the side. "Blackgate has different ways to dispose of its dead," she said to the others. "They used incinerators back when my grandfather was on the throne, but nobles complained about the smoke. They claimed they could smell it all the way in the palace." She nodded at the tombstones. "Blackgate built five cemeteries as a compromise—one for each of the cell blocks. And unlike the rest of the prison, these have next to no security."

"No surprise there," Kyra said nervously. "Isn't it bad luck to rob the dead?"

"Good thing we don't need luck," Enna said, a sliver of metal materializing between her fingers. She pranced to the main gate, held together by a rusted chain. One jimmy later and the lock had cracked open. The thief swept into a bow, her chest puffed with pride. "Behold."

"A human lockpick," Kyra said with complete sincerity. "You must be great at parties."

Enna blinked at Teia. "Is she ribbing me?"

"Kyra's sarcasm is a work in progress."

"Noted."

They knelt beside the mausoleum, among the tangled thatches of weeds. The structure was poorly made—the blocks of stone painted a grayish white, the statue of Armina more clownish than not—but Teia was grateful for the cover. Beside her, Kyra pulled furiously at stray clumps of grass. She fiddled them apart between her fingers, occasionally setting a few blades alight.

"Now that we're here," she said to Teia, "how is digging up graves going to help Alara?"

She'd been waiting for someone to ask the question. "The greenies," Teia said.

"The who?"

"Catchy name," Tobias provided.

"What a stupid title," Enna said.

Teia ignored them both. "The greenies," she said again patiently. "Pembrant mentioned them in Blackgate."

"Right," Kyra said. "Was this before or after we began running for our lives?"

Teia shifted her weight, pressing against the mausoleum's wall. "Blackgate operates on a hierarchy. Greenies are the guards at the bottom of the pack, the ones who have just started out. They get stuck with the worst jobs, which include manning the Dead Run."

"That's actually what it's called?"

"What would you rename it to?" Enna said. "'Nightly Trips to Drop Off Dead Prisoners' doesn't quite have the same ring to it."

Teia waved her hand. "You can call it whatever you want," she said. "But when the greenies make their next drop-off, you better thank the Goddess for the Dead Run."

Kyra winced. "Because?"

"Because it's how we're getting inside Blackgate."

The pieces of grass scattered to the ground as the rebel champion's balance wobbled. "We're going in with the dead?" she emphasized.

"Through a cart used to *carry* the dead," Teia said. "There's a significant difference."

"Won't it be searched when it enters the prison?"

"That's the beauty of things. The cart is padlocked shut once the bodies are emptied out. No open windows, and the door is covered. The guards don't bother checking the carts until they're unloaded in the stables."

"And you know this how?"

"I do my research." After she'd seen the greenies carry out the corpse in Blackgate, it had been easy to pay for information on their routines. There were plenty of street urchins in the Flats who were happy to stake out the cemetery in exchange for some guilds.

Kyra didn't seem particularly convinced. "And how reliable are your sources?" she said.

"Reliable enough," Teia answered briskly, as she flicked a speck of mud off her trousers. "We just need to get to Alara and smuggle her out in the cart. The greenies go on Dead Runs twice a night, which gives us the perfect excuse to leave the prison."

The Poisons Master wouldn't be thrilled about being packed into a wagon full of bodies, but Teia thought Alara would understand. If this worked, there would be no need for any questionable prisoner exchanges. They could all make tracks to the nearest alehouse in the Flats, getting fantastically drunk and basking in their newfound victory.

And if it didn't, they were about to be in for a world of hurt.

The greenies were both incredibly timely and vociferously loud. Teia could hear them from where she hid behind a tombstone, grousing about how they'd drawn the short straw for this shift.

"The selection is rigged," one of them complained, hacking a cough that rattled across the cemetery. "How is this my third Dead Run of the week?"

"You shouldn't have gotten on the commander's bad side." This from a fellow with a lisp. "I heard you made eyes at his girl."

A third greenie, with the deep rasp of a smoker, brayed out a laugh. "Which one?"

"The redhead from the Highlands."

"Goddess, mate. She's thin enough to blow away in the wind."

"So are you," the cougher whined back. "But you don't see me yapping on about it."

There were four of them in total, just as Teia had anticipated. They tied the team of brown horses to a nearby post and bustled to the back of the cart. The iron door was fitted with a padlock, which the smoker clicked open unceremoniously. As the cougher heaved the door aside, the other greenies uttered a collective groan.

"Goddess," the lisper swore, hiking a shovel over his shoulder. "This is going to take us all night."

They made multiple trips between the cart and the edge of the gravesite, where several holes had been dug in preparation. Through the lantern light, Teia caught the occasional glimpse of the bodies they hauled. The corpses were riddled with burn marks, blisters adorning clammy skin. She said a silent prayer that Alara was still among the living, that Jura had managed to constrain himself.

For all their protesting, the greenies made excellent time. It had barely been an hour when they tossed the last body into its grave, fussing tremendously about the strain on their backs. The two in the middle patted down the soil haphazardly, before all four headed to the wagon in a protective cluster. The coughing greenie snapped the padlock back in place, while the others grumbled to one another skittishly.

It was time. Teia focused on the spot next to the mausoleum. She nudged at the strands of heat, and a flame illuminated in midair. It danced the way a torch would, trembling slightly against the night.

The cougher cursed. "Do you see that?"

"Ghosts?" the lisper wailed.

"Monsters?" another whimpered.

"Don't be daft," the smoker declared. "Your eyes are playing tricks on you."

That was when a second flame emerged beside the first. This one was conjured by Kyra and burned a steady crimson as it whipped about cheerfully. Together, the twin fires drifted farther into the cemetery. They bobbed against the wind, daring the greenies to follow.

For all her planning, Teia had miscalculated how cowardly the guards might be. The greenies began to prattle among themselves, debating whether to search for the source of the fire or simply turn tail for the safety of Blackgate. It was a heated disagreement, the men split evenly down the middle, but it was the cougher who finally won the discussion with a single, highly effective argument.

"What if it's still there when we're back?" he said resolutely. "We have another run tonight—and I'm not telling the commander about no flames."

With that, the greenies edged uneasily toward the fires, revolvers out, swords at the ready. Blackgate's finest were flustered, on edge—but Teia knew the ruse wouldn't last more than a handful of minutes. She could already feel the distance that stretched between her and the threads of heat, a canyon that couldn't be crossed. Her connection was slipping fast, the ball of fire dwindling by the second.

The greenies had left one lantern hitched to the side of the cart. It illuminated Enna as she raced from her hiding spot, reaching the cart's padlock to caress it gently. One twist with her lockpick, and the door had given way. The thief climbed inside the wagon nimbly, disappearing into its depths.

Teia's flame had nearly extinguished when Enna popped

back out again. She flashed a signal at the group, the laughter drained from her face. "Hurry," she hissed, leaping outside the cart to hold the door aside.

Tobias went first, with Kyra right behind him. As Teia sprinted toward the wagon, muffled shouts came from the back of the graveyard. Both flames had vanished, which meant their distraction had just gone with them. The greenies would be making their way back to the main path any minute now, spooked by the ordeal and eager to return to the prison.

She hoisted herself inside the cart, and Enna secured the padlock after her.

There was no time to survey the space. Teia stepped over to where Tobias stood, stretching as tall as she could. Together, they wrestled away the grated semicircle from the top of the door—presumably installed to air out any smells—and lowered it carefully to the bottom of the cart. Enna had loosened the grate's bolts after opening the cart door. It was one of the thief's trademark tactics, and something she used when robbing similarly built shipment wagons.

I should buy stock in this manufacturer, Enna had said, when Teia first relayed the description of the cart to her. *Every pinhead in Erisia uses the same design.*

And Teia was eternally grateful. She flattened against the wall while Enna squeezed through the open section at the top. She landed lightly on her feet, barely disturbing the cart at all, and Teia scrambled to replace the grate.

The greenies were mere feet away now, lamenting about superstitious fools and fairy lights. As they ambled toward the cart, Teia dropped to the floor. She hunched behind the iron door, praying that their good fortune would hold. Enna hadn't had a chance to tighten the bolts, and there was nothing keeping the grate in place. If the greenies touched the door—if they jiggled it in the slightest—the semicircle at the top would fall away.

Shuffling came from the front of the wagon. It was paired with the grunts of four men, the whinny of a horse. The entire cart shuddered as the greenies climbed on board, and the grate wobbled in its perch.

Teia lunged upward in the nick of time. She caught the grille by the edges, her palms sweating against the cool metal. Adrenaline buzzed in her lungs, lashing through her body, as Enna rose beside her. The thief produced a heap of silver bolts from her pocket, reattaching the grid with a carpenter's touch before nodding at Teia confidently. *Let go,* she mouthed.

Teia did. She waited for the grate to collapse, for the cart to stop. For something—anything—to go terribly, horribly wrong.

But the wheels turned steadily beneath her. The greenies were oblivious as the horses plodded on, cantering through potholes, dragging the cart behind them.

They were headed back into the shadow of Blackgate.

Chapter Twenty-Nine

The light was low, peeking in through the grate, but it did nothing to disguise the filthiness of the cart. Heaps of bloody rags were scattered about. The smell of decay lingered in the air, and the wagon's floor was slick with grime and mold.

Teia's stomach flipped with each rotation of the wheels. *How long do we have before we arrive?* she thought, as her mind spun with what was to come. With the speed they were going, Blackgate couldn't be much farther, and the realization sent an ache into her side. Dread pulsed in the corners of her chest, willing her to flee.

She couldn't. She wouldn't. She had made a promise that she intended to keep. Teia would get Alara out. She would make it through Blackgate.

And then she was going to claim her throne.

A cough thundered through the cart. Teia whipped around, fully prepared to take off someone's head, when she realized the noise had drifted in from outside. The greenies were getting restless, perhaps sensing the Dead Run was coming to an end.

"Some night, huh?" the cougher stated, his voice muffled through the metal. "Didn't expect to see so many bodies."

"The Golden Prince is leaning hard on the prisoners," the lisper said.

"Makes sense. His coronation is coming up, isn't it?"

"Celebration for the ages."

"Think we'll be invited?"

"Are you out of your mind?"

"He must be," the smoker snarked. "We chased those damn lights for a good bit, didn't we?"

"It ain't my fault that place is haunted."

"Just like it's not our fault you don't got no brains in your head."

The wagon screeched to a halt. There was the sound of heavy footsteps, the faint rustle of documents. Teia gripped at her legs. She hardly dared to breathe, afraid the slightest movement might give them away. The greenies must be at the prison's checkpoint now, parked at the entrance next to the stable. She guessed they were showing their identification papers, as a cursory inspection for reentering Blackgate.

A rough voice boomed out somewhere from their left. "Any trouble?"

"None, sir," the cougher chirped, exactly as Teia hoped he would. It had been a decent bet to make, considering the type of men who were recruited into Blackgate: proud, driven, and eager to prove themselves. Far from the sort to flaunt that they'd pursued a set of ghostly lights into a graveyard and returned empty-handed.

The gruff voice said nothing. Yet he must have motioned the greenies forward, because she heard a whip crack. The cart glided on, the road here smooth as a dream, and they slipped into Blackgate Prison not a second later.

◆◆◆

It was the stench of horses that tipped Teia off.

She beckoned to the others, as the cart squeaked from a change in weight. Somebody rounded the side of the wagon, and the padlock rattled once, twice. The greenie groaned. He huffed something about rubbish quality and stingy budgets, before the door was violently yanked open.

"What the—"

Then Tobias was lashing out, his hand striking the soft of the greenie's neck. The guard crumpled, but Tobias barely spared him a second glance. He swung deftly from the cart, moving from Teia's line of sight. Several more thumps thudded out, interspersed by moans of pain.

Tobias walked back into view looking exceedingly pleased with himself. "Not bad, right?"

"You have a real future as a mercenary," Teia said.

"I'll put you down as a reference."

They had arrived at Block C's stable, which was used solely for Dead Run preparations. The stall they stood in was cramped but clean, the walls neatly lined with tack. The two horses were still tethered to the cart, observing the scene unfold with their enormous placid eyes. They were unusually well-behaved for animals who had just seen their masters ambushed and knocked out, and Teia dared to pat one on the muzzle gingerly.

"Good girl," she said.

Enna smirked. "Goddess have mercy," she said. "Are you talking to a horse?"

"What's wrong with that?"

"I can't believe we're putting our lives in your hands."

"In my extraordinarily capable hands," Teia said, and the horse snorted its assent.

She bent down to help the others, who were stripping away the guards' uniforms. When they'd finished, Enna bound the greenies hand and foot using strips of her cloak. The unconscious men were rolled toward the far wall, shunted behind stacked bales of hay.

Everyone changed in the same stall, their backs facing one another. Teia tried not to choke at the musky scent of the uniform, which was several sizes too large. She tugged on the trousers, tightened the waist, and padded over to Kyra, who slid a tin box from her pocket. The rebel girl set to work at once, folding back the excess fabric, pinning away at the hems. The uniforms wouldn't be a perfect fit, but they would at least be passable from a distance.

Enna eyed one of the pins on her sleeve. "They teach you this in rebel boot camp?"

"I was a tailor before I joined the Dawnbreakers," Kyra answered.

"Sounds frightful."

"Why do you think I left?"

"To escape a life of carrot farming?"

"Carrot farming?" Kyra said, confused, and Enna shot her a wicked grin.

Teia, in the meantime, had shifted off to one side. She was busy scrounging through the uniform's many pockets, some of which extended down to her thighs. At long last, her fingers closed around something bulky and circular. The pocket watch had a plain lid and a thick chain. It was scratched along the rim, the glass badly chipped, but the hands clicked on steadily.

"Standard issue for Blackgate guards," Teia explained. "All of you should have one."

Tobias pulled a pocket watch from his uniform. "Very nice," he said dryly. "Must really help with efficiency."

Teia checked each of their watches, confirming the times, ensuring all were synchronized. When she was finally satisfied, she dug into her pockets once again. This time, she drew forth a key, cut with a square bronze head.

Enna whistled. "And that is?"

"The master key," Teia said winningly. "Gives the greenies access to every cell in the block."

"Hideous," Enna proclaimed. "If I saw that on the street, I'd actively try *not* to steal it."

Kyra stowed away the pin box. She rose from her crouch and lowered her iron mask over her features. It was disconcerting to see her once again in full uniform, down to the bright green stripes denoting her rank. "We should get going," she said tersely. "Isn't the second Dead Run in an hour?"

"Talented and punctual," Enna remarked. "You're starting to grow on me."

"Even though I'm from Set?"

"Don't push it."

The path that left the stables and wound toward Block C was lit by a series of lanterns. They glowed with a sickly light, almost green in the darkness. *Turn back*, they seemed to say. *Turn back*.

Teia stomped forward, approaching a door along the inner wall, reaching out to grasp the handle. She felt the bite of fear, the instinct to run, and for a moment it overwhelmed her. She didn't want to return to these cursed walls, stuffed with the cries of the broken and the damned. She could feel the edge of the sword tearing into her ribs, the agony that came after. It was a memory that expanded in her mind, painting over her courage.

Move, she told herself sternly, and it was the thought of Alara that compelled her forward. Teia would survive this, just as she had everything else. She would take her fear and wield it as a weapon.

She had been doing it all her life, so what was one more night?

The door opened slowly. A vicious stink rose to greet them, one that made the cart smell like a candy shop. Low groans could be heard from down the hall, spilling out from the cells that lined the corridors. A great stone staircase spiraled to their right, the steps climbing upward. Just as the wooden door had been during their last trek through the prison, the stairs were marked with a single half circle, which Teia now understood.

Dawnbreakers.

"Goddess," Enna muttered, pressing a sleeve toward her mask.

"I don't think you'll find her here," Tobias said grimly.

Teia stared up at the flight of stairs. It took barely a second to make her next decision, as she rotated to face the others. "We'll cover more ground if we split up."

"I was afraid you would say that," Enna sighed.

"Enna—you and Kyra search this floor. They might have Alara in one of these cells."

"And you?"

"Tobias and I will take the floor above."

Kyra swallowed. "The white rooms?" she said. "Are you sure?"

Teia wasn't, but she nodded anyway.

The rebel girl glanced down the long hallway. It was a study in shades of gray, a corridor that seemed to extend forever. "What if Alara isn't here?" she said hopelessly. "What if they moved her to another block?"

"They wouldn't have. Dawnbreakers are always kept together. It makes things easier."

"For disposing of corpses?"

There was no point in denying facts. "Yes," Teia replied curtly. She withdrew the pocket watch, prying back the lid so the others saw the time. "The next Dead Run is at three. If either group isn't back at the stables by then, the other leaves without them."

"Is that supposed to be a pep talk?" Enna said.

"No."

"Good. Because I feel much more demoralized than before."

They quieted as a pack of guards came clomping down the hall. They marched in perfect formation, not a single one out of place, their sleeves emblazoned with three red bands. These were no greenies, scuttling about to gather bodies. No—the men passing by were senior officials, well established within the prison, close to the top of Blackgate's pecking order.

There was nothing more that could be said without the officials overhearing. Kyra and Enna started down the cavernous hallway, keeping a safe distance from the other guards. It was a purely precautionary measure, although Teia doubted the officials would notice. Blackgate's hierarchy was known to be rigid, and the greenie uniforms they wore all but guaranteed anonymity.

"Are we sure they should be sent off together?" Tobias murmured, as he and Teia took to heaving themselves up the steep stone staircase.

"We only have one master key, and Enna can take apart any lock. Plus, if we need to fight, Kyra and I have to be separated."

"You think someone might actually confuse you for Kyra?"

"Maybe." She shrugged. "It's dark, isn't it?"

"It's not *that* dark," he mumbled, cupping at the scar on his neck. "Besides, I would know you anywhere."

In spite of herself, of the danger they were so clearly in, Teia almost lost her footing. Thank the Goddess she caught on to the rail, staggering up the final step to reach the sterile white walls. It was like walking into the cold nothingness of a snowstorm, a scene drained of any life. She found herself comforted by the sheer number of cells that stood empty, the doors propped to the far right.

Yet far more rooms were secured shut than there had been before. She and Tobias were nearing one now, the door positioned on Teia's side as she steeled herself for what she might see. Would there be another tortured soul, a Dawnbreaker driven mad? A graying corpse, speckled with burns?

Through the door's rectangular glass panel, she saw a figure strapped to the metal slab. Their wrists and ankles were cuffed down, and a shard of metal had been embedded into their thigh. A Blackgate guard stood above the prisoner, a clip of papers wedged against his arm as he leaned forward casually. He dragged the metal shard farther into flesh, scrutinizing the prisoner for their reaction.

Each room was soundproofed, but Teia recoiled anyway. Goddess. It was no wonder Block C required two Dead Runs a night. Leaving in a body bag was its own brand of mercy.

"It's not Alara," she managed, but Tobias shook his head. "Does it matter?" he said back.

He was right. It didn't, not really. Even Kyra hadn't dared argue the merits of helping anyone they encountered along the way. They were getting Alara out, but could they say the same for the other Dawnbreakers? How many rebels had to be left behind, sacrificed because they weren't deemed important enough? How many of them had yearned to spark a revolution, to be the hero, but had ended up chained to a slab and thrown to the wolves?

They combed through another few rooms, each one awash with blood, when a new set of voices echoed from down the hall. Teia didn't think much of it—they had already passed another patrol group since reaching the white rooms—but Tobias came to an unexpected stop. Suddenly, his hand shot out. He grabbed Teia by the wrist, yanking her back around the corner.

"Tobias?" she hissed, but he just gritted his teeth. Underneath the iron mask, any color had drained from his face.

A man was speaking rapidly from the other end of the corridor. His voice quavered with each syllable, words blurring as he rambled on. "We have nothing on their base, but we're close to a breakthrough. We've been using new methods, testing different levels of pain. The rebels we've interrogated—"

"Don't bother," said a second voice calmly, and Teia's blood instantly ran cold. Every nerve in her body screamed at her to run, although her legs remained rooted to the spot. That voice had haunted her since she was seven, chasing her throughout the Golden Palace.

Just like that, Teia was a child again. She was napping in the shadow of an apple tree. She was waking to the crackle of flames.

This was a nightmare. It had to be. But when Teia opened her eyes, the voices had drawn nearer, the footsteps unrelenting.

Jura Carthan had come to Blackgate.

CHAPTER THIRTY

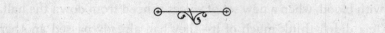

Tobias stiffened beside Teia.

Something hollow flickered behind his eyes, carved from the ruins of the St. Clair name. Tension roped through his muscles, his shoulders. His knife shimmered in his fist, the blade beaming against the white of the hallway.

It was the sight of the weapon that shocked Teia into motion. Tobias was going to kill Jura. He was going to avenge his family.

And Teia couldn't let him.

In the next instant, she was catching Tobias by the hand, trying to force the knife back into the sheath. The movement took him by surprise; he reeled back, his expression twisted in anger. "What are you doing?" he rasped, his voice low.

He deserved his revenge. He deserved to take Jura's head, to cut the crown prince's heart from his chest. But when Teia thought of Alara, of Kyra and Enna, she darted again for the knife, locking her hand over his. If Tobias attacked Jura, they would never reach the Poisons Master. They would alert every guard in the prison to their position and kiss away any possibility of escape.

"Tobias," Teia whispered furiously. "Don't."

In the background, the first voice fussed on. "Not a bother at all, Highness!" the man was saying. "The rebel base has eluded us for too long. I'll have my men double their force on the prisoners. Triple!"

Jura responded with a laugh. Genuine mirth underlined his tone. There came the sound of him thumping someone on the back, and a gasp from his companion at such informality. "Relax, Hadic," he admonished. "This isn't a test to pass."

"Highness?"

"Let's just say the location of the Dawnbreakers' base won't be relevant for much longer."

The statement rang in Teia's ears. She thought there might be something more to what Jura had said, a mystery to be unraveled, but there was no time to decipher riddles. The Golden Prince's footsteps had become disturbingly loud. He would be on them any second now, colliding directly with her and Tobias.

Teia lifted her gaze to Tobias's, her fingers still curled around his. She didn't know if he registered her touch—didn't know if he could hear her from whatever place he'd gone to. "Please," she breathed. "Trust me."

When she brought the knife once more toward its sheath, he let her. Then Teia gave Tobias a shove, forcing him around the corner before striding out alongside him. Her shoulders were pushed back, her spine ramrod straight.

Jura hovered at the edge of Teia's vision, so close she could count the freckles on his cheeks. He was dressed in filmy black robes, the hem fanned in an arc of golden embroidery. Behind Jura, a hulking giant of a man trailed his movements. He was outfitted in the dark uniform of a commander, a bushy beard poking out from under his mask.

Teia dropped into a bow.

Her pulse beat in double time, a bird frantic to escape,

throwing itself against the bars of its cage. She hoped Tobias would follow suit, that he wouldn't cave to impulse and lunge for Jura's throat. If there was ever a time for stellar acting—to convince the crown prince that they were two lowly greenie guards, paying their respects to the royal family—it was now.

She felt the weight of Jura's stare as he considered her bent form. Her back had begun to ache when he laughed heartily, clapping his hands together in delight. "Your men are well trained," he said to Hadic.

"We aim to please, Highness."

"I would expect nothing less."

The click of boots started up once more. It was the sweetest sound Teia had ever heard, but she didn't dare raise her head. She stayed in her bow until Jura's voice had receded altogether, sucked away into the silence of the white rooms. When she finally righted herself, Teia was shaking uncontrollably. Sweat dotted the back of her neck. It trickled down her skin, cold enough to make her flinch.

Beside her, Tobias was motionless. And when she looked toward him, he met her gaze with eyes like heartbreak, like the world would collapse if they took another step. "He was right there," he whispered. "He was right there, and I let him go."

She wanted so desperately to allow him to grieve. Yet the hand of Teia's watch ticked on, catching them all in its wake. If Tobias didn't move, she suspected he never would again, and so she pulled at him forcefully, grabbing at his sleeve.

"Tobias," Teia said, his name falling from her lips. "We have to keep going."

He inhaled shakily. Some of the emptiness disappeared as he blinked hard, his gaze clearing. "I know," he said. "I'm here."

They moved faster through the white rooms, fueled by fresh

urgency. Teia would check on the left, Tobias on the right, updating the other as they went, bracing for disappointment with each response. Teia was beginning to despair as they entered the final hallway, which was far shorter than the others. What if Kyra and Enna hadn't located Alara either? Had the Poisons Master truly been kept in another section of the prison?

Then they reached the last room in the wing.

A girl lay inside, cuffed down to the central slab. Burn marks puckered along her left arm, creeping to her shoulder. Jagged blond hair hung over one ear, hacked through with a pair of scissors.

Unsteadily, Teia fit the master key into the lock.

A skylight had been built into the ceiling, and the moon cast a pallid glow down from its perch. Alara lay limp on the table, her eyes closed, her skin waxy. Bruises mottled her face. Her tunic had been torn down the side, the skin beneath wreathed in blue.

"Goddess," Tobias swore, as he unclasped the shackles around Alara's wrists. "Is that—"

Teia said nothing. The Carthan crest had been seared above the Poisons Master's heart, imprinted in horrifying detail. Blackened bits of flesh peeled away from the brand. The redness of an infection had set in, and pus bubbled at the edges.

Alara stirred. Her lashes fluttered slightly, her head drooping to the side. "Teia?"

A lump formed in Teia's throat. She smoothed back the remains of Alara's hair, rage kindling in her chest. "You didn't make this easy."

Alara made a painful sound, somewhere between a sob and a laugh. "I'll send a flare next time," she mumbled.

"There won't be a next time."

"I'll hold you to that."

There was a scuffling from the doorway. Teia started, already summoning a flame. She wasn't afraid anymore—not of the guards, not of Jura. She wanted to burn. She welcomed it. Her body thrummed in anticipation of a fight, ready to incinerate whoever came into the room.

Instead, two greenies rushed inside. The taller one hung back, keeping a respectful distance, but the shorter one went straight for the Poisons Master.

"Alara," Kyra gasped. She sank down, grasping for Alara's hand, squeezing it in hers. "You're all right."

"Funny definition," Alara creaked, her fingers tightening around Kyra's. The movement was small, but there was something so fiercely intimate that Teia looked away, heat licking up her cheeks. She stepped away from the pair, shuffling back toward the door, coming to a stop beside Enna.

The thief's eyes were fastened on the brand. "Jura?" she said flatly.

"Who else?"

She made a noise of disgust. "He practically led us here, you know. Kyra and I figured wherever he was coming from, it was worth looking into."

Teia adjusted her uniform, sliding a stray pin back into place. "We saw him, too," she said with a frown. "He was . . . happy."

"Seems out of character for the prick."

It was, and that was what worried her. Yet Teia couldn't afford to dwell on things here, so far from freedom. She inclined her head at the thief and fished the pocket watch out to examine it. "We don't have long until the Dead Run starts," she said quietly. "If you want the Star, this is your chance."

Enna glanced at Alara again. "Right," she said, after a brief pause. "Which way do I go?"

"Back down the hall. Take two turns to the right, and the walls should fade back to gray. Follow that path the entire way down—the entrance to the Vault should be at the end."

"Should be?"

It was as good a guess as any. Teia remembered how the walls had slanted inward as Pembrant guided her and Tobias through the gray corridor. She was no architect, but she had noted the tell-tale signs, the sloping ceilings that hinted they were approaching the tip of the prison's pentagonal structure. If they hadn't veered from that hallway—if the soldier hadn't gone mad—Teia suspected they would have arrived at the Vault.

"Yes," Teia said firmly. "If something goes wrong and you can't meet us at the stable—"

"There's a door built behind the Vault. I know."

"Just try to make it out alive. I don't want your death on my conscience."

"You still have one?"

"It resurfaces on occasion." Teia stowed away the watch. "You're prepared for the traps? The guards?"

"I'm insulted. You almost sound worried for me."

"Don't let it go to your head."

Enna patted her breast pocket securely. It was where the thief kept a pouch full of nasty tricks: smoke pellets, flash bombs, brass knuckles. She'd probably packed her favorite ice pick, too, for the sake of sentimentality. "I'll be fine. Save your prayers for someone who needs them."

"Then it's a good thing I don't pray."

A wry smile crossed Enna's face. She dipped into the sleeve of her greenie uniform and withdrew an intricate bracelet. Teia recognized it immediately as Enna set the band in Teia's open palm. She'd given it to the thief all those weeks back, when Teia first asked for information on Kyra. It had been the request that set off this chain reaction of events, the beginning of the end—Teia just hadn't known it yet.

"Just in case," Enna said. "Give my ma my love."

"Tell her yourself, when you have Erisia's crown jewel in your pocket."

It was as close to a goodbye as they could manage. Enna ducked into the hallway, her footsteps silent against stone, and Teia returned to the metal slab. She laid a tentative hand on Alara's shoulder, careful not to disrupt any injuries, but her next words were aimed at Kyra. "It's time."

The rebel girl's brow furrowed. "Where did Enna go?"

"She's running an errand." It wasn't a complete lie, considering Enna's usual routines. "You have the serum?"

Kyra obliged. She took out her pin box and rolled a single syringe from a scrap of cloth. The glass reflected dully against the light as she held it up for Alara to see. "This will help with the pain."

The Poisons Master hesitated. "Wait," she said. "Teeth. Between my back molars."

Tobias reacted first. He reached inside Alara's mouth to extract a transparent disc, no larger than a fingernail. His expression tightened as he studied the clear substance caught inside. Kyra looked horror-struck, but Teia blinked in confusion.

"What is it?"

"Suicide tablet," Alara managed. "Just in case."

"You had that on you?" Kyra said. "And you didn't use it?"

At this, the Poisons Master broke into a beatific smile. It was one the Goddess herself must have worn when she descended from the skies, taking in the lush fields and the sparkling streams, the animals that snuck through the grass and the people that still brimmed with hope.

"Why would I?" she said. "I knew you would come."

Tobias passed the tablet to Teia. He took the syringe from Kyra and injected it deftly into Alara's upper arm. Alara's eyes drooped. A sigh whistled through her lips as her hand went slack in Kyra's. She was asleep within a matter of seconds, a welcome respite from the pain.

Teia gestured to Tobias. "Can you carry her?" she said, and he nodded. He bent down, scooping Alara effortlessly into his arms.

And that was when the bells began to clang.

The sound screeched through the room, lancing through Teia's skull. *One, two, three, four. One, two, three, four.*

No, Teia thought wildly. *Not again.*

She turned—just as the cell door slammed shut before her.

CHAPTER THIRTY-ONE

◈━❖━◈

"**N**o!" Teia growled, hurling herself at the door. She jammed the key into the lock. She wrenched at the handle, saying a silent plea that it would give way.

Nothing. The door refused to budge.

"The greenies," Kyra groaned. "They must have gotten free."

Or Enna had been caught on her way to the Vault. Or Jura had come back to finish Alara off. Teia could think of any number of explanations for why a Red Alert had now overtaken the prison, none of which she cared to share, none of which were good.

Tobias set Alara down. He examined the glass window fixed to the door, before slicing forward with his knife. The blade all but bounced off, nearly taking out his eye.

"Bulletproof?" Teia said.

"That would have been nice to know."

"Would fire work?" Kyra suggested, touching the glass cut-out. A flame burned red under her palm, smoke rising into the air—but when she withdrew to check on her progress, the glass was as pristine as ever.

"Our flame isn't hot enough," Teia said. She, too, laid a hand against the glass. When nothing happened, she pulled away from the door, muttering a curse under her breath. The bells trilled on, piercing through her ears. Teia felt the edges of a headache setting in as she paced a frantic lap around the room.

There had to be some other means of escape.

There were no ducts, no windows. The only way out was the door, which was sealed from the outside and unbreakable from within. *They learned from last time,* Teia thought darkly. No doors had bolted shut before, but Blackgate had clearly improved its methods. This was the perfect cage, at least until someone came along to pepper them with bullets.

Frustration sank into her. She hadn't come this far only to fail, boxed in by the shriek of bells. *Come on,* Teia commanded herself. *Think.* She was no stranger to improvisation when a scheme went awry or a plan fell to pieces. There were close calls, of course. There always were. But whether she'd lied through her teeth or threatened someone with fire, Teia had emerged each time on the other side, scratched and bruised and marred with threats, but alive.

Always alive.

There was nobody to blackmail here, nothing to threaten. An airtight room. No ducts, no windows.

No windows except for one.

Teia's eyes went high above her. They stopped on the glittering skylight, where the moon was a pale sliver. It shone feebly through the glass, daring her to follow.

It was an impossible task. Even with the proper climbing equipment, the skylight was too far away. Teia could neither scale a vertical wall nor sprout a pair of wings, and the room was heartlessly bare, devoid of anything useful. There was nothing here but the metal slab, a sagging tin cart full of bloodied instruments, and the drain installed into the floor.

The drain.

Inspiration struck like a moving train. For the most part, the room's four white walls were constructed from the same marble that lined the halls outside. Every so often, though, the texture changed. She saw a section now where patches of the wall had been replaced with plaster, painted white to match the stone.

And beneath that, Teia could feel the carefree gurgle of water, running cheerfully through an array of metal pipes.

"Teia?"

She must have looked insane as she pawed through the tools on the metal cart. At long last she came across the drain cap, nestled under a grubby towel, and gestured to the others. "Kyra," Teia said. She thought back to when they first met, how the rebel champion had shied away from a puddle on the ground. "How do you feel about water?"

"Water?"

"Large quantities," Teia specified. "Like an ocean or a small lake."

"Neither sound very pleasant."

"And if it's a matter of life or death?"

"I would hope it was a strictly hypothetical scenario."

Teia locked the drain cap in place. "Just answer the question."

Kyra cringed. "I suppose I would manage," she said unhappily.

It was an encouraging enough response. The sound of bells had been permanently etched into Teia's ears. She fully expected a platoon of guards to burst into the room at any second, armed and at the ready.

"Can both of you swim?" Teia asked.

Tobias stared. "What?"

"Yes or no: Can you swim?"

"Yes," Tobias said.

"Not well," Kyra provided.

It would have to do. Teia narrowed her concentration as she imagined a skein of rope connecting her to the pipes. Working with a half-empty bucket was infinitely different from disturbing the plumbing network of Blackgate Prison, but she refused to let it matter. Teia was her mother's daughter. She was Shaylani, and the ocean was in her blood. She sensed the giddiness of water brewing within the pipes, coursing through the metal. It knew she was there. It frothed to join her. It sang about the adventures they could seek once they were united.

A creak emitted from inside the wall. Teia squeezed her eyes shut, digging her hands into plaster. *Come to me*, she thought. She was desperate for the comfort of water, for the moods of the waves and the darkness beneath.

Come to me.

Something cracked behind the plaster. By the door, Kyra blanched at the sound. "Teia—"

Then came the flood. Countless metal pipes exploded from the wall, spewing a waterfall into the room. Water burbled around Teia's feet to span the length of the floor. It explored the space it'd been given, the newfound freedom she had offered it, and Teia laughed as the iciness tickled her ankles.

Kyra, in comparison, was far less amused. "Your solution," she said forcefully, raising a dripping foot before her, "is to drown us?"

"Not drown," Teia said. "Float."

She pointed to the skylight, and Kyra's mouth dropped in disbelief. "All the way up there?"

"It's not *that* far."

"It's fifty feet up," Tobias said stoically.

"Yes," Teia agreed. "But once we reach the skylight, you break the glass with your knife and we're home free."

"What about your powers?"

"What about them?"

"Can you direct the water toward the skylight? Force it to crack?"

Teia shook her head. "There's too much to focus on. I'm best with small amounts."

Kyra glanced down. The room was filling astoundingly quickly, with the waterline now at their knees. Every drop in the building seemed to have heeded Teia's demands, ecstatic that she'd given her call. "I wouldn't say this is small."

"This might be somewhat unintentional."

Tobias coughed. "One more question," he said.

"What?"

"How do you know that the skylight isn't bulletproof?"

Teia didn't. It was all a gamble, like hatching a plan or taking a risk. Two sides of the same coin—victory on one, failure on the other. She didn't usually leave things up to chance, but she had no other choice. Her luck was gone, her fortune spent. All Teia had left was intuition. That, and the budget plan she'd once seen for Blackgate, where the amount surely wasn't enough to fit bulletproof glass over each door *and* skylight.

"I'm almost positive it isn't," she ventured, and Tobias groaned.

"*Almost* positive?" he repeated.

There was no going back, not anymore, not with the water well over their waists. Teia and Tobias supported Alara together, keeping her head above the surface. Kyra bobbed nearby with an injured expression, splashing against the current.

They were rising at an alarming pace, past the damaged chunks of plaster, the metal cart floating alongside them. Water gushed steadily under them, as more pipes broke to join the cacophony below. Suddenly, the distance to the skylight seemed much too close. They would have less time than Teia had anticipated before water shrouded them.

"Go!" she yelled to Tobias, shifting Alara's full weight onto her shoulder. She was treading with all her might, her legs pumping as Tobias withdrew his knife. He drove the blade up, metal piercing toward glass.

The window held.

Teia cursed. "Again!" she said. And Tobias thrust his knife up once more. This time, she spotted a minuscule crack running diagonally along the pane, expanding toward the corners.

Water had brought them this far—and yet it had distorted into their enemy, intent on forcing them under. The earlier playfulness had disappeared. What was left was a cruel sort of glee, a desire to claim another victim. Waves collided against Teia as she struggled to keep her hold on Alara. Kyra spat out a mouthful of water, her movements becoming less and less controlled.

Only a few inches remained between the lapping surface and the ceiling. There was an added resolve to the way Tobias raised his knife, an understanding that time had truly run out. Another crack formed, crisscrossing the second. It was progress. It was good.

It wasn't enough.

Teia fought to stay afloat. She could have sobbed aloud, but she no longer had the energy. Instead, she inhaled one final gulp of air before water blanketed over her, pushing her into a haze of blue.

How would Erisia react when they heard about her death?

No doubt Jura would flaunt this to every dignitary that entered the Golden Palace. They would learn how her body had been discovered in one of Blackgate's torture chambers, in the company of several Dawnbreakers. They would mark her as a traitor to her country and scrub her name from history.

Teia's mother had died in a cold room, with a physician bearing over her. Years later, her father had passed the same way, his heart fractured, his liver soiled. Compared to her parents, Teia thought this was a far better way to go.

It wasn't the worst thing to die among friends.

A current shifted to Teia's right. She was knocked to the side, buffeted into a wall. When she looked over again, there was Kyra, paddling her way to Tobias. The rebel girl stretched her arms above the waterline, where an inch of open air persisted. She pressed her palms flat against the skylight, and the window glowed a deep red.

Kyra jerked her head at Tobias.

He slammed the knife into the glass, making contact just as water overtook it. For a long second, there was nothing. A swirl of bubbles danced past them, eerily beautiful as they drifted by.

The sound of the window breaking reached Teia even underwater. Shards scattered outward violently, waves battering her from all sides. *Swim*, a voice inside her demanded, and so she did, kicking at the water, straining toward the opening. Her hand burst through the surface, then her head. Her ribs raked against something hard as she dragged herself onto the roof, one inch at a time, her arm fastened around Alara. Her breaths came out in cloudy puffs. The moon was the smallest slice of silver.

She managed to reach out, touching her face with a trembling hand. She saw the darkness of blood and the wetness of tears—but Teia Carthan could no longer tell which was which.

CHAPTER THIRTY-TWO

Teia didn't know how long she lay there. The world around her was muted, sound and color siphoning away. Fatigue washed over her, dampening the pain in her ribs. Teia let out a sigh. She lodged one arm beneath her to cushion her head, ready to sink into a deep sleep.

But when her fingers brushed against something cold and clammy, Teia's eyes flew open. *Alara,* she thought. The Poisons Master lay unmoving on her back, her arms outstretched, her legs tucked beneath her.

Panic shot through Teia. How long had they been submerged? How much water had the Poisons Master taken in? As she hauled herself into a sitting position, Teia placed her hands on Alara's chest. Water sloshed in the other girl's lungs. It protested mightily at her touch, refusing to leave easily.

Slowly, Teia coaxed each droplet out, forming a sphere that hovered in midair. When she had drawn out as much water as she could, Teia pressed down solidly. She started a pattern with the compressions, something she'd seen a sailor do once for a drowned man. One, two, three. One, two, three.

"Come on, Alara," Teia muttered. "We both know this is an idiotic place to die."

That must have done the trick. Alara doubled into a fit of coughing, water dribbling down her chin. She gulped in a mouthful of air, wheezing as she did. Her breathing became more measured, her heart resetting to a firm tempo.

Lovely, Teia thought. She fell back down with an immense sense of satisfaction, content with the knowledge that everything had been resolved. They had escaped. Alara was alive. There was nothing more she needed to do, save for take a gloriously long nap.

She was beginning to drift when someone latched on to her arm. "Teia?" a voice panted, firm and insistent and so incredibly annoying. "Teia—you have to get up."

"I do?" she mumbled.

"The alarm? Jura?"

Jura.

Teia forced her eyes back open, and the comfort of the roof fell away. Tobias and Kyra stood above her, both soaking wet and shivering from the chill. As Tobias crouched to pick Alara up, Kyra offered one hand to Teia, who took it without hesitation. She struggled to her feet, her boots crunching over remnants of the skylight. Bits of glass littered the rooftop, glistening like diamonds against the moonlight.

"The skylight," Teia said. She remembered Kyra's palms against the glass, right before the window blew apart. "You heated it?"

"Thermal fracturing."

"Excuse me?"

"Hot glass can crack after it's suddenly cooled." Kyra smiled. "I learned about it after my powers came in. I set most of my furniture on fire—and broke all my pitchers in the span of a day."

"Seems like a productive afternoon," Teia replied. She

rotated cautiously to her left, testing out her side. The skylight had shredded through any partially healed flesh, but she'd inspect the wound later. She would put herself on bed rest, maybe pressure a healer into stitching her back up. For now, they still needed to reach the lights of Bhanot, which gleamed beyond the black walls.

They began hobbling to the edge of the roof, where a rusted ladder had been secured against the wall. Teia risked a glance behind them. Blackgate was an endless extension of turrets and towers, which rose in odd spurts against the sky. The central guard tower had been erected in the middle of the five blocks. It was fitted with external platforms for sharpshooters and a separate ring of artillery. The guns were massive, imposing, each one as large as a wagon.

And as Teia watched, the ones on the far left adjusted position.

She gripped her side, clutching at the wound as she stumbled forward. "The guns," she choked out. "They're moving."

Kyra's expression was bleak. "Don't look," she commanded, even as the guns creaked behind them.

They'd reached the rickety metal ladder, which was a sorry excuse for a fire escape. Rust had eaten through several rungs, and bolts hung loose at the top, with the frame barely attached to the side of the building. When a strong gust of wind tumbled through the air, the entire ladder quaked precariously.

Tobias eyed the ladder with open apprehension. "That's a tragedy waiting to happen."

"So is staying here," Teia reminded him, as a spate of gunfire cracked through the night. She hurled herself onto the roof, swearing mightily. The control tower's guns clicked into place, repositioning themselves for a second round, and she threw a hand out at Tobias, who was still carrying Alara. "Go. Go!"

A second volley erupted through the air, just as Teia pulled herself onto the ladder. Kyra was already below her, and Teia felt the fire escape shudder with their combined weight. She clung to the rungs as the bullets pattered over her head. Her arms quivered, her wet clothes suctioned to her skin. She was colder than she had ever been, trembling with exertion, terrified of what she would find at the bottom.

The answer was absolute pandemonium.

Block C's courtyard was in disarray. The Red Alert had squashed any sense of order as bells boomed out from inside the building, echoing down from the central watchtower. Guards hurried about, shouting instructions and hoisting weapons high. Several directed their companions into the building, waving their arms frantically.

Teia joined Tobias and Kyra, who were observing the scene from the shadows. Kyra glanced back toward the prison, biting at her lip. "Teia," she said softly. "How will Enna make it out?"

With great difficulty, Teia thought. But there was the Vault's back door and the thief's trusty bag of tricks, as well as her unmatched ability to stay alive. Enna had once stolen the front wheels off a moving pram, so Teia wasn't ready to discount her just yet.

"She'll be fine," Teia said bracingly. "Do you have what I asked for?"

Kyra opened her hand in reply. There, resting in the center, was a small silver key. It would unlock any of the prison's outer gates, identical to the one Pembrant had carried.

This, among many other reasons, was why Teia had timed their entrance into Blackgate. Senior guards patrolled the halls every half hour. Each held a copy of the silver key, and Teia had instructed Enna to lift one, just in case of trouble.

The original plan had been to load Alara onto the cart, use the greenies' identification papers, and drive back out the way they came. She'd deduced the guards at the gate wouldn't look too closely anyway. What was the point, when they'd seen the greenies an hour before?

Except the Dead Run had been blown to hell, and Teia would have to rely on her contingency plan. She could see an outer gate ahead, less than forty feet away, where four guards stood tall on the other side of wrought iron. Storming the gate might not be the most graceful exit, but it would have to do in a pinch.

Tobias followed her gaze. "That one?" he said.

Teia nodded in confirmation.

"I don't suppose they'll just let us pass?" Kyra asked hopefully.

"Always a pacifist," Teia said. "You really are in the wrong business."

They slunk through the courtyard, using both the chaos and the shadows as cover. Thirty feet. Twenty. Teia could make out the Serkawr design on the back of the guards' uniforms when a thunderous shout arose from the block. It spiraled above the bells, cutting through the din. A door clapped shut from the building, accompanied by the thump of a rifle as it rammed against the ground.

Blackgate's guards snapped instantly to attention. Any ongoing havoc flattened into nothing, as the men moved as one. Their arms rose into salutes, their sabers stiff at their waists. The ones with revolvers replaced their guns, and the collective rustle of leather holsters rippled through the space.

Aside from the bells, the courtyard fell disconcertingly quiet. In spite of herself, Teia took a step back.

"Teia," Kyra whispered nervously. "I don't suppose you know what's happening?"

"Nothing good," Tobias replied.

A burly man had taken up residence on Block C's outer steps. His black uniform was immaculate, the unruly edges of his beard visible beneath the iron mask. It was Hadic, the commander who had escorted Jura through Blackgate, the one who'd seemed petrified of the crown prince.

It was a pity he no longer appeared afraid. Hadic radiated confidence as he studied the sea of guards, scanning each of his men thoroughly. His demeanor was relaxed, unhurried—the manner of a predator that had already trapped its prey.

When his eyes stopped on them, Teia knew it was over. They might be in the cover of darkness, but they were also soaked to the bone, completely bedraggled, and holding an unconscious prisoner. It would have taken a blind man to miss them in the crowd.

Hadic spun a pearl-handled revolver from his holster. He aimed it directly at Teia's head and lifted his voice to the other guards. "Those four," he announced. "They're Dawnbreakers."

"Shit," Kyra said.

Under any other circumstance, Teia would have been delighted to hear her curse. Except now was a definitively poor time, as four dozen guards swung to face them. Teia saw the shine of their weapons with renewed clarity, metal in the moonlight, polished blades begging for a target.

They would need a miracle to survive the onslaught.

Then came a peculiar hissing noise. A veil of smoke puffed up over the masses. It blanketed the courtyard, obscuring everything from sight. Shouts swelled from the guards. A gunshot fired into the night. Hadic's booming orders were muffled by the turmoil, as his men floundered to regain their bearings.

A hand wrapped around Teia's arm, dragging her unceremoniously to the ground. Smoke was thick around her, scratching at her every breath, but she could hear Kyra's voice in her ear, a guiding star against the madness. "Move!"

Teia did. She pulled herself forward on her elbows and knees, letting Kyra lead the way. When there was another yank on her arm, Teia rose to her feet. A clatter ahead was followed by the snap of a revolver. She lifted one hand to squint against the smoke, dumbfounded by the sight in front of her.

The gate had been opened, with the guards outside toppled onto the ground. Teia directed a dazed look at Kyra, but the rebel champion shook her head. "No time!" she snarled. "We need to go!"

They might have a head start, but they were no match for the guards that chased them. Teia ran as fast as she could, pain gnawing at her ribs, but the men behind her were gaining. She listened to the whiz of their guns firing, the murmur of blades being drawn. The smoke in the courtyard had bought them a few precious seconds, but their borrowed time was at its end.

Teia had imagined her death a thousand times, but never quite like this.

If she couldn't outrun the guards, she needed to fight while she still had the strength. She would go down swinging, wreaking as much havoc as she could. This wasn't something she could win, not by a long shot, but it was better than a slab in a white room.

Teia had started to turn when she saw the two horses, cantering gracefully from a nearby alley.

She lost her footing, stumbling against the cobblestone streets. *I've died*, Teia thought with absolute conviction, staring down the horses that had materialized before her. This was some final delusion from her dimming brain, or perhaps a spiritual encounter with the creatures who would guide her into the next life. She'd never heard of horses escorting a soul to Armina, but maybe another deity had laid claim to her instead.

But when she spotted the figure perched atop one of the horses, Teia knew death would have to wait. The stallion on the left had a rider—not Armina at all, but a girl with dark curls and crafty green eyes, dressed in the torn uniform of a Blackgate guard.

There, in all her glory, sat Enna van Apt.

Teia was moving before she even realized it. She hoisted herself onto the stallion while Tobias and Kyra mounted the other horse, Alara wedged safely between them. "You all look awful!" Enna shouted happily, spurring the stallion forward with a practiced movement.

Blackgate shrank from view. The guards behind them screamed their frustrations, firing off a fruitless round of bullets. They had dwindled to the size of toy soldiers, their weapons useless, their guns out of range.

Teia crumpled forward, her side on fire. Her ribs felt like they were tearing through her skin. "You stole a *horse*?"

"Two horses. I'm a *thief*. It's in the job description."

"And the Star?"

"Do you have to ask?"

She didn't. Enna's grin was wide enough to crack her jaw. It was as good a confirmation as any.

It was done. The Star was safe, away from Lehm's grasp, away from Jura's. Teia wanted to whoop in celebration. Instead, she settled for a clipped smile. She could envision Blackgate in the recesses of her mind, the guards they had outpaced, the plan that had inexplicably worked. A flash of pride surged inside her, giddiness cresting on a wave as her eyes slid shut.

"So much for impenetrable," Teia said, before she fainted dead away atop the chestnut stallion.

CHAPTER THIRTY-THREE

Teia woke in a cocoon of buttery sheets.

As she glanced around, the room nearly blinded her with its finery. The finishes here rivaled the Golden Palace, with everything tailored to the highest caliber of luxury. Sapphire-encrusted lamps, blue velvet headboards, pillows fluffed with goose feathers. A champagne flute stood on the ornate night-stand, and a bottle of imported bubbly nestled inside a bronze ice bucket.

"Kyra?"

The rebel girl was curled at the foot of Teia's bed. She stirred drowsily when she heard her name, sitting up with a yawn. "You're awake!"

"I'm not entirely certain I'm not dead."

"We weren't either, when Enna pulled you off the horse." Kyra drew her legs to her chest. "How do you feel? A healer patched you up, but there might still be some pain."

Her ribs were sore, but it was nothing compared to before. Teia waved away the question and propped herself up against one of the pillows. "How is Alara?"

"She was awake a few hours ago. Kept insisting she would poison the next person that tried to coddle her."

"Did the healers take that well?"

"No," Kyra said happily. "I think they're afraid of her."

Teia cocked her head. "And you?" she said lightly.

She'd expected Kyra to bat away the question, or perhaps blush another fascinating shade of red. But the rebel girl just slid her legs forward, gazing at Teia through ink-black lashes. Teia had never seen a look like that before: quiet, clear, and full of conviction. "She terrifies me," Kyra admitted. "But I wouldn't have it any other way."

She spoke so firmly, so unwaveringly, that Teia felt a quick stab of jealousy. What was it like to be so certain about another person? To see the tempest on the horizon, gray clouds gathering, and choose to weather it anyway?

Teia didn't know. She might never. The relationships in her life were fragile, delicate things. If she held one too close—if she brought it toward the light—it was a matter of time before something shattered.

She motioned to the grandeur around them, eager for a distraction. "Speaking of things that shock and terrify—did you strike gold? Uncover a lost family fortune?"

"Rob a bank?" Kyra supplied.

"Sounds like a typical morning for Enna."

"I know. She was telling me about some of her heists."

"And?"

"Something about impersonating a priest to steal an icon from a temple, and auctioning it off to the highest bidder afterward?" The rebel girl shook her head. "Either way, I need to go to confessional."

The image of Enna regaling Kyra with one of her stories, one leg planted on a chair, arms waving vigorously, made Teia laugh. "Is this how it feels to corrupt the great Kyra Medoh?" she asked.

"You don't have to seem so proud about it."

"Please. This is the highlight of my year."

"And living through two runs of Blackgate isn't?"

"You're right. I should start penning my memoir." Teia smoothed the quilt on her lap. Despite the comfort of the room, the mention of Blackgate sent a flutter up her spine. She thought of those last minutes in the prison, the commotion in the courtyard. "The smoke. Do you know what happened?"

The rebel girl's expression grew very smug. "I might," Kyra said, reaching into her pocket to bring forth a tiny silver sphere. Teia accepted it warily. She'd seen similar smoke pellets before, stocked throughout the Flats' crowded storefronts. This one was small enough to hide in the lining of a shoe, which would have made it far more expensive.

"Enna gave me a dozen when we were checking the cells," Kyra explained. "She said to use them in case of an emergency."

"She must have liked you."

"Why?"

"Enna doesn't give away anything for free. I don't think that word is in her vocabulary."

"Oh, it wasn't for free," Kyra assured her. "She made it clear I'd owe her interest. But considering we faced a block's worth of guards, I'm glad I took her terms."

Teia regarded her with wonder. "You opened the gate."

"I did," Kyra said modestly.

"And the guards outside?"

"Tobias."

"With his knife?"

"A revolver."

"Ah." She didn't need more of an explanation. Teia had

already seen the damage Tobias could do with his knife. She couldn't imagine the extent of destruction if he was given a gun.

Teia stretched toward the nightstand. She uncorked the champagne and filled the glass to its brim, passing it over to Kyra before holding up the bottle solemnly. "Does this mean I owe you my life now?"

"I'd say we're even." Kyra's grin was as bright as the sun. "What's a little blood between friends?"

"Spoken like a true rebel."

They tossed back their heads and drank, just as the door opened. Tobias swept inside. He wore a fresh set of clothes, his hair characteristically disheveled. "Isn't it a little early for that?" he asked, taking in the champagne with a smirk.

"It's a celebration," Kyra said defensively.

"I can tell." His eyes fell on Teia. "Hi," he said, and she hated that his smile split her heart wide open.

"Hi yourself," she responded.

He threw a look at Kyra. "Has she seen it yet?"

"I was waiting until you were ready."

Teia wasn't one for surprises, and yet another near-death experience had done nothing to change this. "Seen what?" she asked suspiciously. She wondered if there was a way to politely refuse whatever was coming.

Kyra grinned. "Can you stand?" she said.

"I think so."

"Good. We have something to show you."

The hallway was somehow more elaborate than the room. Red carpet lined the floors. Oil paintings of women on schooners and men with rifles decorated the corridor. The walls were covered with silver accents, creating a distinctly ethereal effect, and three words had been monogrammed infinitely across the wide center ribbon.

The Absinth Hotel.

Teia had been kidding when she asked if they'd struck gold. Now, she wasn't so sure, especially with what she knew about the hotel. The Absinth was renowned for its opulence, where any sin could be forgiven for the right price. Booking a reservation was akin to a blood sport, although that hadn't discouraged people from trying. It was said the Absinth's lobby was perpetually crammed with tourists, men and women who sipped on drinks, glaring at guests lucky enough to snag a room.

She lowered her voice into a hiss. "You do realize we're in the most famous hotel in Bhanot?"

"I know," Kyra chirped, blissfully unaware of Teia's dismay. "It's really something, isn't it?"

Easy for her to say. Kyra's wanted poster might not capture her likeness, but Shaylani were a rare sight in Erisia. Teia would be made in minutes, identified by one of the servants who roamed the halls, taken back to Blackgate or spirited away to the palace.

"Of course," Teia said brusquely. "I'll be sure to remember how the chandelier sparkles when we're hauled away in chains."

The rebel girl smiled mischievously. "What if I told you we're among friends?"

"In the Absinth?"

"Yes."

"I'd tell you money has a funny way of winning people over."

"Most people," Kyra said. "But not all."

They had slowed before a door, indistinguishable from all the others. The room number was plated in gold. The handle was shaped like the letter *a*, and Tobias wrenched at the tail, which curved upward in a flourish. He must have pressed a hidden button, because a gentle *click* sounded through the hall.

"You first," he said to Teia, holding the door aside.

The blinds were down, the lanterns unlit. Teia's vision dimmed as she stepped cautiously over the threshold, blinking rapidly against the darkness. Furniture hunched in one section of the room, tables and chairs stacked atop each other. In the back, away from the covered windows, a second door cut against the mahogany panels.

Teia picked her way toward the strip of light filtering through the door's bottom crack. And when she turned the knob, pushing the door back, she found herself in the most beautiful place she'd ever seen.

High ceilings stretched overhead, intersected by wooden beams that framed the cavernous space. Metal staircases spiraled from different entrances toward the floors below, with lamps illuminating everything in a gauzy glow. People bustled about, shuffling through files, comparing sheets of paper. A vivacious energy crackled in the air, the sensation of being on the cusp of greatness.

Teia's eyes widened. "Is this . . ."

She didn't want to finish the sentence, afraid of breaking some spell, but she thought Kyra understood. The rebel girl laughed, one hand extended in a flourish.

"Teia Carthan," she said, "welcome to the Dawnbreakers' base."

CHAPTER THIRTY-FOUR

Teia drank in the sight before her. She stood speechless at the top of the banister, her hands trembling around the metal, her legs weak beneath her.

Tobias smiled. "Good," he said to Kyra. "I think she likes it."

The rebels led her down the winding staircase to a set of plush chairs positioned near the bottom. Teia hardly noticed. She was still marveling at each exquisite detail—the space they were in was as large as the palace's main banquet hall. "How did you manage to hide all of this?"

"With great difficulty," Tobias answered.

Kyra nestled into one of the seats. "Lehm owns the Absinth under a false name," she said. "It's an easy way to explain away the flow of people."

"Do guests actually stay here?" Teia asked.

"Where do you think the guilds for this"—Kyra gestured to the base—"come from? There's no shortage of rich men in Bhanot."

"Thank the Goddess," someone drawled from behind them, "because that means there's no shortage of pockets to pick."

Of all the revelations so far, this was the least unexpected.

Teia wasn't at all shocked to see Enna van Apt sauntering up to them. The thief dropped sideways into the seat opposite Kyra. She propped her feet on the armrest, crossing her legs at the ankles, and bestowed a roguish grin onto Teia. "Took you long enough to wake up."

"Let me guess—you've been a Dawnbreaker since the beginning."

"Don't be ridiculous," Enna said with a shudder. "I'd have to work on a volunteer basis. *Without pay.*"

"I know what volunteering means."

"Then you're aware I don't even speak to people without charging for my time. But after you paired me with Kyra in Blackgate, I got a fantastically long lecture about the merits of joining a just movement—"

"It wasn't a lecture," Kyra grumbled.

"It was most definitely a lecture," Enna said, "and you would fit right in with the merchants in the Financial District. I've never heard anyone sell their cause with such passion."

"It worked, didn't it?"

"Sure. Enough to make me realize that I needed to come back for your sorry hides or I wouldn't get my full payment. Good thing I did, too, since you were almost carted away in body bags."

"What an inspiring visual," Tobias said.

Teia lifted a brow at Enna. "So how did you end up here?"

"Your friends contacted Lehm. Your Poisons Master needed medical attention, and he agreed coming here was the best course of action."

"And you were allowed to stroll right in?" Teia thought it over-whelmingly unfair that she had spent the past weeks in limbo, while Enna had all but skipped into the rebellion's headquarters.

"Lehm has wanted to recruit me for ages." Enna thumped herself on the chest vigorously. "Best thief in Erisia, remember? I would be a tremendous asset."

Kyra nodded. "You would be," she said eagerly. "Imagine the impact you could have on the Dawnbreakers—on Erisia."

"I'll think about it," the thief said back, in a tone that heavily implied otherwise.

"Would another lecture help?"

"It most certainly would *not*."

"I wouldn't speak so soon," another voice chimed out. It was sweet and lyrical, honey dissolving into a teacup. "When she wants to be, Kyra Medoh can be extremely persuasive."

Teia whirled around. Alara stood several paces away, a smile on her face, one arm caught in a sling. Her trusty leather belt was once again slung over her hips, although far fewer bottles remained. Her blond hair was cropped short, stopping just below the nape of her neck.

"Utter betrayal," she said cheerfully. "You know I love a good party."

That was as far as she got before Teia pulled her into a hug. Then Kyra and Tobias were there as well, embracing Alara fiercely, asking how she was. Everyone spoke over one another, their voices clashing together, their sentences melding into one. It was only when the Poisons Master held up a hand, her laughter rippling out, that some semblance of calm returned.

"To answer any burning questions," Alara said, adjusting the sling over her arm. "Yes, I'm fine. No, nothing hurts. And yes, when I see Jura Carthan again, I will be force-feeding him my most painful poison."

"You'll have to get in line," Kyra said.

"That's fine. As long as I get my turn."

There was a strangled cough from the chairs. Enna walked forward, shrinking before Alara's presence as she offered a timid wave. "Enna van Apt," she said. "We haven't formally met, but I'm a big fan."

"You are?" Teia said.

"Huge, actually," Enna amended, blinking shyly at Alara. "You're something of a celebrity in the Flats."

Alara beamed. "You know my work?"

"The sellswords study your methods. They're thinking about transitioning to poisons."

"Really?" said Alara, looking ecstatic.

"Really?" Tobias repeated dubiously.

"It's genius," Enna gushed. "*You're* genius. I have a few ideas for new poisons, too, if you have a minute . . ."

They began chattering about chemical compounds and potential use cases, jabbering so fast their words became indistinguishable. It appeared all those stakeouts in Bhanot University's classrooms really *had* paid off for Enna. The thief seemed ready to break out her best pen and ask Alara for her signature.

Kyra prodded at Teia's shoulder. "Look," the rebel champion said happily. "They're bonding."

"More than that. Do you think Enna will explode from pure joy?"

"Alara would be flattered. She'd find a way to work it into every conversation."

"Understatement of the century," Tobias put in. "She would probably have it inked on her forehead."

Alara and Enna were still speaking, oblivious to the conversation around them. Tobias and Kyra debated the limits of Alara's ego. And as Teia looked at the people before her—the

Poisons Master, the thief, the champion, the rebel—something tugged at her heart. An invisible string, a weeping warmth. A sensation she'd never experienced before, even when her parents were alive.

This felt like she had finally come home.

Chapter Thirty-Five

After the conversations had slowed—Enna did not, in fact, ask for an autograph—Kyra insisted on providing a tour of the base. "There's a spa in here," she gushed. "A *spa*. With *attendants*."

Enna rubbed her hands together. "If this is your new recruitment pitch, you're doing an excellent job."

They followed Kyra, Alara, and Tobias through the meandering halls of the base. Each room was a wonder of glass and wood and metal, astoundingly captivating despite the lack of windows. The furniture had been selected with a curator's eye, and expensive art pieces graced the walls. Lehm had managed to squeeze an entire world within the false walls of the Absinth, one that brimmed with purpose and life.

Teia couldn't hold back her questions. "What's that?" she said, pointing at an engraved double door.

"The library."

"And that?"

"Lehm's study."

"What about that?"

"Alara's lab."

Another corridor later, they had arrived at the mess hall. It rivaled the palace's mighty sprawl of kitchens in size, filled with rebels and ringing with the cheerful clatter of cookware. An impressive line snaked toward the counter. Workers distributed heaping trays of food, and a great wooden clock kept track of time, its hands shaped like spoons.

Enna's eyes lit up. "I'm ready to chew off my own arm," she declared. She was halfway to the line when Kyra snatched her wrist.

"Try not to steal anything while you're there."

"You're kidding, right? I'm a thief. It's what I do."

"Some thieves pay."

"Not the good ones."

Kyra shot Enna a hair-raising look. The thief groaned pitifully and slouched back to the rebel girl. "All right," she griped. "Can I take out a loan?"

Kyra provided a fistful of guilds, which Enna stared at with obvious reluctance. Teia could tell she was debating what to do next—refuse the coins, make a scene in front of Alara—before deference won out. Enna sighed, closing a mournful hand around the guilds.

"I'll go with you," Teia said.

"Hungry?" Enna asked.

"Entertained. You look like you're going to stab someone with a fork."

The line moved at a glacial pace. Twenty minutes had crawled by before Enna deposited the coins—"People do this *every day*?"—to receive her cornbread. She nibbled at it halfheartedly, making a face as she tasted the crust.

"Satisfied?" Teia said.

"Marginally so," Enna answered.

They trekked back to where the others had gathered, close to two pillars made of swirling gray marble. As she and Enna neared the group, Teia's pace slowed. From a distance, she recognized the coiffed silver hair, the sweeping greatcoat.

A few steps later, Cornelius Lehm had come into full view. "Halfling," he said in greeting. "Enna."

"Lehm," Enna acknowledged. It was evident from the thief's voice that there was no love lost between the two of them. Teia wondered what had happened during those failed attempts at recruitment. What had Lehm tried to entice her with?

"You returned my Poisons Master to me."

"It was a team effort."

"I can see that." His gaze jumped to Teia. "I assume the break-in was your idea?"

"You assume correct."

"After I specified we would accept the crown prince's deal?"

"Good thing I'm not a Dawnbreaker. You've made that abundantly clear."

Lehm's lip curled. "You haven't earned your stripes, girl. I'm not running a charity."

Teia bit back a retort, something about not having the sufficient kindness needed to do so. "I suppose I have many, many years ahead to prove myself."

His eyes seared into hers. Teia had the disconcerting notion that he was privy to every last one of her thoughts, her discoveries, her notions for the future. *It doesn't matter,* she told herself firmly. The Star was safe in Enna's possession. If Lehm had dreamed of commanding the oceans, all his ambitions had been ground to dust in Blackgate.

Lehm broke his stare first. "I suppose you do," he said at last. With that, he swung his attention back toward the others, his expression frosty. "Rennert. I need you for a briefing."

"Now?" Tobias said.

"Yes. Now." Lehm nodded briskly at Enna and Teia. "By all means—enjoy the base."

Enna hesitated. She extended a stiff hand in Lehm's direction, an act that seemed to pain her. "It was good to see you again."

His knuckles cracked white as he folded his hand over hers. "Likewise," Lehm said. Then he was gone, parting the crowd as he went, leaving a trail of admiring whispers in his wake.

"Well," Kyra said brightly, "that went well."

"I believe the appropriate thing to say," Alara said, "is that it could have gone worse."

"Seems like morale is high around here," Enna piped in. She might have said something slightly more damning, if an odd look hadn't muddied her features. Her left hand flew to her stomach, her right still clutching the cornbread. "Goddess. I feel terrible."

Teia winced. "Now that you mention it, I've had better days."

Alara eyed the cornbread. "Oh," she said. "That might be a problem."

"You didn't poison us, did you?"

"It certainly feels like it," Enna grunted.

"I didn't," Alara said, sounding alarmed. "But we might have forgotten to mention—"

"The food here is notoriously bad," Kyra finished. "Though it seems to be affecting you worse than most. Maybe you're just not used to it?"

There was a beat of stunned silence. "You're telling us *now*?" Enna yelped, at the same time Teia said, "You have a *spa*."

Alara shrugged helplessly. "It's hard to find chefs who want to join the cause."

"But you managed to recruit a tailor?" Teia said.

"I," Kyra said haughtily, "am an anomaly."

Enna shook her head impatiently. She had sagged down to

her knees, supporting herself against the pillar. "Washroom," she croaked, and Alara hurriedly pointed out directions.

Enna and Teia set off in a furious sprint, doubling back through the mess hall to skirt around the corner. A room stood empty to the right, and the thief beckoned Teia inside, latching the door firmly behind them. After Teia sent heat into a nearby lantern, they discovered they'd found refuge inside a meeting room, fully stocked with butcher's paper and fountain pens, a paradise for any wandering scholar.

Enna fell into the nearest chair. She dropped her head to the table with an anguished sigh, all traces of the stomachache melting away. "That," she moaned, "was the most humiliating moment of my life."

"I wouldn't say that," Teia said, as she sat on the edge of the table. "You have a real future in theater."

"I pretended to have the runs in front of my idol."

"Alara?"

"Who else?"

"Do you also sleep with her picture under your pillow?"

Enna scowled. "Is this the thanks I get?" the thief said. She held her fist high, where something small and silver glimmered tauntingly. It was Lehm's pendant—the one with the semicircle charm. The one he always wore.

The one Teia would use to break into his study.

She had seen the door to Lehm's office during the tour. It was hardly remarkable at first glance: embellished with a lion's head knocker, outlined in gold leaf. There had been no lock. Instead, a small metal panel was attached to the center of the door. A distinct half-circle shape was indented in the middle, stamped an inch into solid silver.

Teia knew on sight where she'd seen its match.

But when she'd outlined her plan to Enna, the thief was assuredly unimpressed. "Let me get this straight," Enna had said, as they trudged forward in the mess hall line. "You want me to rob Cornelius Lehm—in the Dawnbreakers' own base—due to a *feeling*?"

"Not a feeling. A hunch."

"That's the same thing."

"It isn't. You weren't there when he floated the prisoner exchange, Enna. Not to mention how badly he wanted the Star."

"Except the exchange doesn't matter anymore, and I wouldn't give Lehm a handkerchief, much less the Morning Star. What's the purpose of snooping around his study?"

Teia lowered her voice. It was the enduring question that remained, refusing to allow her rest. "He had Jura's *ring*, Enna. He wears it around his neck, under his tunic."

"He must have hired a good thief."

"So why not show it off? Flaunt it on his finger?"

"Nerves? Anxiety? The fear that yours truly might try to rob him?"

Teia clenched her jaw. "Come on," she said. "Don't tell me there's not something strange about him."

"I'm not saying I disagree," Enna admitted. "Why do you think I turned down his offers to join the Dawnbreakers?"

"Because you like money?"

"Because I have basic critical thinking skills. That man is a viper in a pit. He'll bleed you dry and smile over your corpse."

"Isn't that all the more reason to lift his pendant?"

"No," the thief retorted. "Because just about everyone I know—including you, Teia Carthan—would likely do the same. Being a viper doesn't make Lehm special. It makes him dangerous. And I already have an extensive list of people who would like my head on a stick."

Teia's patience was fast unraveling. She needed that pendant—and while she might not have Kyra's powers for persuasion or Alara's ability to make friends, what she did possess was the common language of crooks and con men and, yes, thieves. The flow of guilds had cemented her relationship with Enna for years. Why should this be any different?

Teia released a breath. "How much?" she said.

"Excuse me?"

"How much for stealing me the pendant and buying me some time?"

"Goddess. You're serious?"

"Whatever your price, I'm willing to pay."

The thief grew quiet. They'd almost reached the counter—where stacks of cornbread had been piled onto tin trays—when Enna spoke up. "Fine. If it really means that much to you, I'll do this one for free."

"You will?"

"You want me to change my mind?"

"No."

"Then shut up and accept my generosity." Enna scrubbed her palm over her face. "Goddess," she muttered. "We're going to be thrown from the top floor of the Absinth."

But they hadn't been—at least not yet. Running into Lehm had been a stroke of luck, which the thief had taken full advantage of. Enna had swiped the pendant from Lehm's neck as she'd shaken his hand, moving so fast that Teia hadn't seen a thing.

Now, Enna bobbed her head at Teia. "I can buy you ten minutes."

"What do you plan on doing?"

"Trip an alarm. Or potentially commit some casual arson. I haven't decided yet."

"What a diverse range of options."

"You're making me blush." Enna held up her fingers. "Ten minutes," she said again. "I hope you find what you're looking for."

Teia did too.

A staircase and a half later, Teia was positioned before Lehm's study, looking up at the lion's head knocker. She slipped the pendant from her pocket, the metallic chain digging into her skin—and she hesitated.

Was it recklessness that brought her here? Determination? Was this a byproduct of her time in the palace passageways, learning secrets and gathering information?

Perhaps it was as simple as instinct, honed within Teia throughout the years. She didn't know what she hoped to find, aside from a solution to the missing pieces, fragments that didn't align when placed alongside one another. Mysteries that Teia wanted the chance to untangle. An opportunity that came once in a lifetime.

Power is currency, Teia.

She surged forward, fitting the pendant against the door's central panel.

CHAPTER THIRTY-SIX

The door cleaved apart, the two sections fanning open toward her. Teia stole inside, her heart pounding, her mouth dry. What if Lehm had sentries lying in wait? What if he'd rigged another security system?

She needn't have worried. The room was quiet. No guards, no alarms. The study itself was gorgeous, decorated in a similar style to the rest of the base, paneled with mahogany planks. There wasn't a single item out of place—not a loose file on the couch or a pen that had been left out. The tassels on the rug had been carefully combed straight, the books on the shelf arranged by color.

Lehm's desk was positioned near the wall. It was an imposing thing, hewn from a block of granite, ornamented in geometric designs. The surface was more polished than any mirror, but it was the framed picture in one corner—sandwiched behind two cuts of crystal—that caught Teia's eye. She assessed the sketch of the young woman, who had the sultry elegance of a performer. She looked vaguely Shaylani, with coffee-colored eyes that curved at the edges.

Was this Lehm's sister, the one killed in the Bhanot Uprising? There wasn't any immediate resemblance, but Teia committed the face to memory anyway. If she did a passable job describing the woman to Enna, the thief might be able to chase the lead through her contacts.

She turned her focus to the drawers and began rifling through each one meticulously. The compartments were crammed to the brim, as messy as the room was clean. Teia dug through a mountain of crumpled reports, wood shavings, cigars, rusted brooches, and inexplicably, a scattering of wrappers. Apparently Lehm had a fondness for toffee candies. Who would have thought?

Teia swatted at the detritus. She was exasperated, ready to move on. And that was when her fingers rustled against the silkiness of fabric.

She grimaced as she brought forth a wad of bloody clothes. They had been buried in the back of the drawer, hidden beneath a stack of blank notebooks, and Teia held them tentatively to the light. Was it a souvenir from someone Lehm had killed? A token from a hard-earned victory? She hadn't taken the old man to be sentimental, but she thought anything was possible.

Then Teia saw the pattern of snowflakes stitched along the front. The clothes weren't a uniform at all, but a child's dress, smocked in the latest fashion. It was so bloody that Teia couldn't distinguish the fabric's original color, the lace collar mangled by knife marks.

Shock tore through her like lightning. Teia's mind flew back to Blackgate, past the cells and white rooms to swerve into an isolated gray hallway. Johns Pembrant had pressed his revolver to Tobias's chin. He had threatened to pull the trigger, caught in the throes of madness, shaken by an unexplainable vision.

I thought I could trust you. You gave me your word.

Teia's pulse quickened. She shoved the dress back and slammed the drawer shut. The bloodstains couldn't be recent.

Wynter was alive and well. Teia had seen to the girl's safe return herself, while the bill from the Imperial Hotel spanned the length of her room.

But Johns Pembrant hadn't known that.

She'd assumed he'd gone mad, driven insane by the pressure of the heist, his mind fractured when Teia killed the guard in the white room. There was nothing she could have done, no way to have saved him. Pembrant's delusions had overtaken his senses, and that was the end of that.

Except the bloody dress told a different story. Pembrant hadn't snapped. Far from it. Rather, he'd seen clothes that he'd taken for his daughter's, which had solidified his worst fears about the Halfling Princess. It had laid bare a desire for vengeance, setting Pembrant onto a doomed path.

And Cornelius Lehm had been the one to do it.

But why? Teia's head spun as she raked through his stack of files. Hadn't Lehm been adamant about getting the Star? Why would the rebel leader have betrayed them? Their trip to Blackgate would have been Lehm's best chance at receiving the jewel and accomplishing whatever foul thing he intended to do with it.

The rest of the desk yielded nothing. Teia stood hastily, walking around the study, lifting the rug to check beneath. She could feel the seconds bearing down on her, an unseen clock that ticked relentlessly onward. It was hard to say how much time had passed. Three minutes? Four?

Inspiration blazed through her. Teia spun on her heel and settled into Lehm's chair. She bent toward the wall, searching for a telltale indent, a crevice in the shape of the pendant.

There it was. As she placed the pendant against the indentation, a section of the wall sprang open. The space behind it had been converted into a safe, and a handful of items sat inside. Teia saw a single slip of paper, along with three maps, folded into squares.

She reached for the scrap with a sharp sense of dread. The message she read had been written in black ink, the script thin and spindly. It was nothing extraordinary—a note scrawled as an afterthought—but each word sent a tremor through her.

A token of things to come.

What had Teia wanted to find, when she first came here? Answers to her questions, a way to root out any lingering concerns. Lehm might wear Jura's ring, but there were a thousand explanations for how it had come into his possession. A hired thief. A backroom auction.

But as Teia stared at the note before her, she felt the world tremble. This was unmistakably Jura's handwriting. She had seen the contracts he'd signed, the decrees he'd drawn up. She was well aware of the curl of his *t*'s, the slight slant of each letter.

Jura Carthan—the Golden Prince, the future King of Erisia—was working with the Dawnbreakers.

Teia's brain revolted. This didn't make sense. None of this did. When she'd first seen Lehm with the ring, she had considered the thought for the barest second, before dismissing the idea altogether. Jura hated the Dawnbreakers. He killed them with an inhumane brutality; he would do whatever it took to rid Erisia of them. Lehm alone had a price on his head that would decimate the country's treasury.

What would have possibly prompted them to work together?

She moved automatically, seizing a map next. Teia unfurled a blueprint of Blackgate, with each of the gates painstakingly marked out. There was one in particular that caught her eye, near the edge of the page. It had been circled in red, with a line of text scribbled in Jura's handwriting.

Military will be stationed at the East Gate.

Goddess. When Teia had first revealed how she would steal the Star, Lehm had insisted on the East Gate. He'd peddled her a strategic reason at the time. She'd accepted it stonily, writing it off as nothing important, but the map before Teia implied something else entirely.

Lehm had known the military would be at the East Gate—and he'd done all he could to steer them there anyway. They would have been arrested, placed in cells or taken to the white rooms. Lehm would have lost his Poisons Master, his best fighter, and his champion in one fell swoop. The rebellion would have been thoroughly gutted by the loss, if not permanently crippled.

Except wasn't that the inevitable result of the prisoner exchange as well? It was the same outcome, just packaged into a different form. Alara and Tobias would have likely been killed in the crossfire, along with a good chunk of any accompanying Dawnbreakers. Kyra would have been spared, but that was because Teia had been charged with protecting her. *I have every confidence you'll think of something,* Lehm had said.

It had been a wholly ridiculous notion. Even if Teia could redirect the trajectory of a bullet, she and Kyra would have been stuck behind the Crown's line. Kyra would be a prisoner and Teia unmasked as a traitor. Their chances for escape would be as slim as they came.

Maybe that was exactly what Lehm wanted.

The faintest trace of an idea swam through Teia's mind. It was a ghastly thought, a scenario that created a chasm in her stomach. When she opened the other maps slowly, she found

herself grateful that she was already sitting down, positive her
legs would have given way beneath her.

The second drawing was of Fairweather Banks, with the unmistakable remnants of the drowned mansions. This, too, was
paired with Jura's untidy scrawl. He'd circled several spots on the
paper—points where Lehm had wanted to position the sharpshooters, when he'd laid out his plan in the safe house.

*Exchange details understood. My men can take out your
snipers.*

The final map was the largest. It reached corner to corner on
Lehm's enormous desk, as Teia stood on the chair for a better
view. There were the towers that marked Bhanot and the mountains of the Highlands. Quarries dotted the coast and forests extended along the southern shoreline, but there was more on the
map, too, which expanded beyond Erisia. Each of the other kingdoms had been represented. Shaylan's soaring peaks. K'val's lush
fields. And between that, dividing the Five Kingdoms, stretching
like blots of ink—the wide expanse of the Dark Sea.

Teia didn't need Jura's notes anymore, but she saw them
anyway. His writing was tucked to the side, jotted over Ismet's
swaths of deserts.

The sea beast first, the kingdoms tomorrow.

Teia could finally see the full picture, and she didn't like it
one bit.

If she had to guess, it was Jura who had approached
Cornelius Lehm. He'd delivered the ring as a show of good faith;
she couldn't remember him wearing it after the Autumn Ball.
After that, his actions spoke for themselves. He brought Lehm
pages from *Legends of the Serkawr* as further proof of the Star's
power. He had betrothed Teia to Abbott to keep her—and her
abilities—close.

Necessity drove decisions. Pride could be set aside for a common goal. Maybe the two had no option but to work together, if both noble's water and commoner's flame were needed to raise the sea beast. Jura had access to the Star—to Teia—but not Kyra. And while Lehm might create an elaborate ruse to tap into Teia's and Kyra's powers, he had no means of retrieving the Star.

It was a tactically brilliant decision, a way for Jura and Lehm to get access to what each of them lacked.

Lehm hadn't believed in Teia's ability to steal the gem at all. The infiltration of Blackgate had been orchestrated to start and end at the East Gate, where the military lay in wait. And if that didn't work, the rebel leader had ensured Johns Pembrant was a contingency, a way to derail the heist and hand them over to the guards. All too similar was the prisoner swap—an intentional tactical blunder, a plan designed to isolate Teia and Kyra.

Over and over, time and time again, Lehm and Jura had devised their schemes to snare the two together. They'd found ways to concoct Teia's and Kyra's arrests, to secure them in the palace.

To force them to summon the Serkawr.

Goddess, Teia thought, as a sick feeling flooded through her. *They're going to carve up the Five Kingdoms.*

She reread the notes, digesting each word, searching the maps for more clues. For all the cordiality, Teia was certain the rebel leader and the crown prince had a tenuous alliance. This was all smoke and mirrors, a false promise that both were aware of. Lehm and Jura would shake hands and break bread, up until the Serkawr had risen. Then the two would sever whatever ties they'd had, leveraging resources to dive into civil war.

After all, this was everything Jura had ever wanted: power to spare, the kingdoms groveling at his feet. *But what about Lehm?* Teia thought, as she leaned her head back. What happened to his hopes of a bright democracy, where he carried out his sister's dreams? Was her death in the Bhanot Uprising just a stray piece of gossip?

Teia didn't know. Maybe Lehm's sister had been the catalyst for his grand revolution, but the lure of power became too much. With the Serkawr by his side, Lehm could remake the kingdoms to his will. He could sculpt a new version of a better world, refashioned to fit his own image. He could fulfill what his sister had wanted.

Teia shut her eyes. A visceral pain had split into her chest, picking apart each nerve. It was a knife to the heart, a dagger through the ribs. Family legacy. Wasn't that what things always came back to? The path she'd chosen, the one she'd forged from fire and ash. Everything had changed in the quiet of Lehm's study, but what she needed to do hadn't.

Teia had known since the second she ached for the throne. She had thought there might be another option, to have her cake and eat it too, to hold the Dawnbreakers close while wearing a crown. Somewhere along the way, she had managed to convince herself it was possible. People could be reasoned with. Movements could change.

It was a wonderful lie. A happy one. And yet the truth had come knocking, more persistent than ever, and it refused to be denied. Here, sitting in Lehm's study, the remnants of his plan strewn around her, Teia was reminded of what was to come.

Her future was calling, and it would not wait a moment longer.

CHAPTER THIRTY-SEVEN

When Teia arrived back at the meeting room, Enna was waiting inside, doodling coins on a sheet of butcher's paper. "Well?" the thief prompted.

"Well what?"

"Did you find what you were searching for?"

"Yes."

"Really? You don't sound too pleased."

"I never am."

"You aren't wrong," Enna said amicably, which did nothing to improve Teia's mood.

The thief pranced off, Lehm's pendant cupped inside her hand. She was back minutes later, shaking her head in disgust. "He'd just left his briefing. It was like returning candy to a very ugly baby."

They navigated back to the mess hall, where Alara and Kyra had claimed one of the great oak tables. Teia was racking her brains for an adequate excuse to leave the base when the Poisons Master raised her good arm. She brandished the largest bottle of champagne Teia had ever seen, holding it aloft with the magnificence of a sword.

"We," Alara proclaimed, "are having a toast."

"In the mess hall?" Teia said.

"Say that again, and I'll poison your afternoon tea. Do I seem like the kind of heathen to have a toast in the mess hall?"

"No," Teia said doubtfully.

"Absolutely not," Enna trilled.

"I've seen the way you drink," Kyra said slyly, "and I wouldn't be so quick to throw stones."

"Shut up," Alara said to Kyra, affection shining through each word. She inclined her head at Teia with a smirk and jabbed the bottle in her direction. "I blame you for this. Now that you've taught Kyra sarcasm, there's no going back."

"My influence is extraordinary," Teia said.

"Who said I was being sarcastic?" Kyra protested.

Alara led them away from the commotion of the mess hall. They advanced up another spiral staircase before stopping in front of a door. Teia recognized the metallic sheen, the engraved handle. It was a location they'd passed on the tour of the base, although they hadn't ventured inside.

Alara shoved the door open to reveal a wide rectangular space. Planters cluttered the length of the room, with lanterns strung above them. Overflowing cabinets decorated the walls. Test tubes sat in wooden holders, lining the metal countertops. They were filled with an array of mysterious liquids, some of which bubbled ominously when Alara illuminated the lanterns.

The Poisons Master bowed. "Welcome to my workspace," she said.

"It's *amazing*," Enna cooed.

"It's smaller than I thought," Teia said.

"You try manufacturing a toxic garden in the heart of Bhanot," Alara replied. "I had to create makeshift sunlight, Teia.

Makeshift sunlight. The Minister of Agriculture couldn't do better."

This wasn't a traditional garden, not by any stretch of the imagination, but there was something strange and fantastic about what the Poisons Master had cultivated. The stems here grew greener than normal, each petal alight in a cascade of color. Teia could sense the love and care that went into each planter; it held the same touch of a girl from years before, who had awaited her brother's return and tended to his garden.

Her eyes fell on a snowy flower tipped in light blue. "I wouldn't touch that," Alara warned, but Teia had already crouched near the clay pot, poking the petals with a stray fountain pen.

"*Flora teian,*" she said, as she bit back a rueful laugh. Of course Alara would manage to grow this flower here, far from the rolling fields and muddy banks of Set.

"You know it?"

"My namesake." Teia set the pen aside. "What do you use it for?"

Alara looked somewhat sheepish. "It kills when ingested," she said. "It's the source for the suicide tablets."

Convenient. "Glad to be of service," Teia said, and the Poisons Master flashed an apologetic smile.

"Alara?"

Kyra and Enna had assembled five chairs in the center of the lab, away from any noxious flowers and poisonous herbs. They were waved over to the seats, where Kyra gestured at the bottle, still in Alara's grasp. "I thought we were preparing for a toast?"

Teia glanced at the fifth chair. "What about Tobias?"

"He's with Lehm," Alara said airily. "We'll save him some champagne."

"Debatable," Enna said, as she pushed her flute forward and propped a leg on the empty seat.

Liberal amounts of champagne were poured for the group. The glasses were filled to the brim, liquid frothing over the sides, before Alara lifted hers forward. "Here's to good friends," she said. "Good friends and excellent homecomings."

They drank deeply, the champagne light and crisp, the lab awash with a rainbow of plants. "Excellent," Alara said contentedly, swirling the liquid around in her glass. "This is going so much better than last time."

"What happened then?" Enna said curiously.

"Another celebration," Kyra provided. "Alara had just finished working on one of her sleeping draughts—"

"No small feat," Alara said. "My test subjects kept falling into comas."

"We had another bottle of champagne—"

"Awful stuff. We would have done better with rubbing alcohol—"

"She convinced Tobias to drink with us—"

"You would've thought he was being asked to run naked through Bhanot—"

"And we came back into the lab to celebrate," Kyra finished. She smiled piously. "I had a great time."

"You threw up on my test tubes and fell asleep in a planter."

Enna choked on her champagne. Teia had to lean over to pound the thief on the back, who folded in two to mimic curling into a planter. Kyra scowled—"I was much more comfortable than that"—while Alara roared in laughter and Enna wheezed for breath.

Teia had never known the world to be so bright, so alive and full of color, painted in every shade. As she watched Enna imitate

Kyra, the thief now attempting to stuff herself into a nearby pot, she took another sip. She held back a laugh.

It was the stuff that forever was made of, if only time would slow down.

◆◆◆

Teia held her liquor surprisingly well.

After three servings of champagne and one of brandy, everything had merged into a haze. She was on the cusp of being drunk, teetering right on the fringe, although she thought she'd done much better than Kyra. The rebel champion hadn't destroyed any test tubes, but she was fast asleep in a sitting position, her head resting against Enna's shoulder. The thief didn't seem bothered. She was fiddling with one of the stoppers in deep concentration, making it vanish into the folds of her sleeve, reappear, then vanish again.

Teia set down her drink unsteadily. She had made it to the door when a voice sounded from behind her.

"You're going to look for Tobias?" Alara said. She smiled at Teia with all the wisdom of a prophet.

Somewhere deep in her heart, locked away behind the bristles and thorns, Teia knew it was a mistake. Here she was, two steps from the throne, one foot out the door. Here she was, so close to the end, and yet Tobias Rennert still lingered in her mind.

"Yes," Teia said reluctantly, and Alara grinned.

"I thought so," the Poisons Master said, her tone brimming with satisfaction. "Anyone with a pulse can see what the two of you have."

"A healthy working relationship?"

"If you say so." Alara gave Teia a sage wink. "He's in the last room on the right. Although I would knock if I were you—he likes to answer the door with his knife."

Teia's *thank-you* died in her throat. Her gaze strayed lower, inching toward the covered area above the other girl's heart. Alara's shirt was high-necked and woolly, stylishly cut, wrapped in the middle with a bright yellow ribbon—but Teia knew what lay beneath.

"Alara," she said, in a startling moment of clarity. "Are you sure you're all right?"

"Why wouldn't I be?"

"Because . . ." *Because Jura branded my family's crest into your chest. Because you barely survived a place that took your brother.* "Just because."

Alara's expression was as calm as water. "Not yet," she said. "Not completely. But I will be."

Then she was shooing Teia into the hallway and shutting the door after her.

The light was dimmer in the corridor. Faint murmurs swelled from down the staircase, but most of the earlier activity had faded away, replaced by the creaks of a building settling in for the night. Rebels planned their next attacks. They spoke of their dreams, made friends, fell in love, flush with a yearning pride for their inevitable victory.

Teia's feet carried her to the end of the hall. Her heart had begun beating erratically, falling into a haphazard rhythm, but she had the presence of mind to follow Alara's advice. As she lifted her hand to the sanded wood, she wondered just what the hell she was doing here. Why muddle things any further? Why break her own heart?

The door opened. Tobias stood before her, knife in hand, features bemused. The top button of his shirt was undone, revealing a faded white scar, and this, for some reason, set her nerves aflame. "Teia?"

She let herself in, satisfied he wouldn't stab her. The room was sparsely furnished, with a lantern glowing on the desk. A map of Erisia had been tacked to the wall. Notes were jotted over each major town, and a suitcase lay open on the bed, clothes strewn about inside.

Teia stared at the bag uncomprehendingly. "You're leaving Bhanot?" she said.

"Lehm wants me in different parts of Erisia."

"For what?"

He closed the door behind her. "Champagne?" he asked, amused.

"We were toasting Alara's return."

"Must have been quite some toast."

"It was. Or at least, the first one was. The other six—" She frowned, trying and failing to recall any specifics. "Never mind. Stop avoiding my question. Why does Lehm want you out of Bhanot?"

"He thinks I have a talent for recruitment."

"You?"

Tobias's mouth lifted. "Give me some credit. I was your handler, and you're still alive. That has to count for something."

"An unrelated correlation."

"Rude."

"Accurate." She perched on the mattress to peer into the suitcase, shifting aside a collection of trousers. Several maps lay inside; she picked up the one on top and studied it methodically. There were the many deserts of Ismet, charted to their fullest extent, the unknown regions highlighted with question marks. "Am I intruding on Dawnbreaker secrets?"

"Not quite." He took a seat beside her. "They're the places I have yet to go."

"That's a lot of traveling."

"This fight can't last forever. Once it's over—" He shrugged. "I'll need to fill my time."

The next map took her aback. "Shaylan," Teia murmured. She traced the mountain ranges, the winding rivers. Her finger landed on a cramped line of writing—and when she flattened out the wrinkled paper, Teia laughed in pure astonishment. "Mooncakes?"

"Filled with red beans and lotus paste," he said. "They're a tradition in Shaylan."

She glanced at him. "I didn't think you would remember."

"How could I not?" Tobias was inspecting the map with remarkable interest, his voice barely audible. "You're hard to forget."

Her throat squeezed. Teia set the map aside quickly, searching frantically for another subject. "When are you due to leave?"

"My train is in three days."

"That soon?"

"Jura's coronation is the day after next. Things are bound to get worse once he's king."

Teia fell silent. They hadn't spoken about what had taken place in Blackgate, where Tobias had been seconds away from killing Jura. She'd seen how much he'd wanted to, every muscle in his body pleading to attack. And while they were alive because Tobias hadn't struck, some part of him must regret the decision.

There was so much she longed to say, thoughts she could never articulate aloud. That he had done the right thing, against all his other judgments. That he might be ruthless and broken and stubborn, but there was a goodness that remained intact, one that scared her to no end.

In another lifetime, maybe they could have saved each other.

Teia cast her eyes to the far wall. "The timing works out," she said nonchalantly. "Kyra and I leave for the palace in the morning."

"You have another assignment?"

"No. But I can't be away for too long. People talk."

He did a spectacularly poor job of hiding a grin. "Rumor has it that you developed a nasty case of boils."

"I've made an astounding recovery."

"It's almost like they were never there at all."

"My immune system—" She fluttered a hand before her. "It's very fast acting."

His laugh made her stomach clench. It was a sound she would miss, one she was certain would haunt her. She could scour all of Erisia for a replacement and still yearn for that incredible warmth.

There was no point in delaying any further. Teia laced her fingers together and said, "This is the last time we'll see each other?"

His smile dipped. "For a while," he agreed, and she dared to look at him. His mouth was set in a line, his jaw tight. "I'll write to you," he said roughly. "If that's what you want."

"I don't know. Pretty hard to pass letters into the palace."

"I know people. Some owe me favors."

"Friends?"

"You could call them that."

"Sounds complicated."

"Maybe. But it would be worth it."

She shouldn't have said yes—shouldn't have said anything at all. But her reply came on a sudden tide, and she heard herself speak before realizing what she'd done. "I'll describe every event that takes place in the palace. Although fair warning—my letters might put you to sleep."

"I highly doubt that. Aren't you there to liven things up?"

"There's only so much I can do."

"Ah," Tobias said knowingly. "Naps under tables?"

"I'd sooner drop a suitcase in the ocean."

"Amateur move. It takes at least two to draw a crowd."

"Don't worry. I can take care of myself."

"I know," he assured her. "I pity anyone who tries to stand against you."

The words dug into Teia. She rose without warning, scattering the maps onto the floor. As she refolded them one by one, setting them back into the suitcase, Teia nodded vaguely toward the door. "I should go. You need to finish packing."

"Ah yes," he said dryly. "Mankind's favorite activity."

"Other than starting wars and imposing taxes?"

"I'd say it's a close third."

She was going to miss this. She was going to miss *him*. It wasn't a groundbreaking revelation, not really, but her resolve wavered all the same. Her hand stilled on the handle. She met the dark blue of his gaze, the ocean with its gentle waves, the current that had pulled her under.

"You'll think of me?" Teia said softly.

It took a moment before Tobias replied. And when he did, Teia saw the barest hint of a smile, flashing faster than any shadow.

"Every day of my life," he said back.

CHAPTER THIRTY-EIGHT

Teia sensed something was wrong from the second she stepped into the throne room.

It was supposed to be a routine rehearsal, the last before Jura's coronation later that evening. When Teia answered the summons, the stammering page boy had led her through the halls and down the stairs, pushing open the soaring doors with trembling hands. Inside, both sides of the carpeted aisle were filled with dignitaries and nobles alike. Erisia's many ministers had been called into attendance, along with a dozen uniformed guards stationed by the front.

Jura himself sat on his throne, resplendent in scarlet robes, a crystal glass glittering in his fist. His circlet sat low on his forehead, the rubies catching the light. It would be replaced with a crown in a matter of hours, and the circlet whisked off to the Erisian Royal Museum for preservation.

"Halfling," Jura said, waving to the spot at his feet. "Come—join us."

The walk to the throne took a decade off Teia's life. It would have been polite for her to kneel, but she stood firm, staring up at Jura steadily. He wore the vicious smile he reserved for special occasions, and her heart sank into her stomach.

"What a momentous day," Jura crooned. "Your half brother ascends the throne tonight."

How could she forget? He'd practically written the date into the sky. "I'm aware," she said.

"That's it? No well-wishes? No words of congratulations?"

Did he want her to break into song? "I'm delighted," she ground out. "Truly."

Jura coughed out a laugh. "Delighted, are you?"

"Yes."

"Fascinating," he mused. He pulled his robes around him, his green eyes narrowing. She had the foresight to think that this wouldn't end well, before he said, "Then perhaps you can enlighten me. If you're so *delighted* by my coronation, why have you been conspiring with the Dawnbreakers?"

The room was in free fall. It plummeted away from Teia, dissolving into a whirl of sound. "Excuse me?" she managed to say.

She could tell how deeply he savored this victory, reveling in the grand reveal. Really, she should have been flattered. Leave it to Jura to fashion an entire event around her demise, gathering Bhanot's officials for her downfall. He would most likely have her paraded around the streets, too, towed through each district in a prison cart until an executioner lopped off her head.

"I've been gathering proof," Jura said. "Mysterious disappearances. Venturing into the city at odd times."

"Is it a crime to take walks?"

"At two in the morning?"

"I'm an early riser."

"Spare me the excuses," he sneered. "One of the guards at the servants' entrance was more than happy to give us his statement." When she said nothing, he took her silence as an admission, barreling ahead with, "I take it you're familiar with Alara Armitov?"

It was too late to play dumb, but Teia would do her damnedest anyway. "Who?" she said blankly.

"The Poisons Master," Jura said, and their audience sank into a round of jeers. "We were able to capture her—at no small expense to the Crown, might I add. But she disappeared from Blackgate, broken out of her cell by a group of Dawnbreakers."

"You should invest in better security measures."

"Perhaps I will, once I exterminate the rats from the palace." His eyes gleamed. "Witnesses say you were among the rebels that night."

"What witnesses?" Teia said. "The birds in the sky? The beetles on the ground?"

"Multiple guards posted within the block," Jura snapped. "Trustworthy men who are prepared to take the stand."

Goddess, Teia thought. So this was how it ended. There was no point in pretending anymore. Jura would have men stretched as far as Dvořáki, ready to swear up and down that they'd seen Teia in Blackgate. And they very well might have, for all she knew. The prison's courtyard had been overrun with guards when the smoke pellets exploded. One of them could have easily identified her through her iron mask.

She had thought this would be done under more private circumstances. An intimate setting, with just a few officials present. But if Jura wanted to be theatrical, then Teia would oblige.

All her years in the palace had taught her how to put on a show.

Teia smiled. "You're right," she said to Jura evenly. Her voice rose over the crowds, and the courtiers' whispers died away. "I *was* at Blackgate. I needed to rescue the Poisons Master to win over the Dawnbreakers."

His features tightened. Jura had planned a spectacle—but this was something else entirely. "You're admitting to treason?" he said.

"On the contrary. Because while you failed to discover the Dawnbreakers' base—to locate any shred of information that might prove remotely useful—I've been undercover with the rebels. I gathered information on them. I learned about their weaknesses." She spread her hands. "And now, I've brought some gifts for you."

Her eyes met General Miran's. He had been positioned with the rest of his troops, but he peeled away now to walk forward, the rows of medals adorning his chest. Miran stopped short of the throne. He placed a fist over his heart and delivered two curt bows—one to Teia, one to Jura. "Highness," he said.

"Miran," Teia acknowledged. "I believe you have news to share?"

"Yes, Princess." A wolflike smile stretched over his narrow lips. "We discovered the Dawnbreakers' base in the Absinth Hotel, based on the intelligence you provided."

"You raided the facility?"

"Thoroughly. The Absinth is now under the Crown's protection."

"Any prisoners?"

"Fewer than we would have liked." While he spoke, Miran reached leisurely into the folds of his uniform. His expression oozed satisfaction as he withdrew a silver pendant, which he set in Teia's hand. The half-circle charm was streaked with blood, yet the chain links shone beneath the lights.

"I'm pleased to say," Miran informed her, "that Cornelius Lehm will no longer be a problem."

Teia closed her palm around the pendant. "Good," she told the general, relishing every ounce of her audience's attention. "And what of the special request?"

"Waiting for you outside, Princess."

"Excellent. You can bring her in."

He clapped his hands smartly, and the doors burst open on command. Two guards hauled a thrashing figure into the center of the room. Swiftly, one of the men yanked the hood from her head. The girl's face was covered with cuts, her left eye swelling shut. White cuffs shimmered on her wrists— soapstone welded with diamond, designed to contain someone who could control fire.

"Jura," Teia said, "allow me to introduce you to Kyra Medoh— the Dawnbreakers' illustrious champion."

The throne room exploded into pandemonium. There was a cacophony of noise, which broke away from the masses to surge over the crowds. *She said what? That's who?* The braver courtiers peeked brazenly out at Kyra, eager to scrutinize this new prisoner.

The rebel girl made no sound as she knelt on the floor. Kyra lifted her head slowly, painfully. As she took in the sight before her, something shattered behind her eyes. "Teia?" she whispered.

Teia was silent. She felt the smallest sliver of pain, just enough to hurt. She didn't look at Kyra, didn't react.

She hadn't come this far to break.

On his throne, Jura had turned the same color as his robes. He wet his lips as he surveyed Kyra warily. "An impostor," he said. "A trick."

Teia laughed. "If you don't believe me," she challenged, "why don't you see if she can burn?"

The words had scarcely left her mouth when a pillar of fire erupted around Kyra. Nobles gasped, squinting into the blaze. The flames crackled orange, so hot that the fresco paints bubbled on the ceiling. Here was a tangible incarnation of Jura's fury, a display of power that he needed to make.

But once the fire had died away, once Jura retracted his hand and the smoke petered from the room, the court saw the truth. The walls had become smudged with soot. The carpet was torched in a perfect circle, everything charred within its radius.

All that destruction, and yet Kyra Medoh remained perfectly fine.

A pulse beat against the side of Jura's forehead. "The Dawnbreakers' champion," he repeated.

"In the flesh," Teia said.

"You captured her."

"I won her over, and she led me straight to the rebel base."

"No."

It wasn't Jura who'd spoken, but Kyra. She staggered to her feet, straining against the cuffs. Confusion melted into anger, blistering against her gaze. "You used me," she spat. "I trusted you. *We* trusted you."

Teia kept her tone even. "Do you remember the first day we met?"

"I wish I didn't."

"Either way." Teia tucked Lehm's pendant into her pocket. "I warned you that you shouldn't trust me."

Then Kyra was screaming at her, yelling insults that would have horrified any hardened Flats veteran. Some of the courtiers shuffled about nervously, but Teia merely signaled for Miran's guards. She wasn't interested in the rebel girl's insults. She was here to hold court on her own terms, to demand Erisia's respect.

"I believe the title you're looking for," Teia said, "is princess."

It took four guards to drag Kyra from the throne room. Her shouts were audible until the doors clanged shut. The crowd turned back to Teia, rapt with anticipation for what came next, but her eyes remained on Jura. Jura, whose jaws had locked into a fawning smile. Jura, who seemed seconds away from disintegrating into a heap of ash. She wanted to crystallize this moment, capturing it in amber to relive when she wanted.

Teia hadn't simply made a fool of him—she had single-handedly neutralized the Dawnbreakers, bringing down the base and capturing the rebellion's champion. She had proven her loyalty to both court and country. She could feel the begrudging admiration from each person in the room, spectators that had been won over.

Teia Carthan had become power incarnate.

Jura downed the remainder of his drink. He stood, adjusting the circlet on his head. "Halfling—"

Suddenly, Jura reeled back, his hands grabbing at his throat. The glass shattered on the ground as he crumpled with a hideous gargle, his limbs askew. Purple liquid seeped down his face. It lathered his robes as he seized against the floor.

Shrieks rattled the walls. Miran's guards leapt forward, drawing a protective arc with their swords. Nobles cowered in alarm.

Teia yelled for a healer as she dropped down beside Jura. She cradled his head in her lap and begged for him to stay with her. She swore she'd make the rebels pay.

The barest spark of recognition twitched in Jura's gaze. Something fought to crawl back from the light, battling against the poison that consumed his heart. There was even a minute when Teia wondered if he would make it after all, borne on the winds of pure spite.

Yet in the end, it was *Flora teian* that won out. Teia had held fast to Alara's suicide tablet after Blackgate, stowing it into the lid of the greenie's pocket watch for safekeeping. After venturing back into the palace with Kyra, it had been easy enough to dart into the passageways and step into the kitchens. None of the cooks had been in the ice room as Teia dissolved the coating around the poison. She'd frozen the tablet's contents within a tray of water, and slid her creation into the jeweled ice box, the one reserved for Jura's evening drinks.

When the coroner examined the corpse later, he would find traces of the Dawnbreakers' trademark poison. The entire affair would be connected back to Kyra, who had pretended to be a servant. She'd had ample opportunity to sneak into the kitchens, and had struck right before Jura's coronation, as any black-hearted villain would do.

Erisia would mourn. It would grieve and it would heal, but Jura would be around for none of it.

The Golden Prince died with his eyes wide open, staring up at the ceiling, his mouth curled into an endless scream.

CHAPTER THIRTY-NINE

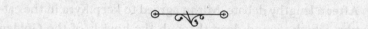

The palace was in an uproar.

Jura Carthan had been dead for several hours now. His body had remained in the throne room, covered by a white sheet, before it was carted to the morgue with the utmost ceremony. The court had been stunned. They spoke about the Halfling Princess, who had been understandably distraught, weeping for her brother after he'd passed. They talked about the *nerve* of those awful Dawnbreakers. How dare they come into this place of power? How dare they commit regicide within such hallowed halls?

Kyra's transport to Blackgate was delayed. There wasn't the personnel, with every guard in the palace sweeping the grounds for more rebels. When Miran suggested deferring a few soldiers to escort Kyra to the prison, he was instantly overridden by a stampede of panicked nobles.

"We need protection!" Abbott had squawked, punctuating each word with a stab of his pudgy finger. "What if there are more intruders? What if one of us is next?"

Miran had given Teia a questioning look, and she'd responded with a shrug. "Best to wait until morning," she'd recommended. "She doesn't seem the type, but Kyra Medoh can fight."

"Against a sword? Against a phalanx of archers?"

"She has her ways. Blackgate isn't going anywhere, Miran. Let's not do something we'll regret later."

"Exactly!" Abbott piped from his seat. "I'm thankful *someone* is talking sense around here."

After a lengthy debate, Miran agreed to keep Kyra in the catacombs, which wound deep through the bowels of the Golden Palace. They had been constructed for Eris the First, who had been keen on stockpiling the skulls of his enemies. The catacombs had been meticulously designed to house Eris's collection, before architects decided on more cost-efficient measures. They'd installed a series of cells near the beginning of the catacombs, where unlucky prisoners rotted away until their execution day. After all, why board captives separately, if their skulls would end up back here anyway?

The cells might have been abandoned once Blackgate was commissioned, but they were an acceptable solution for the Kyra Medoh problem. The locks worked fine, and the sole entrance was a barred iron door atop a musty staircase. Any of Kyra's potential rescuers would need to slip past Miran's guards, who would be on high alert throughout the night.

It was a good thing the palace passageways granted a second way in.

As Teia entered the endless stretch of darkness, she remembered exactly why the catacombs had gained such notoriety. The dungeons made Blackgate look like a tropical paradise. Rows of skulls lined the ridges in various states of decay, leering out at her with empty sockets. Cells had been cut straight from stone, with rusted chains affixed to the doors. There was no source of light aside from the flame above Teia's palm, which cast a ghastly shadow as she walked down the hallway, skirting around dirty puddles of water.

"Teia?"

Kyra was several cells down, her arms still pinned behind her. She clambered awkwardly to her feet, starting to say more, but Teia put a finger to her lips. Miran's guards were painfully superstitious, too afraid of ghosts to patrol the actual catacombs. Sound shouldn't carry up the stairs and through the door, but Teia wasn't eager to test that theory.

She withdrew a key from her pocket and set to work on the rusted lock. Teia had made copies of the cell keys years ago. At the time, she'd been afraid Jura would stage her disappearance and stash her inside the catacombs. She'd carried the keys with her for months, fashioned into makeshift bracelets beneath her sleeves.

The lock creaked open with a groan. Teia undid Kyra's cuffs before helping her into the passageways. She snuck one last glance at the catacombs, the lines of grinning skulls, and slid the tunnel's panel gently back in place. With any luck, the escape would be chalked up to some unexplainable brand of magic. Kyra could already wield fire. What was one more stunt to a magician who could do the impossible?

Neither of them spoke as they set off down the passageways. Teia was immensely grateful for the silence. She basked in it. She was just hoping they could reach the end of the tunnels without saying anything at all when Kyra's hand shot outward, bringing Teia to a halt.

"Teia," she said, a tremor snaking through her voice. "Tell me the throne room was an act. Tell me Jura threatened you, that he forced you to say those things."

She could. It would be one more tall tale, one more lie in an infinite ledger. But as she opened her mouth, the truth bubbled up on Teia's tongue. "I can't."

"You mean—"

Teia looked away. "It was my idea," she said. "I was the one who gave up the Absinth."

She felt something crack between them, a ravine poised to swallow her whole. *Let it.* As Teia watched the light dim in Kyra's face, she would have welcomed any respite from the conversation to come.

"The raid," Kyra whispered. "The soldiers."

"Yes."

"Your military stormed our base. People *died*, Teia."

"I know."

"And what about Tobias? Alara?" Threads of heat collided around them. Bursts of flame wove themselves together and broke apart in midair. "I lost track of them before the raid started. If they were hurt in the commotion—"

"They're safe."

"How do you know?"

"I sent Enna ahead. She'll take you to meet them once we exit the tunnels."

"But the other rebels? The ones who were arrested at the base?"

"They'll await their trial and sentencing in Blackgate."

"A *trial*? That solves everything, doesn't it?"

"They could be found innocent."

"Nobody is ever found innocent once they go to Blackgate." Kyra flung out a furious hand. "And what about Lehm? Is he also sitting in a cell, awaiting his turn before a magistrate?"

Teia swept her fist to the side, extinguishing the different pockets of flames. The passageways seemed to extend on forever, and it took her several more steps to pry loose her next sentence. "Lehm was working with Jura."

Kyra's laugh was jagged. "Have you gone mad, Teia? Do you know how absurd you sound?"

"He was sabotaging our assignments. Feeding information to Jura—"

"He was our leader."

"He was a traitor. He was trying to raise the Serkawr. He would have destroyed the Dawnbreakers to get what he wanted."

"The Serkawr? The one from legend?"

"Legends stem from truth."

"Don't get philosophical with me. Legends stem from lies too. It just depends on who you ask." Kyra's shoulders trembled. "Is that why you sold us out? You listened to a fairy tale told to children? You decided one man's life was worth hundreds?"

"No."

"Then what?"

"It doesn't matter."

"It matters to *me*," Kyra snarled. Her eyes were pools of ink, unreadable, indelible. "Did we really mean that little? Was our friendship worth nothing to you?"

Pain ripped through Teia. Every emotion she'd tried to stem tore loose, leaching through her veins. She exhaled a shaking breath, and the secret she had been guarding tumbled out in a rush. "Jura is dead," she said. "I killed him."

Kyra stopped. "You *what*?" she said, her expression stunned.

"It's a cliché, really." The words tasted strange in Teia's mouth, as if this triumph belonged to someone else. "Poison in the cup. Who would have thought?"

"When?"

"After they took you away."

"How long have you been planning this?"

"Not long," she admitted. "After our first run through Blackgate."

Kyra shook her head. "But why betray us? If you were going to kill Jura, the Dawnbreakers—" Comprehension sank into the rebel girl. An awful emptiness crept into her tone. "You want to take the throne."

The seat of power that the rebels despised, the twisted path that she'd set herself on. What had Teia given up to come to this moment? Alara, Tobias, Kyra—they had been everything. They were her family, her home, a place where she could brave the harshest storm. They had carved a hole inside her that she could never fill, even if she ruled for a hundred years.

Was our friendship worth nothing to you?

Kyra couldn't know how close Teia had come to turning back. That she'd paced her room for hours before meeting Miran in his study. That she'd nearly provided false instructions as she mapped out the Absinth's hidden rooms. The shame she'd felt had eaten her alive, whittling away at her resolve. She could choose the rebels; she could find a new cause.

And yet the crown was a tether, a promise that carried through the din. She'd shaped her own future, set the pieces in motion. She'd discovered her purpose, as true as her pulse.

Teia's heart might not break clean, but she was determined to hold on to whatever remained.

She clenched her jaw. "I do," she said, and the words reverberated through the passageways in a continuous echo.

"You gave up the base because you needed us out of the way."

"Would you ever have accepted Carthan rule?"

"Did you think to give us a choice?"

She hadn't. She had done what others had before her: imposed her will, moved forward with her plan. Her family tree was full of murderers and monsters, but maybe that was what it took to survive the Golden Palace. Good people didn't belong in the Erisian court, which chewed them up and spat them back out.

"I can be different from Jura," Teia said. It was a lackluster defense, but she thought it better than none at all.

"Funny how things go. Carthans sit on the throne, and ordinary people die."

"It won't be like that this time."

"How do you know?"

"I'll enact new policies. I'll treat people fairly."

"Is your word supposed to be reassuring? I trusted you, and it landed me in a cell."

"A cell that I broke you out of."

"Well," Kyra said icily, "doesn't that resolve everything?"

They had neared the end of the passageways. A gate stretched wide across the opening, the ivory white long rusted to copper. The lock had been sawed in preparation for the escape. When Teia touched the gate, it swung aside easily. The sky was flecked with stars, constellations twinkling high above.

"Follow the path," Teia said. She shrugged off her wool cloak and bundled it into Kyra's arms. "The guard at the back entrance won't give you any trouble. Once you reach Mourner's Bay, Enna will guide you to the schooner. Tobias and Alara should be on board, and the crew is paid for in full."

"Where will it take us?"

"Wherever you want. Cross the Dark Sea to Shaylan. Go south to K'val, or seek your fortune in Ismet." Teia paused. "Anywhere in the Five Kingdoms, as long as you don't come back here."

A howling wind had started up outside. As Kyra draped the cloak around her shoulders, Teia caught a glimpse of the rebel girl's face. Rage lined her features, shadowing her eyes. Her hands were unsteady as she tugged on the hood, but her next words were measured, restrained.

"If I ever see you again," Kyra said quietly, "I'm going to kill you."

"I believe you," Teia said wearily. And she did, truly. She could already imagine a knife in the back, a revolver to the head. It might take years. Decades. But at some point or another, she and Kyra would inevitably meet again.

When that time came, Teia knew things wouldn't end well for either of them.

Kyra nodded. She walked through the gate, her movements heavy.

She didn't look back as the night swallowed her into its embrace.

CHAPTER FORTY

Teia saved Minister Abbott for last.

It was more for practical reasons than anything. Along with being an unbearable lecher, the Minister of Contracts and Coin was renowned throughout the palace for his endless complaints, which spanned from the temperature of his meals to the springiness of his mattress. Teia hadn't been afraid of the minister, nor did she pity him. She simply couldn't be bothered to deal with his whining earlier.

When Teia arrived at the War Room, Abbott was in the throes of his latest rant. She could hear him faintly as she strode down the hallway, his voice grating against her ears. "It's witchcraft, Miran. Mark my words. If your men hadn't been so lax, Kyra Medoh's head would be on a pike—"

Teia glided into the room, letting the doors thud after her. Abbott started at the sound, the wine sloshing from his glass, but Miran remained expressionless at the table. When his eye met hers, he gave Teia the slightest nod.

"Hello, Minister," she said carelessly. "General."

Abbott took a swig of his wine. She noticed he was sitting in Jura's former seat, that his gaze lingered a bit too long on her chest. "My deepest condolences, Princess. The Golden Prince was a shining star among men."

It was certainly the most flattering analogy Teia had heard so far. She had been routinely stopped by officials throughout the past week who had murmured out sympathies about the Blessed Heir's death. Jura had been compared to a stalwart bull, a galloping mustang, and an evergreen pine that had been uprooted too soon.

"I appreciate the sentiments, Minister."

He grinned, his teeth stained purple from the wine. "You see, we were just discussing His Highness's death. You wouldn't be familiar with the Erisian line of succession, of course—this is a terribly formal, highly complicated matter. But should a ruler pass away with no heir, there's a certain order to who receives the crown next."

Teia nodded along innocently. "Is that so? And who would be next in line?"

"Make no mistake," the minister said, trying and failing to maintain an air of solemnity. "It's a time of great mourning in our country. This isn't an obligation I bear lightly, but Erisia needs a leader."

Well, she was hardly one to keep him from his mountain of responsibilities. "About that," Teia said, as Abbott gulped down another third of his drink. "I do have something to show you, if it's not too much trouble."

"Which is?"

"A contract I need advice on. Very formal. *Very* complicated." Teia set the rolled-up document on the table. "All it needs is your signature."

Abbott reached forward greedily. He broke the wax seal in one motion, his eyes veering across the page. Teia watched as the smile slid off his face. He thrust the contract in her direction, his jowls quivering. "Is this a joke?" he said imperiously.

Teia picked up the page delicately. "I don't see anything funny," she said, assessing the contract with a forced concentration. "This looks like a proposed change in law to me."

"What you're asking for is preposterous! Outrageous!"

"Careful, Abbott," Teia said amiably. "At the rate you're going, you might exhaust your vocabulary."

Abbott pounded his fist on the table. "You're asking to be crowned as the next Erisian monarch."

"I'm glad to see you can read at an advanced level. You had me concerned for a moment."

His cheeks reddened. "This is treason."

"How? Jura is dead, murdered at the hands of those vicious Dawnbreakers. You haven't been sworn in yet, with all that's happened. And you mentioned it yourself—Erisia needs leadership. Stability." She tipped her head. "Me."

"It can't be done."

"And why is that? Am I not a Carthan?"

"You are," Abbott forced out.

Teia smiled indulgently. "Then what seems to be the problem?"

"You're seventeen. You must be twenty-one to assume the throne."

"Good thing Provision Eight"—she tapped the line with her finger—"makes that change."

"Not to mention only a male heir—"

"Provision Nine. Goddess, Abbott. Maybe I misspoke about the reading level."

He snatched the document away from her. She saw the paper

give way under his fingers. "Women aren't fit to rule. It isn't their place—"

"In the government? Spare me. K'val and Ismet are both governed by women. And Shaylan passes the throne to the next eligible heir, male or female."

The minister muttered something not quite audible, and Teia tugged at her ear. "Is there more you have to say, Abbott?"

He glowered at her with unmistakable loathing. "Those countries are barbaric," the minister said.

For a man of so few morals, Abbott was astonishingly self-righteous. Teia lifted her chin at the minister. "Any other words of wisdom you'd like to share?"

He slapped the crumpled document against the table. "I can't sign this," he growled. "I won't."

"That's your final stance?"

"The law stands. It's not my place to change it."

"And where was that persistence when you voted to employ children in the salt mines? If I remember correctly, you had mentioned bending rules for the greater good?"

His shoulders tensed. "How did you—"

"You keep your secrets and I keep mine."

Abbott gave a mighty shake of his head. "Regardless," he blustered. "I don't know what forms of duress you used on Miran"—he scowled at the general, who was impassive in his seat—"but you'll never have my support. It's my job to preserve the integrity of the law."

Good. She'd been hoping he'd say that.

Teia took the chair opposite Abbott. His eyes followed her cautiously as she placed both elbows onto the table. Instantly, the minister's hands flew upward. Water leaked from his mouth. It dribbled down the rolls of his neck, and Teia flexed her fingers expertly. She let the minister's lungs fill, the seconds compacting in on themselves, until she abruptly relaxed her hold.

Abbott fell into a fit of hacking coughs. Fear shone in his face as he sucked in a tremulous breath.

"Abbott," Teia said softly. "If I'm not mistaken, we are the law."

A pitiful whimper escaped the minister's lips. So much for the grandstanding, the haughtiness—both were gone, replaced instead by the true Minister of Contracts and Coin. Abbott might be all powder and silk on the surface, but he was, at his core, a coward. A man who liked to have his way. A man who'd kneel to save his own hide.

"You'll defile the throne," Abbott croaked. "You'll lead Erisia astray."

She reached into her pocket and slid a pen across the table toward him. It gleamed black against the gray soapstone, rolling to a stop before Abbott. The man flinched as Teia gestured at the contract.

"Abbott," Teia said. "I won't ask again."

The minister signed. His signature was wobbly but discernible, blotted with smears of ink. When he finished, he dropped the pen like it would bite him. "This is a mistake," Abbott quavered. "You're prepared to dissolve six hundred years of tradition."

She didn't spare him another glance. "What's six hundred years?" Teia answered. "I'll build something that lasts an eternity."

Erisia buried Jura two weeks later.

The wake was spectacular, with all the fanfare that Jura would have insisted on. The Golden Prince lay in a crystal casket with the Carthan crest engraved on the lid. Flowers blanketed any available space, spilling out in shades of gold, red, purple. The entire room was lit by the dying sun, light settling over the crowd of mourners.

Teia sat directly in front of the casket. She wore a white gown that dripped with diamonds, a lace handkerchief dangling in her fist. She dabbed at her eyes when appropriate, providing a watery smile to any nobles that passed. All attention in the temple was fixed on her, gauging her reactions, but that suited Teia just fine. It was why she had chosen this seat.

When the ceremony was over, Teia laid down her offering of roses. She shook hands with every official that came her way. She thanked the new Minister of Contracts and Coin for coming. They made small talk in the gardens outside and murmured about how his predecessor, the late Lurel Abbott, had succumbed to a mysterious heart attack.

"The tragedies don't seem to end," Teia told the new minister somberly, "but I trust you'll do Abbott proud."

Afterward, she separated from the crowds, walking toward the ash trees that rustled by the temple's back entrance. It was considered unseemly for any surviving family members to accompany the funeral procession, which was why Teia would meet the casket at the Splendid Graveyard. The pallbearers would wind through the Royal District. They would pass the pyres that the commonfolk had prepared, effigies laid out by the people of Bhanot. Jura would receive his final blessing from the palace's head priest, who would pray that the crown prince's soul returned safely to Armina.

It was a pleasant sentiment, although entirely unnecessary. Wherever Jura was now, Teia would wager that it wasn't with the Goddess.

Behind her, someone coughed. Teia glanced back to see General Miran, who lowered his head respectfully. He, too, was dressed in all white, with an ivory sash looped across his uniform and a snowy flower tucked in his chest pocket.

"Highness," he said.

She indicated the dwindling funeral march. "What an awful affair, General."

"Indeed. I never thought I'd see the day."

His tone gave nothing away. And as they stood there, the waving banners of the pallbearers growing steadily smaller, red flares that punctuated the horizon, a whisper bloomed in Teia's mind.

Did Miran know she'd poisoned Jura?

The general had to harbor his suspicions. Miran might have agreed to help her in his study, but he hadn't been privy to any plans for an assassination. It had taken all Teia's leverage to convince him of a coup. Regicide would have been too much to ask.

Does he know? Teia thought. *Does he care?* Yet even as the concerns sprang into her head, she knew her secret would be safe with him. If there was anyone in Erisia who needed a fresh start, it was Miran. His daughters were back in the palace, and he had tacked Lehm's pendant to the wall of his study. Teia had given the general everything she'd promised. With any luck, they could both dispose of their skeletons here, burying the past alongside Jura.

Miran's gaze was still on the procession, barely visible against the budding dusk. "It was a beautiful ceremony," he said mildly. "The late prince will be missed."

"Not too much, I hope."

"I believe that will depend on his successor."

"I can assure you that I'm up for the challenge."

They listened to the sounds of the procession fade away, the drums and wails flattening to silence. That was when Miran spoke again. His spine was rigid, his arms clasped behind his back, but his voice was calm as he said, "The military will be watching, Highness."

He shouldn't have bothered with the sugarcoating. Teia had lived seventeen years in the Golden Palace, with half a decade under Jura's thumb. Once she peeled away the layer of courtroom civility, she could see Miran's words for what they were. A promise of life to come. A threat if things went awry.

But really, what was there left to take from her? Her family was gone, the Dawnbreakers dismantled. All that remained were the throne and the crown, and she intended to make the most of both. She would create her happiness from the fragments that remained. She would design something that tried out whatever equality—whatever fairness—the rebels had dreamed about.

And if she didn't think too hard about it, it was almost a fair trade.

So Teia just gave a sparkling laugh, one borrowed straight from a storybook. She stepped closer to the general, her hair falling in a curtain over her face. She wondered what they looked like from a distance.

The Halfling and her adviser. A queen and her confidant.

"Watch away," Teia said sweetly. "At least you'll finally see something worth looking at."

CHAPTER FORTY-ONE

Three Months Later

Over the past months, Teia had grown accustomed to reading General Miran's moods.

He didn't have much of a range, but he did harbor a few tells. He was rarely pleased, but his gray brows would lift if he agreed with a decision. And when he was dissatisfied—which was more often than not—the lines on his forehead chiseled deeper. He would readjust his eyepatch in displeasure, the remnants of an old wound that would not be forgotten.

As soon as Miran entered the throne room, his features etched in a permanent frown, Teia knew it was bad news. "Highness," he said, kneeling to the floor.

"General."

"There are protesters at the front gate."

Was that all? It was hardly something to be upset about. "More than last week?"

"Fewer. Far fewer."

That meant her strategies were working. The imported bags of spices weren't cheap, nor were the sacks of fine sugar she'd had shipped from Ismet. But when word spread about the new queen's generosity—and how the goods were distributed to families who didn't attend protests over Teia's coronation—many of the commonfolk had taken down their banners. Most of the others folded when Teia began sending flagons of mulled red wine, stewed with luxuries like oranges and cinnamon.

All those months back, Teia had mocked Jura for distracting Erisia. Now, she could admit he'd had a point, if merely to curry favor with the commonfolk. Once they'd stopped railing at the palace's gates, she'd been able to direct her focus to more legislative matters. Outlawing torture. Redistributing land. Opening the public courts to all of Bhanot. Some changes had been met with apathy, others with reluctant approval—but everything could be softened by a scoop of sugar and a tankard of wine.

Miran's forehead creased. Unless the demonstrators had brought a warship to their latest rally, there was something more to be said.

"I have news on the Dawnbreakers," the general said gruffly.

She suppressed a sigh. "Is it the villages up north again? I thought I'd made myself clear—if there's one thing I won't tolerate, it's a rebellion."

"It's not the north," Miran assured her. "My men say it's been quiet since the trouble there last month."

"What about in the capital?" The Dawnbreakers had been decimated in Bhanot, but there might be some pockets still remaining.

When he again shook his head, Teia's patience dipped. "Then what? Don't tiptoe around me, General. We both know I don't have the time."

His fingers dug into his knee. He pulled heartily at his eyepatch. "There are rumors," Miran said.

"About?"

"Former Dawnbreaker leaders."

Teia stiffened. The crown might rest heavy on her head, but it was nothing compared to the past's many burdens. She thought about the others more than she should—Alara and Tobias and Kyra, their names burned into her mind, their faces slipping into her dreams. In the months since she'd ascended the throne, Teia had learned that ghosts didn't need to be among the dead.

It was them. It had to be. And Kyra was the one leading the charge, seeking the justice she'd promised to carry out in the passageways.

Teia braced herself for the general's response. "Kyra Medoh?" she said.

"Cornelius Lehm," Miran said instead, and Teia's heart plunged. It was a name she hadn't wanted to hear again.

"What about him?" Teia said sharply.

"Our scouts say they saw him boarding a ship from Mourner's Bay."

"When?"

"This morning, just before dawn."

"Tell them to get their eyes examined," she said tartly. "Cornelius Lehm is decaying in an unmarked grave, not commissioning trips out to sea."

"One would think, Highness."

"Excuse me?"

"I checked the gravesite. I thought it best to put any questions to rest."

"And?"

Miran hesitated. "It's empty. The ground was disturbed and the shroud missing."

"Animals. Robbers." The world was full of infinite

possibilities. Surely there had to be some reasonable explanation for the gravesite. "Really, Miran. Don't tell me you buy into this nonsense."

"No, Highness. Although I had my men visit the Absinth out of an abundance of caution."

The general had wanted the hotel permanently closed after the raid, but Teia insisted it remain functional. The Absinth would serve as a constant reminder of the Crown's might, while doubling as a healthy source of revenue. Miran had been understandably skeptical, even speaking out during a Council meeting, but Teia's intuition had proven correct. The Absinth was booked solid until the following spring, and the lobby's bar packed out the door. Travelers flocked from all over to see where the Dawnbreakers had fallen, captivated by the morbid sight.

"I assume your soldiers found the usual," Teia said. "Drunk diplomats. Tourists flaunting their guilds."

Miran's eye twitched. "Rabble."

"Rabble with deep pockets," Teia corrected. "That makes all the difference. Besides, unless Lehm is impersonating a tourist, there's no cause for concern."

"Anything is possible," the general bit out. He extracted something from his pocket and held it up for her to see. Teia opened her hand, and he pressed a curled scrap of paper into her outstretched palm. "This was left with the Absinth's clerk."

If the note had contained anything else, Teia would have shaken off her worries and gone about her day. She would have likely replaced the scouts, too, for imagining they'd seen Lehm's phantom, floating casually aboard a schooner.

On the paper was a crudely drawn star, colored the brightest shade of red.

Memories collided within Teia, discoveries she'd have

preferred to forget. A pulse of fear prickled against her chest. She fought to keep her composure, scrunching the drawing into her fist. "Who left this behind?" she demanded. "Did the clerk remember a description?"

"Nothing helpful. They said the gentleman was older, well-dressed."

She bit down hard on the inside of her cheek. "Miran," Teia grated. "I went to the morgue. I saw Lehm's body."

"There are ways to fake death."

"You ran him through."

"Yes."

"With a *sword*."

"Yes."

"So how is this possible?"

The general looked positively miserable. "I've heard of concoctions that can slow the heart," he said helplessly. "Perhaps it also helped clot any injuries, until he was revived by a remedy."

She shouldn't have been as shocked as she was. Hadn't Teia known that Alara was capable of incredible things? Hadn't Alara already designed potions that would induce sleep and poisons that would kill on contact? Concocting a paralytic toxin would be no challenge for the Poisons Master. If anything, she would probably consider it a fun afternoon pastime.

Teia should have expected Lehm to be prepared for the worst, even if that entailed being thrown into a shallow grave. Men like that didn't go down easy. She had been foolish to think she'd outwitted him, and now she was paying the price.

She should have burned his body when she had the chance.

A sour taste filled Teia's mouth as she glanced down at the wrinkled note. He knew. Goddess, he *knew*. The drawing clutched in her hand was a taunt, a confirmation of her greatest fear. The dream that should have died with the crown prince and the rebel leader had resurfaced, rearing its ugly head, its shadow enveloping the Five Kingdoms.

The old myths longed to come alive—and Cornelius Lehm was after the Serkawr.

Fog misted over the lapping waves.

Mourner's Bay was empty. The boats had all been docked in the harbor, with the inhabitants off to the city's livelier districts. As Teia waited on the shore, she wondered which spot Lehm's ship had taken up. Had he bribed his way onto a merchant's boat? Had he always had a schooner in place, ready to extract him in case of an emergency?

Someone brushed her shoulder, lighter than any feather. "Highness."

"Don't call me that."

She heard Enna's laugh, wild and breathless, as the thief sat gracefully beside her. "Are you still allowed to do this?"

"Do what?"

"Play dress-up. Sneak out."

"Pay your commissions?"

"I'm hurt. You know these meetings are the highlight of my evening."

"You need better hobbies."

The thief rolled her eyes. "Did you bring me here just to insult me? Because I'll have you know that I'm extremely busy—"

"The Star."

Enna's smile faltered. "What about it?" she said.

"You took it from Blackgate."

"Yes. And?"

"I need to know what you did with it."

"I thought you didn't care."

"I didn't. But I do now."

Discomfort overtook Enna's face. Teia was suddenly struck with a dreadful revelation, an option she had assumed the thief wouldn't take. "You didn't sell the Star, did you?"

"Of course not," Enna snarked. "But things are—complicated."

"Meaning?"

Distress softened into embarrassment. Enna picked at a hangnail, deliberately avoiding Teia's gaze. "It was stolen."

A shard of ice lodged into Teia's stomach. "What?"

"Someone broke into our headquarters."

"At the Society of Thieves?"

Enna nodded. "They killed Kolt and Dival. Absolutely sacked the place too. Pulled up the floorboards, rifled through every safe."

"And you didn't tell me?"

"It's not something I like to advertise." She scoured a hand over her eyes. "It's not important, is it? Things can be re-stolen. It might take some time, but we'll track the bastards down."

Teia said nothing. She sat deathly still, listening to the roar of the tide. Up until this instant, she could have pretended that things were a fantastic mess of chance and coincidence. The scouts needed spectacles. The drawing was a perverse joke.

But her proof was here, written in the Star's disappearance, laid out before her. There was no denying things anymore. Teia's heart pounded, each beat slashing through her. She had a vision of the Serkawr roaring up from the water, tearing apart the seas and thundering onto land. It would decimate the Five Kingdoms. It would eradicate whoever stood against it.

"Enna," Teia said faintly. "I know who raided the Society of Thieves."

"You do?" Enna's eyes danced with an unmistakable fury. "Well? Don't make me beg for a name."

Teia's jaw tightened. "It was Lehm."

Enna did a double take. "Sorry," she said. "The wind is a bit loud, and I think I just hallucinated."

"You didn't."

"I did. Because I'm positive you said *Lehm* took the Morning Star." When Teia nodded, Enna paled. "He's *dead*, Teia," she sputtered. "Didn't your military take care of him?"

"That's what I thought too." Teia grabbed at a fistful of pebbles. "It's him, Enna. I don't know how he slipped the noose, but he did. Lehm is the one who broke into the Society. He killed your friends and stole the Star."

"That son of a bitch." Enna's expression twisted. "Why the hell does he want the Star, anyway? He lost his precious rebellion, and this is his consolation prize?"

Teia winced. "Not exactly."

"What do you mean *not exactly*?"

"I mean . . ." She said the words in rapid-fire, flinging their weight off her chest. "The Serkawr. Lehm will raise it with the Star."

She sounded ridiculous, even to her own ears. If Teia had heard the statement just months before, she would have burst into hysterical laughter. It was the type of talk that deserved to become a rumor, transforming into another drunken story told over a hefty pint.

Except Enna wasn't laughing. Maybe it was the thief's beliefs in the legends, coupled with whatever interactions she'd had with the rebel leader. Or maybe it was her upbringing, where she'd been inundated with tales about the sea beast by Ystrad locals. Either way, Enna took a jagged breath. Her voice was hoarse as she said, "You're telling me the Serkawr is *real*?"

"Lehm thinks it is. It's why he took the Morning Star."

"You can't be serious."

"What happened to your unshakable faith?"

"It's as sturdy as ever," Enna retorted. "But you don't believe in the legends. You once told me the temples housed more con men than the Flats."

"Maybe I've changed my ways."

"I highly doubt that."

Teia rolled a pebble between her fingers. "What I believe in are facts. I found notes in Lehm's study, maps making his intentions clear. He's after the Serkawr, Enna. Trust me."

Enna's response was an impressive string of curses. "So that's it, then?" the thief said, once she'd ground to a halt. "Lehm hightails for the ocean, drops the Star into the water, and gets a sea beast for his troubles?"

"It's more complicated than that."

"You say that like it's a bad thing."

"He would need someone with powers to help him. One with fire, one with water."

"How poetic," Enna said. "And since Kyra hates you—"

"Lehm will seek her out. He'll hide his true motivations and persuade her to join him."

Was there anything she could do to safeguard Erisia? Teia didn't think so. A thousand options flitted through her mind—a barricade around the kingdom, a dam of stone to keep back the sea—but they wouldn't be enough. Nothing would. If the

Serkawr really did come calling, it would scatter her army to the wind. Men would be tossed aside as easily as dolls, metal shredded through like sheets of paper.

Next to her, Enna brightened unexpectedly. "Hold on," she said. "There's good news, isn't there?"

Teia would settle for anything that wasn't remotely terrible—good news seemed too much to ask for. "Which is?"

"He needs you for this to work. If someone who controls water has to help summon the Serkawr, Lehm's plan falls apart without you."

It was true, at least in theory. Yet Teia had the sinking suspicion that Lehm had already accounted for her refusal. Kyra might uniquely possess commoner's flame, but Teia wasn't the only noble who could manipulate water. There were royals who had never heard of Cornelius Lehm, who sat oblivious across a foaming sea, waiting to be charmed and duped.

She sat straight up, a pulse of energy spiking through her. The beginnings of an idea blazed to life, unfolding in the recesses of her mind. It was spiny and uncertain, more hope than logic, and yet Teia felt a flicker of promise.

Lehm thought the fight was over. He thought he'd gained the upper hand, rendering Teia powerless. But wasn't there always something more to be done? Hadn't she meandered her way out of closer scrapes than this? Lehm was a strategist, a man of great ambition, but she was the Halfling Princess, the Half-Witch, the girl who'd taken the Golden Palace and made it her own.

He might be a monster, but so was she.

Teia offered the thief a thin smile. "Enna," she said. "I know what we're going to do."

"We?"

"If you'll join me."

Enna groaned loudly, but Teia glimpsed pure steel behind her gaze. Nobody had stolen from Enna van Apt before—the ones who'd tried ended up without one eardrum, sometimes both, bleeding from a multitude of places. Teia almost pitied Lehm's fate if the thief got her hands on him. "I must have a weakness for suicide missions."

"Or a fondness for great company."

"I'm not admitting to anything." Enna considered Teia carefully. "So what now, Boss? We put out a hit on Lehm? We track where Kyra went?"

"You'd like the first option, wouldn't you?"

"Immensely so."

"You'll have to keep that in reserve," Teia said. "I have something a bit different in mind."

Somewhere past the horizon—beyond the Dark Sea and all its dangers—lay another kingdom. It was one with icy peaks and shadowed ridges, terraced fields awash in a vibrant green. If the stories were to be believed, dragons roamed the cerulean sky, keeping watch over the land, darting among the clouds.

It would have been hers to rule in another life.

The waves bled into the pebbled beach. The tide stirred sleepily. And Teia looked at Enna with a new determination, a spark prepared to catch alight.

"Now," Teia said, "we set sail for Shaylan."

ACKNOWLEDGMENTS

It really, truly takes a village. *Inferno's Heir* would not exist without the backing of some amazing people, and this book wouldn't be complete if I didn't at least try to express what their support has meant to me.

It would be impossible to write this acknowledgments page without first mentioning my powerhouse agent, Kelly Van Sant, who plucked this book out of her slush pile to become Teia's biggest advocate. Thank you for always being in my corner, for answering every frantic text, and for believing in this story. Here's to many more books to come!

Kevin Norman, who read this book and saw straight to its heart. I couldn't have asked for someone better to partner with on Teia's story. Your ideas have made this book that much better, and thanks to you, Teia and the Dawnbreakers are out in the world. I will forever be grateful.

The entire Bindery team—Matt Kaye, Meghan Harvey, Charlotte Strick, CJ Alberts, and Zack Jordan—has made this debut experience a dream. The amount of time, care, and patience put into bringing this book to life has gotten me the closest I could be to achieving inner peace during the publishing process.

On a similar vein, thank you to the Girl Friday team—Reshma Kooner, Mari Kesselring, Katherine Richards, Kelley Frodel, and Melody Moss—for their support, especially all the work they've done behind the scenes. And an additional, huge thank you to Tegan Tigani, whose developmental edits and guidance brought this book into a whole new light.

Writing is often considered a solitary practice—and it can be sometimes, when I'm holed up in my room, hunched over my laptop like a gremlin. That said, the friends I've made in the writing community have made the journey much less lonely. A special shout-out to the original Hydrate or Diedrate group chat: Kalie, Anahita, Aymen, and Gab. Also sending the biggest hug to Nessa Le, who absolutely floors me with her writing and patiently listens to me scream via text.

Sarah Street, who is literally this book's number one supporter and who I send every one of my manuscripts to—I'm so lucky to call you a friend. Thank God for that happy hour!!

Andrew, who is—simply put—the best partner I could have ever asked for. Thank you for balancing me out, and for being my biggest fan. You finally get to read this book now!!!!!! (melon)

My wonderful friends, who've listened to me lament endlessly about edits and still swore they would read this book when it comes out ("For Christmas, I'm getting every person in my family a copy"). Lina, Kli, Yunhee, Chris, Kat, Abhi, Howie, Maggie, Ross, Jessie, M, Angela, Eric, Ada, Erik, Carol, Wing, Nicole, Rohit—the list goes on, and I couldn't be more thankful.

Mindy, my (former) roommate, who listened to me catastrophize whenever I got a new set of edits. Hopefully you find at least some parts of this book funny.

Throughout everything, my family has been my rock. Thank you to my parents for always encouraging me to write, and buying me all those composition notebooks so I could scribble my stories inside. And, of course, a thank you to Mo, who keeps me humble no matter the circumstances.

Finally, to everyone who has made it this far—this book is for you. Thank you for following Teia's journey.

THANK YOU

This book would not have been possible without the support from the Violetear Books community, with a special thank-you to the Associate Publisher members:

Ashley Odriozola
BecosIRead
Cassidy D Gomez
Christian Bellman
Courtney Doerr
Cristina Rowe
Dani Paez
Fairiedancr
Holly Blakemore
Jeffrey Tristan Thyme
Megan Gallardo
Paprika
William Dozier

About the Author

© Andrew Cui

TIFFANY WANG hails from a town in North Texas, although she's currently wandering her way through New York City. She studied communication and international relations at the University of Pennsylvania. In her spare time, she enjoys searching for a quiet place to write and snacking on a questionable amount of Cheetos.

Want to be the first to hear about the
best new teen and YA reads?

Want exclusive content, offers and giveaways?

Want to chat about books with people who
love them as much as you do?

Look no further...

Sign up to our newsletter now!